**W9-CBW-312**

Dear Reader,

I hope you're enjoying this special collector's edition of the original CODE NAME: DANGER series. It's a blast for me to kick back and watch OMEGA's operatives wiggle out of all these impossible situations.

In this edition, you'll meet two of my favorite characters: the smooth operative called Doc and his timid fiancée who—as much to her surprise as his—goes undercover as a secret agent.

Then there's Maggie Sinclair (aka Chameleon) and her enigmatic boss, Adam Ridgeway. The attraction that has sizzled between them for so long glows white-hot in the final book of the original series.

But don't despair. In response to your many letters and e-mails, the adventures continue in a whole new set of CODE NAME: DANGER books. *Hot as Ice* (IM #1129) was a February release and *Texas Hero* (IM #1149) will be available next month.

Here's hoping you have as much fun reading these new CODE NAME: DANGER stories as I had writing them!

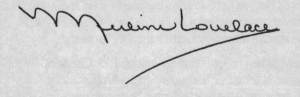

## THE OMEGA AGENCY

*Top secret government agency charged with keeping peace throughout the world—by just about any means possible. With a few exceptions, the operatives generally live their own lives until they are called into action. They work under the direction of special envoy Adam Ridgeway—and they always get the job done.*

Jaguar and Cowboy have concluded their missions— and succumbed to passion. But OMEGA's jobs are never done....

**Doc:** Book smarts matched by physical strengths give David Jansen an edge, but he hides both behind a diffident air. What will happen when his resolve is truly tested...?

**Chameleon:** With an ear for languages and a quick mind, Maggie Sinclair can be anyone she wants to be. But will she let Adam see her true self?

*And don't miss the adventures of the next generation of OMEGA agents:*

**Artemis:** Like the huntress, Diana Remington always bags her prey. But her arrows miss the mark when she's sent to recover a downed pilot in *Hot as Ice*, a February 2002 release from Silhouette Intimate Moments.

**Renegade:** The last thing ex-marine Rick Carstairs wants is to act as bodyguard to an Ambassador's fiery niece—especially after he meets her....

Watch for *Texas Hero*, an August 2002 release from Silhouette Intimate Moments (IM #1165).

# MERLINE LOVELACE

## DANGEROUS TO KNOW

Published by Silhouette Books

**America's Publisher of Contemporary Romance**

If you purchased this book without a cover you should be aware that this book is stolen property. It was reported as "unsold and destroyed" to the publisher, and neither the author nor the publisher has received any payment for this "stripped book."

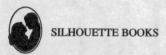 

SILHOUETTE BOOKS

DANGEROUS TO KNOW

Copyright © 2002 by Harlequin Books S.A.

ISBN 0-373-48482-8

The publisher acknowledges the copyright holder of the individual works as follows:

UNDERCOVER MAN
Copyright © 1995 by Merline Lovelace

PERFECT DOUBLE
Copyright ©1984 by Merline Lovelace

All rights reserved. Except for use in any review, the reproduction or utilization of this work in whole or in part in any form by any electronic, mechanical or other means, now known or hereafter invented, including xerography, photocopying and recording, or in any information storage or retrieval system, is forbidden without the written permission of the editorial office, Silhouette Books, 300 East 42nd Street, New York, NY 10017 U.S.A.

All characters in this book have no existence outside the imagination of the author and have no relation whatsoever to anyone bearing the same name or names. They are not even distantly inspired by any individual known or unknown to the author, and all incidents are pure invention.

This edition published by arrangement with Harlequin Books S.A.

® and TM are trademarks of Harlequin Books S.A., used under license. Trademarks indicated with ® are registered in the United States Patent and Trademark Office, the Canadian Trade Marks Office and in other countries.

Visit Silhouette at www.eHarlequin.com

Printed in U.S.A.

# CONTENTS

PRAISE FOR

# MERLINE LOVELACE

"A fabulous mixture of intrigue, adventure and romance.
The sexy fantasy scene is delicious, the action non-stop,
and the super spy gadgetry loads of fun."
—*Genie Romance Exchange* on **UNDERCOVER MAN**

"There are not enough tales as good as this
in the genre to satiate today's reader."
—*Affaire de Coeur* on **PERFECT DOUBLE**

"Lovelace has made a name for herself..."
—*Romantic Times*

"Merline Lovelace delivers top notch romantic suspense
with great characters, rich atmosphere
and a crackling plot!"
—*New York Times* bestselling author Mary Jo Putney

"Merline Lovelace writes with humor and passion."
—*Publishers Weekly*

# UNDERCOVER MAN

To Al, who's given me a life filled with wonderful adventures. Who would've thought that bowl of raspberries would someday show up in a romance!

# Prologue

*H*er heart thumped painfully against her rib cage as she approached the security station. Only one more checkpoint to pass through. One more screening.

Despite the chill March air pervading Washington's Dulles International Airport, sweat trickled down between her breasts. But she allowed no sign of her inner trepidation to show as she strolled toward the conveyor with a long-legged grace that made men crane their necks to watch her and women sniff disparagingly.

Smiling at the wide-eyed girl on the stool behind the X-ray screen, she dropped her white chinchilla coat and her little leather purse, with its discreet designer logo, onto the conveyor, then moved toward the metal detector with an air of assurance. When she caught the hefty, red-faced guard's openmouthed stare, her smile deepened into the sensual, teasing pout she'd perfected for hicks like these.

Without seeming to, she rolled her shoulders. The narrow, slithery front panels of her gold mesh halter shifted, baring most of her generous breasts. The guard's mouth sagged, and she *sailed through the detector. No alarms sounded. No beeps distracted the security specialist from his gawking.*

Almost choking with relief, she retrieved her purse and her coat and joined the stream of elegantly dressed passengers heading for the Concorde's gate. With each step, her terror lessened by imperceptible degrees.

Still, she wished she hadn't let herself get talked into this. It was too nerve-racking. And too damned dangerous. The last woman who followed this route hadn't ever returned. Sure, the money was fabulous, but she made enough from her regulars to live well, very well, in L.A. She didn't need this kind of—

"Miss Ames?"

Her stomach heaved. Swallowing the sudden, acrid taste of bile, she turned to face the broad-shouldered man who stood behind her.

Under any other circumstance, she might have appreciated his square, cleanly shaven jaw and severely cut brown hair, with its subtle mahogany tints. She liked a man who dressed in his conservative style. They usually paid most generously for the decidedly unconservative services she provided.

But the expression in his gray blue eyes killed her flicker of professional interest instantly. There was no trace of the admiration she was used to. No masculine appreciation of her well cultivated beauty. Instead, those steely eyes slicked through her with an intensity that made her tremble in pure, unadulterated fear.

"Are you Meredith Ames?" His deep, even voice sent danger signals screaming along her nerves.

"Y-yes."

"Come with me, please."

She threw a frantic glance around the waiting room, seeking an escape route.

"Don't even think it," he growled, taking her arm in an iron grip.

# Chapter 1

Cold March winds swirled along the uneven brick sidewalks of a quiet side street just off Massachusetts Avenue, in the heart of D.C.'s embassy district. Late-afternoon shadows marched down the facades of the elegant Federal-style town houses on either side of the street, casting many of them into preevening darkness.

The shadows dulled the sheen on the discreet bronze plaque mounted beside the door to a brick-fronted three-story structure midway down the block. Anyone who glanced at the plaque would learn that this particular town house was home to the offices of the president's special envoy—a nebulous position created a decade ago to give a wealthy campaign contributor a fancy, if meaningless, title and a chance to rub elbows with the Washington elite.

Only a handful of the most senior government officials were aware that the president's special envoy also served as director of OMEGA, a secret agency whose initials comprised the last letter of the Greek alphabet. An agency that, as its name suggested, served as the president's last resort in certain situations with international implications.

Not ten hours ago, an urgent call from the president to the current director had activated an OMEGA response. Now, a small team of dedicated professionals was gathered in the control center on the third-floor of the agency's headquarters, preparing to send two of their own into harm's way.

"Now *this* is more like it!"

Maggie Sinclair twirled slowly in front of the crew room's full-length mirror. A wide, sequined gold band circled her throat like a shimmering dog collar. From the collar, narrow folds of gold mesh draped sensuously over her breasts to be caught at her waist with another band of sequins. Everything else above her waist was skin.

She faced the mirror once more and grinned at the men hovering just behind her.

"You guys should take notes. This is just what every well-dressed secret agent should wear into the field."

The pudgy, frizzy-haired genius who headed OMEGA's field dress unit snorted. "I'm just glad the suspect was carrying a purse. Even I couldn't figure out how to conceal a weapon in that outfit."

Her grin widening, Maggie smoothed her palms down over hips encased in sleek, cream-colored spandex leggings.

"This outfit *is* a weapon," she purred.

Splaying a hand across her chest to keep the narrow ribbons of mesh in place, she leaned toward the mirror and squinted at the glittery collar through green-tinted contacts.

"Which one is the microdot?"

Maggie still found it hard to believe that one of the tiny disks sewn to the collar contained over a million lines of computer code. Code that translated into the latest secret technology in fiber optics. Code that was worth hundreds of millions of dollars on the black market.

She'd known, of course, that both the FBI and CIA had been watching the cadre of very beautiful and very expensive call girls jetting between L.A. and the pleasure centers of Europe for some time, suspecting them of acting as couriers in the dangerous and often deadly game of industrial espionage. But until the president called the director with the shocking news that highly classified fiber-optic technology was at that moment being smuggled out of the country, Maggie hadn't realized just how high the game stakes were.

This technology had been developed by the military and now formed the backbone of their command-and-control networks. Using the new optical fibers, electrical impulses could be transmitted at many times the speed and a hundred times the capacity of the old cables.

The same technology would soon be available for civilian use, with certain modifications. To say it would revolutionize the global transfer of visual or digital information was a gross understatement. Huge broadcast news and entertainment conglomerates, particularly, were clamoring for its release.

The sequin-and-fur-clad woman who'd been eased off a plane at Dulles International Airport a few hours ago and whisked away to a secret holding center in Virginia hadn't known what information she carried. Nor had Meredith Ames known who she was delivering it to, only that someone would contact her after she arrived in Cannes.

Now Maggie would make contact for her.

The chief of the field dress unit squinted at the collar, then pointed to one of the small gold circles. "That's the microdot. I think. You need a hand-held infrared scanner to tell for sure."

Maggie squinted at the tiny dot, no different to the naked eye than any of the other glittery sequins. "You could have fooled me," she murmured.

Rolling her shoulders to settle the slithery gold halter into more graceful folds, she picked up a leather purse and a cream silk jacket that matched her leggings.

"If you guys will pack the rest of this stuff for me, I'll go downstairs. Doc's waiting with the director for our final mission clearance."

"Will do, Chameleon."

The chief clucked disapprovingly as one of his subordinates started to transfer the rest of Meredith Ames's wardrobe, hastily altered where necessary to fit Maggie, into her suitcases. "Careful! Those Guccis aren't knockoffs, you know."

Maggie snapped open the flap of the white-and-gold Paloma Picasso purse to make sure it held her lipstick, her newly doctored passport, the diamond-studded compact the Special Devices Unit had given her an hour ago, and her Smith & Wesson .22. Satisfied that all items rested securely in their special nest that would shield them from airport metal detectors, she hooked the bag's chain over her shoulder and strolled out into the control center.

A long, low wolf whistle rolled across the banks of communications equipment. Grinning, Maggie did a slow pirouette for Joe Samuels, the senior comm technician, with whom she'd shared many tense hours and cold cups of coffee.

"Not bad for a small-town Oklahoma girl, huh?"

"You look like a million dollars."

"Well, a couple thousand, maybe," she countered with a laugh. "Which is about what this little ensemble cost, and about half what the woman I'm impersonating earns a night."

The other occupant of the control center, a serene, dark-haired woman with dove gray eyes and a luminous ivory complexion, smiled. "You look stunning Maggie."

"Thanks, Claire. Do I fit the profile you compiled on Meredith Ames?"

"Perfectly."

A psychologist with a string of degrees, Claire Huffacker had quietly become one of the world's foremost experts on hostage negotiations after the death of her husband some years ago at the hands of terrorists. Not content just to passively provide information to those combating terrorism's deadly effects, Claire had recently joined OMEGA as an agent. Her code name, Cyrene, was drawn from Greek mythology, and alluded to her hard-won serenity.

Maggie couldn't think of anyone she'd rather have acting as headquarters controller for this mission than this remarkable woman. Her tranquil expression hid a mind as keen as any in the organization, and an astounding ability to anticipate the re-actions of the sort of dangerous characters that Maggie and Doc, her partner for this mission, might have to tangle with in the field.

"Generally, the more expensive call girls dress rather conser-vatively," Claire commented, surveying Maggie's dramatic ap-pearance. "They tend toward neat suits, pearls and leather pumps, particularly when meeting their clients in public. The businessmen they service don't want it known that the deal being negotiated over drinks and dinner is for sex, instead of stocks and bonds. But Meredith is in a different class."

"*Was* in a different class," Maggie interjected. The tall, sultry blonde in the Virginia interrogation center would be out of busi-ness for some time.

"Was in a different class," Claire agreed calmly. "The women who work the international scene, as Meredith did, are at the absolute peak of the prostitution hierarchy. Their clients are usually so wealthy, they're beyond the reach of the law. These men want their escorts to dress with style, and a sensual allure." She hesitated, then tacked on a quiet warning. "Because they're so powerful, however, they can be absolutely ruthless. Be careful, Maggie."

"I will," she promised, heading for the door to the control center.

"Good luck on this one," Joe called out. "Soak up some of those Riviera rays for me."

"Will do. You just keep Terence away from the twins' home-work. You know how he likes to eat paper."

"Yeah. He's a ready-made excuse when the boys 'forget' to get their assignments done."

Joe shook his head, mumbling something about not quite knowing how he'd ever gotten talked into babysitting for Maggie's pet in the first place. Wisely, she kept silent. There were few enough people willing to watch the German shepherd-size blue-and-orange striped iguana while she was on assign-ment. The creature had been a gift from a certain debonair

Central American colonel who wanted to establish much more than a working relationship with her. Joe's twins had unofficially adopted Terence, and Maggie secretly hoped to make that arrangement official one of these days.

With Joe mumbling behind her, she flattened a hand against the hidden sensor beside the control center's door, spoke her code name and waited for security's computers to process the positive palm, voice and video identification. In a few seconds, the heavy titanium-shielded oak door hummed open. She swept down the stairs that led to the second floor, the heels of her cream-colored ostrichskin boots beating a tattoo on the oak treads. After a quick scan of the monitors to make sure the second-floor offices were clear, she stepped into the reception area. The gray-haired, matronly receptionist glanced up at her entrance.

"You look like one of those angels on top of a Christmas tree," Elizabeth Wells exclaimed, beaming. "All spun gold and cream."

"Good grief, I hope not! I was aiming for the other end of the spectrum! You don't think Field Dress overdid it a bit on the hair?"

"That particular shade of ash blond is very attractive on you," Elizabeth declared staunchly.

"Think so?" Maggie wrapped a finger around one of the wispy tendrils that escaped her smooth French twist. "Well, at least this is a commercial color, right out of the box. I'm not trusting those guys upstairs with dyes anymore, not after that so-called temporary blemish they tattooed on my chin for the last mission. It took two months for that thing to fade completely."

When she dipped a shoulder to examine the pale white-gold strand of hair, the halter slid to one side.

So did Elizabeth's smile. "Er, won't you be a bit cool in that top, dear?"

"Not in the least. Honestly, Elizabeth, there's a white chinchilla coat waiting with my bags that you have to see to believe.

Apparently high-class hookers don't worry about being politically correct. They're still into real fur!"

"If you say so." The grandmotherly woman cast another doubtful glance at the skimpy halter and picked up the intercom.

When Maggie walked down the short corridor that led to the spacious office of the president's special envoy a few moments later, excitement bubbled in her veins, as it always did at the start of a mission. But this time the bubbles were two parts professional and at least one part personal. With an unabashedly feminine sense of anticipation, she couldn't wait for Adam Ridgeway to see her in this particular field uniform.

During her three-plus years as an OMEGA agent, Maggie's unique ability to alter not only her physical appearance, but also her very personality, to fit whatever role she was playing had earned her the code named Chameleon. She had gone underground as everything from a nun to a streetwalker. Had slathered every substance on her skin, from camouflage soot to bone-white makeup. Had traveled in every conveyance from a mule cart to an air force jet.

For the first time, she was going first class. In slinky, sinfully expensive clothes. Bathed in the subtle scent of Bal de Versailles, at three hundred dollars an ounce. Flying via the Concorde to Paris, and then by chartered jet to a sun-soaked playground for billionaires on the Mediterranean. She was definitely going to enjoy this mission.

She stopped just outside the director's office and drew in a deep breath. Feeling the effects of that breath on the slippery halter, she hastily let it out. If this little number didn't get a reaction from the iron-spined Adam Ridgeway, she thought with an inner grin, nothing would.

It did.

With a dart of sheer feline satisfaction, Maggie saw his blue eyes narrow sharply as they swept up from the tip of her silverblond head to the toe of her thousand-dollar-a-pair ostrich boots, lingering for long, heart-stopping moments on parts in between. When his gaze worked its way back to her face, it held a combination of blatant masculine appreciation and an almost reluctant approval.

Feeling unaccountably pleased with herself, Maggie sauntered into his spacious office and took her favorite perch, on the corner of the huge conference table.

The two men who waited while she made herself comfortable couldn't have been more different. Tall, dark, and leanly handsome, Adam exuded an aura of unshakable authority and sophistication that only a moneyed background and a Harvard education could produce. Most Washington insiders thought he'd been appointed to the juicy sinecure of special envoy because of his hefty campaign contributions and first-name familiarity with the man who now occupied the Oval Office. Few knew that, in addition to his largely ceremonial duties as special envoy, Adam Ridgeway also directed a dozen or so highly trained OMEGA agents.

The operative who stood beside him was one of the most skilled in the agency, although few would have guessed it to look at him. If Maggie had been forced to come up with one word to describe David Jensen, it would have been *solid*. Brown-haired, broad-shouldered and square-jawed, he had honed his muscular body to tempered steel through rigorous self-discipline and regular exercise. He moved, spoke and thought with the precision of an engineer, which he was. His code name, Einstein, referred to his reputation in his civilian life as a world-renowned expert in electronics, although the OMEGA agents had shortened that to Doc.

Doc had been recruited into OMEGA from the navy, where he'd been their foremost demolition expert. He'd pulled a number of combat tours, and could detonate explosives underwater, on land or in the air. Maggie sincerely hoped he wouldn't have to use his expertise on this particular mission.

His smoky gray blue eyes now looked her up and down with careful precision. Maggie hid a smile, knowing that Doc was cataloging her appearance in minute detail and filing it away for future reference. When they met again in Cannes tomorrow afternoon, he would know if she'd altered so much as…

Well, there wasn't much she could alter about the two pieces of clothing she wore.

"Nice," he told her with an approving smile.

"How nice?"

Doc's brows rose at the husky, sensual purr. "Very nice. Did you pick that accent up from Meredith Ames?"

Maggie nodded. With her extensive training in linguistics, duplicating Meredith's distinctive southern-California accent had been a piece of cake.

"Miss Ames was *very* cooperative," she confirmed. "In fact, she was so frightened, she spilled her guts—literally and figuratively—as soon as I got her alone. You must have scared her half to death at the airport."

"I had her under surveillance from the time she left L.A.," Doc said with a small frown. "She was scared before I approached her."

"With good reason," Adam put in dryly. "She faces espionage charges for trying to smuggle technology that's still highly classified. What's more, the last courier suspected of carrying information like this was found dead in a Cannes hotel room, of a supposedly accidental drug overdose."

Maggie tucked a strand of hair behind her ear, taking in Adam's cool air. Although he rarely displayed any emotion, she knew that even the unshakable Adam Ridgeway had to have his breaking point. One of these days, she sincerely hoped, she'd find it.

"Supposedly?" she asked, watching his face as he tapped a gold fountain pen against his desk blotter.

"Supposedly. There's no proof her death wasn't accidental, but she was transporting a prototype of the same technology you're now carrying." Adam's blue eyes skimmed her face, their expression unreadable. "A lot of people would go to any lengths to get their hands on that microdot. Be careful."

"I will, Chief."

"Have you memorized the list of potential buyers I put together?" Doc asked quietly.

Maggie smothered a grin. Doc's lists were famous around

OMEGA. In his quicksilver but methodical way, he could pull together seemingly random facts and scraps of information, analyze them, and draw parallels others had missed. He also made lists of his lists, and occasionally cross-indexed them. People like Maggie, who tended to operate more on instinct, could only watch him in awe.

"I've memorized the list of buyers," she assured him. "And the list of possible middlemen. And the long list of ramifications to international command-and-control systems if this technology is compromised. I've got so many lists floating around in my head, it's a wonder there's any room for anything else under this fluff of—" She brushed a hand through the wispy tendrils. "This fluff of white."

"Silver," Adam said.

"Platinum," David amended in his precise way, then his handsome face softened into a crooked smile. "It happens to be one of my favorite shades. It's very similar to my fiancée's, although perhaps hers has a few more gold tints."

"Really?" Maggie titled her head in surprise.

Although David had been engaged for almost a year now, he kept his civilian life and his undercover activities so separate, so compartmentalized, that none of the close-knit OMEGA cadre had ever met him outside the environment of a mission. And no one had even glimpsed so much as a photo of his longtime fiancée.

"Really," Doc replied.

Maggie tapped an ostrich boot impatiently. When no more details were forthcoming, she shook her head in exasperation.

"Just when are we going to meet this elusive fiancée of yours, Doc? You could introduce us without blowing your ties to OMEGA. A few of us have socially acceptable covers in our civilian lives, you know."

The tanned skin at the corners of his eyes creased. "You wouldn't think so, to look at you now. But I was hoping I could convince you to stay an extra day or two in Cannes after this mission," he added, reaching for his trench coat. "To act as a witness. I've already cleared it with Adam."

"Witness?"

"At the marriage ceremony."

"Wait a minute!" Maggie yelped. "You're getting married? In Cannes?"

"If we complete this mission within acceptable time parameters. If not, I'll have to reschedule the ceremony for after our return." He picked up his briefcase and turned to Adam. "I'll leave this list of contacts with Elizabeth and—"

"Doc!" Maggie jumped off the edge of the conference table, remembering just in time to keep her shoulders back and the halter snug against her chest. "For Pete's sake! You can't just announce you're getting married and leave me hanging like that."

"Like what?"

"How on earth can you plan a wedding when you're about to leave for a mission?"

He stared at her in genuine puzzlement. "The two are hardly incompatible. I've built enough flexibility into the agenda to allow for unforeseen circumstances. My fiancée understands that the 'symposium' I'm attending may extend indefinitely. Assuming I don't pack it in on this mission," he added with a small shrug, "she'll fly to France when I call her."

"I should have known," Maggie groaned. "I'll bet she has a detailed timetable sitting on the kitchen table."

His lips curved. "On the nightstand, actually. I've laid out her agenda from the hour she leaves L.A. to the minute she arrives in Cannes."

Maggie couldn't help wondering what kind of woman would live her life to one of Doc's precise schedules. "I'm looking forward to meeting her," she said honestly.

"You'll like her. She doesn't have your confidence and exuberance, perhaps, and she's a little timid at times, but she's…she's…"

Maggie waited in surprised anticipation. If the articulate, precise Doc had to fumble for an adjective to describe this woman, he must have it bad. A tiny pang of envy curled through her. Carefully she avoided looking at Adam.

"She's sweet," Doc finished.

With a final nod to Adam, he picked up his trench coat and folded it over his arm. His eyes held a gleam that only two people who have shared dangerous, desperate hours could understand.

"See you on the Riviera, Chameleon."

"See you, Doc."

Maggie's soft sigh floated on the air for a moment after Doc left to catch his plane. She turned to find Adam's inquiring gaze on her.

"I wish I could manage my life as well as Doc does," she said with a small shrug. "I have enough trouble just working in the care and feeding of one small house pet, let alone a fiancé or even a significant other."

"Perhaps if you got rid of that repulsive reptile you call a pet," Adam suggested dryly, "you might find it easier to acquire a fiancé or a significant other."

Maggie refused to rise to the bait. She and Adam had agreed to disagree about the relative merits of a large iguana as a companion.

"Something tells me I won't have too much trouble 'acquiring' male companionship in this little outfit," she responded, with a seductive toss of her shining white gold hair.

To her absolute delight, Adam's jaw squared a fraction. Maggie couldn't have pinpointed exactly when ruffling his formidable equilibrium had become such a personal challenge to her. In the three years they'd worked together, he'd never given any indication of anything other than a professional interest in her well-being. And she would've died before admitting how much the media shots of the dashing special envoy out for an evening on the town with any one of his several elegant and very eligible companions disturbed her.

Yet there was no denying the intensity of the awareness that arced between them. Or the way her heart seemed to flip-flop in her chest whenever they were alone together. Or how much it secretly delighted her when Adam raked her face with those steel blue eyes, as he did now.

''I have no doubt any number of men will try to purchase your services during this mission,'' he said after a moment.

Flashing him a mischievous grin over one shoulder, Maggie headed for the door. ''I just hope they can afford my price.''

For long moments after she left, Adam stood still and silent, one hand in the pocket of his tailored gray suit. Without realizing he was doing so, he fingered a gold money clip that held a fold of hundred-dollar bills.

# Chapter 2

$P$aige could sense the Mediterranean before she saw it. As her tiny rental car putt-putted up steep hills, then coasted down winding inclines, the air took on a softer, balmier feel. Even the scent from thousands of acres of roses and jasmine and mimosa and wild lavender around the mountain town of Grasse, the perfume capital of France, couldn't disguise the tang of the sea only a few more miles ahead.

Double-clutching to downshift around a hairpin curve, Paige winced when the gears growled a protest. After three days of driving through the French Alps, she still hadn't quite mastered either the winding roads or the art of changing gears or an incline. Sending the gearshift an apologetic glance, she wrapped both palms around the steering wheel and aimed the little car forward.

When she crested another steep hill, she gave a sudden gasp. Tires crunched on loose shale and brakes screeched as she pulled off onto a narrow overlook. While the engine shuddered and died, Paige gazed, awestruck, at the dazzling vista before her.

Laid out below in a hazy, shifting pattern of azure and ultramarine and indigo was the Mediterranean. Far out to sea, huge tankers plowed through the waters, while closer in, smaller ships weaved through the waves and left sparkling white wakes. They were cruise ships, Paige mused, or those fabulous yachts she'd read about, with their own helicopter ports and twenty-six state-rooms. In the distance, a gray green island rose out of the blue. Corsica, she thought. Or Sardinia.

But it was the spectacular shoreline that drew her awed gaze. The famous, sun-drenched Riviera.

Almost directly below her, the city of Cannes clung to the curve of the bay. A narrow strip of sand and a wide boulevard lined with palms and flowering shrubs separated the city from the sea. Tall luxury hotels faced the Mediterranean on the inland side of the boulevard, like a row of white-fronted sentinels guarding Europe's most unselfconscious pleasure port.

Crossing her wrists on the steering wheel, Paige propped her chin on top of them. She couldn't believe she was here. She couldn't believe she'd actually torn up David's careful, typed instructions, called the airline and booked her own flight. She wasn't supposed to arrive in France for another week, at least. She certainly wasn't supposed to have rented a car in Paris and driven the long, tortuous route through the Alps to reach the sea. By herself, yet!

The first few days on the road, she'd been terrified of losing her way, of unintentionally offending someone with her execrable French, of ordering the wrong things from the menu. Even now, her stomach gave a funny little lurch every time she remembered the calf brains in a rich brown sherry sauce she'd been served her first night on the road. She hadn't realized what they were until the second or third bite.

She'd almost turned around right then. Almost scurried back to Paris and called home to leave a message for David on her recorder that she'd wait for him there. But the same desperate need that had driven her to leave L.A. early had kept her on the road. She'd needed this time by herself, away from the bustle of the city. She'd needed quiet to think. Privacy to sort through her jumbled feelings. She'd needed to find a way to tell David she wasn't going to marry him.

Painfully, Paige swallowed to ease the lump that seemed to have taken up permanent residence in her throat since the day David had calmly suggested they combine his business trip to the south of France with their honeymoon. Blinking back a sting of tears, she shook her head. She wouldn't cry again. She wouldn't! She'd cried all she was going to.

Still, her throat was raw as she lifted her left hand and stared at the square-cut emerald on the plain white-gold band. The ring was simple. Unadorned. Filled with a quiet, soothing beauty, David had said, like Paige herself.

So quiet, she could only nod when he'd slid the ring onto her finger.

So simple, she'd believed that his deliberate restraint when he made love to her was a mark of respect.

So soothing, that even now, after almost a yearlong engagement, he still kissed her with that same combination of fond affection and control. He could ignite every one of her senses with his skilled hands and mouth, yet he always kept a small part of his inner self distant from her.

Only a woman who loved a man as desperately as Paige loved David Jensen would ache with longing at the memory of his kisses. And be so devastated by the knowledge that she wasn't woman enough to engage his whole heart.

He deserved better, Paige told herself in a now-familiar litany. He deserved a woman who would make him lose himself in her arms. One who would throw him into a tailspin once in a while. Would make him forget his careful schedules. Toss out his endless lists. One whose wedding he wouldn't work in neatly with an international symposium on digital electronics, she thought with a little spurt of resentment.

That tiny spark of indignation gave her the courage to tug the emerald over her knuckle and off her finger. She fumbled in her purse for a tissue, then wrapped it around the ring. Still, she had to blink furiously to hold back her tears as she tucked the wad of tissue into the zipper pocket of her purse.

Drawing in a deep breath, Paige reached down to shove the little car into gear. An agonized screech made her jump, then hastily tromp down on the clutch. This time the gears engaged, and the mini edged back onto the road.

As perspiration gathered between her breasts, Paige pressed the heavy knit of her sweater with one hand to blot the dampness and tried to ignore a small niggle of guilt. David had left specific instructions about what clothing to bring. He'd even given her the range of temperatures to expect, and the average number of sunny days—three hundred!—that the Riviera enjoyed each year. But the weather in L.A. had been gray and overcast and decidedly chilly when she impulsively tossed her things in a suitcase and dashed to the bank to transform her entire savings account into travelers' checks. It had been just as cool in Paris when she landed, and downright cold driving through the Alps.

Now that she'd left the snowcapped peaks behind, however, Paige was forced to admit that David had been right. As usual. The Riviera was not the place for heavy sweaters and plaid wool jumpers.

Feeling utterly depressed, she realized that the first thing she'd have to do after checking into her hotel was buy some clothes. She sighed, thinking of the neat list of shops David had left for her. Boutiques suitable for her own quiet style, he'd told her, in the deep voice that always sent shivers of delight down her spine. Shops where she could pick out her trousseau.

As she inched around the hairpin turns, Paige sighed again. She'd left the careful list of shops in L.A., knowing that she wouldn't be shopping for her trousseau. She'd just have to find something suitable on her own before the shops closed for the afternoon.

Two hours later she pushed open the door of yet another boutique. The store window displayed only one item, a sequined ball cap in lavender on a black marble stand, so Paige wasn't quite sure exactly what she'd find inside.

As soon as she saw the single rack that ran the length of the small shop, she almost turned around and walked back out. A quick glance told her the beaded and jeweled garments weren't the kind of clothing she wore. What was more, she knew they would be well out of her price range.

Paige paused with her hand on the door latch. She was tired and hungry and absolutely appalled at the prices she'd encountered. Unfortunately, she was also smotheringly hot and not in the mood to search for the kind of shops David had indicated carried items more to her taste. Gritting her teeth, she closed the door and walked over to the rack. Maybe they'd have something on sale.

The shop attendant called out a musical greeting, advising Paige that she'd be right with her. A moment later, the dark-haired woman glided into the back room in search of some item for the only other customer in the boutique, a tall, leggy blonde in a short tomato-red jacket worn over a gold mesh halter.

Paige flipped through the few padded hangers on the rack, without much hope. She suspected that the prices for these sequined, Madonnna-ish corsets and lacy see-through tank tops would be in direct inverse proportion to the amount of material that went into them. The skimpier the article of clothing, she'd discovered in the past hour, the more outrageous the price.

She lifted a hanger from the rack and gazed at a narrow band of gold lamé. The stretchy loop couldn't be more than a couple inches wide. Steeling herself, she glanced at the tag.

"Good Lord!"

The sound of a soft chuckle brought her stunned gaze from the handwritten tag to the shop's other customer.

"Kind of hits you right in the solar plexus, doesn't it?"

Surprised and unaccountably pleased to hear another American accent after so many days on her own in France, Paige sent the stunning blonde a weak smile.

"Is this the price or an inventory number or something?"

The American's vivacious laughter added a gemlike sparkle to her green eyes. She strolled out from behind the rack, and Paige blinked at her short—*extremely short*—shorts, which were in the same eye-catching shade of red as her jacket.

"It's the price. The starting price. One doesn't pay that, of course."

"One doesn't?"

"No. Don't you know that Cannes is the world's most opulent bazaar? You don't quite haggle like a street merchant, but you certainly don't pay the asking price. For anything!" She nodded toward the tag still clutched in Paige's hand. "Besides, that figure includes the TVA."

"The TVA?"

"*Taxe à la valeur ajoutée.* A luxury tax. About forty percent on that little piece, I'd guess. You have to deduct the TVA when you calculate the cost, since you'll get reimbursed for it when you leave the country."

"Oh." Paige stared down at the tag dubiously. She'd never been good with numbers, and the simple mathematical exercise required to estimate the price of this strip of gold daunted her.

"It's not that difficult," the other woman assured her with a grin. "Really. Just divide that figure in half to incorporate the TVA and a ten percent-discount, then convert to dollars, and you have the approximate cost."

Scrunching her forehead, Paige struggled with the mental calculation. "So this…this…"

"I call it a boob tube, but I think a more polite term is bandeau."

"So this bandeau only costs the equivalent of my monthly car payment, and not what we're planning to put down on our house in—"

Paige broke off, biting her lip against a wash of pain. The realization that she'd never live on the hillside home she and David had made an offer on just two weeks ago closed her throat.

The other woman cocked her head. She didn't say anything, but she couldn't have missed the sudden, bleak expression on Paige's face.

Shy and somewhat withdrawn, Paige rarely confided in her few friends. To her shame, she couldn't even fully express herself to David. He was so self-contained, so confident, that she'd always felt a little intimidated by him. Yet she found herself responding to the unspoken question in the other woman's eyes. Drawing in a slow breath, she articulated the decision she'd come to so painfully over the past few days.

"I was engaged...until very recently. We were planning on buying a house together."

"And now?"

Paige swallowed the constriction in her throat. She wouldn't cry. She wouldn't!

"Now?" She lifted her chin. "Now maybe I'll buy this bandeau instead."

A smile curved the blonde's generous mouth. "Good for you. I can't think of any better cure for a broken engagement than a new wardrobe. And Cannes is just the place to acquire one."

Paige eyed the woman's flamboyant red jacket and minuscule shorts. They would look just as stunning when worn with the gold lamé breastband she clutched in her hand as with that glittery mesh halter.

"Did you get that outfit here?" she asked.

"The shorts and top? Yes, earlier this morning. This is my second foray into the shops."

"I wonder if they have another one, in a size eight. My name's Paige, by the way. Paige Lawrence."

"I'm Meredith," the other woman replied. "And if they don't have this in your size, they'll have something just as sinful."

The saleswoman produced the red hot pants and jacket in a perfect size eight. Clutching the bandeau, Paige followed her to a small curtained fitting room that smelled of lavender potpourri and money.

For the next half hour, Maggie pushed her simmering tension to one corner of her mind and indulged in the serious pleasure of shopping.

When Paige Lawrence first walked into this shop, she'd wondered if the younger woman could possibly be the contact she'd been waiting for since she'd arrived in Cannes early this morning. A few moments of idle conversation with the younger woman had killed that idea. If Paige had any connection with the ring of high-class hookers that Meredith Ames was a member of, Maggie would eat the pink satin bustier she'd purchased just two shops ago.

Still, she had to give the slender young woman credit. She'd gulped once or twice, but she'd soon got into the spirit of things. One by one, she'd shed her layers of worsted wool and cable knit. What had emerged was a delicate beauty, less dramatic than Maggie herself, in her carefully orchestrated role, but similar enough to make Maggie feel like a mother hen with a newly hatched chick.

When they'd finished outfitting her in the jaunty red two-piece outfit and matching three-inch-high platform shoes, Paige struggled with the effort to convert the bill from francs to dollars.

"Can I help?" Maggie asked.

"Would you? I don't do well with numbers," she confessed.

Maggie did a quick conversation, skillfully negotiated the saleslady down to a less outrageous commission, and computed the amount of the TVA so that Paige could complete the necessary forms.

The younger woman managed not to flinch at the total, although she did turn a little pale and her fingers fumbled with the pen as she signed the traveler's checks.

"Shall I have your packages sent to your hotels, ladies?" the attendant asked.

"Yes," Maggie replied. "I have more shopping to do yet."

The real Meredith Ames had indicated that she'd been instructed to stroll the shops that lined Cannes's world-famous boulevard, the Croisette, until the nameless, faceless individual who'd arranged shipment of the stolen technology made contact. Maggie had followed the same routine, secretly delighting in the fact that she'd been *forced* to purchase an item or two to keep up her cover. Still, she'd be glad when she finally made contact and got this mission under way.

"Send my things to the Carlton, suite 16," she told the attendant.

"I'll take mine with me," Paige murmured as she stuffed her

traveler's checks into her purse. Gathering up her various bundles, she tugged self-consciously at the back hem of her shorts to make sure the red material covered both cheeks. It did. Barely.

"I haven't found a hotel room yet," she said with a hesitant smile. "When I do, can I give you a call? Maybe I could buy you lunch sometime, to thank you for all your help."

"Maybe," Maggie returned easily, although she had no intention of responding if Paige called. She wasn't about to draw anyone else into the games she'd be playing once the operation swung into high gear.

The tension she'd kept at bay during the interlude in the boutique flickered along her nerves. She should've met her target by now. She'd been in Cannes for six hours, and she'd been strolling the shops off and on for three. The sixth sense that had served her so well during her years with OMEGA told her the contact had to come soon.

"Well, thanks again," Paige said shyly. "I'd...I'd better go find a hotel." She flicked an uncertain glance at the front door and tugged once again at the back hem of the shorts.

Maggie hid her amusement at the younger woman's obvious reluctance to step outside in her new, abbreviated look. Slipping a pair of star-shaped sequined sunglasses off the top of her head, she held them out.

"Here. You need a finishing touch. Try these."

Paige slid on the bright red shades with barely concealed relief.

"Perfect," Maggie told her, grinning.

An answering smile tugged at the other woman's lips as she glanced at herself in the wall of mirrors behind the rococo desk that served as a sales counter.

"Perfect," she agreed.

With a rustle of tissue paper and a final farewell, she gathered her bags in one hand, opened the shop door and stepped out into the late-afternoon sunshine.

She was still smiling when she turned left to walk along the palm-lined boulevard.

And when the long, sleek Rolls-Royce slid to a halt beside her.

Her smile slipped a bit when a dark-haired chauffeur stepped out of the car and took her arm.

It disappeared completely when he hustled her toward the rear passenger door.

Watching through the shop's tinted window, Maggie gave a sudden gasp. "Oh, my God!"

She raced for the boutique's door and dashed into the street just as the Rolls merged into the traffic flowing along the Croisette. Before Maggie could catch more than a few numbers on its license tag, it disappeared into the streaming flow.

"Dammit!"

She stood on the sun-washed pavement, her mind racing with a dozen different possibilities. Unfortunately, only one of them made any sense.

Unless she missed her guess, Paige Lawrence had just made the contact Maggie had been waiting for all afternoon!

# Chapter 3

Great! Just great!

Grinding her teeth in frustration, Maggie searched the lanes of traffic for a likely pursuit vehicle. Just as she stepped off the sidewalk, intending to flag down a sleek German sports model, the flow of cars slowed. To her intense disgust, traffic quickly ground to a halt.

She'd seen some horrible traffic snarls in her lifetime, but few to match those of the Croisette. In the short time she'd been in Cannes, she'd discovered that these hopeless backups occurred frequently, usually when carloads of tourists slowed to gawk at the sun-bronzed, topless and often bottomless bathers on the beach.

While she waited with mounting impatience for the tangled, honking vehicles to sort themselves out, half a dozen possible courses of action flitted through her mind, only to be immediately discarded.

Given the sensitivity of her mission, she couldn't involve the local authorities and ask them to track the Rolls for her. Only two French officials at the highest government levels knew

OMEGA operatives were in place on the Riviera. One was the French president himself. The other was the chief of security, who would supply any assistance Maggie might need in-country.

She'd have to work through OMEGA control to extract Paige Lawrence from this situation without compromising her own or Doc's cover. And she had to do it immediately, before the shy, innocent tourist was harmed!

To her intense relief, the traffic began to flow again. Hailing a cruising cab, she flung herself into the back seat and instructed the driver to take her to the Carlton, fast! While the swarthy Mediterranean weaved back and forth across three lanes, gesturing obscenely but good-naturedly at every angry honk, Maggie dug in her purse for her diamond-studded compact. Flipping open the lid, she pressed the square stone in the center of the lid with one finger.

"Doc, do you read me?" she murmured. She doubted the driver would hear her or notice her talking to her own reflection, seeing as he was engaged in a shouting match with a trio of youngsters on motor scooters who seemed to think they had some right to use the road, as well. Just to be authentic, however, she stabbed at her nose with the powdered sponge.

Pressing the stone once again to shift the communications device in the compact's lid into the receiver mode, Maggie waited impatiently for Doc to respond. His own device, an elegant gold cigarette case, would hum with an ultralow-frequency resonance only he could hear until he acknowledged her transmission. While she waited, she searched her mind, trying to remember just where he would be at this moment. He'd given her a detailed schedule to memorize, then destroy. She hoped he hadn't yet left for the international symposium that was providing his cover.

"Doc here," he replied calmly a few moments later. "Go ahead, Chameleon."

Maggie threw a quick glance at the cab's rearview mirror. The driver was still too engrossed in his vociferous argument with the teens on the scooters to notice her prolonged preoccupation with powdering her nose.

"Doc, get hold of control, quick. Have Cyrene run a check through the IIN on a silver Rolls, 1991 or '92 make, French tags, the first two digits of which are *74.*"

"Will do."

That was Doc, Maggie thought with a surge of sheer relief. No questions, no panic. By the time she got back to the Carlton, he'd have all the information immediately available on the owner of the Rolls through the IIN, the International Intelligence Network. And probably have it synthesized into a list of possible connections with all known fiber optics firms in Europe and North America. What was more, Claire would have started a psychological profile on the possible target.

"I'll be back at home base in five minutes. Make that three," Maggie gasped as the driver swung recklessly across two lanes of traffic, cutting ahead of the motorbikes and a rather large truck in the process. "Meet me in my suite."

"Roger."

"Oh, and ask Cyrene to check out an American by the name of Lawrence. Paige Lawrence. I think our friends have just picked her up by mistake."

Maggie grabbed at the handgrip as the cab swerved around a corner. Righting herself with some effort, she pressed the stone again.

"Doc?"

There was no response. She pressed the transmit button again.

"Doc, did you copy that last transmission?"

"I copied it."

Frowning, Maggie stared down at the compact. She'd never heard quite that element of savage intensity in Doc's voice before. It was clearly audible, even after being bounced off a communications satellite orbiting some two hundred miles overhead.

"Where are you?" he growled. "Right now."

Maggie glanced through the windshield. Just ahead, the distinctive twin cupolas of the Carlton rose above a wavy line of palm fronds. Supposedly modeled after the breasts of a gay French mistress of the Prince of Wales—before he became King

Edward VII—the conical domes crowned either end of the hotel's fanciful facade.

"I'm about a half mile from the hotel," Maggie responded.

"Get the hell up here. Fast! Out."

She blinked at the abrupt termination, then shrugged and tucked the compact in her bag again. She wasn't any more pleased than Doc at this complication in their mission before it even got started. She only hoped she could extract Paige from this damnable mix-up before the players in this deadly game of industrial espionage discovered they had the wrong woman.

Clenching both hands around her purse, she scooted to the edge of her seat and waited for the driver to sweep to a halt in front of her hotel.

A preposterous, thoroughly marvelous wedding-cake structure, the Carlton had been built just prior to World War I. White-painted bricks set in intricate patterns decorated its caramel-colored facade, and gleaming marble columns rose in majestic splendor at the colonnaded entrance. A stately, liveried doorman marched forward to open her door, but before he reached it, Maggie was already out of the cab and rushing for the entrance.

She thrust a wad of francs into his gloved hand, asked him to take care of the fare and add a substantial tip, and hurried inside. Wrought-iron elevator doors clanged shut behind her as she waited, foot-tapping in impatience, for the old-fashioned cage to take her to the fifth floor. She had barely thrust her room key into the lock when her door flew open and a hard hand yanked her inside.

Years of intense training kicked in immediately. Without thought, without hesitation, Maggie swung at her attacker.

Luckily, Doc had undergone the same training she had. He threw up an arm to deflect her blow just in time, then hauled her inside and slammed the door.

"What in the world—?" she exclaimed in astonishment.

Frustration, and an emotion Maggie couldn't quite identify, blazed in his gray blue eyes as he swept the sitting room. She knew he was searching for a place where they could talk undisturbed. A place where he could be sure they wouldn't be "overheard'' by the anonymous individual who'd reserved this opulent, high-ceilinged suite for Meredith Ames in the first place.

"It's clean," she told him, still stunned by his uncharacteristic behavior. "I cleared it this morning."

Using the electronic "sweep" Special Devices had designed to fit into the handle of her hairbrush, Maggie had surreptitiously checked for bugs and hidden cameras when she first arrived.

She'd found one, a sophisticated listening device that she'd foiled with a simple countermeasure. The small gadget looked like a travel clock, and would filter a conversation just enough to make the words indistinguishable. It would also drive any listener batty with the effort to make them out, the chief of Special Devices had informed her smugly.

Doc, however, didn't appear particularly gratified by the knowledge that they could talk in the open.

Although dressed in a conservative business suit of fine gray worsted, his powerful body radiated a fierce, controlled tension as he swung Maggie around to face him. His dark brown hair, gleaming with subtle mahogany tints, lacked its usual neat style. In fact, it looked as though he'd thrust his hand through it. Several times.

"Control is checking the license tag. Claire should get back to us in five minutes or less," he informed her in a low, ominous voice. "Which means you have exactly four minutes and fifty-nine seconds to tell me just how Paige Lawrence got into the picture. And what do you mean, she got picked up by mistake? By whom? When? Dammit, Maggie, how in the hell did you get her involved in this?"

Maggie took an involuntary step backward as Doc leaned over her. She'd never seen him like this. And she'd never realized just how intimidating he could be when all one hundred and ninety pounds of him emanated a cold, hard fury.

"I didn't get her involved," she protested. "Well, I did, I suppose, by encouraging her to buy an outfit similar to mine. That must have been what caused the mix-up. That, and our coloring. But…" She craned her neck back and stared up at David in utter perplexity. "But…"

"But what?" he snarled.

Enough was enough. This was her partner, for heaven's sake. She would trust David Jensen with her life. She'd done just that, in fact, one hot, muggy night in Malaysia, two years ago.

"But what's with this 'Paige' business?" she retorted. "You say her name as if you know her."

His smoky eyes narrowing to dangerous slits. "Of course I know her. She's my fiancée."

*"Your fiancée!"*

Ignoring Maggie's surprised gasp, he pinned her with a hard look. "What I *don't* know is why she came to Cannes before I called her, and why you involved her in this operation."

She debated which issue to address first—the fact that David apparently no longer had a fiancée, at least according to Paige Lawrence, or the fact that Maggie hadn't involved the younger woman in this operation. After another quick glance at Doc's tight jaw, she decided to take the easy one first.

"I don't know why she's here a week early, and I didn't involve her in the mission. It was a mistake. A mix-up. My contact evidently mistook her for me."

Doc ran an eye down her bright gold-and-red-clad form. "Unless your contact is completely blind, there's no way he could mistake Paige for you. She wears dresses, not spangles. And sensible shoes, not elevators."

"Platforms," Maggie said, trying to find a way to break the news that the last time she'd seen Paige Lawrence, she was wearing spangles and three-inch platforms and not much else.

"Look, Doc, I don't understand this any more than you do. It's incredible that she's here and we just happened to bump into each other. Just a crazy coincidence." She paused, her brows drawing together. "Or is it?"

"What the hell is that supposed to mean? What else could it be?"

Still frowning, Maggie folded her arms across her chest. "Just what do you know about Paige Lawrence? Who is she, Doc?"

He stared at her for a long, incredulous moment. "I know all there is to know about her," he stated with savage intensity.

"I've been engaged to her for over a year, and we dated for almost that long before deciding to marry."

"You don't know what she's doing in Cannes," Maggie pointed out.

He drew in a sharp breath, obviously struggling to contain himself.

"No doubt she got the dates confused. She does that occasionally. Well, regularly. Last month, she took me to her parents' home for their fortieth anniversary party. She got the date right. Even the day of the week. Just the wrong month."

The tenderness Maggie had glimpsed in his eyes when he told her of his wedding plans a few days ago flickered in their depths once again.

"Paige has a mild form of dyslexia. One that causes her to transpose numbers. It's what drew me to her in the first place," he added wryly. "That, and the two-hundred-dollar fee she mistakenly charged my department for a two-dollar technical publication. She's smart and generous, and far too trusting for her own good, but she gets a bit muddled at times. She needs someone to look after her."

The tenderness vanished, to be replaced by a fierce, flaring protectiveness. "Which is why I intend to find her, and quickly. However she got involved in this operation, she's out of her depth here. Way out of her depth. Tell me exactly what happened," he ordered.

Maggie did, although she found herself glossing over Paige's hesitant confession that she and Doc wouldn't be making a down payment on a house together. When they located the young woman and extracted her from the situation she'd inadvertently been drawn into, Paige could tell Doc about that herself, Maggie decided.

He listened to her brief account without interruption, absorbing every detail. When she finished, he began to pace the spacious suite.

"All right. We know the problem. This driver appears to have mistaken Paige for you. Now let's break it down into small pieces and find the solution."

Maggie felt a surge of admiration at the way Doc deliberately, ruthlessly controlled his emotions and engaged his mind. She tended to operate more on instinct, yet she knew firsthand how many potentially dangerous situations Doc had neutralized with just this kind of swift, brilliant analysis.

"The driver will have instructions to take her someplace private. Someplace where your contact can remove and examine the chip. Someplace with access to a computer sophisticated enough to read the lines of code and verify that they contain the fiber-optic technology."

His face set with intense concentration, Doc paced the blue-and-green Savonnerie carpet that covered the sitting room's parquet floor.

"I'd guess we have a half hour, an hour at most. When this contact discovers that Paige doesn't have the microdot, he'll either let her go or…" His jaw worked. "Or he'll make sure she doesn't tell anyone about her visit to wherever he's taken her."

"We'll find her, Doc."

"Yes, we will. All right, here's how I think we should—"

He broke off and dug in his pocket. Maggie's pulse leapt in anticipation as he pulled out his gold cigarette case. With the information control would provide, they could kick into action.

"Doc, here. Go ahead, Cyrene."

For a second or two, the only sounds disturbing the sunny stillness of the sitting room were the wash of the waves on the beach across the street and the hum of traffic that drifted in through the open balcony doors. Then Claire Huffacker's calm voice filled the air.

"There are more Rolls-Royces per capita in Cannes than in any other city on earth…" she began.

"Why doesn't that surprise me?" Maggie murmured, glancing at the priceless antiques scattered about the sitting room.

"But I found two that fit your description. One belongs to a reclusive film star, Victor Swanset. He's an English expatriate who owns a villa on avenue Fiesole, in La Californie."

From her intelligence briefings prior to this mission, Maggie knew La Californie was an exclusive residential area that clung to the rugged hills above Cannes. According to the intel briefer, its grandiose Edwardian villas had once been home to a sparkling mix of European royalty and distinguished diplomats and their bevies of mistresses. They sat tucked away among the fragrant stands of pine and eucalyptus trees, and the only access to them was via a steep, winding mountain road.

"No one has seen Victor Swanset in public for over a decade," Claire continued. "My sources indicate he's an anonymous, driving force behind the Cannes Film Festival. Supposedly he's donated millions to preserve his art. I don't have anything else on him right now, except…"

"What?"

"The computer cross-referenced a missing-persons report with Swanset's name listed as a contact. The report was filed about a year ago, on a cook who disappeared from his villa. I'm following up on that now."

"What about the owner of the other Rolls?" Maggie asked.

"It checks to a French banker. Gabriel Adrenne. He was in Tokyo at an International Monetary Fund conference until two days ago. He supposedly stopped over in Cannes for a few days' rest before flying back to Paris."

Claire paused, then added softly, "I've verified that he was also in Cannes last month, when the prototype fiber optics technology was smuggled out of the States."

Maggie and Doc exchanged swift looks.

"Do you have a fix on his location here?" Doc growled.

"Nothing firm. He keeps a condominium in one of the beachfront palaces, but isn't using it on this trip. His staff doesn't have a clue why. From what I've been able to gather on him so far, he's a Donald Trump type. Early forties. Wildly extravagant. Overextended financially. Enjoys the finer things in life, including a string of very expensive ex-wives and mistresses, but is having trouble paying for them. I'll have more for you when I get his health and social history over IIN."

"Thanks, Cyrene," Doc replied, then quickly signed off. "Get changed," he told Maggie, his eyes a flat steel blue. "We're going hunting."

She nodded, already on her way into the bedroom. Slamming the door behind her, she peeled off the halter and stuffed it into her purse. That little dot was going with her wherever she went.

Working frantically at the zipper of her red shorts, she hurried toward the ornate wardrobe that held Meredith's clothes. She had the shorts halfway down her hips when she heard a sharp pounding on the door to her suite.

Kicking off the clingy shorts, Maggie grabbed a pale lavender silk kimono from the wardrobe door and flung it on. She dug in her purse for her .22 and dashed out of the bedroom as another staccato rap sounded on the oak panel.

His weapon in his hand, David melted back into the shadows beside the huge nineteenth-century armoire that housed the suite's entertainment center.

"It's probably the boutique, delivering my purchases," she told him softly.

"Could be," he replied. "Or it could be one of Meredith Ames's customers, sent up by the accommodating concierge. Whoever it is, get rid of him. Fast!"

"Right."

Tucking the .22 into a pocket of her kimono, Maggie pulled open the door.

If the individual standing in the corridor was a delivery boy, he'd forgotten his packages. If he was one of Meredith's customers, he was a precocious one. Small and wiry, with a shock of red hair and a splash of freckles across his thin nose, he couldn't have been more than ten or twelve years old.

To Maggie's considerable amusement, he gave her a cheeky grin and ran his eyes over her bare legs with a blatant masculine approval that was all French.

*"Mademoiselle Ames?"*

*"Oui?"*

*"Bon."* He turned and called out, to no one in particular that Maggie could see, "Your friend is at home, *mademoiselle.* You can come out now."

Keeping a firm grip on the weapon in her pocket, Maggie leaned out the door and peered down the corridor. When a pile of laundry in a wheeled hamper a few yards away began to heave, her eyes narrowed. Sheets and towels tumbled over its sides, and then a disheveled blond head poked its way out of the mound.

While Maggie gaped in astonishment, the street urchin went to help Paige Lawrence climb out of the laundry cart.

The woman looked as though she'd run a marathon—and finished dead last. Her hair straggled down her back in wet, tangled snarls. Her bright red jacket had disappeared, along with one of her shoes. The narrow gold bandeau covered only the center of her breasts, leaving the full curves above and below bare. Her shorts rode down in front and up in back as she clambered awkwardly over the side of the cart and clumped down the hall on one high-soled platform shoe.

"I'm sorry to bother you like this," she murmured distractedly, "but I'm in something of a predicament."

"So I see."

Paige shoved her wet, tangled hair out of her eyes with one hand. "I fell into the bay and lost my purse, along with my passport and all my money."

She'd lost a lot more than that, Maggie thought wildly. She couldn't even begin to anticipate Doc's reaction when he saw his sweet, demure former fiancée.

"Why don't you tell me about it inside?" she suggested faintly.

Paige flashed her a relieved smile. "Thank you. I was hoping I could count on you. This is all so embarrassing."

When she limped awkwardly into the foyer, the cocky boy strolled in right behind her. Hooking both thumbs in the waistband of his rather scruffy-looking shorts, he gave the ornate sitting room a quick once-over and whispered softly.

"A palace, *mademoiselle*," he commented in swift, idiomatic French. "You must do very well of a night."

"I do all right," Maggie returned dryly.

It didn't surprise her that this young tough had guessed Meredith's occupation with one sweeping glance. In fact, it wouldn't have surprised her to learn that he occasionally acted as a middleman in negotiations for just the type of services Meredith offered. His thin, pinched face and shrewd, too-knowing eyes hinted at a life on the streets.

"May I borrow fifty francs?" Paige asked, wrapping her arms around her chest to ward off the cool, breezy air in the suite. "Just until I arrange to have my traveler's checks replaced? I promised to pay—"

She broke off, her mouth dropping, as a tall, broad-shouldered figure stepped out from beside the armoire.

Glancing from her to Doc and back again, Maggie couldn't tell who was the more thunderstruck.

"Paige?" he growled.

"David?" she squeaked.

A cheerful young voice broke the stark silence that followed. "Me, I am Henri. Someone will pay me fifty francs, yes?"

# Chapter 4

Stunned, Paige stood unmoving.

Some distant corner of her mind registered the whisper of cool air that raised goose bumps on her damp skin. She heard the muted roar of the sea across the street. She tasted the tang of salt as she ran the tip of her tongue along suddenly dry lips.

"David?" she repeated weakly.

He didn't answer, except to stride forward and sweep her into his arms.

With a tiny sob, Paige lost herself in his solid, comforting warmth. Her fingers clutched at the scratchy wool of his jacket, and she strained against him for endless, wonderful moments. Then his hand tangled in her hair. He brought her head back and crushed her mouth with his. For once, he didn't control his emotions.

His rough kiss was all that she'd dreamed of. Hard. Searing. Scorching in its intensity.

And over too soon.

Far too soon.

Paige gasped an indistinct protest as he dragged his mouth

from hers and held her head steady in both hands, scrutinizing her face with narrowed eyes.

"Are you all right?"

Still dazed by the raw power of that kiss, she could only stare back at him. It took her a moment to realize that whatever he'd experienced in that brief, shattering moment, he'd already managed to bring it under control.

While her heart was thudding erratically in her chest, David showed only an icy calm.

While her lips ached for his touch, his were drawn into a thin, tight line.

"Are you all right?" he repeated, his eyes searching hers.

Still unable to speak, she pushed herself a little way out of his arms. Or tried to.

As she stumbled back, the narrow lamé band caught on David's tip clip. To her horror, the fabric dragged downward. She splayed one hand across her breasts and tugged frantically at the soggy band with the other.

David unsnared her and shrugged out of his jacket. "Here, take this."

Her face flaming, Paige stood rigid as he dropped the worsted around her shoulders. She heard a stir behind her and remembered that there were others present. The heat in her face intensified even more.

She glanced behind her and caught the other woman's eyes. Friendliness shone in their green depths, and a carefully banked curiosity. Paige started to respond to the unspoken question there, and then noticed for the first time Meredith's short dressing gown. The pale lavender silk brushed the tops of her legs. Her very long and very bare legs.

The soaring combination of relief and joy that had swept through her when she saw David faltered.

Meredith moved forward, the silk swishing against her bare skin. "Why don't you bring her into the sitting room, Doc? So we can find out what happened?"

*Doc?*

The easy familiarity with which this woman addressed David

plummeted through Paige like a stone dropping into a well. Numbly she felt him take her elbow and steer her toward the huge, vaulted room.

Glancing down at the woman beside him, Doc struggled to bring his soaring relief and astonishment under control. His senses were still reeling from the vivid image of Paige standing before him, her green eyes huge in her pale face, wearing only a narrow strip of gold, a pair of red shorts that displayed a good portion of her firm, rounded rear cheeks, and one ridiculously high shoe. He gripped her arm in a tight hold, as if to reassure himself that this wet, unfamiliar creature was actually Paige.

They hadn't taken two steps when a high, piping voice stopped them.

"But first my fifty francs, no? Me, I have business I must attend to."

Doc turned back, wrenching his attention away from his bedraggled, nearly naked fiancée to survey the boy. The youngster cocked his head and waited expectantly, his thumbs hooked in the waistband of his grubby shorts and a confident expression on his freckled face.

Malnourished, Doc noted in a swift mental list. Undersized for his age, which was about eleven or twelve. A faint scar on his chin that probably hadn't come from falling off a bike. Tough as shoe leather, if the cocky expression on his face was any indication.

"Fifty francs?" Doc asked. "For what?"

"For fishing *mademoiselle* out of the sea."

At Doc's quick frown, the boy gave a little wave of one hand. "She wades ashore some distance from here, you understand, and I bring her to the hotel. Fifty francs is a small fee, no? For such a service?"

Reaching into his pocket, David withdrew his wallet and pulled out a hundred-franc note. *"Merci."*

To his surprise, a white-faced, trembling Paige pushed his hand away before he could pass the bill to the youth.

"No."

Her voice wavered and almost broke on the single syllable.

His protective instincts soaring, David moved to take her into his arms again.

"No!" she repeated, backing away.

Sudden, swift fear curled in Doc's belly. Although she appeared unhurt and had walked into the suite unassisted, something must have happened to make her shy away from him like that. Exerting immense control, he remained still. "What is it? What's the matter?"

"Before I let you pay my debts for me, I think you'd better explain—" She swallowed and darted a quick look at Maggie's bare legs and scantily clad body. "I think you'd better explain what you're doing here, in this woman's suite."

Cursing to himself, Doc realized that he'd made a tactical error. He, the precise, flawless engineer, who always thought problems through step by step before acting, who never made mistakes, had screwed up. Royally. He'd let his concern for Paige drive clear out of his mind the fact that she had no idea why he was here, in "Meredith Ames's" suite.

And he couldn't tell her.

He met Maggie's eyes in swift, silent communication and gave an almost imperceptible shake of his head, determined not to involve Paige in this any more than she already was. Still, the agent in him had to draw whatever she knew out of her.

"We'll talk about what I'm doing here later," he said. "Right now, you need to tell me what happened."

"No, I think we'd better talk about it now," she insisted, squaring her shoulders under the gray wool suit coat.

Despite himself, Doc felt heat spear through his belly as her small movement threatened to dislodge the thin strip of gold once more.

Rigidly he controlled the urge to reach out and tuck the folds of his jacket across her front. He'd seen Paige in less than she now wore, he reminded himself. He'd caressed and kissed her soft flesh a number of times in the past year. Not as often as he'd wanted to, but he'd deliberately held himself back. He hadn't wanted to overwhelm her, to frighten her with the passion he kept ruthlessly in check. She was so shy with him, so delicate in her responses.

Yet seeing her there, with that barbaric band around her breasts and her eyes flashing a challenge he'd never seen in them before, he had difficulty remembering that this was Paige. Sweet, shy Paige.

"I can't explain it," he replied in an even tone. "Not now."

Henri gave a small, derisive snort and lifted one red brow. "Me, I can."

"Keep out of this, half-pint," Maggie murmured, jerking at the back of his ragged, less-than-pristine navy sweater.

Doc ignored the two of them. "You'll just have to trust me," he said quietly.

When she hesitated, her eyes searching his with desperate need, he smiled reassuringly.

"Come on, sweetheart, we'll sort this out later. Right now we need to talk about what happened."

Ever afterward, Paige would wonder what might have happened if he hadn't used just that tone with her, as though he were speaking to a recalcitrant child.

If he hadn't assumed she would meekly comply with his soft but unmistakable order.

If she hadn't seen the swift, silent communication between David, *her* David, and this sophisticated, elegant…female.

It galled Paige no end that she'd actually liked Meredith! That she'd come to her for help after losing her passport and her money. That she hadn't wanted to contact David, because she hadn't been ready to face him yet.

She was ready now. Jerking her arm out of his hold, she lifted her chin defiantly.

"I'd like an explanation, David. Now."

He blinked, looking as surprised as if a pet kitten had suddenly arched its back and dug its claws into his hand. Over her head, he sent Meredith a quick, puzzled look.

When she saw the exchange, hot, fierce jealousy seared through Paige. It was emotion she hadn't ever felt before where

David was concerned. In its wake came another, even more shattering emotion. Pain. Pure, unadulterated pain.

She'd been right.

In those moments perched high above Cannes, in that little turnout, when she slipped her engagement ring from her finger, she'd been right.

She wasn't woman enough for this man.

In her heart, she believed David, *her* David, had some logical explanation for being in this suite. In her soul, she knew he wasn't the kind of man to dally with one woman while he was engaged to another.

But that quick glance, that unspoken communication between the two of them, told Paige that David shared a special bond with Meredith Ames. She was a part of his life Paige hadn't known about, for some reason. A part of himself she'd often sensed that he held back. A part that, despite the fierce, searing kiss of a few moments ago, he still kept separate from her.

"Paige…" he began, once more in that placating tone she suddenly despised.

"Never mind! It doesn't matter anymore." Blinking furiously to dispel a sudden sheen of tears, she lifted her chin. "I'm sorry I arrived in Cannes early and disrupted your…your business conference. I'll let you get back to it."

Spinning around on her one platform heel, she limped toward the door. "Come on, Henri. I'll get the francs to pay you from the American Express office."

"Dammit, Paige! Wait!"

She flashed him a furious glance as he planted one big hand against the painted door and prevented her exit.

"Get rid of the kid," he instructed Meredith tersely, then took Paige's arm in a hold that wasn't quite as gentle as before.

She started to resist, but one look at his face quelled her brief spurt of rebellion. She'd never seen David look so hard. Or so determined. Biting her lip, she allowed him to lead her a little way into the suite.

"Here, Henri." Meredith shoved a bill into the boy's hand and gave him a little push toward the door.

His birdlike black eyes darted from one adult to the other, then fastened on Paige. "I am often at the telephone kiosk at the corner of the Croisette and the Allées de la Liberté. The kiosk is my headquarters, you understand. You will find me there, yes? If you need me."

Paige swallowed. "Yes. Thank you."

He lifted his hand and rubbed the bill between his fingers. "I thank you, *mademoiselle*."

With a wide grin and another quick glance at Meredith's legs, he was gone.

For a long moment after the door closed behind the boy, no one moved. It was as though they were all measuring each other, mentally adjusting to the unfamiliar personalities that had just emerged.

David, as Paige might have expected, recovered first. His hand gentled on her arm, and his gray blue eyes shaded with concern as they swept over her.

"Sit down, sweetheart, and tell us what happened."

Mutely Paige sank down on a damask-rose satin settee swirling with ornate curves and exquisite detailing.

David sat beside her. Reaching out, he took her cold hand in both of his and began to rub some warmth into it.

Meredith curled a leg under her and occupied a rose-and-green patterned armchair.

Confused, hurting, and close to the tears she'd held at bay until this moment, Paige stared down at David's large, square hands. Those blunt-tipped fingers had worked such magic on her body. Those palms had shaped her breasts and her waist and her future. Now she had no future. Not the one she'd envisioned with David, anyway.

With a fresh wave of pain, she tried to tug her hand free. David's fingers suddenly tightened on hers.

"Where's your ring?" he asked. His face subtly altered, taking on stark planes and rigid angles. "Did those bastards take it?"

She blinked, startled by the savage fury in his voice.

"Did they hurt you?"

"Did who hurt me?"

His jaw worked. "You can tell me, sweetheart. What did they do to you?"

"They?"

"Let her tell us what happened, Doc," Meredith interjected.

The quiet words tore at Paige's soul. If she'd needed any proof that the man she loved and the woman she'd admired during their brief encounter in the boutique shared a special bond, that casual nickname was it. She couldn't imagine any of David's associates at the engineering firm where they both worked calling him "Doc." His impressive credentials and professional stature were such that everyone, from suppliers to the president of the firm, regarded him with a respect bordering on awe.

As chief of the technical library, Paige had been more than a little intimidated the first time she'd been summoned to David's office. Especially since she'd overcharged his department by several hundred dollars for a publication he'd requested.

She'd been equally overwhelmed when he followed up that first meeting with several visits to her crowded little work center. So overwhelmed, she hadn't even realized he was asking her to dinner one drizzly Saturday morning, until he tilted her chin and smiled down at her in a way that made her stutter in confusion.

Correctly interpreting that stammering reply as an affirmative, he'd picked her up that night. And the next. Shortly afterward, he'd begun a slow, measured courtship that left Paige simmering with anticipation for each new plateau in their relationship and aching with loneliness during his frequent business trips abroad.

With a slow sinking sensation, she wondered how many of those business trips David had taken with Meredith Ames. And just what their relationship was.

She glanced at the other woman now, cataloging her vitality, her glowing beauty. Paige's hurt became a dull, throbbing ache.

"What happened?" Meredith asked. "After you left the boutique?"

"A limousine pulled up," Paige replied, with a small, defeated sigh. "No, not a limo. A Rolls-Royce. It was sent for you, you know. The chauffeur called me Mademoiselle Ames several times.''

''That's what I was afraid of.''

''I tried to explain, but I was so surprised that my little bit of French deserted me.'' She made a little grimace of distaste. ''Besides, the driver was rather rude about it all.''

David's hand tightened on hers. ''Rude?''

''Yes. He practically pushed me into the back seat. Then there was a glass partition between us, and I couldn't even talk to him until we pulled up at the marina.''

''What marina?''

''I don't know. One of the ones along the Croisette.''

''And then?''

''And then he gestured toward the boat. Since he didn't seem to understand me and I couldn't get through to him, I decided to explain the situation to whoever was on the boat. But when I tried to walk up the ramp in these shoes, I fell off.''

''What?''

''You did what?''

The simultaneous questions jumped at her from opposite directions.

The swift, startled look that passed between David and Meredith set Paige's teeth on edge. These two might not be lovers, but they certainly could communicate with an economy of words. A tiny, healthy anger began to nibble at the edges of her hurt.

She pulled her hand free of David's tight hold and wove her fingers together in her lap.

''I fell off the ramp,'' she repeated through stiff lips. ''The gangplank. When I was walking up it, onto the yacht.''

''What yacht?''

''I don't know. A big one. With white sides.''

''Did you see the name?'' David asked.

''Or the registration number?'' Meredith added.

''There were some numbers painted on the side of the boat. Three-six-one something.'' Her forehead scrunched. ''Maybe it was six-one-three. Or three—'' Embarrassed by the disability that had dogged her all her life, Paige clamped her lips shut.

"Never mind," David replied. "We'll check all possible combinations. What happened after you fell off the gangplank? It's important. Tell us everything, exactly as it happened."

Gripping her hands together in her lap, she recounted the details of her unexpected swim in the Mediterranean.

"The tide swept me under the dock. There were so many boats berthed at the marina that when I finally surfaced, I didn't know where I was. I could hear shouting some distance away. I thought I heard a splash or two, like oars hitting the water. But by that time, I'd started swimming for shore. I had to shrug out of my jacket, and I lost my purse, but I made it."

David's brows drew into a dark slash, but he didn't interrupt.

"That's when Henri came along," Paige finished. "On his scooter. He saw me wading through the water and helped me to shore. I...I remembered that Meredith had told the saleslady to send her packages to the Carlton, so I asked Henri to bring me here."

With a challenging tilt to her chin, she met Meredith's eyes. "Other than David, you were the only person I knew in Cannes."

David shifted beside her, drawing her attention back to him as he stared at her in some puzzlement. "Why didn't you just come to me? You knew I was staying in this hotel, as well."

It was here, the moment Paige had dreaded and worried about and cried over for weeks. She wet suddenly dry lips, unable to speak.

"Why didn't you come to me, Paige?" A small frown etched across his forehead. "And you still haven't told me what happened to your ring."

In the small silence that followed, Meredith uncurled her long legs and rose. "Why don't I go get dressed?"

Neither of the two people facing each other on the settee paid any attention to her as she moved across the wide, luxuriously furnished sitting room. The tall double bedroom doors closed behind her.

Paige ran her tongue along her lower lip, her whole being focused on the man beside her. She let her eyes drift over the strong planes of his face, storing up memories of the lines at the corners of his eyes, the slight bump in the bridge of his nose, the square chin.

"My emerald ring is in my purse, David," she said slowly. "Which is resting somewhere at the bottom of the bay right now. I took it off before I arrived in Cannes."

"Why?"

"Because I was going to give it back to you."

He went completely still.

Her heart hammering, Paige searched his face. She thought she saw confusion, and hurt, and a sudden fierce denial, flicker in his intent eyes, but in typical David fashion, he didn't express any of that. Instead, he sought to understand the root cause of the problem.

"Why?" he asked again.

Paige groped for some way to explain the feelings that had haunted her for weeks. "Because we have different ideas of marriage. To me, it's a communion between two beings, an equal partnership, with nothing held back." Her gaze flickered to the closed bedroom door. "To you, it's obviously something else."

"I see. You think that I—"

He broke off as the door flew open and Meredith burst into the sitting room.

"I just went to draw the curtains and saw Paige's little friend, Henri, on the sidewalk below. He's talking to someone who looks very much like the chauffeur of the Rolls."

"Hell!" David surged to his feet. "Stay with Paige. And lock the door behind me."

In a few swift strides, he was out the door and into the corridor.

Meredith turned the dead bolt behind him and hooked the old-fashioned chain into the guard for good measure. Without speaking, she crossed the wide expanse of carpeted floor and flattened her back against the wall beside the open balcony doors. She peered out for long, tense moments, while Paige watched in growing confusion.

After a few seconds, Meredith shook her head in disgust. "I can't see anything from here. The palm trees block the sidewalk."

She came back to the grouping of graceful carved rosewood furniture and dropped into the chair she'd vacated just moments before.

"What's going on?" Paige asked. "Why did David rush out like that?"

"We'd like to know who the chauffeur's working for."

"You don't know? I thought…I thought the driver came to the boutique for you."

"He did."

"But you don't know who he's working for?"

Struggling to make sense of the confusing situation, Paige tucked a strand of limp white gold hair behind her ears. "Who are you?"

The tall, self-assured woman hesitated, then gave a small shrug. "I told you. I'm Meredith Ames."

"How do you know David?"

"That's something he'll explain to you."

Frowning, Paige stared at Meredith, then did a slow survey of the opulent suite.

"What do you do? For a living?"

Maggie stifled a groan. She hated having to perpetuate this deception on a woman she was coming to like, for herself as much as for the fact that she was Doc's fiancée. Had been Doc's fiancée. Whatever. But she had no choice, not if there was any chance at all that she could maintain her cover and salvage what was left of her mission.

She drew in a slow breath, suspecting that Paige wasn't going to appreciate the answer to her question.

# Chapter 5

"A call girl?" Paige looked Meredith up and down, then shook her head emphatically. "I don't believe it."

"You believed it, or something close to it, when you first walked in the door."

"That was then," she stated with irrefutable logic. "This is now."

Meredith hesitated, then made a small gesture that encompassed the elegant suite. "Do you think your average American tourist can afford to stay at the Carlton or shop on the Croisette?"

Paige glanced around, taking in the opulent furnishings and the huge vases filled with freshly cut flowers that were scattered on every level surface. Her work as a technical librarian involved her more with research in engineering and the applied sciences than with general references, but she'd studied enough sourcebooks in college to recognize a few of the priceless antiques that graced the sitting. A beautiful rosewood secretaire, its roll top inlaid with an intricate mother-of-pearl woodland scene, sat in one corner. The ornate, marble-topped table set against the opposite wall was Italian, she guessed, as was the massive gilt mirror that hung above it.

No, she acknowledged heavily, your average American tourist couldn't afford this suite.

Still, Paige refused to accept that Meredith and David, *her* David, shared an illicit relationship. "You may be a…a call girl, but I don't believe David's one of your customers."

An understanding smile tugged at the other woman's full lips. "No, he's not one of my customers."

Paige stared at her for a long moment, and then her eyes widened in startled disbelief. "Good heavens, you're not trying to tell me he's your…your pimp?"

Half groaning, half laughing, Meredith shook her head. "Women at my level of the profession don't have pimps. Our clients are referred to us by reliable sources, and usually contact us over the phone, which is where the term came from in the first place."

Paige chewed on her lower lip, thinking furiously. She might be naive, and a little timid on occasion, but she wasn't stupid.

"I don't believe it," she said flatly. "There's something else going on here, something you won't tell me. Either of you."

The other woman hesitated, then gave a small sigh. "Look, I'm not cleared to tell you anything. Obviously you realize you've stumbled into the middle of something Doc and I are working on together. All I can say is that it's dangerous. Very dangerous."

Meredith threw a quick glance over her shoulder as a soft knock sounded on the door. She rose, her hand slipping into her pocket. Paige's eyes widened at the faint outline of a gun she saw in the lavender silk. Open-mouthed, she watched Meredith glide to the door on bare feet, not making a sound, then peer through the peephole.

Her shoulders lost their coiled tension, and she opened the door for David.

"We're okay," he said quietly. "It cost me another fifty francs, but I verified that our pal Henri didn't disclose anything to the chauffeur other than the fact that he brought an American woman back to this hotel. Apparently the driver still thinks it was Meredith Ames who went into the sea.''

''We're close enough in appearance,'' Meredith said. ''Maybe we can still pull this operation off.''

''What operation?'' Paige asked.

David walked to her side. ''You aren't cleared to know. Tell me, did anyone besides this driver get a good look at you before you nose-dived into the bay? Anyone on board the yacht?''

''I don't know. There were some people—crewmen, I think— on the back deck. But I didn't see anyone else.''

''We'll just have to chance it,'' Meredith said quietly to David. ''We've taken greater risks before. Or we can take the chauffeur out for a little while.''

''Right.'' He gave Paige's hands a little squeeze. ''Come on, let's get you out of here. I'll take you back to your hotel so you can get your things.''

''My things?'' she asked, startled.

''You're flying out of Cannes in forty-five minutes—sooner, if Meredith can arrange it.''

''Leaving? But what about my purse? My passport? I don't have any papers, or money.''

''You won't need any,'' the other woman assured her, moving toward the bedroom with a confident stride. ''I'll take care of everything.''

''Let's go,'' David said, tugging her to her feet. ''I'll write out your itinerary for you as soon as it's confirmed and make you a list of contacts at each stop, in case you need them.''

Her forehead creased as she rose, still wrapped in the soft wool of his suit coat. ''How can you get me out of France with no papers?''

His mouth firmed in an effort to control his impatience as he tugged her to her feet. ''I can't explain it to you. Not right now. But you don't have to worry. I'll make sure you're safe. Someone will be covering you every second until you walk in your front door. When I return,'' he added firmly, ''we'll work through this matter of our engagement.''

It was that firm, no-nonsense tone that did it.

At that moment, Paige decided she would not walk out of this hotel room like a chastened child, to be sent home to wait and wonder and worry. If there was any hope for her and David at all, if he was ever going to share this private part of his life with her, it had to be now.

Digging in her one bare and one shod heels, she resisted his efforts to escort her to the suite's door. "I'm not leaving."

"I know this is confusing for you," he said, in that even voice that made Paige's back teeth grind together. "I'll explain what I can when I get home."

"I'm not leaving," she repeated, folding her arms across her chest. "I want to know what's going on."

His jaw squared a bit at that. "We don't have time for this."

"Then we'll just have to make time."

His blue eyes hardened for an instant, and he gave her slender form a quick, assessing look that suddenly made Paige just a little nervous. How ridiculous, she thought, dismissing the shivery sensation that darted down her spine as the product of overstretched nerves. David would never use his physical strength against her. He was always so careful with her, so solicitous of her comfort. The thought reassured her, yet somehow depressed her at the same time.

"You weren't listening before," she told him, with a tilt to her chin. "I was trying to say that marriage has to be an equal partnership. All the strength can't be on one side, nor all the sharing."

"What about all the trust?"

"I trust you. I trust you enough to believe you're not one of Meredith's customers."

"Thank you for that much, at least."

Paige's back stiffened at the hint of sarcasm in his voice. She tossed her damp hair over her shoulders in a gesture that held an uncharacteristic rebelliousness.

"Someone has mistaken me for Meredith, correct?"

"Correct. And we're getting you out of here before they discover that mistake."

"What happens if they do discover Meredith isn't me? Or I'm not her?"

"That's not your concern."

There it was again. The closed door. The sealed chamber. The locked part of himself that he refused to allow Paige into. Her mouth settling into mulish lines, she met his look.

"I'm not leaving, David."

"It's not your choice," he told her, his face hardening.

"Is that right? Just what are you going to do? Drug me and carry me unconscious aboard the plane?"

"If I have to."

Paige's jaw dropped. Shock held her immobile for long, silent moments. Then the welter of emotions that had weighted her down for so many weeks exploded. Uncertainty, wrenching unhappiness, insecurity and a debilitating sense of inadequacy all erupted into searing anger.

Planting her hands on her hips, she glared at David. "Now you listen to me, Mr. Take-Charge-Stone-Face-Macho-Man! I don't know who you think you are or where you got the impression that I'm some kind of windup doll you can play with when it suits you, then set conveniently out of the way when you've got better things to do. But we're going to correct that impression right here and right now."

"Calm down, Paige."

"Don't 'Paige' me. And do not, *do not ever,* use that patronizing tone of voice with me again. Assuming I allow you to speak to me at all, that is. I want to know what's going on here."

They faced each other like two combatants, arms crossed and bodies tense. Neither one heard Meredith walk back into the room.

Maggie could see at a glance that the course of true love hadn't run smooth during her brief absence. David and Paige stood toe-to-toe, looking for all the world like a sleek, well-muscled California brown bear squared off against a delicate gazelle. He towered over Paige, his face set in hard, unyielding lines. Chin lifted, eyes flashing with a surprising bravado, she glowered up at him. The gazelle wasn't giving an inch, Maggie realized with a start of surprise.

"It's all set," she announced, drawing their reluctant attention. "A helicopter will pick Paige up at the heliport atop the Carlton in thirty minutes. She'll fly to the U.S. air base at Ramstein, in Germany, then take a transport to the States."

"I'm not going."

Her eyes widening in surprise, Maggie glanced from Paige's set face to David's thunderous one, then back again.

"Someone thinks I'm you," the younger woman said belligerently. "Or rather that I'm the person you're obviously pretending to be."

"What makes you think I'm pretending?" Maggie asked sharply.

Paige waved an impatient hand. "I admit I don't know anything about call girls or pimps or this particular line of work. But I do know David. He may be overbearing and obnoxious and entirely too arrogant in his own quiet way," she said acidly, "but he's not the kind of man to become involved with...with prostitution."

Doc didn't look particularly pleased with her somewhat backhanded vote of confidence.

"Besides," Paige added, with a cool look in her forest green eyes, "a call girl doesn't just whisk a person out of a foreign country aboard military transports. Who do you work for? Military intelligence? The CIA?"

Maggie and Doc exchanged silent looks.

"If you two do that one more time," Paige stated through clenched teeth, "I'm going to throw something."

Her mind racing, Maggie assessed the situation. Obviously, there was more to Paige Lawrence than the shy, somewhat timid young woman she'd met in the boutique this morning. She was intelligent, too intelligent for her own good. She'd guessed enough to put herself in danger if those on the yacht managed to connect her with this operation. OMEGA would have to send her to a safe haven for the duration of the mission.

Assuming the mission wasn't already hopelessly compromised, Maggie thought with bitter honesty. She and Paige were close enough in appearance to be mistaken for each other at first glance, but not close enough to carry off the deception if the driver, or anyone else, had gotten a clear look at either of them.

Which was why, when Paige suggested a few moments later that she stay in Cannes and meet with whomever had sent the Rolls, Maggie didn't object immediately.

David, however, did.

"Absolutely not."

Paige ignored him, addressing herself to Maggie. "The driver thinks I'm Meredith Ames. I never managed to correct that impression before I fell into the bay. Those people aboard the yacht may have seen me. Whoever was waiting on that boat now expect me, not you."

"True."

"Why were you going there? Other than the obvious reason?" She stared at Maggie, her eyes thoughtful. "You must be delivering something. A message. Or information. Or money."

This woman was definitely too intelligent for her own good.

"That's enough," David interjected. "You've just run out of time to gather your things, Paige. I'll have them sent to you. Come with me."

"No."

"Dammit, you have no idea what's going down here."

"No, I don't. So tell me."

"You don't need to know. I'm not going to allow you to—"

She interrupted him in a soft, dangerous voice. "David, if you harbor even the faintest hope that we might marry someday, which I'll admit appears very unlikely at this moment, you won't finish that sentence."

His jaw tight, Doc refrained from finishing his sentence.

While he scowled down at her, Paige fired the final shot. "I love you, David. I think I've loved you since the moment I walked into your office and you helped me sort out the mix-up on that rather expensive publication I ordered for you. I…I know you love me, too." She held up a quick hand when he moved towards her. "Let me finish!"

"You've just said all that matters."

"No. No, I haven't." She drew in a deep breath. "I see now that we don't really know each other. You think I need to be coddled and protected and cherished all my life, and..."

She slid Maggie a quick, sideways glance. "And I think you need a more adventuresome partner, a woman who stirs more than just your protective instincts. I want the chance to prove I'm that woman. I need to do this. For you. For me. For us."

Maggie held her breath, feeling much like a voyeur watching a riveting, compelling personal drama. She probably should've gone back into the bedroom some time ago, she told herself ruefully. But there wasn't any way she was going to miss the ending to this particular scene.

"Whatever you're doing must have some desperate consequences," Paige added softly. "For you, or for our country. I can help. I have a right to help."

When he didn't respond, she drew in a deep breath. "I'm not leaving, David. Not willingly. I'm going to deliver whatever it is that Meredith's supposed to deliver. When this is over, we'll decide who we really are and where we go from here."

Endless seconds ticked by. Outside the open balcony doors, a shrill horn honked on the boulevard below. Inside the suite, a soft breeze stirred air redolent with the scent of white carnations and tall velvet blue irises.

"When this is over—" Doc snapped "—I just hope we *know* who the hell we are."

Sometime later, Maggie studied the two figures on the settee as she waited for control to acknowledge her transmission.

Paige fidgeted a little, hunching shoulders still wrapped in Doc's coat against the cooling breeze. Her eyes were wide with excitement.

David didn't move. Not a muscle. Not an eyelash.

Maggie had worked with him on a number of missions in the past three years. She'd seen him up to his elbows in an Asian swamp and flat on his stomach, inching his way across a thin crust of ice that cracked ominously under his weight with every movement. She'd watched him at the high-speed computer in the control center, his jaw tight and small beads of sweat rolling down the side of his brow as he pulled together a list of possible Irish terrorists just hours before visiting British royalty were scheduled to land in Washington, D.C.

But she'd never seen him as tightly coiled as he was now.

Claire's clear voice cut through the heavy silence at last.

"Cyrene here. I've got Thunder with me. Go ahead, Chameleon."

Maggie smiled as she lifted the transceiver. She'd just won a bet with herself. She'd fully expected Adam Ridgeway to come up to the OMEGA control center once Claire had given him the startling news that Doc's fiancée needed immediate extraction. The director would make it his personal responsibility to ensure his agent's loved one was out of danger.

"The situation I briefed you on a few moments ago has changed a bit," Maggie announced, with slight understatement.

"How so, Chameleon?"

"We won't need the transportation I requested for the subject. Not just yet, anyway."

"Why not?" Adam asked sharply. "Is she all right?"

"She's fine. She's right here, with me and Doc. But she understands that she's been mistaken for me. She wants to make the contact in my place." Flicking an apologetic glance at Doc, Maggie finished her transmission. "I think we should let her."

For several long moments, Adam didn't respond. Maggie held her breath, not quite sure whether or not she wanted the director to approve this highly irregular request. What they were proposing was well outside OMEGA's operating parameters. As far as she knew, Adam had never allowed anyone other than fully cleared, well-trained agents to become involved in the organization's desperate and often deadly operations.

On the other hand, he had two of his best-trained operatives in the field with Paige right now. If anyone could keep her safe, and still pull off this dangerous charade, Maggie and Doc could. She hoped.

"Let me get this straight," Adam said at last. "You want me

to authorize a civilian to impersonate a secret agent who's impersonating a call girl?''

"That's it," Maggie confirmed.

"Does Doc concur with this?"

Maggie flicked a quick glance at David's rigid face. Strange she'd never quite appreciated the phrase *carved in granite* before. Without a word, she handed him the compact.

David sent his former and perhaps current fiancée a cold stare.

Paige started to shrink back into the cocoon of his wool jacket, but caught herself just in time. Squaring her shoulders, she returned his look.

His mouth compressed to a thin line, David lifted the compact. The gold case looked tiny and fragile in his big hands, but he operated the transmit button with a sure, competent touch.

"Doc here. I concur. With specific conditions."

Maggie frowned. In the heated discussion that had preceded this transmission, David hadn't mentioned any conditions.

"The subject isn't to be out of our contact, not for a moment," he stated with grim emphasis. "I want to know where she is every second. She'll need a tracking device implanted under her skin. Today."

"I can have someone there in a few hours," Adam replied slowly.

"Wait a minute!" Paige protested. "What tracking device? Implanted where under my skin?"

"Don't worry," Maggie assured her. "It's just a small chip. So tiny, you won't even know it's there."

"I won't know it's *where?*"

Ignoring their exchange, David continued laying out his conditions. "I'm altering my cover to provide her closer surveillance. I haven't worked out all the details yet. I'll get back to you as soon as I do."

"Fine."

The lines bracketing either side of his mouth deepened. "And I reserve the right to extract her without prior consultation. Anytime I deem it necessary."

"Agreed."

"Not by me!" Thoroughly indignant, Paige reached for the compact. "I want to talk to him."

With obvious reluctance, David handed her the communications device. "Press the stone in the center of the lid once to transmit, twice to receive."

She fumbled with the small gold case for a moment or two, then held the mirror up in front of her face.

"What did you call him?" she asked Maggie, peering over the lid. "Thunder?"

"Thunder," Maggie confirmed. "It's his code name."

The satellite transmissions were secure, and so scrambled they couldn't be interpreted even if they were intercepted. Still, none of the OMEGA agents ever took unnecessary chances.

Paige squeezed the small stone. "Mr. Thunder, this is...this is Jezebel."

David grimaced in disgust.

After a pregnant pause, Adam replied. "Go ahead, Jezebel."

"I just want to let you know I'm well aware of Dav—of Doc's concerns. I'll do whatever he and—?"

"Chameleon," Maggie supplied.

"Whatever he and Chameleon say. Within reason. I want to check out this implant before anyone pokes it under my skin."

"I can understand your reservations," Thunder replied. "However, Doc has made the tracking device a condition of your involvement in this operation. If you don't agree to it, you'll be out of Cannes within twenty minutes."

*Whew!* Maggie had felt the whip of Adam's authority a few times herself in the past. It wasn't a particularly pleasant experience, even at a distance of some five thousand miles.

To her credit, Paige didn't wilt under the force of Adam's edict. The prospect of adventure, Maggie decided wryly, must have brought out some inner qualities that she suspected the younger woman hadn't displayed very often in the past.

Paige scowled at the compact, then at Doc, then at the compact again.

"Fine," she said testily into the transmitter. "But the thing had darn well better be removable. I don't want to walk around on an electronic leash for the rest of my life.''

Fumbling with the receive button, she didn't catch the hard glint that deepened David's eyes to a gunmetal gray.

Maggie did, however.

Something told her that Paige was going to find it a lot more difficult to shed her leash after her adventure than she imagined.

*Chapter 6*

For Paige, the next few hours seemed like something right out of a spy novel.

David made no effort to hide his anger at her stubbornness, but as soon as Thunder confirmed the decision, he moved into action. Coolly directing Paige to slip into something more suitable for an intense training session, he sat down at the secretaire and pulled a sheet of the hotel's elegant stationery in front of him.

Chameleon, who had confided that her real name was Maggie, took Paige into the bedroom and dug out a pair of tan linen slacks and a sleeveless, backless silk top in a vivid jade.

"Come out as soon as you're changed. We've got a lot to do, and not much time to do it in. Our…your contact could call at any moment."

Maggie paused, her hand on the door latch. "Are you sure about this, Paige? Or I suppose I'd better call you Meredith?"

Paige glanced over her shoulder into the sitting room. David's broad back was to her. She could see the play of his muscles under his starched cotton shirt as he wrote. The afternoon sunlight picked out the deep reddish tints in his brown hair. He seemed so achingly familiar to her, and yet suddenly such a stranger.

Her heart thumped with the knowledge that she was going to discover a side to him she'd never known before.

"Yes, I'm sure."

When she emerged from the bedroom a few moments later, David held several neat handwritten lists.

"All right," he said, "let's get to it."

She'd known he was a skilled engineer and a born leader, of course. The several hundred electronics engineers and technicians who worked for him at the huge firm where they were both employed worshiped him. Personnel turnover in David's division was minimal, and output was well above that of any other department in terms of both quality and quantity. He'd rarely talked about his work when he and Paige were together, preferring instead to explore their similar preferences in old movies and spicy foods and biking through Cali-fornia's glorious national parks. But she'd heard enough cafeteria scuttlebutt and office gossip to know that when David set his mind and his energy to a problem, everyone considered it solved.

He now orchestrated Paige's transformation from technical librarian to high-class hooker with the same skill he brought to his job. And with a merciless, unrelenting thoroughness that almost overwhelmed her.

The first task was to teach her the emergency signals.

Taking into account her difficulty with figures, David and Maggie grilled Paige on each and every signal, over and over. By the time they were done, she was sure she'd be able to verify everything from "Agent in place" to "Situation desperate, request immediate backup" sixty or seventy years from now.

Then they instructed her in the use of the various implements Maggie laid out on the square, marble-topped coffee table. Paige fumbled a bit with the electronic "sweep" in the hairbrush handle, and gasped when a small but lethal projectile shot out of a tube of mascara and embedded itself in the opposite wall. On her second try with the mascara, she aimed for a thick folded

pad David had propped against a chairback and hit a rare
Meissen figurine of a young girl on the mantel. While David
picked up the shattered porcelain pieces, Maggie quietly tucked
away the evil-looking gun she'd laid on the table, saying that
Paige would be safer without anything more lethal than the mascara.

When a fussy little waiter knocked at the door to the suite an
hour later, Paige, in her new role as Meredith, answered. But it
was David who took charge when the waiter set the silver tea
tray on a marble-topped table and extracted a set of surgical
tools from the snowy linen napkin.

"Is this the chip?" David asked, holding up a clear cellophane
package containing a paper-thin sliver of plastic no bigger than
a newborn baby's thumbnail.

"Yes, Dr. Jensen," the waiter confirmed in a clipped
European accent Paige couldn't place. "It's been tested in labs
both here and in the States, and several times in the field. It has
not failed us. Not once."

David sent the man a cold look. "It had better not fail now."

"No," he replied, blinking. "No, of course not."

When the little waiter picked up what looked like a scalpel,
Paige swallowed nervously. "Is this absolutely necessary? I
mean, I'll have the compact with me, and you've said that one
of you will be in visual contact at all times."

The look David turned on her was almost as cold as the one
he'd given the waiter. "It's not too late to get you out of here."

Paige gulped. "Bring on the knife."

Still, she couldn't help tensing as the waiter wiped the scalpel
with an antiseptic gauze, then approached her.

"This won't hurt, *madame*," he assured her. "I will deaden
the area a bit. Just sit there, in that chair, and relax."

"Easy for you to say," Paige muttered as she perched on the
edge of a side chair.

Her nervousness evidently communicated itself to the little
waiter-surgeon. He hovered over her, frowning.

"*Madame,* you must relax. I make only the slightest of incisions, no more than the scratch of a pin. Just here, at the back of your neck, where your hair will cover it.''

He indicated the area with a swipe of the anesthetizing pad. Despite herself, Paige flinched.

With a small, savage curse, David strode to her side. Lifting her bodily out of the chair, he resettled her on his lap. Gratefully Paige turned her face into his shoulder. He brushed her hair to one side with a big, warm hand, then cradled the back of her head.

Closing her eyes, Paige buried her nose in his jacket. The distinctive blend of fine wool, woodsy after-shave and the subtle masculine scent that was David's alone filled her senses. She felt the strength of his arms around her, the solid security of the body pressed to hers.

What in the world was she doing? she wondered for a wild, tumultuous moment, burrowing deeper into his hold. How did she think she could play this dangerous game, when she trembled at the thought of a scalpel? Why didn't she just nest here, in David's arms, for the rest of her life?

Because she didn't want to nest, Paige reminded herself. Because she wanted to…to soar with the eagles. Or at least with David. To share whatever danger and excitement and…

"So, *madame,* it is done."

"What?" Paige turned her head sideways and opened one eye to peer up at the little man standing beside her.

"It is done."

"It is?"

Cautiously she lifted her nose from David's shoulder. His arms tightened around her for a fraction of a second, as though he were reluctant to let her go.

When he eased his hold, Paige tried to convince herself she didn't miss the security of his arms. She moved her head a few careful degrees in both directions, but didn't feel a thing.

"This is the receiver," the waiter-surgeon said, holding out a small, flat rectangle that looked much like a miniature calculator with a liquid crystal digital display. "Using the signals from the chip, it will pinpoint the subject's exact location, either in global coordinates or in radial meters from a specific center.''

"I'll take that." David slipped the small device into his suit pocket.

Paige watched it disappear with an odd sensation. She might have lost her emerald ring, but she was now bound to David by a stronger, far more intimate link. One she couldn't take off if she wanted to.

The thought unsettled her. And reassured her. And confused her.

Once the odd little waiter departed, the pace became frantic. Maggie and David worked through each item on his list to complete Paige's transformation.

A summation of Meredith Ames's leisurely, pampered lifestyle. Check.

A rundown of the wealthy, elite clients she catered to. Check.

A brief description of the technology she'd carried from L.A. and how she'd carried it. Check.

A precise step-by-step plan for Paige to hand over the microdot, then disappear from the scene. Check.

And in the event the unknown contact didn't surface within the next few hours, a detailed schedule for the rest of Meredith's day and night. Check.

Paige stared at the schedule. "The casino? I'm supposed to go to the casino?"

"It's part of Meredith's normal routine when she's in Cannes," Maggie explained.

"Does she gamble?"

"Occasionally."

"You won't, however," David interjected, his face softening for the first time in what seemed like hours. "You'd probably put down a five-thousand-dollar chip, thinking it was five."

"Probably," Paige agreed, more relieved by that almost-smile than she'd allow herself to admit. "So what do I do at the casino, if I don't gamble?"

Maggie gave her a wry grin. "You advertise. You're a businesswoman, remember? In addition to acting as a mule for smuggled technology, you have a product to sell. One that commands rather incredible prices here in Cannes.''

"Oh. Yes.''

Ignoring David's sudden frown, Maggie rose to her feet. "Come on, Meredith. It's time we went to work on packaging your product.''

David rose also, only to be stopped in his tracks when both women murmured protests.

"We can handle this part,'' Maggie assured him. "We don't need one of your lists for this.''

His gaze rested on Paige's face for a moment. "I have a pretty good feel for what she looks best in.''

"Doc,'' Maggie replied gently, "what you think Paige looks best in and what Meredith Ames looks best in might be two entirely different bests.''

Closing the door to the huge, luxuriously appointed bedroom, the two women went to work adapting Maggie/Meredith's working wardrobe for Paige/Meredith's more slender frame.

Digging through the drawers of a high chest-on-chest, Maggie pulled out a stunning silver belt, Italian leather sandals, and a jaunty emerald green rhinestoned ball cap. They would add Meredith's distinctive touch to the linen slacks and green top Paige was now wearing, she explained. Just in case the contact called and she had to go out immediately.

That done, Maggie threw open the doors to a magnificent walnut armoire that must have once belonged to French royalty. Paige's mouth sagged at the array of silks and satins, seductive teddies and whisper-thin negligees, see-through organza blouses and stiff-boned bodices displayed within.

"The Grand Casino is one of the most exclusive men's clubs in the world,'' Maggie told her as she flipped through the padded hangers. "It's patronized by movie stars and oil sheiks and billionaires who like their play deep, their cigars hand-rolled, and their women elegant. Here, try this little number.''

Dubiously Paige eyed the two-piece ball gown she held out.

While the full, floor-length black taffeta skirt was demure enough, the bustier that went with it was something else again. An eye-catching, glowing fuchsia in color, the strapless bodice was trimmed with black satin ribbon along its heart-shaped upper edge and the deep V of the lower edge. More ribbon traced the stiff boning that ribbed its front and covered the front closure, which hooked together like an old-fashioned corset.

Paige slipped on the skirt, then struggled with the hooks of the constricting bodice. As she tugged it into place, she discovered that it was fitted with padded lifts that pushed her breasts up to create a dramatic cleavage. Far more cleavage than she'd ever dreamed she possessed.

Maggie handed her a black velvet ribbon with a heart-shaped diamond pendant. "Here, this is perfect with that outfit."

Paige tied the thin ribbon around her throat, then stared at her image in the floor-to-ceiling dressing room mirror.

"Now *that's* what I'd call superior product packaging," Maggie said with a grin.

Paige nodded, ashamed to admit that she wasn't sure she'd have the nerve to go out of the bedroom, much less to a crowded casino, in this decadent, delicious, totally erotic gown.

Yet, she would, she told herself fiercely. It was time a certain broad-shouldered, overprotective engineer learned that there was more to her than long bike rides through the California parks and lazy Sunday mornings sharing the paper. There was excitement. Romance. Mystery. Adventure.

She gave the bustier a last, uncertain look, then changed back into the tan slacks.

Laying the eveningwear on the bed, Maggie smiled as she trailed a fingertip along black satin piping. "This was one assignment I was planning to enjoy."

Paige glanced up from working the buttons on the green blouse. "Do you go out on assignment often?"

"Often enough."

"Always with David?" Despite her best efforts, she couldn't keep a faint trace of jealousy out of her voice.

"Not always." Maggie gave Paige a bland look. "But regularly enough to know what kind of man he is."

Paige fought a little dart of resentment. The other woman certainly didn't make any bones about her intimate knowledge of someone else's fiancé. Former fiancé.

"And what kind of man is he?" she asked, a trifle coolly.

"The best," Maggie replied bluntly.

Paige's resentment melted, and she gave a small sigh. "I know."

Maggie nibbled on her lower lip for a moment, as if wanting to say something. But a glance at the ornate little clock on the dresser evidently made her decide not to share any further details about the man they both appeared to appreciate, if in vastly different ways.

"I'd better get out of here," she said, tossing a few items into a small overnight case. "I'm moving into the suite across the hall with Doc."

Busy with her packing, she didn't see Paige's shoulders stiffen.

"We've got a surveillance camera rigged that sweeps the hallway every few seconds. No one can get in or out of this suite without our knowledge."

She gave the bedroom a last, assessing glance, before turning back to Paige.

"You've got the compact in your pocket?"

"Yes."

"The gold halter is in your purse?"

"Yes."

"And the mascara?"

Evidently David wasn't the only member of this team who made lists. "Yes."

"Just be careful where you aim it, okay?"

With a final, encouraging grin, Maggie led the way out of the bedroom. "We've got our own bugs planted in each room. We can hear every word spoken anywhere in the suite. Just say the word, and we'll be here in three seconds flat."

Paige nodded, feeling a slight constriction in her throat. Now that the actual moment had come for her to begin her big adventure, she was a little nervous about it. More than a little. But she would've died rather than admit it to David.

She didn't have to.

He was too attuned to her, too sensitive to her every movement, to miss the sudden uncertainty in her eyes. Crossing the plush carpet, he curled a knuckle under her chin.

"You don't have to do this."

Paige stared up into his face, as if memorizing the handsome, regular features. The tiny lines at the corners of his gray blue eyes. The faint shadow that darkened his chin this late in the afternoon. The small, almost invisible scar on one temple that he'd never quite explained.

"Yes, I do," she replied quietly.

He expelled a slow breath. "I'll be just across the hall."

"I know."

Bending down, he brushed his mouth across hers. His touch was light. Warm. Possessive.

"I won't let anything happen to you."

"I know," she replied, sighing.

Long after the door had closed behind him, Paige felt the touch of that soft kiss.


Minutes slid into hours. The balmy breeze from the sea picked up a slight nip. The phone didn't ring.

Shadows slanted across the pale blue carpet as the afternoon faded into evening. No one knocked on the door, except Maggie once, to check on her, and David twice. Neither lingered more than a few moments. They expected a call from the contact at any minute. Or the chauffeur to show up at her door with another summons.

Growing more nervous by the minute, Paige called room service to order one of Cannes's famous *niçise* salads. She paced the sitting room while she waited for it, arms locked across her chest. Every so often she slid a hand under her hair to touch the skin at the back of her neck with a light, questing finger.

The chip was there somewhere, she knew, but she couldn't feel it.

The discreet tap on her door a few moments later sent adrenaline shooting to her every extremity. Her shoulders knotted, her fingers shook, even her toes curled inside the Italian leather shoes, as she stared at the door.

David was watching, she reminded herself.

Maggie was listening.

Paige had insisted on this crazy scheme. She'd wanted to prove something to David. To herself. Yet for a moment, as she stared wide-eyed at the door, she couldn't for the life of her remember what it was.

Another discreet tap sounded.

Her feet dragging on the plush carpet, she crossed the spacious sitting room. With trembling fingers, she unhooked the heavy chain. A cold palm wrapped around her brass door latch.

"Your dinner, *mademoiselle,*" a dark-haired young woman announced cheerfully as she wheeled a cart into the suite.

Paige sagged in relief.

After arranging the domed dishes on a small side table, the maid pocketed a generous tip and left.

The minutes crawled by as Paige picked at her salad. The tart dressing coated her empty stomach with an oily residue. To soak it up, she crumbled a crusty baguette and nibbled at its soft white interior. By the time she'd finished, crumbs lay scattered all over the table and a good part of the floor.

And still the phone didn't ring.

David came across the hall to tell her they'd had no luck yet tracing the yacht. Neither of the two owners of the silver Rolls kept a boat at Cannes with a registration number that included the digits *6, 1* and *3.* Of course, the boat could have been rented.

"Or I could have mistaken the numbers," Paige admitted.

"Don't worry," he told her. "We'll find it."

When the sky outside the open balcony doors had darkened to a star-studded black velvet, Paige went into the bathroom to bathe and dress for the casino.

It was almost ten o'clock. No one in Cannes began the evening's pleasures until midnight, David had explained. The city's inhabitants played until the early hours, slept late, then took lunch at one of the elegant seaside hotel restaurants or strolled the Croisette or drifted on the azure sea in one of the fabulous yachts until it was time for a leisurely drink and dinner. Then the cycle began again.

Paige was a morning person. Her energy levels were highest then, her attention was sharpest, her senses were most alive, early in the day. The times she and David had made love in the early dawn, still warm and flushed from sleep, were among her most precious memories.

Yet, as she soaked in a sinfully rich bubble bath and slathered a creamy lotion on her skin, it seemed as though she were slowly coming alive in a way she'd never experienced before. Maybe it was the unaccustomed luxury of the enormous bath. Or the heady mixture of nervousness and excitement that tripped through her veins. Or the knowledge that David was going to see a different Paige tonight. A very different Paige.

After her bath, she brushed her hair back from her face in soft wings and let its shining length fall loosely down her back. She applied the expensive makeup Maggie had left with a heavier hand than usual, then reached for the small crystal bottle on the dressing table.

Just in time, she remembered Maggie's warning. A woman in Meredith's profession didn't use perfume on the job. Her clients didn't want to go home with a woman's scent clinging to their clothes or their skin.

Paige's fingers trembled as she tied the black velvet ribbon around her neck and felt the cool sting of the diamond-studded heart against her skin. When she finished dressing, she clutched her small evening bag to her chest and surveyed herself once more in the floor-to-ceiling mirrors.

This exotic creature in fuchsia and black looked as different from the shy, demure technical librarian who'd left L.A.—was it only a few days ago?—as it was possible to look.

With all her heart, Paige wished David was waiting for her

in the sitting room. She wanted to sweep in, to show him this sophisticated side of herself that he'd never seen before. She wanted to take his arm and stroll out to enjoy the sights and sounds and serious pleasures of the Riviera.

She wouldn't be with David tonight, however. She'd be unescorted...until Meredith Ames's nameless, faceless contact finally met with her. Or a prospective client arranged for her services.

Gulping, Paige swept out of the bedroom in a rustle of taffeta skirts.

As the cab pulled away from the Carlton, she stifled the urge to twist around and check the rear window. Her mind told her Maggie wouldn't lose sight of her taxi. Her heart told her David wouldn't lose sight of her. Still, she had to swallow a lump in her throat when the cab turned onto the Croisette and left the stately hotel behind.

After a leisurely drive along the well-lit boulevard, the taxi swept up a curving drive to a gleaming vanilla villa on a high promontory overlooking the sea. A uniformed valet helped Paige out and escorted her inside, where a man who might have doubled for a Russian grand duke bowed over her hand.

"Good evening, *mademoiselle*," he murmured in flawless English, having clearly identified her age, her marital status, and her nationality in a single glance.

"Good...good evening."

"Welcome to the Grand. May I have your passport, please?"

"Oh. Yes. Of course."

Fumbling in the evening bag, Paige dug out Meredith's hastily doctored passport. She checked to make sure the large-denomination bill Maggie had tucked inside it was still in place. It would signal her profession to this sophisticated head croupier more clearly than a printed announcement. Her fingers trembled as she handed the small leather-bound passport over.

With an unruffled savoir faire, the duke pocketed the bill and placed Meredith's passport in an old-fashioned walk-in safe, then gestured her inside with a charming old-world bow.

"Good luck this evening, *mademoiselle*."

"I beg your pardon?"

"At the tables."

"Oh. Thank you."

That was it! Her first…business contact as Meredith Ames. A little dazed by the smoothness of it all, Paige stood at the top of a wide, curving marble staircase and tried to still her fluttery pulse.

Maggie had explained in detail how these matters were arranged among the elite. A note passed to a maître d', or in this case the head croupier. A murmur here, a whisper there. A glass of champagne, if she wished it. Perhaps a chip or two tossed onto one of the felt-covered tables. Then either the client himself or perhaps the croupier would approach her. To request her companionship. To arrange a meeting later. Only if *mademoiselle* wished it, of course.

It was all so civilized. So polite. So seemingly safe.

At this moment, the uglier aspects of Meredith's profession seemed to belong to another world. The somewhat shocking description of the various services a woman in her business might be requested to provide took on a hazy, surreal distance.

Paige stared at the sea of hushed elegance below her, trying to absorb the impact of its opulence. The sounds that drifted up the stairs were far different from those that had assaulted her ears in the Las Vegas casino David had taken her to one weekend. There was no raucous clatter of coins hitting the trays of slot machines. No exultant shouts and delighted exclamations. No loud music blaring from a lounge band to distract the gamblers.

Here, music from a string quartet floated above the low murmurs of laughter and muted conversation. Fine crystal champagne flutes tipped against each other with melodious clinks. The only discordant note was the subdued rattle of little wooden balls in the roulette wheels, and even that was muted by the plush carpeting and the acres of thick felt on the tables.

Paige swallowed, wondering if Meredith's contact was among the glittering crowd that swirled through the high-ceilinged room. Gripping her small black evening bag with both hands, she started down the stairs.

Two hours later, she ached in every bone.

She'd never realized how much effort it took to appear relaxed when every muscle and tendon in her body was tight with tension. Her mouth hurt from keeping it curved into a small, provocative smile, and her eyes felt dry and strained from trying to search the crowd without appearing to. She wasn't sure whether she'd spent more time looking for David or for her prospective contact.

She hadn't seen either one.

She'd been approached several times, however.

Once by a rather florid-looking man in a tux and a stand-up collar that appeared to be choking him. Her heart had nearly jumped out of her chest when he stared at her from across a felt-covered table, but she'd managed what she hoped was a seductive smile. To her secret, infinite relief, he'd been detoured at the last moment by a chesty woman with short-cropped iron gray hair and a steely glint in her eyes. The man had sent Paige a regretful glance over one shoulder as he was led away.

Another potential client had materialized at her elbow not long after that. Bowing over her hand, he'd presented her with a fresh flute of champagne. After a few moments of murmured conversation—smooth on his side, somewhat stilted on hers—he'd brushed a knuckle down the curve of her cheek and asked if she included a certain rare skill in her repertoire. Paige had stared at him blankly. Smiling, he'd elaborated. When she finally understood exactly what skill he referred to, she could barely contain her shock.

Speechless, she'd shaken her head. Maggie had definitely not included that particular vice on Meredith's list of offered services. With a murmured expression of regret, the disgusting pervert had moved away.

At that moment, the glamour had faded from Paige's grand adventure. For the first time, she'd understood the darker side of this mission. And the danger if she didn't do just as David had instructed.

Her fingers had trembled as she slid them to the back of her neck, searching in vain for the tiny embedded chip. Suddenly her electronic tracking device felt less like a leash and more like a safety line. Only the knowledge that David was here, close by, a part of this glittering, swirling crowd had given her the courage to lift the crystal goblet to her lips and continue the charade.

Although there were no clocks anywhere in the casino, Paige guessed it was now close to 3:00 a.m. She was feeling the effects of one of the longest, most emotional days of her life. She couldn't believe that just this morning she'd pulled off onto a little overlook and gazed down at the Mediterranean for the first time. That just this morning she'd choked back tears as she slipped David's ring over her knuckle.

Since then, she'd lost her purse, her ring, and a little of her timidity. In return, she'd gained a new wardrobe, a new identity, if only for a short while, and an eye-opening insight into—

*"Mademoiselle?"*

Paige jumped. Delicate pale gold champagne splashed onto her chest. Blotting it with her palm, she stared at the man she'd labeled the grand duke.

"Yes?"

"One of our guests much admires your charm."

"He…he does?"

"He does. He comes to us well vouchered, you understand? Very well vouchered."

Paige understood. This unnamed patron represented the elite of the elite.

"Do you wish to meet him?"

So sophisticated, she thought. So polite. Unable to speak, she nodded.

"At your hotel? Within the hour?"

She swallowed, trying to find her voice.

"Within the hour, *mademoiselle?*"

Her powers of speech had completely deserted her. She could only stare at the duke and nod.

## Chapter 7

Paige scarcely drew a full breath during the long drive back to the Carlton. The aching exhaustion that had racked her just moments ago was gone. In its place was a shimmering, shivering excitement.

She'd done it! By God, she'd done it!

Paige Lawrence, full-time technical librarian and sometime mouse, had just successfully passed herself off as Meredith Ames, woman of the world.

The gentleman who'd requested her company might not be Meredith's contact, she reminded herself. If he showed no interest in a certain microdot, he might have to be eased out of Meredith's suite, using the ingenious plan David devised earlier.

But then again, he just might be the individual trying to acquire stolen technology that would allow him to transfer millions and millions of bits of data at twice the current capacity. If he was, David would have identified his target, and Paige would have participated in the adventure of her life.

By God, she'd done it!

As the taxi swept along the broad, brightly lit boulevard, a gathering tension gradually replaced her initial spurt of exultation. She wasn't quite home free, she reminded herself. The adventure wasn't over yet.

When the Carlton's caramel-and-cream facade came into view, she quivered with a combination of nervousness and anticipation. Stiff black skirts rustling, she slid out of the taxi and fumbled in her bag for some francs to pay the driver. While the doorman sorted through her wad of notes and bent down to negotiate a respectable fare, a small, slight figure detached itself from the shrubbery along the curved drive.

"So, *mademoiselle,* you have recovered from your swim in the sea, no?"

Startled, Paige swung around. "Henri?"

"Yes, it is me."

Sauntering forward, the boy hooked his thumbs in the waistband of his rumpled shorts and looked her up and down. A long, low whistle drifted across the night air. "Of a certainty you have recovered."

"What in the world are you doing here? It's almost four in the morning. You should be in bed."

"Me, I do my business at night," he announced with a cheerful insouciance. His red brows waggled. "As do you and your friend, no? The one with the so lovely legs."

"What? Oh, yes."

"Is this boy bothering you, *mademoiselle?*"

The deep voice at her shoulder made Paige jump. She turned and hurriedly assured the frowning doorman that, no, the boy wasn't bothering her. Rocking back on his heels, Henri waited while the dubious doorman gave her the change, then moved away to assist another patron into the cab. Even at this late hour, a steady stream of limousines and taxis glided along the wide curved drive in front of the hotel, picking up and discharging passengers. Paige wondered if one of those vehicles held David. Or Maggie. Or her prospective client.

Nervously, she turned to bid the boy good-night, only to have him forestall her with a shrewd assessment.

"You have the customer, no?"

She nodded, her face heating. This youngster's frank knowledge of the world astounded her.

Henri smirked and rocked back on his heels. "It is the big man who takes you in his arms this afternoon, no? Of a certainty, he has the passion for you."

Arrested, Paige stared at him. "Really? You saw that, did you?"

"*Mais oui!* He will be generous, that one, as much as he desires you. You must make sure you ask a proper fee."

"Fee? Oh. Yes. Yes, I will."

A look of complete disgust crossed his freckled face. "Do not say you failed to establish the price before you make the assignation with him?"

"Well, I…"

"Just how long is it that you do this type of work, *mademoiselle?*"

"Not very long."

Paige couldn't believe she was standing outside one of the world's most elegant hotels, discussing such matters with a grubby-faced boy.

"Look, I have to go inside," she said, a little desperately. "It's late and I, uh, have to get ready."

The boy planted himself before her. "No, no, you must not. Not until we decide your fee."

"We?" she echoed weakly.

"But of course. Unless you have the manager to do this for you?"

"Er, no."

The boy frowned. "One can tell you need someone to assist you, *mademoiselle.* One who knows the value of the service you provide."

He looked her up and down once more, then suggested a figure that almost made Paige gasp. Just in time, she remembered she was supposed to be among the best of the best.

"Yes, that's about what I had considered. Well, good night."

"Wait. You must pay me fifty francs, *mademoiselle.*"

"For what?"

"For my consultation."

Sure that David would come along at any moment and ask what the hell she was doing, Paige fumbled in her purse. She dragged out a note and thrust it in the boy's hand.

Clucking, he shook his head. "It is too much. Of a certainty, *mademoiselle,* you have need of the manager."

He reached into a pocket of his shorts and pulled out a fat roll of bills.

Paige blinked in astonishment. "Do your parents know you carry all that money around with you?"

His lips pursed in concentration, he counted out her change with careful deliberation. That done, he stuffed the roll back in his pocket and gave a nonchalant shrug.

"Me, I have no parents. This money is not mine. I deliver it for certain patrons who wish to place the bets with Antoine." He gave her a cheeky grin. "Antoine, he breaks my legs if the money does not arrive intact, you understand."

Paige stared at the boy incredulously. She wasn't exactly sure, but she thought he'd just admitted that he was a runner for the local bookie. Among other things, it soon appeared.

"So, *mademoiselle,* shall I be your manager?"

"No! No, thank you, Henri." Flustered, Paige knew she had to end this incredible conversation. "I'm, um, an independent."

With that, she bade him a quick good-night and hurried inside. Her nerves, already strung taut by the interminable ride back to the hotel, were now stretched to their limits.

As the wrought-iron elevator cage creaked and groaned its way to the fifth floor, Paige forced herself to repeat over and over the list of instructions David had prepared for just this situation. Still muttering under her breath, she unlocked the door to the suite and stepped inside.

First, sweep the suite for any devices that might have been planted in her absence.

She fumbled with the hairbrush handle for a moment, twisting it this way and that, then waited until a small red dot glowed in its end. With a sob of relief, she tossed the brush on the dressing table. No hostiles, as Maggie had termed them, only the devices she herself had planted.

Second, test friendly system.

"This is Jezebel," she whispered to the bedroom at large. "Can you hear me?"

"We have you covered, Jezebel," a feminine voice assured her.

Startled, Paige glanced up at the cherubs atop a high carved chiffonier. One of the plump little angels on the chest of drawers seemed to have spoken directly to her.

"Is...is Doc there?"

"He's on his way up."

"Okay."

"Just stay calm."

If she hadn't been rather shy by nature, and speaking to an angel, Paige might have made a very rude response to that comment.

Third...

Oh, Lord, what was the third item on David's list? Or had she already done the third? What was the fourth?

Frantic, Paige searched her mind. Oh, yes. She was supposed to leave the lights dimmed, to keep her client from seeing the nervousness in her face.

And leave the door to the suite unlocked.

David had stated calmly that he could take the door down without much difficulty, but he didn't want even that much of a barrier if Paige needed him. Her skirts swishing, she hurried into the sitting room and turned off all but one lamp. That done, she took the chain off the door.

When someone rapped softly against the door a few moments later, the knowledge that David was watching and listening and waiting just across the hall was the only thing that kept her knees from crumpling under her.

"Come in," she called out, her heart thumping.

The tall oak panel opened with agonizing slowness.

Throat tight, fists clenched in the folds of her full skirt, Paige stared at the figure silhouetted against the glow of the crystal chandelier in the corridor.

He wore a black tuxedo that shaped his broad shoulders like a mantle of night. The diamond studs in his white dress shirt caught the chandelier's light. He stood unmoving for a long moment, yet Paige sensed immediately the coiled power in his tall, muscled frame.

"David?" she whispered.

With an unhurried calm, he locked the door and walked into the sitting room. In the dim shadows, he loomed large and re-assuringly solid.

Paige did a quick mental inventory of the possible contingency plans he'd made her memorize. His presence in her suite when the contact arrived wasn't one of them.

"What are you doing here? I thought I was supposed to meet my—" she swallowed "—meet Meredith's client alone."

"You are."

She glanced at the clock on the mantel. "He should be here at any moment."

David shrugged out of his tux jacket and tossed it on one of the chairs. "He's here."

"What?"

"I saw how tired you were, and decided to pull you out of the casino," he told her, tugging at one corner of his white tie.

Stunned, she stared at him. "But...but I..."

"No buts, Paige." He dropped the tie on top of his tux. "The situation is too dangerous for you to muddle through with drooping eyelids and sagging shoulders."

Stung, Paige recalled the knife-edged tension that had racked her during the interminable drive back to the hotel. The buckets of adrenaline that had pumped through her veins. The wild exultation at the thought that she, timid little Paige Lawrence, had actually been mistaken for someone like Meredith Ames.

"I thought I did a little better than muddle," she retorted. "And you might have asked me if I was ready to leave before making a unilateral decision like that."

Curbing both his impatience and his mounting need to crush

Paige in his arms, Doc slipped his Smith & Wesson Model 39 out of the holster at the small of his back. Specially bored and made with an alloy frame, the gun was light and flat and incredibly accurate. While Paige watched, wide-eyed, he checked to make sure a round was chambered, then laid the weapon aside.

In the little silence that followed, Doc walked over to the cabinet that housed the suite's bar. From his own years of experience, he knew she needed time to work the tension out of her system. Time to decompress after being plunged into an alien and unfamiliar world.

And he needed a drink badly. He couldn't remember the last time he'd been so tense, so wired, during an operation.

After following Paige into the casino, he'd taken a seat at one of the chemin de fer tables, which were set on a raised dais that gave an unobstructed view of the casino floor. Normally, Doc would've been able to engage one part of his mind in the complicated high-stakes card game while another kept track of his target.

Tonight, he'd found it impossible to concentrate on anything but Paige. He'd watched her every move as she wandered hesitantly through the casino. He'd counted every sip of champagne she took. He'd tensed at every male who looked at her with more than passing interest. And he'd just about lost it completely when one of the jet set's better-known perverts sauntered to her side.

She'd handled that little encounter well. Doc had to give her that. Still, the idea of Paige, *his* Paige, being exposed to a man like that made his gut twist.

Although, he thought savagely as he splashed a generous amount of cognac into a crystal snifter, she sure as hell didn't look much like his Paige tonight. Christ, that pink thing she had on had just about destroyed his ability to function at all. He'd felt himself harden when he first glimpsed her full, rounded breasts plumped up above that heart-shaped bodice and saw the shimmer of light on her pale, golden hair. What was more, he'd stayed hard as a rock most of the night. She'd looked so seductive, yet so fragile, that it took all his control not to sweep her out of the casino and into his bed.

Which was what he intended to do. As soon as they settled a few things.

Turning, he held out the snifter. "Do you want a drink?"

When she shook her head, Doc took a long, satisfying swallow. Liquid heat curled in his stomach, fueling the tiny flames of desire he'd kept banked all afternoon and evening. He waited until the heat had distributed itself more evenly throughout his body, then dealt with Paige's indignation at his decision to pull her out of the casino.

"Let's review the bidding one more time," he said evenly. "This isn't a committee. You don't get a vote on each course of action."

She stiffened. "Is that so?"

"Yes, it is. You're in over your head here. Way over your head. I allowed you to continue the charade against my better judgment, but I'm not going to let you take any unnecessary risks."

"You know, David, I'm discovering that you have a rather nasty autocratic streak under that protective layer of yours."

"I do, where you're concerned."

"I'm beginning to wonder just what other traits you've hidden from me these past months."

Doc cradled the brandy snifter in one palm. This discussion had to come. He knew that. They hadn't been alone for more than a few moments since she'd stumbled into the suite this afternoon, half-naked and wholly wet. He hadn't had a chance to work through the desperate fear that had gripped him when he learned she'd been taken. Or the surging relief at her safe return. Or her sudden doubts over their marriage.

They'd work them through now, he decided with grim determination. The way they'd worked through their minor differences in the past. With a calm meeting of their minds and a slow, sweet joining of their bodies. Anticipation curled low in his groin as he took another swallow, then set the snifter aside.

Without taking his eyes off Paige, he lifted his chin and spoke over his shoulder. "You can switch off the cameras and the microphone, Chameleon. I'll send you an emergency signal if I need you."

"You sure, Doc?"

Paige gave a little start as Maggie's voice floated out of the bronze bust of some long-dead Roman emperor that sat on a pedestal by the foyer.

"I'm sure." Doc's shadowed gaze drifted over the woman facing him. "I'll provide Jezebel cover for the rest of the night."

After a slight pause, Maggie murmured, "Right."

Doc signed off, watching with silent amusement the bright wash of color that flooded Paige's delicate face.

"If that means what I think you meant it to mean," she said, wrapping both arms around her waist, "you're getting way ahead of yourself, David. We need to talk."

Doc's brief amusement disappeared as her movement caused her creamy breasts to swell above that damned pink-and-black thing. He'd never considered himself a particularly possessive or primitive type, but Paige's repeated appearances in Meredith's working clothes were stirring some deep, surprisingly atavistic urges. This was the twentieth century A.D., not B.C., he reminded himself savagely. He couldn't just sling her over his shoulder and carry her off to his cave. Not until they'd had their talk, anyway.

Paige drew in a slow breath, unaware that the simple act ripped away one more layer of Doc's civilized veneer. Swearing under his breath, he reached up to loosen the top stud on his dress shirt.

"I'm not going to sleep with you, David," she announced, in a small, determined voice. "Not until I know who you are."

"You know who I am."

"No, I don't! Until a few hours ago, I thought you were an engineer."

"I am an engineer. I've never lied to you, Paige. Except by omission."

"Well, you omitted a few rather significant details. A whole secret identity, in fact. A life completely apart from me. How could you do that, David? How could you deliberately exclude me from this part of yourself?''

She searched his face, her eyes cloudy with the need to understand. ''Didn't you trust me?''

''It's not a matter of trust.''

''Then what? Have I been indiscreet? Am I too stupid? Were you afraid I might give you away?''

''No, of course not.''

''Then what?''

Doc raked a hand through his hair, knowing that he owed her an explanation. ''I wanted to keep you separate from this side of my life. It's too dark. Too dangerous.''

She hugged herself more tightly.

Doc gritted his teeth as the creamy flesh swelled higher.

''I...I see,'' she said. ''So you divided your life into nice neat compartments labeled Engineering, Undercover Work, and, oh, yes, Paige.''

''That's one way of putting it.''

''I see,'' she repeated in a small voice.

He waited while she struggled with the hard, undeniable truth. There was a part of him he'd withheld from her. A part he would always withhold.

Even if he'd wanted to, Doc wasn't cleared to tell her about his work with OMEGA. About the dark, twisted people he dealt with. The lonely days and weeks in the field, when an agent lived on the knife edge of danger, with only his wits and his skills to keep him alive. He couldn't even tell her about the debt he owed Adam Ridgeway, who had personally recruited him for OMEGA.

That debt originated far back in their navy days, when Doc had commanded an underwater demolition team and Adam had flown carrier-based jets. Most of the world assumed the wealthy Bostonian had simply been pulling a well-publicized stint in the military before dabbling in politics. Yet Doc could recall in vivid, minute detail the day his team had come under hostile fire while clearing a mine field in the Persian Gulf. Although low on fuel, Adam had coolly disregarded orders to return to his

ship. Single-handedly he'd held the attacking small boats at bay
until reinforcements arrived and a rescue helo was able to pluck
the demolition team out of danger.

Since the attackers were at that time supposedly U.S. allies,
frantic diplomatic efforts had hushed up the incident. All partic-
ipants were sworn to secrecy. But Doc would never forget those
moments when bullets had sliced through the waters all around
him and a lone navy jet had repeatedly dived out of the skies
overhead.

He couldn't speak of that day to Paige, any more than he
could tell her about the missions he'd undertaken since joining
OMEGA. Not just because she wasn't cleared for such information. Because he didn't want her to know.

Maybe he'd been wrong to try to shield her, he acknowledged
silently, studying her pale, set face. Maybe he shouldn't have
tried to protect her. But she symbolized all that was good and
pure and innocent in his life. He hadn't wanted to contaminate
that purity with what he did for OMEGA.

Not that she looked particularly innocent at this moment, he
thought wryly. Not in that blasted pink contraption.

As she stared at his shadowed face, Paige tried desperately to
contain her hurt. Even now, even after her brief foray into his
world, David wanted to shut her out. To shield her from the man
he really was.

Maybe she should let him, she thought with a touch of despair. Maybe she wouldn't even like the unknown David once
the layers of his varied identities were peeled back to reveal the
man beneath.

No! No! She couldn't spend the rest of her life wondering,
unsure of him or herself.

As she grappled with her hurt and confusion, Paige tried to
find a way to bridge the gap between the David she knew and
the stranger he seemed to be. Maybe, she thought hesitantly, she
had to show David a side of herself he'd never seen before he
would risk opening those closed, secret compartments of his.
Maybe he needed to discover she wasn't all sweetness and light.
Maybe she needed to discover it herself.

"Look at me, David," she whispered.

A faint half smile curved his lips. "I'm looking."

She wet her lips. "What do you see? Who do you see? Paige? Or Meredith?"

The smile faded.

"Maybe I'm not quite the woman you thought you knew, either."

She was.

And she wasn't.

Until this moment, Doc had believed he could identify Paige in a crowded room by her scent alone. That he'd explored every nuance of her personality. That he'd discovered all her strengths. Accounted for all her weaknesses.

Yet now, as his gaze slid down her throat to the narrow velvet ribbon that banded it, he saw a tiny vein throbbing just beneath the circlet of black. He'd never noticed that vein before, and he'd sure as hell never felt anything as potent as the raw need that slammed into him as he watched that fluttering pulse.

"Do you want me, David?" Her whisper held a nervous, totally erotic huskiness. "You can have me…if you can afford me."

"What are you talking about?"

"Are you willing to pay for your pleasures?"

Afraid she was going to lose her nerve, Paige turned away. Her eyes sought his rigid figure, reflected in the huge Italian giltwood mirror that hung above the table directly in front of her.

"You can have the woman you see in this mirror," she told his shadowy image. "For a fee."

She stated the staggering figure Henri had suggested just moments ago. At least she hoped it was the figure. The swift narrowing of David's eyes made her fear she might have mixed the numbers up.

For long moments, he didn't move. Didn't speak. Then he moved slightly, and the light from the single lamp illuminated his expression.

At the expression in his eyes, Paige felt a sudden tiny dart of sensation. Not fear, exactly. Not apprehension. Just a shivery, nerve-tingling ripple of something similar to it.

He slid one hand into his pants pocket. Without speaking, he tossed a neat fold of notes onto the table.

"That should cover it."

Henri would be proud of her, Paige thought wildly. She'd negotiated her contact and even been paid in advance. Or was about to be.

Moving slowly, David came to stand behind her. Her pale hair and bare shoulders gleamed in soft contrast to the stark whiteness of his shirt. The only color in the shadowed scene portrayed in the huge mirror was the deep rose of her bodice. Paige stared at his image in the silvered glass, sure he would say something. Anything.

Instead, he placed his hands on the curve of her waist.

It was such a simple gesture. Such a small touch. But so warm, even through the layers of satin and stiff boning. So firm. So familiar.

This was David, her heart cried. *Her* David, at least as much of him as he allowed her to possess. She stared at the big blunt-tipped fingers that shaped her waist, then lifted her eyes to his.

The man who stared back at her wasn't her David, she realized with a shock. His face was taut with a need she'd never seen before. His eyes glittered with an intensity he'd never shown her before. His hands, those strong, safe hands that had caressed her so tenderly in the past, now tightened around her waist like an iron band.

Paige had wanted to discover what lay beneath the assured, loving exterior David had always shown her. She saw it now in the mirror. And her pulse leapt in wild, unfettered response to this stranger's blatant desire.

His fingers splayed downward, following the V-shaped bottom edge of her corset. The taffeta skirt whispered a protest as he spread his hands over her stomach and pressed her back against the rock-hardness of his body.

Then his hands, those sure, strong hands, moved to the bottom hook on the stiff-boned bustier. The hook gave with a soft snicker of sound.

"You're every man's secret fantasy in this thing," he growled, his warm breath stirring the fine hairs at her temple.

The second hook separated, and his hands slid up to the third.

"Your waist is so small."

Unconsciously Paige sucked in her breath to make it even smaller.

The third hook gave.

"That pulse in your throat is driving me crazy."

He bent and brushed her neck with a kiss.

Another hook came open.

"And your breasts, my sweet, seductive Jezebel, your breasts have made me ache with wanting you all night."

The last hook came undone, baring her from the waist up. She kept her arms stiff, her fists buried in her skirt as he eased the stiff corset from between their bodies. It dropped to the carpet, unheeded.

Her breath suspended, Paige watched him watching her. Their images seemed to blur. To merge in the dimness.

Her nipples peaked, either from the cool air or from the fierce masculine hunger in his eyes.

She thought he'd touch her then. She wanted him to touch her. She arched her back a little, offering herself.

Yet when his hands reached for her, they flattened against her midriff. With slow, sure strokes, he soothed the red marks left by the bodice's stiff ribs. His touch was gentle, so gentle, and erotically possessive.

Then his fingers brushed the underside of one breast, and she shivered.

"David…"

His name on her lips was a sigh. A plea. A promise.

"No, little Jezebel," he told her, bending down to nuzzle her neck once again. "Not yet."

His mouth and teeth and tongue played with the soft skin of her throat. His breath was warm and moist in her ear, his lips were firm. Fires curled in her belly. When she thought she would go wild from wanting more than just his lips, he kissed the spot at the base of her hairline where the tiny chip had been inserted, then moved back half a step.

Paige felt his fingers at the small of her back. The skirt's buttons slipped free, and then the taffeta slithered to a black pool at her feet.

Embarrassed and more than a little shocked by the image in the silvered glass, Paige fought the urge to close her eyes. Never, not even in her most secret fantasies, had she imagined herself standing before David clothed only in sheer black bikini panties, a black lace garter belt, thigh-high stockings and a velvet ribbon around her throat.

His palms planed her hips, her bottom, then slid around to her stomach. One moved up to cup her breast and played with the stiff, throbbing nipple. The other moved down to shape her mound. Paige felt the heat of his hand through her sheer panties.

"Open for me," he ordered softly.

Laying her head back against his shoulder, she eased her legs apart. He tugged the nylon aside, exploring her, preparing her. The pressure of his fingers against her core sent hot, liquid desire spiraling through her loins. She gasped and pressed her bottom back against his rampant arousal.

Was this really her? she wondered wildly. Was she really standing here like a...like a high-class call girl, in diamonds and velvet and black lace, while this shadowy stranger played with her body?

"I told you we might not recognize ourselves when this is all over," David murmured, as if reading her mind.

His fingers probed deeper, and suddenly the thought that a stranger was touching her so intimately frightened her. Suddenly she didn't want to uncover any more of the man in the mirror. She wanted David. *Her* David.

Twisting around, Paige flung herself against him. The diamond studs cut into her flesh as she dragged his head down. Her mouth was demanding, insistent, anxious.

With a low, savage sound, he wrapped his arms around her waist. She strained into him, both relieved and excited by the faint tremor in the muscles of his shoulders as he fought to control his passion. Whoever she might have seen so briefly in the mirror, this was *her* David.

She felt his rigid member against her stomach. She tasted the raw hunger in his mouth. She was gasping with need when he swept her into his arms and carried her into the bedroom. He dumped her on the wide bed with a noticeable lack of his usual gentleness and ripped off her panties.

She didn't stay prone for very long, however. As he yanked at his shirtfront, she scrambled to her knees. Her fingers tore at the studs while he shrugged out of the white suspenders. Tiny diamonds flew in all directions, followed in short order by his shirt, then the rest of his clothes.

When he tumbled her onto the satin coverlet and covered her body with his, Paige was ready for him. More than ready. The flesh between her legs was hot and slick and tight with anticipation.

He filled her, as he always did. And stroked her. And fanned the flames higher and higher.

But this time, his careful control slipped its bonds. For the first time, he let her feel the full weight of his body. For the first time, he lifted her hips clear off the bed with the force of his thrusts.

And this time, for the first time, when she arched her back, groaning with the force of her climax, he slammed into her with a shattering force and spilled himself into her.

# Chapter 8

Restless and edgy, Maggie wandered out of the darkened sitting room and onto the small balcony. Although this suite faced the mountains instead of the sea, the view was almost as magnificent, especially in these last few hours before dawn.

Cannes slumbered peaceful, its subdued lights glowing like yellow diamonds against the inky blackness. In the distance, the city climbed upward at a sharp angle, clinging to the steep slopes of the Maritime Alps. The golden lights grew sparser there and appeared at higher and higher intervals, until a scattered few seemed to hang freely in the night sky.

Maggie wrapped both hands around the balcony's wrought iron railing and stared up at those distant pinpoints of light. These were the villas of the ultrarich, she knew, sumptuous turn-of-the-century mansions that clung to the high hillsides or perched atop almost inaccessible peaks.

Her fingers tightened on the railing. In one of those villas resided Victor Swanset, the reclusive English expatriate whose classic films and right-wing political views had made him legendary in the thirties. He descended from his hilltop aerie only on rare occasions, Claire had reported. When he did, it was in a silver Rolls-Royce like the one that had whisked Paige off this afternoon.

Of the two possible suspects Claire had identified, Swanset was the only one whose location they had a fix on right now. The French banker, Gabriel Ardenne, had gone underground somewhere in this glittering city.

As she studied those soft, flickering lights, Maggie toyed with the idea of taking a little night reconnaissance trip into the hills. She knew the aging film star's private fortress sat in isolated splendor atop one of those high peaks. Unfortunately, Claire had ascertained that the villa was accessible only by helicopter or via a narrow, winding mountain road guarded with state-of-the-art security surveillance systems. Without Doc's backup, Maggie didn't dare try a reconnaissance.

And Doc was otherwise occupied.

Providing Paige close cover.

A rueful smile tugged at Maggie's lips as she recognized the source of her late-night restlessness. Ever since she'd turned off the cameras and listening devices, she'd alternated between a hope that Doc and his fiancée would work through their differences and a sneaking, silent envy that they had differences to work through.

It wasn't that Maggie was lonely, exactly. Her life was too full, her career too challenging, to allow time for loneliness. Nor did she lack for male companionship when she desired it. In addition to the circle of friends she'd established in her civilian life, she'd met one or two men during her missions for OMEGA who desired something far more intimate than friendship. A certain drop-dead-gorgeous Central American colonel made it a point to call her whenever he was in Washington. And a brilliant, somewhat clumsy young physicist was still pestering the president to have Maggie permanently assigned to the United Nations nuclear-site inspection team he headed.

Yet she had no desire to share this balmy night with either of those two men. She closed her eyes and breathed in the heady scent of primroses and cyclamens and tamarisks that drifted from the lush gardens below. Instantly, a vivid mental image rose of just the kind of man she'd like to have beside her on this small balcony.

Someone who could move easily amid the rarefied atmosphere of a city like Cannes, yet enjoy a quiet moment in the still hours before dawn.

Someone who combined a powerful masculinity with an inbred elegance that was all that more potent for being understated.

Someone like Adam Ridgeway.

A stab of pure physical desire tightened the muscles low in Maggie's stomach. Startled, she opened her eyes.

Damn! She was going to have to do something about her growing preoccupation with OMEGA's aristocratic director. Soon. She wasn't sure exactly what, since both she and Adam were too professional, too dedicated to their work, for either of them to step over the invisible line between boss and subordinate. Of course, Maggie admitted with a wry grin, she wasn't above bending the rules on occasion, but Adam...

No, not Adam Ridgeway.

None of the dozen or so OMEGA agents were privy to the exact details of their director's past, but they trusted him with their lives. His cool, ruthless logic and absolute authority were legendary. Maggie knew Adam would never allow personal considerations to color his judgment or his decisions when directing his agents. What was more, she valued her independence in the field too much to give him any more control over her activities than he already possessed. They'd had some rather strenuous differences of opinion in the past over her somewhat unorthodox solutions to problems she encountered in the field.

Still, if she could've chosen one man to stand beside her on this tiny balcony and breathe in the heady, perfumed air, she knew darn well who it would be.

It was this city, Maggie decided as she surveyed the dim, glowing lights. This center of sybaritic luxury. Cannes saturated the senses with its breathtaking vistas, pristine white beaches and fragrant air, not to mention its unapologetic devotion to pleasure.

In a place like Cannes, it was easy to fantasize and forget such things as working relationships and—

Maggie stiffened, her fingers clutching the railing. There was another side to Cannes, she reminded herself. One that rarely pierced the consciousness of the pleasure-seekers. A small army worked behind the scenes to keep those beaches so white. Fishermen got up before dawn to drag from the seas the mussels and bream and other local delicacies that appeared on the linen-covered tables each night. The crews manning the yachts had families tucked away in the old town who depended on their wages.

A whole population of city dwellers out there actually worked for a living, Maggie reminded herself. What was more, those workers maintained an informal intelligence network that operated at warp speed. Word had probably already circulated among the dockworkers about the American tourist who'd fallen off the gangplank of a yacht this afternoon. Those workers would know the name of that yacht, and its current location.

Shedding her unaccustomed lethargy like a butterfly sloughing off its cocoon, Maggie headed for the small briefcase that housed the master communications unit. She hated to do this to Doc, but duty called. Biting her lower lip, she punched in his code.

The ultralow-frequency hum emitted by the elegant gold cigarette case he would've placed within easy reach would wake him, but not Paige, Maggie knew. It was tuned to the absolute end of the spectrum of sounds he could hear.

"Doc here," he replied after a few moments. "Go ahead, Chameleon."

If she'd pulled him from sleep—or from any other bedroom activity—she couldn't tell it from his voice. He sounded calm, and wide-awake.

"I'm going out for a while, Doc. Down to the wharves. To see what I can learn about our unidentified yacht. Can you, ah, cover Jezebel for the rest of the night?"

"I'll do my best," he replied dryly.

Maggie grinned.

"Try the rue Meynadier first," he added. "It's in the heart

of the old city. The town's wealthier merchants have their establishments there. Then the Vieux Port, particularly the quai Saint-Pierre. That's where the ship chandlers who sell everything from fishing nets to diesel engines are located.''

Maggie blinked in surprise. ''When did you gather all this information?''

''This afternoon, when you were packaging Meredith's product.''

She might have known! While she and Paige were sorting through bustiers and ball gowns, Doc had been at work on one of his lists.

''Pretty good packaging, wasn't it?'' she asked lightly.

He hesitated a moment before replying. ''Let's just say it was very effective.''

Grinning, Maggie signed off and headed for the bedroom she'd appropriated from Doc when she moved out of Meredith's suite. She dug through the items in the hastily packed overnight case, with little expectation of finding what she needed. There wasn't much in the wardrobe she'd brought on this assignment suitable for a late-night excursion to the old town. She tapped her foot for a moment, thinking, then reached for the phone.

The concierge assured her that he would have someone from housekeeping bring her fresh towels immediately.

Twenty minutes later, Maggie left the suite wearing a beige-and-white-striped maid's uniform. It hung a little loosely over her hips, but otherwise fit perfectly.

The housekeeper had departed just a few moments ago, having exchanged the spare uniform she'd fetched from a supply closet for a thick wad of notes. The worldly Frenchwoman had been most sympathetic to Maggie's desire to don a disguise and slip away from an overbearing husband to meet a young and most virile lover.

After a quick glance at the closed door across the hall, Maggie stifled another small pang of envy and hurried toward the stairs.

Behind that closed door, Doc stood unmoving. He'd pulled on his slacks and padded barefoot into the sitting room to acknowledge Maggie's signal, not wanting to wake Paige.

Now he needed to think through his partner's late-night excursion. He and Maggie had planned to operate independently during this mission, as they had on past assignments, so her decision to go down to the old town this late didn't surprise or particularly concern him. Maggie Sinclair wasn't the type to sit quietly by and wait for events to unfold.

Nor was he, normally. Since Paige's appearance on the scene, however, Doc had had to modify both his cover and his method of operation. He wouldn't be making more than a token appearance at the international symposium of engineers that was his cover for being in Cannes. He'd already dropped a subtle hint or two in a phone conversation with one of his colleagues that he'd found something more stimulating than the sun and the beaches to occupy his days and nights on the Riviera.

Paige didn't know it yet, but she wasn't going to be doing any more advertising. She didn't need to. When Meredith Ames left the casino tonight, she'd accepted more than just a onetime client. She'd entered into an exclusive contract for the duration of her stay in Cannes. Whoever wanted to claim the microdot from Meredith would have to work around Doc's visible presence. Now he just needed to find a way to let Paige know about the change in her professional status. She'd been surprisingly stubborn this afternoon, and again this evening, about her involvement in this operation.

He turned to head back to the bedroom, and a splash of deep rose pink snagged his attention. Doc smiled to himself as he moved toward the assorted articles of clothing still scattered across the plush carpet. Scooping up the stiff-boned top, Doc admitted that Paige had shown several new facets to her personality tonight.

He'd never seen her explode with quite that wild abandon before. Or felt himself drawn over the edge like that with her. He'd never quite lost all control with her before.

As he fingered the smooth satin, his smile faded.

With a painful honesty, Doc forced himself to acknowledge

that until tonight he'd deliberately tried to fit Paige into one of those nice neat compartments she'd complained of. The day he met her, he'd formed an image of her in his mind that he'd both cherished and tried to perpetuate. An image that didn't allow for either her stubborn insistence on carrying out this dangerous mission or her unsettling appearance tonight as Meredith Ames.

It disturbed Doc, as a man and as an agent, to realize that he'd underestimated her.

"David?"

He turned, still clenching the thick satin.

The wanning moon cast a silvery glow over Paige's pale hair and delicate features. Her makeup was gone. Her hair was tousled. Her skin was flushed from sleep. She'd wrapped a sheet around herself, toga-style, and Doc thought he'd never seen anything more beautiful in his life. Or more erotic. He loosed his grip on the pink top and tossed it aside.

"What is it?" she asked, her voice anxious. "Is something wrong?"

"No. I just got up to take a message from Maggie. She's going out. To do some surveillance."

Paige hitched the sheet up and padded into the room. "This late?"

"This early, you mean. She's going to try to catch the fishermen and dockworkers before they begin their day, to see what they know about your yacht."

"Won't they think it odd that an American woman is up before dawn, asking questions like that?"

"I doubt they'll know she's American," Doc replied. "And depending on the disguise she uses for this little outing, they may not even know she's a woman."

The mingled affection and respect in David's voice didn't trigger any of the jealousy Paige had felt earlier. Thinking about it, she wasn't surprised. Not after what had just passed between her and David. Not after she'd shared, even in a small way, some of the stomach-twisting tension of their mission.

Still, she wouldn't mind hearing a little of the same quality in his voice when he talked to her. Gathering the folds of the voluminous sheet, she sat down on the sofa and tucked her knees under her.

"What do we do if she finds the yacht? What's my next assignment?"

She wasn't sure, but she thought she caught a glimmer of amusement in his eyes. That wasn't quite what she'd hoped to generate, but at least it was better than the cold disapproval he'd displayed earlier this afternoon. Deciding she wanted to see his face during this discussion, she reached up to snap on the lamp.

When the light bathed him in its soft golden glow, it took Paige a while to raise her eyes to David's face. They seemed to snag at the level of his waist and get stuck there. She'd seen David half-dressed before, of course. She'd seen him wholly undressed before. But now, observing the play of the spotlight across his stomach and chest, she realized she'd never quite appreciated the reasons for his sleek, muscled power.

Paige had always assumed he exercised so rigorously every day from an innate sense of discipline. She now knew he did so to hone his physical and mental faculties for this secret life he led. And well honed they certainly were.

The lamplight played on the bare skin of his upper torso, casting it in subtle shades of bronze and tan. A light sprinkling of reddish-brown hair dusted his chest and curled around his flat nipples. She'd always considered David handsome, but seeing him now, with his slacks hanging low on his lean hips and his pectorals bulging slightly as he crossed his arms, Paige made a startling discovery. His body turned her on. Totally. Completely. In a way she hadn't thought much about before. In a way she didn't have to think about at all. Her body was responding with no input from her brain whatsoever.

Beneath the swaddling sheet, her nipples peaked, and a gush of damp heat moistened the juncture of her thighs.

"Your next assignment will depend a great deal on what Maggie uncovers," David said casually, leaning one hip against a marble-topped sofa table.

Paige dragged her eyes from her intense contemplation of his navel.

"If she gets a lead on the boat you were taken to," he continued, "we'll arrange a meeting with whoever's on board. We'll have to make it seem accidental, but…"

"We?"

"We. As you pointed out this afternoon, you're part of this team, whether I like it or not. Until the contact is made, anyway."

He paused, his lips crooking in a rueful smile. "But I can't take another night of watching you make yourself available to the highest bidder."

"You can't?"

"No, I can't. So I think we should alter your status a bit. From available merchandise to reserved stock. For private enjoyment only."

At the look in his eyes, the moist heat between Paige's legs grew hotter, wetter.

"What about the contact?" she asked around the sudden tightness in her throat. "How will he get to me if you're…privately enjoying the stock?"

"Meredith indicated that the women who acted as couriers were free to indulge their own pursuits before and after delivering the merchandise. We'll just let word leak out that you've entered into an arrangement for the period of your stay in Cannes. Whoever wants that microdot is resourceful enough to work around an apparent lover."

"Apparent?" she echoed. Her gaze slid down the broad expanse of his chest as she recalled just how far beyond *apparent* they'd gone tonight. The memories made her clamp her thighs together.

Really, this adventure business was a sort of an aphrodisiac, she decided. The danger, the excitement, the experience of playing a role so different from life's ordinary routine, all contributed to a sense of heightened awareness, a feeling of being intensely alive. No wonder James Bond had such a devoted following, Paige mused as she slid her legs off the sofa and rose.

Hitching the wadded sheet under her arms, she walked over to stand before him. While one hand held the material more or less in place, the other reached out to touch the warm steel of his skin.

"We shouldn't have too much difficulty playing the role you just described," she murmured, tracing a whorl of hair lightly with one finger.

A flicker of regret crossed David's face. His hand closed over hers, stilling the small movement.

"It might be more difficult than you imagine. It has to be only a role."

Sure that she hadn't heard him correctly, Paige tugged at her hand. David held it captive against his chest.

"Listen to me, sweetheart. I lost control tonight, which is dangerous for someone on a covert mission, not to mention stupid as hell for us personally."

"Wh-what?"

"I didn't use anything," he reminded her softly. "I forgot all about the need to protect you."

"Wait a minute. There were two of us in that bed tonight, as best I recall. I think I deserve a little of the credit or the blame, whichever it is you're apportioning here."

"There were two," he agreed, with a wry twist of his lips. "But from now on, sweetheart, there will only be one."

Paige knew very well that her sudden surge of irritation had nothing whatsoever to do with the fact that David still assumed responsibility for her "protection." Although the status of their engagement was somewhat fuzzy at this particular point, in her heart of hearts she wanted desperately to have his children.

What rankled was his unilateral decision to put their sexual activities on hold. Especially now, when just the sight of him had her feeling so damn…aroused.

"Fine," she told him, hanging on to her dignity, and the sheet, with both hands. "I've got the bed. You can take the sofa."

So much for James Bond, she thought in disgust, trying hard not to slam the bedroom door behind her.

# Chapter 9

Maggie hid a smile as she glanced around the small, crowded bistro, the third one she'd visited since slipping out of the hotel less than an hour ago. So much for the glamorous, deliciously decadent undercover role she'd thought she was going to play while in Cannes.

Instead of breakfasting at one of the linen-draped tables in the Carlton's palatial dining room, she was wedged into a tiny café filled with a few oilcloth-covered tables and an astonishing number of people. She shared a narrow bench with a red-faced fisherman who exuded the pungent aroma of his trade and a voluble gray-haired woman who stabbed her croissant into a small cup of café au lait, then waved the soggy pastry in the air to emphasize every point. Maggie didn't mind the enforced intimacy in the least, however, since the woman beside her possessed just the information she'd been seeking.

"But no!" the sweater-clad woman exclaimed. "No, I tell you. The boat you seek is gone."

Maggie ducked as drops of coffee flew in all directions.

Despite her evasive action, several more splotches appeared on the once pristine front of her beige-and-white-striped dress.

The various occupants of the bistro had recognized the Carlton's distinctive uniform immediately, of course. With gruff good cheer, they'd squeezed closer together to make room for another working woman. Just as cheerfully, they'd answered her careful, casual questions.

"This boat," the woman beside Maggie declared with another dramatic wave of the croissant, "the one the American tourist falls from yesterday, was docked at the marina where my Georges works. He operates the fuel station, you understand. Georges filled the tank not long after the woman falls, and the boat slipped its mooring."

"How unfortunate," Maggie murmured in soft, idiomatic Provençal. French—and its related but quite distinct sister dialect of the south of France—were among her favorite languages, and she hadn't needed any refresher training to prepare for this mission.

"The woman is staying at the Carlton," Maggie continued with a small shrug. "She lost her purse when she fell into the sea. She hopes perhaps someone aboard the boat might have fished it from the water."

"Not with the tide that swirls around those docks," the man beside her pronounced, reaching for a crock of creamy butter. "Her purse is halfway to Africa by now, you may take my word for that."

He slathered the butter onto a brioche, then popped the whole confection into his mouth. The lift of his arm sent an overpowering waft of fishy air in Maggie's direction. Her eyes watering, she leaned back against the stone wall and breathed in rapidly through her open mouth. When she had herself under control again, she addressed the woman on her other side.

"Do you think your Georges could give me the name or registration of this boat? So *mademoiselle* may contact its owner to ask about her purse, on the off chance it was found? I will share whatever reward she gives me for this information."

The gray-haired woman patted her hand. "But of course. I'll phone my husband. He's at the docks already."

Chair legs scraped the bare tiles to make room as she weaved her way through the close-packed tables. Maggie edged sideways on the bench in an attempt to put as much distance as she could between herself and the fisherman. Reaching for one of the feather-light croissants in a napkin-draped basket, she watched the woman duck under a row of cheeses dangling from the low ceiling and drop a coin into a pay phone. A few moments later she returned.

"It was the *Kristina II*," Georges's wife announced. "She's owned by an agency that rents pleasure craft to the tourists. Or to those who don't wish to maintain their own boats. Georges didn't know who rented it yesterday."

Maggie concealed her sharp disappointment. Whoever had arranged to use the yacht as a place to meet with Meredith Ames would be too smart to leave a trail through a rental agency.

"Thank you," she murmured. "I will tell *mademoiselle* she must speak to this agency. Is it perhaps the one owned by Gabriel Ardenne?"

Maggie's question was a pure shot in the dark. Although the well-known tycoon and international jet-setter had a finger in a great many pies, not all of them legitimate, Maggie had no idea if he operated a yacht rental business.

Evidently he didn't. Maggie's companion shook her head.

"Gabriel Ardenne, the banker? No, I don't think he owns this agency. Georges has never mentioned him to me."

Hiding her disappointment, Maggie took a bite of her pastry. Across the table, a little man in a gray sweater and a black beret gave a snort of disgust.

"Ardenne? Ha! That one wouldn't own boats, even through a rental agency. I've never seen anyone so afflicted by *mal de mere*. He lost his dinner twice when I ferried him to Saint-Agnès last month, and the bay was as smooth as glass."

The woman beside Maggie stabbed a croissant into her cup once more, than sprayed the assembled crowd with both coffee and her opinions.

"These Parisians! They live such lives of dissipation, then come here seeking relief from their sins. To think our blessed saint's own island has become a sanctuary for men such as Gabriel Ardenne!"

At that point a lively argument broke out concerning the relative levels of degradation of Parisian bankers and the international film stars who flocked to Cannes each spring. When Maggie squeezed her way out of the bistro sometime later, excitement sang along her nerves. She now knew that the last time Gabriel Ardenne visited Cannes, he'd been ferried to a small island near the western arm of the bay. This island, named for the virginal, saintly recluse who'd retreated there in defiance of the Romans' ban on Christian practices two millennia ago, was now the site of a very secluded and very expensive spa.

As she walked through the narrow, still-dark streets of the old town, Maggie formulated a quick plan of action. The island was only ten minutes away. She could hire a boat, do a quick reconnoiter, maybe gain access to the current list of guests, and be back before the sun rose.

If she ascertained that Gabriel Ardenne was among the guests, Maggie would then get together with David and Paige to plan their next step. If he wasn't, she decided with a grin, she would've had a pleasurable early-morning boat trip to a scenic little island.

First, however, she needed to change uniforms.

She turned off the narrow lane into a back alley that threaded through the residential area. Peering over crumbling stone walls into tiny gardens and yards, she soon found exactly what she needed. A few moments later, she pinned several high-denomination franc notes to a clothesline with a plastic clothespin and tucked a bundle of dark garments under her arm.

Maggie's first indication that she might have underestimated the difficulty of her task came when she cut the engine of her small boat and drifted toward the island's only wharf. To her intense interest, she saw the jetty was flooded with light and guarded by two health spa attendants with suspicious-looking bulges under their right armpits. Thoughtfully Maggie tugged the billed cap she'd appropriated earlier down over her forehead and continued around the island, as though heading past it for the far arm of the bay.

Out of sight of the guards, she cut the engine and drifted slowly on the rolling swells. The sharp scent of pine and fragrant eucalyptus floated toward her from the tree-studded island as she studied its steep, rocky shoreline.

If she wanted to move about Saint-Agnès unescorted, she'd have to anchor the boat in one of the small coves that dented the island and swim ashore. Now that she'd seen those guards, Maggie's sixth sense—the tingling inner instinct that made her one of OMEGA's most effective and least orthodox operatives— told her she definitely wanted to move about Saint-Agnès unescorted.

Punching in a code on the digital watch that she'd substituted for the gold compact Paige now carried, Maggie waited for Doc to answer. Much as she hated to disturb him yet again, she needed to let him know she was going in.

Maggie's brief communiqué disturbed Doc, but not in the way she'd envisioned. Instead of rousing him from Paige's side in the gilded bed that dominated the luxurious bedroom, her call brought him instantly awake and off the hard sofa in the sitting room.

Massaging the crick in his neck with one hand, Doc listened intently to her brief report. His hand stilled as she outlined her plan to swim ashore and scout out the spa.

"I don't like it," he told her quietly. "Why don't you wait until control can get us some information on this operation?"

"There's still an hour or so until dawn. I might as well have a look around. I have a feeling that our boy's here."

Doc frowned, but refrained from any further protest and signed off. Maggie was a skilled operative, with as much experience in the field as he himself possessed. Like all OMEGA agents, she was trained to operate independently, and didn't take unnecessary risks.

What was more, Doc had a healthy respect for her instincts. Her intuitive approach to a mission represented the opposite end of the spectrum from his own deliberate, problem-solving approach, yet both had proven equally effective in the past.

Still, he didn't like the idea of Maggie going in to Saint-Agnès blind. Nor, he acknowledged with a flicker of irritation, did he like the idea of his partner going into action while he sat idle. If Paige hadn't insisted on involving herself in this mission, he wouldn't be tied to this hotel suite right now. Maggie could have handled Meredith's role without requiring this kind of close cover, but Paige didn't have the skills or the training to protect herself if things turned nasty.

A dozen ugly scenarios immediately sprang into his mind. The thought of Paige in any one of the situations he envisioned added considerably to Doc's gathering tension. Driven by an uncharacteristic edginess, he began to pace the sitting room.

Dammit, he shouldn't have let himself be swayed by Paige's arguments. He shouldn't have overruled his own common sense and allowed her to stay. There was a reason he'd kept the various parts of his life separate and distinct from each other, he told himself in disgust, and this was it!

Several hours later, Doc's mood had not noticeably improved. He'd dressed in a pair of tan slacks and a red knit shirt retrieved from the suite across the hall and had worked with Claire to compile a working dossier on the Saint-Agnès Health and Wellness Center. His pen tapping impatiently against the secretaire, Doc reviewed the information they'd painstakingly gathered.

There wasn't much. A list of the world-renowned physicians and health experts who consulted at the spa for astronomical fees. A brief description of the physical facilities, which included everything from cedar saunas to marble ice pools. And the names of its more notable clients, including one Gabriel Ardenne, but no accompanying information on the state of his health or wellness as documented by the doctors at Saint-Agnès.

Frowning, Doc stared down at Ardenne's name. The banker

had made several secret trips to the spa in the past year. It appeared likely that he was currently on the island. At this point, Doc wasn't sure which worried him more. The fact that Maggie's instincts had proven correct, or the fact that she hadn't checked in yet.

She hadn't signaled for help. Hadn't requested his assistance. She was good, he reminded himself. Damn good. Still, he'd give her another hour, max, and then he'd take a trip to Saint-Agnès himself. Which meant he'd have to secure Paige in the suite before he—

"Good morning."

He slewed around at the somewhat stilted greeting and felt his jaw tighten in annoyance. Christ, wasn't there anything in Meredith Ames's wardrobe that covered more skin than it showed?

The beaded see-through white vest Paige was wearing plunged to a deep V between her breasts. Strategically placed pearls covered their tips, but not much else. The top was paired with a long white skirt that looked conservative enough at first glance. It was only when she moved across the room that Doc discovered it was slit clear up to her thigh on one side. She'd pulled her hair back from her face in a high braid that showed off both her delicate features and a pair of huge, butterfly-shaped white earrings that *his* Paige would never have tolerated.

Doc found himself admiring this seductive creature and at the same time missing the familiar, comfortable woman who usually bundled herself in bright plaids and ankle-length jumpers and never bothered with jewelry.

Once again he experienced the unsettling sensation of seeing the lines he'd drawn so carefully around his different lives blur past all distinction. His voice had a testy edge to it when he responded to her greeting.

"Good morning."

Paige blinked, clearly taken aback by his curt tone. "What's the matter?"

His pen tapped on the desk for a moment. "I've been waiting for Maggie to check in," he said at last, forcing the words out.

His rational mind acknowledged Paige's need to know, but it was tough to overcome both his desire to shield her and a deep-seated, conditioned reluctance to discuss OMEGA matters with anyone outside the agency.

"Check in? Where is she?"

"I'll brief you about it at breakfast."

Doc recognized his response as the feeble attempt to delay the inevitable that it was. Rising, he grimaced and rolled his shoulders to ease their ache.

"Didn't you sleep well?" Paige asked sweetly. Too damn sweetly, in Doc's opinion.

"No I didn't."

"Good. Just remember whose brilliant idea it was to keep our sleeping arrangements separate. Among other things."

With that, she headed for the bedroom to get her purse.

She wasn't in a much better mood than he was this morning, Doc acknowledged wryly. Shoving his hands into his pockets, he leaned against the desk and waited for her to reemerge. This wasn't shaping up to be a good day.

Where the hell was Maggie? And how was he going to explain to Paige without ruffling her feathers further that he'd have to shorten her leash considerably if he needed to make a quick trip to Saint-Agnès?

Not long after they were seated at one of the wrought-iron tables on the Carlton's sun-drenched terrace, Doc heard a low, resonating hum. He'd just filled Paige in on Maggie's early-morning excursion, so she was as relieved as he when he palmed the gold cigarette case and saw that he had a message from Chameleon.

Although most of the other tables on the broad terrace were unoccupied, Doc wasn't taking any chances. With a murmured admonition to Paige to stay put, he went to find some privacy.

Struggling to contain her curiosity, Paige watched the waiters nod deferentially as David weaved his way through the wrought-iron tables. She had to admit he carried himself with an air of authority that commanded respect. His red knit shirt emphasized the straight set of his shoulders and his lean, tapered waist. Paige hadn't seen those expensive-looking tan slacks or those loafers before. With a small shock, she realized that David must maintain a complete separate wardrobe for his various missions.

Frowning, she spooned a bite of the raspberries and cream she'd ordered, then leaned back in her cushioned chair. The flower-decked terrace overlooked the Croisette and gave a spectacular view of the sea beyond, but she was too tightly wound to appreciate the scenery this morning.

She nudged the purse tucked securely beside her on the chair with one thigh, just to reassure herself it was still there. How in the world was she supposed to pass the gold mesh halter inside the purse to this French banker, who might or might not be Meredith's contact and might or might not be locked away on some secluded island?

"So, *mademoiselle,* you are up early, no?"

Paige swiveled around to see a pug-nosed, freckle-faced boy leaning his disreputable moped against one of the palm trees that lined the boulevard just beyond the terrace. With casual aplomb, he sauntered up the broad stone steps.

"Henri! What are you doing here?"

At Paige's startled exclamation, one of the nearby waiters turned. A scowl marred his features when he spied the boy's grubby shorts and ragged sweater. He hurried over, and a rapid, rather heated exchange in French followed. Only after Paige's repeated assurances that she knew the boy did the waiter retire, still scowling.

Henri occupied the seat David had just vacated and poured himself a cup of thick black coffee. Flooding it with cream, he took several satisfying swallows.

"I see you breakfast with the too-large gentleman," he commented smugly. "I told you he had the passion for you. He hires you for the entire night, then?"

Heat crept up Paige's throat, but before she could decide how to answer, he gave her a stern look.

"I just hope you collect the appropriate fee."

She thought about the thick fold of notes David had tossed on the table last night, and the heat spread across her cheeks.

"I appreciate your interest in my, ah, business affairs, Henri, but I don't think I should be discussing such matters with—"

Her voice faltered as the boy reached across the table to snag a croissant from the linen-covered basket. In the process, the sleeve of his sweater rode up, revealing vicious, swelling bruises on his bone-thin forearm.

"What happened to you?" she gasped.

"Pah!" Henri got out around the pastry he'd stuffed in his mouth. "Antoine, he tried to take the commission you paid me last night."

Shocked, Paige searched her memory for a moment before she recalled that this Antoine was the man Henri carried money for.

The boy devoured the rest of the croissant, then grinned at her. "It appears I shall have to find a new business partner. You're sure you don't wish the manager, *mademoiselle?*"

Paige felt her heart constrict at that brave, irreverent grin. She swallowed, noting how his skin stretched across his sharp cheeks and how his thin, narrow shoulders were hunched under the baggy sweater.

"I'm sure," she said slowly, pushing David's untouched bowl of raspberries toward the boy.

She chewed on her lower lip as he attacked the berries with unabashed gusto. The entire bowl of fruit disappeared in less than a minute, as did the thick cream, which Henry slurped noisily from the silver spoon.

"Maybe there's some other service you can provide while I'm here…" she said hesitantly.

Tugging the pastry basket closer to examine its remaining contents, the boy nodded enthusiastically. "Most assuredly, *mademoiselle*. I shall be your guide, yes? I know shops that carry dresses with the labels of Saint-Laurent and Givenchy—but not the price, you understand. And perfumeries that sell scents for a third what you pay on the Croisette." His red brows waggled.

"Not even your so-large gentleman will know it isn't Arpège you wear, and we will split the difference in price, no?"

"No," Paige said hastily.

Good Lord, was there anything this youngster wasn't into? She took another look at his pinched face and swallowed the impulse to ask.

"Look, why don't I order you breakfast and you can...you can tell me about Cannes, and some of the famous people who live here? Like Gabriel Ardenne," she added in a flash of inspiration. If anyone knew about the international jet-setter, she suspected this boy would.

"The banker? Pah, you don't want to waste your time on that one, *mademoiselle*. He is a pig."

"He is?"

Her heart thumping, Paige summoned a waiter. After ordering half the items on the menu, Henri recited a list of the banker's astonishing excesses, some of which he knew for a fact to be true, he swore.

He ran out of information at precisely the moment the first covered dish arrived at the table. His brown eyes alight with pleasure, Henri cut off a chunk of sizzling sausage and popped it into his mouth.

By the time she caught a flash of a red knit shirt out of the corner of one eye, Paige had extracted a few more interesting bits of information from the boy, including one or two about the reclusive film star Victor Swanset. She wondered if David knew that Swanset made private visits to the wing he'd endowed in the huge convention hall that was home to Cannes's famous film festival. According to Henri, his silver Rolls-Royce had been spotted parked at the back of the Palais des Festivals several times of late.

Anxious and excited, Paige scanned David's face as he wound his way through the scattered tables. At the silent, reassuring message he telegraphed to her, she sagged in relief. Wherever Maggie was at this moment, evidently she was all right.

When David approached, he caught sight of the diminutive

figure ensconced in his seat. The array of empty dishes in front
of the boy sent his brows soaring.

"Do you remember my friend Henri?" Paige asked.

"Of course." David eyed him thoughtfully. "Do you breakfast at the Carlton often, or was there some purpose to this
visit?"

"I came to inquire how *mademoiselle* fares, of course. And
to see if she has reconsidered my offer to act as her business
manager."

"Her business manager?"

At David's startled glance, Paige shifted guiltily in her seat.
She'd been so overcome by nervousness last night, she'd ne-
glected to inform him of Henri's previous offer to act as her
agent.

The boy scooted back the heavy iron chair and rose. Hooking
his thumbs into the waistband of his shorts, he rocked back on
his heels. "I fear *mademoiselle* has not the head for numbers.
She needs someone to watch out for her and protect her interests."

"I won't argue with you there," David drawled.

"I've explained to Henri that I am *not* in the market for a
manager right now," Paige put in. "Of any kind. But I'm thinking of engaging his services as a guide."

David's frown told her he didn't think much of the idea.

"He's been sharing some very interesting information with
me. About Cannes, and some of the people who live here," she
added, hinting heavily.

"He has?"

"I have, *monsieur.* Just to entertain *mademoiselle,* you understand, since you leave her unattended for so long." There
was no mistaking the disapproval in Henri's voice, or the im-
plication that he would manage Paige's time far more efficiently.

"Thanks for watching her for me," David responded in a dry
tone. "I'll take over from here."

Paige didn't particularly care for this turn in the conversation.
She felt like a pet poodle being passed from keeper to keeper.

*"Bon!"* Henri announced. "I will go, then." Contrary to his words, he rocked back on his heels and waited expectantly.

David's mouth twisted in a small smile. "Let me guess. I owe you another fifty francs."

*"Oui."*

"For what?"

"For my time, of course. Like *mademoiselle,* I am paid by the hour."

With a shake of his head, David reached into his back pocket and pulled out his wallet.

Henri made an elaborate show of folding the bill and tucking it into his pocket. Then he brushed past David to give Paige a gallant little bow.

"If you wish me to show you the Palais des Festivals, *mademoiselle,* you have only to come to my headquarters. The telephone kiosk at the corner of the Croisette and the Allées de la Liberté," he added, at her blank look.

"Yes, of course."

*"A bientôt."* He took a jaunty step toward his moped.

"Henri?"

*"Oui, monsieur?"*

"I'd like my wallet back before you leave."

Paige gasped, and a look of wounded innocence filled the boy's brown eyes.

"Your wallet, *monsieur?"*

"It's in your left pocket, I believe."

Henri's freckled face scrunched in disgust as he dug into his shorts. "Me, I am losing my touch."

Her jaw sagging, Paige watched him hand over the wallet, then saunter down the steps to his moped. With an unrepentant wave, he was off.

Calmly David took his seat and signaled for the check. During the brief interval while the waiter cleared the table, he scribbled a few quick words in a small leather-bound notebook.

Still struggling to recover from her shock at the attempted larceny, Paige craned her neck and saw that he'd jotted down the location of Henri's telephone kiosk.

"You're not going to have him arrested, are you?" she asked anxiously as soon as the waiter moved out of range. "I'm sure he just needed the money for food. He was so hungry."

David slid the notebook into his pocket, then eyed the five-digit total on the check. "*Hungry* isn't the word for it."

He caught Paige's anxious look and scrawled his name and room number across the bottom of the bill.

"I'm just going to have control check him out," he told her, rising. "Come on, let's go upstairs. Maggie's on her way back to the hotel. She's discovered some rather interesting information about our friend Gabriel Ardenne."

"That one, he's a pig," Paige murmured, unconsciously imitating Henri's scornful tone. At David's quick glance, she lifted her chin. "Maggie's not the only one who can do a little extemporaneous sleuthing. Did she discover that Ardenne's into drugs, big-time?"

"She did," David said, holding the heavy door of the elevator cage. "But not the kind you think, perhaps."

The door clanged shut, and the elevator began to wheeze upward. Ignoring the panoramic vista of the Carlton's gilt- and palm-strewn lobby, Paige turned to the man beside her.

"What do you mean? What kind of drugs is he into?"

"Experimental ones. Very experimental, and as yet unsanctioned by most medical authorities. The clinic at Saint-Agnès is one of the few places in the world that will administer them."

"Why? What's he being treated for?"

"It appears Ardenne is in the last stages of AIDS. According to Maggie, he's on a respirator and IVs. He won't be leaving Saint-Agnès again."

Paige swallowed. "So…so it couldn't have been Ardenne who was waiting for me on that yacht," she said after a moment.

"No, it couldn't." David's jaw tightened. "Which means the only lead we have at this moment is Victor Swanset. And he's locked away in that impregnable fortress of his."

"No, he isn't! At least, not all the time."

The elevator clanked to a halt, but David didn't reach for the heavy lever that operated its door.

"What are you talking about?"

A thrill of excitement shot through her at the thought that she, plain little Paige Lawrence, had uncovered a nugget of information that this powerful secret agency David worked for hadn't.

"Victor Swanset recently endowed a wing at the Palais des Festivals," she said smugly. "The word on the street is that he visits it occasionally."

# Chapter 10

After a debrief with Maggie in the suit across the hall, Paige and David left her to catch upon a few hours of much-needed sleep. They'd hit the Palais des Festivals around noon, they decided, unless the individual seeking the microdot made contact with "Meredith" sooner.

"There's still that possibility," Doc reminded a restless, pacing Paige.

She turned, and her skirt swirled open to reveal a length of satiny thigh.

Doc drew in a quick breath, then suggested casually, "Why don't you get changed while I work out our approach?"

She chewed on her lower lip for a moment. "Good idea. I'd better wear the halter, so the contact can identify me."

Doc stifled a groan as she pulled the slinky thing out of her purse and headed for the bedroom. He experienced a pang of real regret for Paige's plaids and bulky jumpers, which he suspected might now be a thing of the past.

He pulled out his notebook and flipped to a clean sheet to compile a list of items he wanted Control to check for him.

A—the exact physical layout of the Palais des Festivals.

B—the hours it was open to the public.

C—this wing Swanset had reportedly endowed.

Doc tapped his pencil against the notebook, studying the neat, precisely printed letters. A crooked grin tugged at his mouth as he recalled Paige's smug disclosure about Swanset's supposed visits to the Palais. She was so pleased with herself for having uncovered that bit of information. As she should be.

Unless...

Doc stiffened. His grin faded as he flipped back a page and stared at the address of the telephone kiosk.

Unless the information had been planted. By a certain grubby-faced boy.

They'd all assumed Henri's appearance on the scene after Paige fell into the sea was simple chance. Suddenly, Doc wasn't so sure.

Cursing under his breath, he ripped out a clean sheet of note-paper and began a new list. When it was done, he studied the four entries that documented the boy's involvement so far.

Henri had just *happened* to be in the right place at the right time to fish Paige out of the bay.

The chauffeur had accosted him outside the hotel, *supposedly* to find out where he'd taken the bedraggled woman.

Paige had reported belatedly that the boy had popped out of the bushes when she returned from the casino last night.

And now he showed up this morning, running up a breakfast tab roughly equivalent to the U.S. national debt while he cleverly fed Paige nuggets of information.

Christ! Doc shoved a hand through his hair, feeling like ten kinds of an idiot. They'd been sitting here all these hours, wondering just when Meredith's mysterious contact would try to approach her, and it was entirely possible that he had. Several times.

The boy could very well be acting as a courier for whoever wanted the stolen technology. If so, Henri would've grasped at once that Paige wasn't Meredith, when he plucked her from the sea. No wonder he'd been so obliging about delivering her to the Carlton. The boy wanted to find out exactly what Paige's relationship was to the real Meredith Ames.

David's unexplained presence in Meredith's suite must have confused him. Not enough to keep him from extracting his fifty francs, but enough to delay retrieval of the microdot from Maggie. What was more, Paige's emergence as Meredith Ames last night must have added to his confusion.

Anyone else would probably have abandoned his mission at that point. But not this kid, Doc guessed shrewdly. Not someone who lived by his wits and snatched at any chance to make a few francs. What was more, he could very well be too frightened to report failure to the individual who'd sent him. A kid like Henri was expendable. All too expendable, when the stakes were this high.

His face grim, Doc pulled his cigarette case out of his pocket and waited for Control to acknowledge his signal. Everything was conjecture at this point, he reminded himself. Their only recourse was to proceed with the plan to visit the Palais des Festivals this afternoon. But he was damn well going to know everything there was to know about a certain red-haired street rat before Paige set one foot out of the hotel.

Several hours later, Maggie slipped across the hall in response to Doc's signal. Her silvery-blond hair was still tousled from sleep, but her eyes were wide and alert.

Paige sat quietly on the sofa, thoroughly shaken by Doc's suspicions about the boy, while he briefed Maggie.

"Claire can't find out anything about the kid?" she asked incredulously.

Doc shook his head, frowning. "Nothing definitive. A child of his description was picked up for truancy a couple of years ago and returned to his foster home. The authorities suspected abuse, but the boy disappeared again before anyone could check it out. Since then, the local police have heard his name mentioned by several of the kids who work for a local thug by the name of…" He reached for his notebook.

"Antoine," Paige supplied in a small voice.

"Antoine," he confirmed. "The guy's a pretty rough character, from what Claire was able to piece together. He's a member of the Sicilian contingent here in Cannes. Specializes in drugs, prostitution and bookmaking. A few of his money carriers suspected of shorting him have been found strangled in back alleys."

Paige locked her arms around her waist. "Poor Henri."

"So far," Doc continued, "there's no known connection between Antoine and Victor Swanset, or Henri and Victor. I even had Claire check to see if there was any link to Swanset's missing cook, who, incidentally, was found a few weeks after he disappeared, floating facedown in the bay."

"Was there? Any link, I mean?"

"None," Doc admitted.

"If there is a connection, we'll find it," Maggie said. Maggie stretched, then tucked a stray curl behind one ear. "This telephone kiosk the boy mentioned is located on the Allées de la Liberté, isn't it? I'll nose around the area while you guys check out the Palais des Festivals."

"Be careful," Paige cautioned. "I saw the bruises this Antoine gave Henri."

"I will."

Paige's delicate features assumed a stern expression. "Check in with us if you stumble onto something. Don't try to take out this character by yourself."

Maggie snapped to attention and rendered her own, less than precise version of a salute. "No, ma'am."

"I'm serious!"

She abandoned her military posture and smiled at Paige. "I'll be careful. I promise. You just keep yourself covered at the Palais des Festivals."

That might take some effort, Doc thought wryly as the two women gave each other a little hug. The damned halter slithered sideways with the movement, baring a good portion of Paige's small, sweet breasts.

* * *

The sprawling five-tiered tan-and-white Palais des Festivals dominated the western end of the Croisette.

Crammed with every imaginable audiovisual device, the convention center had been designed as a permanent home for the film festival—which, Paige discovered from the guidebook Doc purchased for her at the front entrance, got off to a shaky start by opening on the very day in 1939 that Germany invaded Poland.

"'The festival reopened in 1946, when Ray Milland won the Best Actor award for *Lost Weekend*,'" she read aloud. "'Since then, this glamorous gathering each May has drawn greater and greater crowds and garnered worldwide attention, until Cannes now rivals Hollywood as a center for the serious study of cinematic art.'"

"I suspect the starlets cavorting on the beaches were as much of a draw as any of the films by Bergman and Fellini," Doc suggested with a grin, his eyes on the spectacular view visible through the floor-to-ceiling glass wall in the central rotunda.

It wasn't the panoramic seascape that had snared his attention, Paige saw at once. Her mouth dropping, she gaped at the generously endowed young woman who was using the Palais as a backdrop while she posed for a cluster of reporters on the beach below.

Paige recognized the girl at once. She was the star of a recent Czech release that critics in twenty different countries had raved about. She'd played an insatiable nymphet in the movie, and although Paige hadn't seen the film, she could understand why the critics said the girl had been born for the role.

As she draped herself over a rock on the beach in a series of shocking, suggestive poses, it became immediately obvious that the bathing suit lacked both top and bottom. It lacked everything, in fact, except a tiny twist of fabric that circled her flaring hips and dipped between her dimpled rear cheeks.

Paige gawked with the rest of the tourists gathered at the windows while cameras clicked and whirred and flashed all around her.

"The Swanset Wing is across the gardens," David reminded her, still grinning.

With a last glance over her shoulder at the starlet, Paige followed him through a set of glass doors into the formal gardens. Immediately the seductive scent of roses and a soothing peace enveloped them. After the chatter and the noise of the huge rotunda, the still, unruffled reflecting pools dotting the gardens offered a surprising tranquillity. Few tourists wandered the crushed-shell paths, and even fewer made it to the wing at the rear of the gardens.

In fact, other than a bored, sleepy-eyed guard, David and Paige were the only ones in the modernistic building, dedicated to the movies of the twenties and thirties. Black tile floors and stark white marble walls provided a dramatic backdrop for still shots from classic Charlie Chaplin and Rudolph Valentino films. Screens set into the walls at various intervals flickered with scenes from old black-and-white melodramas.

"Look!" Paige nodded toward a room just off the main hallway. "This alcove's dedicated exclusively to Victor Swanset's films."

"So it is," David murmured, his eyes on the elaborately framed life-size portrait that dominated the far end of the alcove. It showed a brooding, intensely handsome man in his midthirties. He wore formal evening dress, with a dark cape flung over one shoulder and gloved hands curled around an ivoryheaded cane. His glossy black hair was slick with brilliantine, as were his luxuriant mustache and his small, pointed goatee.

"This is a studio shot from *The Baron of the Night*," Paige reported, scanning the information engraved in marble beside the portrait. "Victor Swanset's first film, and one of two dozen he did for Albion Studios."

"Which he later purchased," David added, supplementing the engraved data with the intelligence he'd gleaned from Claire.

"He made his own movies?"

"He made his own statement," David corrected. "The films Albion Studios produced in the late twenties and thirties became vehicles for Swanset's increasingly vocal criticism of British foreign policy. He felt England and the United States should have entered the war long before they did.''

"To stop Hitler?"

"To preserve the old, aristocratic order," David drawled.

Paige studied Swanset's striking features and arrogant pose. She wasn't surprised that his debut as the Dark Baron had catapulted him to immediate international fame. Or that he'd want to maintain the old order.

"The British government appropriated Albion Studios during the war," David continued, staring up at the portrait. "They used it to churn out propaganda films. Victor Swanset was so outraged by this bastardization of his art and his property that he refused to make another movie. He left England in the early fifties, and never returned."

Paige turned away, disturbed by the haunting portrait. As she wandered through the alcove, she had the uncomfortable feeling that Swanset's eyes followed her. Shrugging off the eerie sensation, she studied a series of framed black-and-white stills. Although Swanset appeared to have brought the same dramatic power to all his roles, from defrocked bishop to desert sheik, none of the stills held quite the intensity as the portrait of the Dark Baron.

David bent to examine a typed notice pasted to a bare spot on one wall. "It says that one of the stills was vandalized and has been removed for repair. I wonder which one?"

"The guard will know," Paige offered.

He nodded, then swept the quiet, empty alcove with a keen glance. "I'll go ask. You sit tight."

His heels echoed on the tiles as he retraced his steps to the entrance. Paige drifted to the black leather bench in the center of the small room. She perched primly on its edge, in a vain attempt to keep the high slit in the side of her skirt from showing more than just thigh.

Her gaze wandered to the marble pedestal beside the bench. A small sign invited her to press the black button, so she did. She half turned, expecting to see one of Swanset's films flicker to life on the opposite wall. Instead, a hazy beam of light focused on the portrait of the Dark Baron.

Surprised, Paige watched as the beam increased in both diameter and intensity. The brilliant light dazzled her and gave the figure in the portrait a slowly sharpening three-dimensional quality. The picture's background faded, blurred by the light. The walls on either side seemed to disappear, until there was only Victor Swanset, the Baron of the Night, standing before her.

Her heart thumping, Paige sat rigid on the leather bench. She was suddenly, ridiculously convinced that if she put out a hand she would touch cold flesh and hard bone instead of canvas.

She half rose, wanting out of the alcove, when the image moved. Paige gave a startled squeak and fell back on the bench with a thump.

It was only a movie, she told herself. Some kind of enhanced video imaging or something.

Despite these hasty assurances, she couldn't hold back a small screech when the figure in the portrait smiled at her. He actually smiled at her!

Gasping in fright, Paige scooted backward on the bench. She couldn't breathe. Couldn't speak. Couldn't swallow past the huge lump in her throat. The Baron seemed to be looking right at her.

When the shimmering image hooked his cane over one arm, she scrambled back another few inches.

When he stepped out of the portrait, she toppled backward off the bench onto the black tile floor.

"Don't be alarmed, my dear."

The measured, mellifluous voice raised the hairs on her arms. Crabwise, Paige scuttled back, away from the approaching image. The high slit in her skirt parted as her sandaled feet sought purchase on the slippery tiles.

An appreciative gleam darkened the Baron's eyes, and his waxed mustache lifted in a small smile. Bending over her, he held out a gloved hand.

"Don't be frightened. Let me help you up."

*"Da-vid!"*

"Your friend will return momentarily, I'm sure. Please, allow me to assist you."

Since the shimmering image was at that point hovering directly above her, Paige had to chose between taking his hand and lying on the floor quivering like the spineless, terrified blob she was. Her whole body shook as she lifted her arm, inch by agonizing inch, toward his outstretched hand.

Blinding light from the projector bathed her arm in the same eerie glow it did the Baron's. Paige thought she would faint when she touched the white glove and felt solid flesh inside. She gave a tiny whimper of abject terror, closed her eyes, and let him pull her to her feet.

"Oh, my dear, I'm sorry to have frightened you so. Please, forgive me."

When nothing violent happened immediately, Paige opened one eye. She wasn't quite sure, but she thought she detected genuine remorse on the Baron's handsome face as he led her back to the bench.

"Here, sit down while I turn off the projector."

Paige collapsed onto the padded bench. She would've tumbled right off it again a moment later, if total shock hadn't held her pinned in place.

When the Baron pressed the switch for the projector, the dazzling white light disappeared. So did Swanset's handsome, youthful face. His smooth skin lost its firm tone and sank into wrinkles. Liver spots darkened his forehead. His hair grew thinner, sparser, duller, and his tall frame seemed to shrink into itself, until the Baron of the Night became a stooped, thin man in a conservatively tailored business suit. Only his dark eyes retained their intense, penetrating quality.

Paige glanced from the man before her to the dramatic image in the portrait, then back again.

"How…how did you do that?"

He gave a small, self-deprecating smile. "It's a new process I'm working on. One which digitizes images and projects them onto living objects. When perfected, this process could revolutionize filmmaking."

"Well, it certainly revolutionized me," Paige admitted shakily. "But I don't understand how you walked out of the wall like that."

His smile deepened, and he lifted his cane. Its tip disappeared into the portrait.

"This is what we call a molecular screen," Swanset explained gently. "It's composed of air bubbles, not solid canvas, as are those in movie theaters. The Baron's portrait is projected onto the bubbles, or, at certain degrees of intensity, onto the object behind them."

"Onto you," Paige murmured.

"Onto me," he concurred with a rueful twinkle in his eyes. "I must ask you to forgive an old man's vanity, my dear. I shouldn't have done it, I know, but I simply couldn't resist the chance to appear before a beautiful young woman as I once was."

He gestured toward the spot beside Paige on the bench. "May I?"

At her small nod, he leaned both hands on his ivory-handled cane and eased down. Once seated, he studied her face. "Will you be all right?"

"I doubt if I'll ever be able to walk into another movie without swallowing a few dozen tranquilizers first, but aside from that, I'm fine."

Swanset gave a low, delighted chuckle. The sound rippled over Paige like deep, dark velvet brushing across her skin. Millions of women must have swooned when they heard that husky laugh, she thought in some astonishment. Particularly when it was accompanied by the heavy-lidded, blatantly masculine stare Swanset raked her with.

"You really are a most beautiful young woman," he murmured, his gloved hands curling around his cane. "That costume you're wearing enhances your charms quite deliciously, Miss—?"

Paige went very still as his gaze lingered on the gold collar of her halter. In the terror of the preceding few moments, she'd forgotten the reason she'd come to the Victor Swanset Wing of the Palais des Festivals in the first place. The reason came rushing back with soul-shattering intensity.

He cocked a brow, politely awaiting her response.

"Ames," she supplied, in a small, breathless voice. "Meredith Ames."

Oh, God! Was he going to ask for the microdot? Frantically she tried to recall David's itemized list of instructions for just such a possibility.

First... First... Dear Lord, what was first?

The sound of approaching footsteps reined in Paige's spiraling panic.

David's deep voice preceded his arrival on the scene by a tenth of a second. "No luck with the guard. He doesn't have any idea—"

Both his voice and his footsteps ceased abruptly.

Paige swung around on the bench. She had never been more glad to see anyone in her life. She had never been more glad to see David, *her* David, in her life.

His red shirt and tan slacks stood out in startling contrast to the sterile white-and-black decor. As did his strong, athletic body and gleaming, steel blue eyes. There was nothing sterile about David, Paige thought in a rush of relief. Nothing ephemeral, like the shimmering image of the youthful Victor Swanset. David was real. He was solid. He was hers.

The instant communication she felt with him at this moment went deeper than mere visual identification. With the heightened instincts of an animal for her mate, Paige knew that she would recognize David even if he stepped out of a molecular screen wrapped in the body of Michael Jordan.

Unfortunately, her brief flash of absolute identity with, of belonging to, this man vanished when he caught sight of Victor Swanset on the bench beside her.

David, *her* David, disappeared in an instant. In his place stood the stranger she'd seen last night in the mirror.

Only someone as attuned to him as Paige was could have noticed the switch. It was so soft, so subtle. She caught the almost imperceptible tightening of his jaw. The slight shift in the planes of his face. The hint of menace in his walk as he strolled into the alcove.

"Ah," Victor murmured. "Your gallant returns."

Rising to his feet with the aid of his cane, he nodded politely. "You are this delightful creature's David, are you not?"

"I am," he replied, laying a light hand on her bare shoulder. Neither Paige nor Swanset missed the significance of his possessive gesture. He might be hers, but there was no doubt that she was also his.

This time Paige had no objection whatsoever to being claimed like a lost toy poodle. Even by this stranger, who was almost, but not quite, her David. In fact, she would've been more than grateful if he'd tugged on her electronic leash at this very moment and walked her right out of this bizarre situation.

A life of adventure, she decided, wasn't all it was cracked up to be.

"I fear I frightened your lovely companion," Swanset said, with a charming, apologetic glance at Paige.

*Frightened* wasn't quite how she would have described it, but she never used the kind of words that sprang into her mind at that moment. Not in public, anyway.

"I couldn't resist the opportunity to demonstrate a new technique I'm working on," the aging star explained.

"The Swanset visual imaging ionization process?"

Victor's smile broadened to one of pure delight. "You're familiar with my work?"

"I'm an electronic engineer by trade. My firm is very much involved in preparing for the transition to the information highway. Your pioneering work in visual imaging will ease that transition."

"Ah, yes, this information highway one hears so much about. An interesting concept, is it not? Channeling all information, whether written, visual, or audio, through a single network, into millions and millions of homes around the world."

Victor looked into the distance, his dark eyes gleaming with a vision of a world he might not ever see. A world that would explode with ideas, images, sounds. One that would exploit the new technology encoded on a tiny sequin attached to Paige's glittering gold collar.

Swallowing, she resisted the urge to lift her hand to her throat and cover the gold band.

With a tiny shake of his head, Victor recalled himself to the present. "May I be permitted to make amends for frightening your lovely companion so? Perhaps you both might join me for dinner, Mr.—?"

"Jensen."

His dark eyes widened. "But of course! Dr. David Jensen. I've read the paper you presented at the international symposium this week. It's brilliant, quite brilliant."

If David was surprised that this aging recluse had obtained a copy of the highly technical paper that provided his cover for this mission, he didn't show it.

"Please," Swanset insisted. "You must join me for dinner. To allow me to apologize for discomposing Miss Ames so, and, perhaps, to discuss further your paper."

David glanced down at Paige, as if politely seeking confirmation of her wishes.

"Dinner would be wonderful," she managed with a small smile.

"Fine. Shall we say tomorrow evening? My car will pick you up at the…"

"The Carlton."

"The Carlton. At eight o'clock, then."

With a gracious bow to Paige and a nod to David, he strolled out of the alcove.

When the clicking of his cane on the tiles had faded, David slipped a strong hand under her elbow. "Come on, let's get out of here."

Paige wasn't surprised to find that her knees were still shaky. Grateful for both David's support and for the opportunity to put some distance between herself and the Baron's portrait, she clutched at his arm as he led her back out into the gardens. In the rose-scented arbor, he swung her around and curved a hand around her neck. Tilting her face up to the light, he scanned it anxiously.

"Are you all right?"

"More or less."

His fingers curled into her skin. "I just about lost it when I walked in and saw Swanset sitting next to you."

"I did lose it."

With a small, embarrassed laugh, she described the abject terror that had toppled her onto the floor when the star made his dramatic appearance.

"Damn!" David muttered, resting his forehead against hers for a moment. When he lifted his head, his blue eyes gleamed down at her with a combination of resignation and reluctant admiration.

"You have your own inimitable style, Jezebel, but you do get results."

Paige basked in the glory of his praise for all of twenty seconds, then sighed.

"I'd take full credit for this coup, except for one small detail," she said gloomily. "We really don't know if Victor Swanset invited us to his villa to get his hands on my microdot or to pick your brain about your brilliant paper."

# Chapter 11

When she walked out of the Palais des Festivals, Paige experienced a sharp sense of disorientation. With all that had happened, it seemed as though she and David had been inside the huge convention center for hours, if not days. Yet the sun still hung high overhead, and bright diamonds sparkled on the bay. The scent of spring drifted along the Croisette, and even the traffic moved more slowly, more politely, as though the drivers were taking the time to enjoy the balmy afternoon.

"Do you mind walking a bit?" David asked as they approached a rank of waiting taxis. "We can have lunch at one of the beach cafés, then, if you're up to it, take a stroll through the Allées."

At the mention of the Allées, the nervous tension still gripping Paige shifted focus. She shoved aside the lingering jitters generated by her meeting with the Baron of the Night and instantly started worrying about Maggie's meeting with Antoine the bookie.

By the time this great adventure of hers was over, she thought, she was going to have an ulcer.

"I could use some fresh air," she said truthfully.

David smiled and slipped on a pair of aviator-style sunglasses. "Me too."

At any other time, Paige would have delighted in the spectacle that presented itself as they strolled along the palm-lined boulevard. If ever a city had been made for people-watching, it was Cannes, especially at this time of day. The previous night's revelers were just emerging for a late brunch. All along the Croisette, the idle rich rubbed shoulders with camera-laden tourists. On the white, pebbly beaches, northerners who'd come to escape the cold, drizzly wet stripped down to string bikinis, or less, and displayed their pale bodies beside those of tanned sun worshipers. Paige managed to refrain from gawking the way she had at the well-endowed starlet posing on the beach at the Palais.

They chose a small seaside restaurant run by one of the huge hotels on the other side of the Croisette. The tiny open-air café was dotted with gaily striped umbrellas and tubs of pink geraniums and white primroses. The aroma of hot bread and mouth-watering sauces made Paige suddenly aware of the fact that she hadn't eaten anything since her breakfast with Henri.

Was that only this morning? She sank into the chair the waiter held out for her, feeling as though she'd aged several years since then.

After ordering crabmeat salad and a carafe of wine, David stretched out his legs and folded his hands across his stomach.

He looked so at ease, she thought with a touch of mingled wonder and resentment. She was still tied up in knots from her encounter with Victor Swanset, and David appeared so relaxed. And so darned handsome.

She hadn't missed the looks he'd attracted as they strolled the Croisette. No wonder. The red shirt deepened the hue of his skin to a polished oak and brought out the mahogany tints in his thick brown hair. What it did to his powerful, well-sculpted body made her squirm in her seat.

Strange. Paige had never thought of herself as the kind of woman who could regard a man as a sex object. In fact, she hated the TV ad that showed a bunch of women gathering at an upper-story window every morning at a specified hour to watch some hunk in a hard hat peel off his shirt. She'd always considered the ad sexist and demeaning to both men and women.

Since last night, however, she'd come to the conclusion that she might just be more susceptible to a man's body—to this particular man's body, anyway—than she'd ever realized. And he, in his infinite, irritating wisdom, had decided this wasn't the time to indulge in some serious body wrapping.

Wrenching her gaze, if not her thoughts from David, Paige stared out at the shimmering azure bay. The dazzling, dancing pinpoints of light reflecting from its surface hurt her eyes. She wished she had the deliciously gaudy star-shaped sunglasses Maggie had given her, but they were at the bottom of the bay, with her purse. And her engagement ring.

"Don't you think you should call Chameleon?" she asked, turning back to face David.

"No. Not yet. She's probably still nosing around the Allées. With any luck, we'll run into her there."

"You don't seem nearly as concerned about keeping tabs on her whereabouts as you do mine."

"Maggie's a pro," he replied with a small shrug. "And I'm not engaged to her."

"You're not engaged to me, either, remember?"

"Are you ready to talk about that?"

Paige rubbed her thumb across the base of her bare ring finger, feeling strangely naked without the familiar white-gold band.

"I'm sorry I lost the emerald, David."

"I'm sorry you felt the need to take it off."

She gnawed on her lower lip, remembering the wrenching unhappiness and insecurity that had caused her to slip the ring over her knuckle.

"I sensed that you were holding something back from me," she told him slowly.

"Now you know I was."

Paige forced herself to articulate the feelings she'd been too shy, too timid, to discuss with him before. "I'm not talking about this secret life you lead, although I'll admit that was a bit of a shock.''

''Then what?''

''You were always so much in control, even when we made love. You never seemed to lose yourself. All of yourself.'' Heat crept up her cheeks, but she met his eyes. ''Until last night.''

''Did I hurt you?'' he asked, frowning.

''No!'' She shook her head, her face fiery now. ''I liked it. A lot. I liked thinking that I was woman enough to push you past the limits you set on yourself. On us. I like what I do to you when I'm wearing satin and sequins.''

''Dammit, Paige—what you wear doesn't have anything to do with what I feel for you.''

She cocked a brow.

''Okay, so maybe seeing you in Meredith's working uniform has given me a slightly different perspective.''

''Ha!'' She placed one elbow on the table and leaned forward. The golden halter drooped enticingly.

''A very different perspective,'' he conceded, with a small grin. ''But doesn't that disprove your doubts about us? Evidently I still have as much to discover about you as you think you do about me.''

''What if—what if we never really find the real us, David?''

''I'm not sure anyone can ever know all there is to know about another person. We're too complex, too changeable. But isn't that what marriage is all about? Long years of learning what works, what doesn't. What pleases you, or irritates me. What makes you sneeze or makes me lose control. Think about it, Paige. Think of all those days and nights of exploration.''

She was still thinking about those days and nights—particularly the nights—when they strolled through the Allées de la Liberté, a series of delightful avenues shaded by wide, leafy plane trees.

The Allées teemed with color and humanity. During balmy afternoons such as this, the natives gathered to sip kir, a white wine spiced with black currant liqueur, at open-air cafés or stroll the flower-filled markets and squares.

Her arm looped through David's, Paige paused to watch a lively game of *boules*. The players tossed the heavy, palm-sized balls into a sandy gravel pit some distance away, gesticulating and arguing so vociferously after each throw that she couldn't tell if the object of the game was for the balls to touch or not touch each other when they landed. David was trying to explain the rules when she caught a flash of carroty red hair out of the corner of one eye.

Paige glanced across the small square, then gripped David's arm. "Look! Isn't that Henri?"

"So it is."

As they watched, the boy hurried toward a circular booth plastered with colorful posters advertising everything from toothpaste to what was billed as the most extravagant transvestite nightclub act in Cannes.

"That must be the kiosk he uses as his headquarters," Paige murmured.

When David didn't reply, she glanced up at him. With a small shock, she saw that her relaxed companion of a moment ago had vanished. In his place was another man, not quite a stranger anymore but not one she felt entirely comfortable with.

Eyes narrowed, David watched the boy dig through his pockets, then begin shoving coins into the phone with a frantic disregard for their denominations. Even from across the square, they could see the controlled desperation on his young face.

"Come on."

Paige didn't need David's terse order. She was already heading across the tree-shaded plaza, the gravel crunching under her sandals with each quick step.

When the boy caught sight of them, a look of relief flashed across his freckled face. He slammed the receiver down and rushed to meet them.

"*Monsieur!* I try to call you!"

"Why?"

"*Mademoiselle's* friend, the one with the so-lovely legs. She offers me fifty francs to take her to Antoine's shop. I tried to dissuade her, but she insists."

"Why did you try to dissuade her?"

Doc kept his voice even, allowing no hint of his suspicions to color it. His muscles tightened as he noted the worry that sharpened the boy's thin face. If Henri was acting, Doc thought grimly, he was doing a damn fine job of it.

"Antoine, he is a pig. He has the weakness for beautiful women, but they do not always return his regard." The boy hesitated. "Not without some persuasion, you understand?"

Doc's jaw hardened. "I understand."

"I cannot go inside the shop, since Antoine and I have severed our business relationship, but I point it out to *mademoiselle*. She goes in some time ago, and does not come out."

David ignored Paige's small gasp. "Where is this shop?"

"Two streets over. I will show you."

In the space of a single heartbeat, Doc ran through a short mental list.

A—this could be a setup, an attempt to separate him from Paige so that Henri could retrieve the microdot.

B—Maggie could be engaging this Antoine in idle chitchat while she scouted out the place.

Or C—she could be in serious trouble, even though she hadn't signaled an emergency or requested backup.

Given the very real possibility of A or C, Doc wasn't about to let Paige out of his sight, and he sure as hell wasn't going to waste any more time.

"Let's go."

Without another word, Henri turned and darted off.

Doc took Paige's arm with one hand and slipped the other into his pocket to activate the transmitter in the gold cigarette case, preset to Maggie's code. If she responded to his signal before they got to Antoine's shop, good. If she didn't, Doc would take it from there.

Henri led them down a narrow lane and across an intersection clogged with afternoon shoppers. He turned right at the next cross street, then skidded to a halt halfway down a block lined with shops and pizzerias. Keeping to the shadows, he pointed across the pavement to a narrow facade near the corner.

"It is there, that *tabac*."

Enough afternoon sunlight filtered through the tall windows to illuminate the tobacco-and-sweet shop's interior. Even from this distance, they could see that it was deserted. A sign hanging crookedly on the front door announced that it was closed until four o'clock.

His jaw tight, Doc surveyed the shop. "Is there a back entrance?"

"*Oui*. Through the storeroom. But Antoine, he's very cautious. He keeps the door locked at all times."

"Show me."

By the time Henri had led them down a narrow alley studded with malodorous garbage cans and grocer's boxes overflowing with wilted vegetation, Doc knew he was going in.

He'd spent enough years in the field to recognize when something had gone wrong with an operation, and this situation had all the hallmarks of a major disaster. Maggie would've responded to his signal by now—if she could. Doc still suspected Henri's motives, but he didn't believe the boy was lying or trying to lead them into a trap. Not with that scared expression on his face.

Adding to Doc's worry over Maggie was a gut-wrenching need to shield Paige from what he feared he might find inside the tobacco shop. Every protective instinct in him was on red alert, but he didn't dare take the time to send her to safety.

Edging around an overturned wooden crate spilling soggy, rotting tomatoes onto the cobbles, he glanced down at the woman beside him. She picked her way carefully through the muck in her open-toed sandals, her nose wrinkled and her face pale. Under her evident disgust and natural nervousness, however, was a strength of purpose every bit as strong as his own. Seeing the determined set to her chin, Doc suspected she wouldn't leave the alley even if he dared send her back out onto the street alone.

With a sheer effort of will, he forced himself to accept the fact that Paige, his sweet, delicate Paige, was beside him in this foul-smelling alley. He couldn't shield her from this side of his life any longer. Besides which, she didn't want to be shielded.

Nevertheless, he halted her a safe distance away from the back entrance to the tobacco shop.

"You and Henri stay here," he instructed in a low, clipped tone.

"But, *monsieur!*" Henri hissed. "You have need of me! To pick the lock."

Somehow Doc wasn't surprised that the boy included breaking and entering among his many talents.

"I need you to stay right here, with Mademoiselle Paige."

The boy frowned, then nodded a reluctant agreement. "*Oui,* someone must protect her."

"Take him with you, David," Paige whispered. "I'll be all right. I've...I've got my weapon with me."

"What weapon?"

She fumbled in her purse for a moment, then held up the mascara tube.

"Paige!" Doc shoved her hand to one side. "Watch where you aim that thing."

"I will stay with her," Henri said, shaking his head. "You need not worry. Me, I have the knife."

He unfolded one grubby fist to display an innocuous-looking pocketknife. Curling his fingers around the handle, he pressed some hidden mechanism. With a deadly click, a thin stiletto blade slid out of the handle.

Doc didn't need to ask if Henri knew how to use the switch-blade.

"Both of you, get back in the shadows and stay there."

Paige pressed backward and tried not to shudder as her bare skin made contact with a dank stone wall. God only knew what was growing between the cracks in the stone. Henri scooted back, as well, gouging one of his bony shoulders into her ribs.

"If I'm not out in two minutes, or if you hear shots, get the hell out of here, understand?"

*If he wasn't back?*

Terror clawed at Paige's chest. Any lingering vestige of excitement or adventure was stripped away at that moment. Her fingers dug into Henri's shoulders.

"I won't leave you here!" she whispered frantically.

"You will if you want to summon help for Maggie and me. Get in the clear, and as soon as it's safe, send the emergency signal 311. Got that?"

"David..."

"Three-one-one. Say it, Paige."

"Three-one-one. What does it mean?"

"Agent down, request immediate extraction."

"Oh, my God."

"Say it again."

"Three-one-one. David..."

"I love you. Say it again."

"Three-one-one, dammit. I love you, too."

Incredibly, he grinned. A crooked, slashing grin that showed his white teeth and his heart-stopping handsomeness.

"We'll finish this discussion later."

"Right. Later."

He leaned over Henri to give her a swift, hard kiss. "Three-one-one, Paige."

"I have it! Just...just be careful."

Her heart hammering with a painful, erratic beat, Paige watched David move down the alley. He stopped a few feet away from the green-painted door.

He seemed to draw in a deep breath, then threw his shoulders against the wood panel. It crashed open on the first thrust and bounced inward against the wall.

Through the opening, Paige caught a glimpse of a short, heavily muscled man frozen in place beside a figure slumped over a table. Aghast, she saw a cascade of white gold hair spilling across the table.

"Antoine." Henri spit out the name, just as David launched himself at the man with a snarl of animal fury.

In the shattering moments that followed, Paige discovered yet another David, one she'd never suspected lay beneath his surface. Gone was all trace of the brilliant engineer. Nothing showed of the skilled, considerate lover. What she saw was a powerful, enraged attacker who mowed down his victim with all the finesse of a Mack truck.

This battle wasn't like those in the Karate Kid and Steven Segal movies Paige had seen, in which the good guys moved with a sort of balletic grace, their arms and legs swinging in slow-motion arcs.

There wasn't anything balletic about the fist David slammed into the man's face. Nothing graceful about the blow he delivered to the bookie's stomach. They were brutal powerhouse punches, thrown with every ounce of strength David possessed.

Blood spurted from Antoine's nose with the first hit. He grunted and doubled over at the second, only to connect with David's upthrust knee. Paige heard a sickening crunch, then a gurgle as he collapsed in an untidy heap.

Forgetting David's admonition to stay put, she and Henri ran forward. They rushed through the door just as David gently raised Maggie's face from where it lay amid a litter of cloudy glasses and bottles on the rickety table.

"Oh, my God..." Paige whispered, stumbling to a halt.

David went on one knee beside the slack woman. "Chameleon, look at me. Look at me."

Her eyes wide and unfocused, Maggie stared at him blankly for a moment, and then her head lolled back limply, like a rag doll's.

"Son of a bitch." David slid an arm around her waist and dragged her up out of the chair.

"The pig!" Henri turned and spit on the comatose Antoine. "He has given her the drug."

"What kind?" David snapped at the boy. "What kind of drugs does he use?"

"That one? Anything and everything."

"Son of a bitch." With visible effort, David reined himself in. "Chameleon, can you hear me?"

Maggie made a pathetic attempt to lift her head from his

shoulder. Her dilated pupils tried to line up on David's face, but couldn't seem to focus.

"Get out your compact," he snapped at Paige.

Still clutching the mascara tube with one hand, she tugged at the clasp of her small white shoulder bag and dug inside. After a few frantic moments, she found the diamond-studded compact.

"Open it and press the center stone," David ordered. "Once to transmit, twice to receive. Once, Paige! Once."

"Nuuu…" Maggie's protest was so weak and indistinct, they almost missed it.

David shifted her weight in his arms to look down into her face. "Chameleon! Can you hear me? Do you know what he gave you?"

Maggie tried to swallow. It was a slow, agonizing effort, painful to watch.

"Nuuu…" she mumbled. "Nhat drrr.…" Her hoarse whisper trailed off.

"Press the stone again," David growled at Paige. "Once to transmit, twice to receive."

She squeezed the diamond as hard as she could and shouted into the compact. "This is Jezebel! Can you hear me?"

David began to pace the small room, forcing Maggie to walk with him. "Try again," he told Paige.

"This is Jezebel. Is anyone there?"

"*Mademoiselle!*" Henri reminded her. "You must press the stone twice to hear."

"Oh. Yes." Paige juggled the mascara to her other hand and squeezed the stone twice in rapid succession.

"This is Cyrene," a woman announced calmly. "Go ahead, Jezebel."

Her fingers slick with sweat, Paige engaged the diamond once. "I'm with Doc and Chameleon. She's been drugged. We need an ambulance."

Paige stared at the compact, waiting for a response. Any response.

"Press the stone, *mademoiselle!*" Henri shouted. "Twice!"

As soon as she hit the stone twice, she heard Cyrene's steady voice. "I repeat, Jezebel, give me your coordinates."

Paige sent David a helpless look. "What are my coordinates?"

"Reach into my left pocket," he instructed Henri. "Pull out the small flat pocket calculator."

The boy's nimble fingers quickly extracted the device that the waiter-surgeon had passed David after inserting Paige's little tracking chip.

"Press the switch in the upper left corner," David told the boy. "Now read the numbers on the screen aloud. Slowly!"

His face scrunched up in fierce concentration, the boy started to call out the numbers.

At that moment, Maggie's head lolled sideways. Her eyes seemed to focus for an instant on something over David's shoulder.

"Daf-fid!" she groaned in warning, just as a blood-spattered figure lumbered out of the shadows.

His battered face twisted into a snarl, Antoine charged toward David.

Without thinking, without hesitating, Paige dropped the compact, aimed her mascara and fired.

# Chapter 12

His face blank with astonishment, Antoine stumbled back against the rear wall. He looked down at the bright red blood blossoming on his thigh, and then at the unidentifiable object in Paige's hand. His legs bowed, and he slithered down the wall until his butt hit the floor with a solid *whump*.

"You shoot me?" Dazed, he stared at Paige. "With that?"

"Yes, and I'll do it again, you pig."

She kept the tube pointed at his chest, which took some effort, considering how badly her hand was shaking. For the life of her, she couldn't remember whether the weapon carried more than one projectile, but she figured Antoine wouldn't know, either.

With a savagely controlled gentleness, David eased Maggie into one of the chairs.

"I'll take it from here," he told Paige. A feral light glittered in his eyes as he swung toward Antoine.

He crossed the room in two strides. Reaching down, he wrapped his fists in the man's shirt, hauled him upright, and slammed him back against the wall, with no regard for either his battered face or his bleeding thigh. The powerful muscles in

David's shoulders bunched as he pinned the heavyset Antoine to the wall, several inches off the floor.

"You've got five seconds to tell me what you gave her."

"I gave her nothing!"

"Four."

"*Monsieur!* I swear!"

"Three."

Blood and sweat rolled down the grooves beside the man's mouth and dripped onto his gore-stained shirt. "She comes into the shop! We talk. She smiles. I invite her to the back room to drink!"

"Two."

"I swear, *monsieur!* I swear. We drink the *pastis!* Together! Look, there is the bottle." He gestured wildly toward the middle of the room.

Keeping the man pinned to the wall, David slewed his head around. His narrowed eyes took in the cloudy bottle and glasses that still littered the table beside Maggie.

With a curse that made Paige blink in surprise—she had no idea engineers used such graphic terms!—David dragged Antoine over to the table. He kept a stranglehold on the man's shirt with one hand while he lifted the bottle with the other and sniffed at it.

From her position across the table, Paige sniffed, too, but couldn't detect anything over the strong, tobacco-y aromas that emanated from the boxes stacked haphazardly around the storeroom. She wasn't sure, but she thought *pastis* was some kind of liqueur or local drink. She'd seen it on the menu at both the Carlton and the seaside café where they'd had lunch.

"It is *pastis!*" Antoine choked, clawing at David's hand. "Only *pastis,* I swear. She took but a sip, then her throat closes like…like an overstuffed sausage, and she struggles for the breath."

"Let's see what it does for your throat," David snarled. Twisting the man's collar even tighter, he poured the remainder of the bottle's contents into his open, gasping mouth. He loosened the pressure enough to allow Antoine to gasp and gag and swallow some of the liquid.

For long, tense moments, the only sounds in the small room were Maggie's shallow, rasping breath and Antoine's frightened pants.

"You see?" Antoine sobbed. "Nothing. There is nothing in the bottle, nothing but *pastis*."

"Daf-fid." Maggie's weak call jerked everyone's attention to her.

"What did this bastard give you?"

"Naaht…drugs. He…had…same. Ho-tel. Take me…ho-tel."

With an utter lack of compunction, David smashed a fist into Antoine's jaw. The burly, heavyset man crumpled to the floor.

Scooping Maggie up in his arms, David strode toward the door.

"Come on." He threw the words at Paige over his shoulder.

She stepped over the unconscious body and hurried after him. "Come on," she called to Henri.

The boy spit on Antoine one final time. "Pig!" he muttered as he followed Paige out the door.


The day and night that followed were the longest Paige had ever spent.

David threw a wad of bills at the driver of the taxi Henri flagged down and told him to move it. During the kamikaze ride along the Croisette, Paige fumbled with the compact and managed to give Control a whispered recap of what had happened. Promising to get a doctor to the hotel immediately, Claire signed off.

Maggie was still dazed and struggling for breath when David laid her on the satin-covered bed.

"Doc," she gasped, and clutched his arm. "I… The drink…"

"I know," he murmured, brushing the tangled hair back from her temples. "Just hang on, Maggie. The doctor's coming."

As Paige watched David stroke his partner's face, she felt a huge lump forming in her own throat. This was the man she knew. This was the side of his personality he'd always shown her. Tender, gentle, caring. She felt a wash of love for him so strong it overwhelmed her. Sinking down on the other side of the bed, she took Maggie's hand and murmured soft reassurances.

When David smiled at her across Maggie's prone form, Paige's heart melted. The contrast between this David and the one who had tenderized Antoine's face just minutes ago was extraordinary. And almost beyond her comprehension—until she remembered that she, timid little Paige Lawrence, had shot a man. With a mascara wand, it was true, but she'd actually shot someone.

David was right, she thought. No one could ever know every facet of another person's personality. Or even one's own.

She glanced at the man on the opposite side of the bed. His short, usually neat hair now stuck up in uneven patches. His red knit shirt carried a variety of stains. And his hands, those incredible, gentle hands, sported bruised, split knuckles.

She didn't need to know anything more about him, Paige decided in that instant. It was enough that he was David, *her* David.

The doctor arrived a few moments later. Not the little waiter-surgeon this time, but a tall, chic woman in a two-piece navy blue Chanel suit and an Hermès scarf. Paige recognized the scarf. She'd seen one similar to it during her brief foray into the boutiques of the Croissette. The price tag had nearly put her into cardiac arrest.

Paige and David, with Henri hovering in the background, stood to one side while the doctor examined Maggie.

"Anaphylactic shock," she announced almost immediately. "It is a severe allergic reaction, similar to what some people experience from bee stings. What has she eaten or drunk?"

"*Pastis,*" David said tersely.

"Ah, yes. It is made from Anise, which has carminative and aromatic qualities some people simply cannot tolerate."

At Paige's blank look, the doctor folded her stethoscope and tucked it into her purse.

"Anise, or aniseed, as some call it, is an herb of the carrot family. It's grown locally, and used to make this potent liqueur."

"I...hate...car...rots," Maggie murmured. "Make...me...gag. Al...ways...have."

"Yes, so I would imagine. It's best if you don't talk for a while."

The doctor extracted a hypodermic syringe and a small vial from her purse.

"It will take at least twenty-four hours for the paralysis of the throat to lessen to where it is not painful, but this will help relax the muscles so you can breathe more easily."

Paige shut her eyes as the doctor swabbed Maggie's arm and slid the needle in.

"Someone must stay with her at all times," the woman instructed a few moments later. She drew a package of pills out of that seemingly bottomless pit of a purse.

"She may have water, only a sip at a time, and soft food when she can eat it. And one of these caplets every three hours."

David nodded. "We've got it covered."

*"Oui, madame,"* Henri concurred, reaching gallantly for her bag. "We shall manage. May I escort you out?"

David gave him a warning frown. "I'm sure *madame* can manage her purse."

Henri's small face assumed a wounded look. *"Monsieur!"* You don't think I would steal from her?"

"I don't?"

Paige intervened hastily. "Why don't you come with me while I show the doctor out, Henri? You can check the room-service menu and decide what to order for Maggie. And for yourself, of course," she added quickly as his eyes lit up.


Just after midnight, Paige walked through the tall double doors of the bedroom into the sitting room. She was limp with weariness, but relieved that Maggie seemed to be getting back her color, if not her voice.

Inside the sitting room, she leaned tiredly against the wall and crossed her arms over the little beaded vest she'd changed back into earlier. It wasn't the most appropriate sickroom attire, perhaps, but it was comfortable and allowed her ease of movement while tending to Maggie. When he saw it, David had muttered something under his breath about plaids and jumpers, but Paige had been too busy to pay much attention.

Between them, they had worked out an hourly schedule to take care of their patient. During her shifts, Paige helped Maggie into the bathroom and fed her soup or the smooth, exotically flavored ice creams Cannes was famous for.

During his shifts, David administered ice water and the medicines and sat in an armchair pulled up to the little dressing table while she slept. He'd occupied the quiet hours making lists, Paige supposed.

Throughout all shifts, Henri had offered encouragement and advice. Enthusiastically pursuing his duties as procurer of sustenance for the patient, he'd established a personal hot line to the kitchens, sampled everything that came up and gradually stuffed himself into a stupor.

He was now curled upon the sofa, one fist tucked under his cheek and a litter of empty plates on the floor beside him. Paige smiled at the sight and wandered over to tug a light blanket up over his bony shoulders. He'd certainly gotten enough to eat tonight. A steady stream of waiters had knocked on the door of the suite, bringing dish after dish, delicacy after delicacy.

The last had left a pot of rich black coffee and a silver bowl of ripe strawberries. Paige studied the bowl for a moment, then picked out a huge, luscious berry. She took a nibble from the tip and was savoring the sweet flavor when another knock sounded on the door.

Throwing Henri an amused look, she wondered what else he'd ordered before falling asleep. They'd gone through every item on the menu, plus a few he'd requested that the chef improvise. She ambled to the door, nibbling on the ripe berry.

The man who stood on the other side looked like no waiter Paige had ever seen. He was tall and tanned and carried himself with an air of unshakable authority. A faint trace of silver threaded his black hair at the temples, giving him an aristocratic touch. Although he carried a leather flight bag in one hand, his knife-pleated dark slacks and tailored blue shirt were smooth and crisp, as though they wouldn't dare do anything as undignified as wrinkle during travel.

Paige stood rooted to the floor, her mouth pursed around the fruit, her eyes wide.

He took in her surprised expression, her half-eaten strawberry, and her beaded see-through vest. A smile creased his tanned cheeks, and he descended from the aristocratic to the merely devastating.

"Jezebel, I presume?"

If he knew her code name, he was one of the good guys. She hoped. Reminding herself that David was only a scream away, she pulled the fruit out of her mouth and fumbled for an answer.

"Er, I'm not sure. I mean, isn't there some kind of a code or something you're supposed to give first. So I know who you are?"

The smile widened. "I'm Thunder. Adam Ridgeway. We spoke yesterday."

"Oh. Yes."

Paige remembered Mr. Thunder all right. This was David's boss in his secret life, the one who'd given her the choice of being fitted with an electronic leash or being bundled out of Cannes on the next available plane. She eyed him with a touch of dislike.

"You know, you have a rather nasty manner over the…" She made a small circle in the air with the strawberry, not quite sure what that diamond-studded compact was. "Over the radio," she said.

"So I've been told." He walked into the suite and deposited the leather flight bag on an armchair. "Where's Maggie?"

Paige gestured toward the high double doors. "In the bedroom. David's with her. You can go—"

He didn't wait for her permission.

There couldn't be any mistake. This was definitely Mr. Thunder. Brows raised, Paige trailed after him as he opened the doors. He stopped on the threshold, his eyes fixed on the still figure in the bed.

"Adam!" David kept his voice low, but his face registered total surprise as he rose from the armchair. "What are you doing here?"

Adam Ridgeway's intent gaze didn't leave the unmoving Maggie. "I had planned to come for your wedding, anyway. I decided to move the trip up a bit."

David sent Paige a quick look.

"How is she?"

Adam's question betrayed no emotion, but there was a quiet, almost indiscernible intensity to it that made Paige glance at him quickly.

"She's going to be fine," David assured him. "I gave Claire hourly status reports. Didn't she keep you posted?"

"She did. I got the last report during an in-flight refueling over the channel." His jaw worked. "It appears that Chameleon has a near-fatal aversion to carrots."

"Distilled carrots, anyway. We've been with her every moment, Adam," David said, his voice gentling as he studied his boss's face.

Well, well…Paige thought.

"The doctor says she shouldn't have any lingering aftereffects from the reaction, other than a sore throat as the paralysis wears off. She's supposed to talk as little as possible for a while."

Paige thought she detected a slight softening of the stark lines around Adam's mouth, as if in relief—or was it amusement? Whatever it was, it was gone when he turned to face David.

"I'll take over here," he said with cool authority. "You and Paige had better go across the hall and get some sleep. I understand you have an appointment this evening. With Victor Swanset."

Shock rippled down Paige's bare arms. Good grief, she'd forgotten all about the Baron of the Night and his invitation to dinner!

At that moment, she wanted nothing more than to tell both David and his boss that she was abandoning her role as Meredith

Ames. She no longer cared who got the blasted microdot. Or how. Or when. She'd had enough.

In the past twenty-four hours, a world-class pervert had sidled up to her in the casino and offered her an unbelievable amount of money to do things she was sure were anatomically impossible; she'd been frightened out of her wits by an eighty-year-old man who stepped out of a wall wearing his thirty-year-old body; and she'd capped off the day by putting a mascara-wand bullet through Henri's former business partner. What's more, David, *her* David, had made her repeat over and over again an emergency code to be used in the event he didn't return.

Paige had had more than enough excitement and adventure to last her the rest of her life. She wanted to go home, and she wanted to take David with her.

Unfortunately, he grinned at her then.

It was that slashing, crooked grin he'd given her earlier, just before he went in to make hamburger out of Antoine's face. The grin that finally, unreservedly, said they were in this together. They were a team. Equal partners.

Paige swallowed a sigh and pasted a weak answering smile on her face.

"That's right," David answered, turning to Adam again. "We have an appointment with Swanset tonight. If everything goes as planned, we're going to wrap this mission up, and then…" His glance swung to Paige once more. "And then we're going to arrange that wedding you came for."

She didn't say anything. She didn't have to. David saw the answer to his unspoken question in her eyes. His grin softened into a smile that was for her and her alone.

For a moment, there was just the two of them in the quiet room, Paige and David. Jezebel and Doc. Meredith and… whoever. At this point, Paige was too tired to sort out their growing cast of personalities. All that mattered was the tender smile in David's eyes.

That smile stirred a slow, delicious heat just under her skin. While David gave Adam concise instructions on Maggie's medication, Paige shoved aside her weariness and made a mental list of her own.

First, a bath.

Second, find something sinful enough in Meredith's wardrobe to make David forget both his caution and his control.

Third... Well, she'd improvise on items three through ten.

After all they'd shared today, there was no way in hell she was going to let David occupy the sitting room sofa tonight. Not if he was going to throw emergency codes at her that suggested he might not be around to occupy anything else in the near future. Not if they were getting married.

Which they were. As soon as they could arrange it. As soon as they wrapped up this mission. She'd shed the last of her doubts and insecurities about herself and David somewhere in a dank, garbage-strewn back alley.

Feeling far more determined about the upcoming evening with Victor Swanset than she had a few short moments ago, Paige tucked her hand in David's as they left the bedroom and walked through the sitting room. They were halfway to the door when she caught sight of the small figure curled up on the sofa.

"David! We forgot about Henri."

"So we did."

Turning, he walked back to the door to the double doors of the bedroom.

"The kid on the couch is Henri," he informed Adam. "If he wakes up, make sure you keep one hand on your wallet at all times."

"Roger."

Back in Meredith's suite, Paige ran hot, steaming water into the claw-footed tub. She'd washed her hands and face before tending to Maggie, of course, but there was no telling what her bare back had made contact with in that alley. And her feet... Ugh!

Her plans for the rest of the night definitely didn't lend themselves to dirty feet.

Sweet, tingling anticipation fought its way through her layers of exhaustion. Smiling, she dumped an extra measure of bubbling, perfumed oil into the tub. Tonight, she wasn't worried about Meredith's client walking out of the suite with an unfamiliar scent clinging to his skin. Tonight, Meredith's client wasn't walking anywhere.

Shedding her vest and skirt and white lace panties, Paige sank into the hot water with a groan of pure pleasure. She let the water run until the bubbles reached the tip of her chin, then turned off the old-fashioned ceramic handles with one foot. Leaning against the high, sloping back of the tub, she went completely, bonelessly limp.

She'd soak for ten minutes, she told herself. Then she'd pull on the erotic lace teddy she'd dug out of the wardrobe and demonstrate to David its unique construction. The sinful little scrap of pale lemon lace was designed, she'd discovered to her somewhat embarrassed delight, for immediate carnal copulation.

Doc found her in the bathroom fifteen minutes later, sound asleep. She'd slipped down in the tub until the water lapped at her lower lip. Her slow, deep breathing fanned the bubbles dotting the water's surface into small circles.

Smiling, he bent and scooped her out of the tub.

Naked and wet, she burrowed against his body, seeking his warmth. "David?"

"I'm here, sweetheart."

"I want to go to bed," she muttered grumpily.

"Me too."

Supporting her bare bottom on one knee, he reached up to turn off the bathroom lights, then carried her into the darkened bedroom.

# Chapter 13

A chorus of chattering, chirping starlings woke Page the next morning. The birds were perched on the wrought-iron balcony railing, noisily commenting on the glorious sunshine or the availability of insects in the lush gardens below or whatever it was that birds chattered about at the ungodly hour of...

Paige lifted her head and squinted at the painted porcelain clock on the bedside table.

Ten o'clock? That couldn't be right.

She blinked a few times to clear the sleep from her eyes and checked again.

Ten o'clock.

Flopping back down, Paige studied the ornate plasterwork overhead and wondered what had happened to her normal morning energy. Usually, she jumped out of bed at dawn, eager for the day ahead. Except, of course, on those mornings when David was lying beside her.

Which he was not doing this particular morning, she acknowledged. Her hair slithered on the pillow as she turned her head to survey the empty space on the other side of the bed. She couldn't tell whether or not David had abandoned the sitting room sofa last night. The covers on his side were neatly smoothed, the way they always were when he rose before she did.

A flash of pale lemon yellow just beyond the bed caught her attention. Paige sighed, eyeing the lace teddy she'd laid out in such anticipation. If any carnal copulation had occurred in this bed last night, she'd slept right through it.

Of course…there was always this morning. And this afternoon. And most of the evening, before they were to go to Victor Swanset's villa for dinner.

At the reminder of the Dark Baron's invitation, Paige slipped deeper under the covers. After her surge of determination to see this thing through last night, in the bright light of day she was having second thoughts. And third. And fourth.

Despite his gallant, old-fashioned charm, the Baron gave her the creeps. She'd be glad when her brief association with him was over.

Of course, they still didn't have proof that Victor Swanset was the man they were after. Until and unless he showed his hand, they had to maintain their cover. Paige would be Meredith for another day and night, at least. David would be the engineer who had engaged her services for his own private symposium.

More adventure.

More excitement.

Paige groaned.

Mumbling under her breath about being careful what she wished for in future, she pushed the covers aside. She needed to go to the bathroom, badly, and she wanted to check on Maggie. She was sure Adam Ridgeway had provided their patient excellent care last night, but there were some things a woman would just as soon not have a man do for her. Especially a man who looked at her the way Adam looked at Maggie.

Paige had one bare foot on the carpet when a brisk knock sounded on the bedroom door. She slid back into the bed and yanked the covers over her naked form once more. Maybe

Maggie wouldn't mind waiting for a few more moments, she thought, her pulse leaping.

She cast a quick glance at the lace teddy, but it was too far out of her reach. She'd just have to make do without it, she decided, injecting a note of sleepy-sultry huskiness into her voice.

"Come in."

The double doors were nudged open. A heavily laden cart trundled in, followed immediately by a bright, freckled face.

*"Bonjour, mademoiselle."*

Paige clutched the satin coverlet higher. "Good morning, Henri."

*"Monsieur,* he tells me to order you the breakfast, which I have done. Me, I have eaten already, but I will join you. Just to keep you company, you understand."

A collection of domed dishes and an elegant silver coffeepot rattled as the boy rolled the cart to the edge of the bed.

"We have here the brioches and the croissants," he informed her, lifting the lids for her inspection. "And sausage and fresh fruit. And a seafood quiche of a quality that is not quite what one expects of the Carlton, but it will do."

He plucked a fat pink shrimp from the dill-and-lemon garnish atop the quiche and popped it into his mouth.

"Yes, it will do."

Dragging the dressing-table chair over next to the cart, he plopped down on it and beamed at her expectantly. "So, *mademoiselle,* which shall you have first?"

Paige's need to go to the bathroom had transitioned from urgent to desperate. Moreover, she didn't think it entirely appropriate for her to breakfast naked with this child, as precocious as he was. But the covetous sidelong glance he gave the sizzling sausages tugged at her heart.

"Why don't you pour me a cup of coffee?" she suggested. "I'll start with that and wake up a bit while you, uh, test the dishes for me."

Tucking the coverlet under her arms, she puffed the pillow

up behind her back and accepted the milky coffee Henri prepared for her.

With unabashed gusto, he piled a dish high with delicacies
and dug into them.

"Where is *monsieur?*" Paige asked after a moment, trying to
catch the boy between mouthfuls.

"He goes across the hall, to confer with the other gentleman
and your so-lovely friend."

Tilting his head, Henri eyed her shrewdly. "Your friend is
not in the business I thought, yes? Nor are you, *mademoiselle.*"

Paige took a sip of coffee, hiding behind the cup until she
decided how to answer.

"Why do you think that?" she finally asked, stalling.

"Because the so-large gentleman who has such a passion for
you tells me I must stay here, where he can keep the eye on me.
But I am not—under any circumstances, you understand—to
discuss fees and prices with you."

"Oh."

"And me, I am not stupid."

No, he wasn't stupid. Pitifully thin and bruised, perhaps.
Definitely dirty. But not stupid.

"So, *mademoiselle,* what is it that you do here? And what is
it that we must do tonight that puts the so-serious look in *monsieur's* eyes?"

"We?"

"But of course, we."

If David had been reluctant for Paige to join the OMEGA
team, she could just imagine his reaction to the news that Henri
was volunteering for an active role in their mission. She was
trying to find a way to let the boy down gently when he gave
her a cheeky grin.

"I will stay here with you for a while, no? I cannot go back
to the Allées, you see. Not for a while. Antoine, he sees me
with you before you put the bullet through him. Now he will
break my head, as well as my legs, if he catches me."

"The pig," Paige muttered.

Although Maggie had managed to confirm that there wasn't

any connection between their operation and Henri's former business partner, Paige now wished David had put the thug away permanently, instead of just pulping his face.

Henri was not going back to the Allées, she decided grimly. Not today. Not next week. Not ever. Paige wasn't exactly sure where he *would* be going, but she'd get David to work something out. Or Adam Ridgeway. He could put all that inbred authority of his to work on Henri's behalf.

"Why don't you roll the cart into the sitting room?" she suggested to the boy. "Just leave me a brioche and some coffee. We can finish this discussion after I get dressed."

She waited until Henri had closed the bedroom doors, then made a dash for the bathroom.

Ten minutes later, she'd scrubbed her face, brushed her teeth and her hair, and pulled on a black knit tank dress held up by narrow spaghetti straps that crossed over her bare back. The deceptively simple little dress—what there was of it—clung to Paige's body like a second skin.

Slipping on a pair of strappy black sandals with thin cork soles, she grabbed a few essential supplies for Maggie and stuffed them in her purse, alongside the gold halter, then hurried across the hall with Henri. While waiting for a response to her knock, she rested a hand on his shoulder. The light touch caused the boy to blink up at her in surprise, as though he weren't used to human contact.

Paige smiled down at him reassuringly, although the sensations conveyed from her fingertips to her brain shocked her. She registered both the threadbare quality of the navy sweater the youngster seemed to live in, and the thinness of the shoulder it covered. She'd make an excursion to the hotel's gift shop this morning, Paige decided, her mouth settling into a determined line. Henri needed clothes, as well as nourishment.

When David opened the door a moment later, her inner tension and nervousness eased perceptibly. This was the David she knew. Calm, solidly handsome, his brown hair combed, his gray shirt tucked neatly into a pair of dark slacks. His eyes showed no trace of the so-serious look that Henri had noticed earlier.

"So you've finally decided to rejoin the living," he said, with a small, teasing smile.

Warmed by the intimacy of that half grin, Paige followed Henri into the suite. "You should've wakened me."

"I tried," he murmured, for her ears alone. "Several times. You were unconscious. Naked and sprawled over most of my side of the bed, but unconscious."

"Try harder next time."

That settled the question of whether or not he'd abandoned the sofa last night. Unfortunately, it didn't tell Paige whether he'd tried to wake her in an attempt to abandon his self-imposed restraint, as well. Resolving to put that scrap of lemony lace to work at the first opportunity, she headed for the bedroom, while Henri peeled off to investigate a basket of pastries.

"How's Maggie?"

"Better. Her throat is still a little raw, but she's recovered her energy."

She'd recovered more than just her energy, Paige saw as soon as she walked into the bedroom. Her face had lost its deathly pallor, thank goodness. Her eyes, a deep nutmeg brown without their disguising contacts, sparkled with a combination of rueful humor and relief.

"Morn...ing," she rasped.

Paige had heard bullfrogs with more melodious voices. "Good morning. Sorry I slept so late. Certain people failed to wake me."

"That's probably my fault," Adam volunteered. He pushed back his chair, one of two around the graceful Italian table that had been dragged in from the sitting room and placed next to Maggie's bed.

A total absence of sleep certainly hadn't lessened Adam Ridgeway's air of command, Paige thought. His blue shirt wasn't quite as crisp as last night, and the crease in his dark slacks had all but disappeared, yet he showed no other visible signs of his long night, except the dark stubble shadowing his cheeks and chin.

"Doc and Maggie were bringing me up to date on the operation," he explained.

Paige glanced at the papers and drawings littering the table's tooled-leather surface.

"So I see."

Her respect for the other woman edged up another notch. As sick as Maggie was last night, she'd recovered enough to participate—nonverbally, Paige hoped—in a mission briefing.

"Control came through with a detailed description of Swanset's villa," David told her. "The place has thirty-six rooms, including the servants' quarters. I've drawn out a floor plan for you to memorize before we go in."

Her jaw sagged. "You want me to memorize thirty-six rooms?"

"You can't go in blind."

"No, of course not," Paige said weakly. Good God, while she was sprawled blissfully across the bed, David had been sketching out thirty-six rooms for her to memorize!

He pulled a folded sheet of notepaper out of his shirt pocket. "We've revised the emergency codes, as well."

"New codes?" she asked, her heart sinking. "I've got them down, at least the important ones. One-one-three for emergency assistance. Two-three—"

She stumbled, trying desperately to remember the digitized signal for "Agent in place, backup requested."

"The numeric system allows too much possibility of error during translation at headquarters," Adam interjected smoothly. "We've switched to a selection of code words that allow immediate voice recognition."

"Voice?" Paige threw Maggie a doubtful look.

The patient grinned. "Only...one...word. Can't...mistake... it."

Paige knew darn well that this small, select committee had made the switch from numbers to words for her benefit, not because of any translation problems at headquarters. She was grateful, relieved, and just the tiniest bit annoyed that she hadn't been consulted in the matter.

"I'll study the codes and the floor plan later," she told David. "Why don't you and Adam take a break and go into the sitting room?"

He flipped through his little notebook, frowning at the neat lists. "We've got a lot of work to do here."

"We can do it later," Paige said firmly.

Adam rolled his shoulders a bit, finally demonstrating a little human weariness, but seconded David's opinion. "If Maggie's up to it, we should go on."

"La...ter," the patient croaked.

Paige ushered the two men out and shut the door behind them. Her shoulders sagging, she leaned against it.

"Are they always like this on the job?"

"Doc...is."

"And Adam?"

"Don't...know. Am...finding...out."

Paige caught a flicker of what looked like intense, personal satisfaction in the other woman's brown eyes. She was dying to ask how the long night had gone with the impeccable Mr. Thunder waiting on Maggie hand and foot, but she respected her privacy too much to pry.

Levering herself away from the door, she walked over to the bed and dumped the contents of her purse onto the satin coverlet.

"I brought some essential sickroom supplies," she announced. "Perfumed bath oil. Meredith's complete makeup kit. Silk panties. And your little lavender kimono, guaranteed to make the wearer feel like a million dollars and the observer loose his cool completely."

The private satisfaction in Maggie's eyes went very public. She stroked the short, silky kimono with the tip of one finger and gave Paige a wicked grin.

"You...doll!"

By late afternoon, Maggie's energy, Paige's ability to concentrate and Doc's patience were all wearing thin.

Even Henri's inexhaustible curiosity had petered out. He had stopped trying to listen in while they conferred, and had taken up residence in front of the armoire housing the entertainment center. A huge bowl of sweet black cherries kept him company.

"Let's go over the mission objectives one more time," Doc instructed.

"A—I pass the microdot," Paige parroted. "B—you convince Swanset to demonstrate his digital imaging technique, and in the process insert a virus into his system."

"Go on."

"C—we leave the villa, giving him time to play with the stolen information. You activate the virus by remote signal, thus destroying his system, and that of anyone who tries to access the stolen technology."

Doc nodded. "Right. No heroics. No flashy stunts."

"No making hamburger out of Swanset's face," Paige added sweetly.

"And D—" Maggie croaked, her voice almost recovered, "OMEGA sweeps in for the kill."

Doc rubbed the back of his neck. Compared to many of his missions, this one sounded relatively tame. Passing a subtly altered microdot and slipping an electronic time bomb into a computer wasn't exactly the stuff of an Ian Fleming or Tom Clancy novel.

But this technology was on the cutting edge. Right now only a handful of international military and paramilitary organizations, like police and drug-enforcement agencies, were using its awesome, high-speed video and data imaging capabilities. If an outsider with his own agenda was to tap into or divert the flow of essential security information, he could hold some of the most powerful governments in the world hostage.

The psychological profile Claire had pieced together on Victor Swanset showed them he would be merciless with that kind of power.

It had taken most of the night and all of this morning to sort through Swanset's many dummy corporations and his tangled financial dealings, but OMEGA now knew that Victor Swanset himself had destroyed Albion, the studio he'd built from the ground up. Rather than see it produce what he felt were inferior films after the war, he'd anonymously reacquired large blocks of shares in both the studio itself and its major suppliers. In a ruthless move that sent shock waves through international stock markets, he'd dumped the shares and caused several major entertainment corporations to fold.

He'd brought down two successive governments, as well, all without leaving his mountain fortress above Cannes. Since then, his financial empire had spread around the globe, until he gained controlling interests in several multinational communications-industry corporations.

The man felt no ties, no loyalty to any country, Claire had emphasized. Nor to any other person. Only to himself. And to his art, which was now a thing of the past.

Or was it?

There was something missing in this picture of Victor Swanset, international financier. Something that didn't add up. Some piece of illogic that nagged at Doc, although he couldn't quite put his finger on it.

In his precise, methodical way, Doc had broken everything they knew about the onetime star down to specific categories of information and tied them together in every possible combination. The trail always led back to Albion. To Swanset's days of glory.

And to a dead cook.

The pieces of the puzzle didn't fit, and Doc was not the kind of man to be satisfied until they did.

"Let's go over this again," he said.

Paige gave a small groan.

Even Maggie sagged back on the pillows, protesting. "Doc! E...nough."

"We're missing something," he insisted.

"Maybe we'll see what it is if we come at it from a fresh perspective later," Adam commented quietly.

It was a suggestion only, and Doc accepted it as such. Adam had kept in the background throughout the long afternoon, informing them that he had no intention of second-guessing his agents in the field. This was their mission. Theirs and Jezebel's.

The slow smile that accompanied that remark had gone a long way toward softening Paige's attitude toward Adam Ridgeway.

After half a day in his company, she still wasn't quite sure she liked him. He was too controlled, too enigmatic. She couldn't tell what he was thinking, and that made her nervous. But she could certainly understand why Maggie was attracted to him. Even after twenty-four hours without sleep, he radiated an unshakable confidence, not to mention an undiluted masculine potency.

Paige knew that she could never handle a man like Adam Ridgeway, and she didn't want to. She had David. All twenty or so different versions of him.

She also had Henri, she remembered belatedly.

"Before we adjourn this meeting," she said, lowering her voice so that it wouldn't carry to the sitting room, "I have another item to place on the agenda."

David paused in the act of gathering his notes. "What's that?"

"Henri."

Frowning, David made an automatic check of his back pocket. Satisfied that his wallet was still in place, he glanced at the red head planted in front of the TV. "What about Henri?"

In her best David manner, Paige ticked off her short list.

"A—he needs clothes. B—he needs shelter. And C—he needs protection. All of which OMEGA is going to provide."

Adam sent her a cool look. "It is?"

"Yes," Paige replied. "It is."

# *Chapter 14*

**H**enri glanced at the closed bedroom doors of Maggie's suite, then turned to glower at Doc.

"Me, I do not like this."

"So you've said. Several times."

The boy's face settled into stubborn lines. "I should go with you to this villa in the hills. I am the guide."

"Not this time, Henri."

"Someone must watch Mademoiselle Paige while you are busy," he insisted. "I will protect her, as I did last afternoon in the alley."

"I'll take care of her."

Henri's lower lip jutted out. "I do not like this." He stuffed his hands into the pockets of his new jeans, hunched his shoulders and began to pace the sitting room. It was a measure of his agitation that he walked right past a cart laden with silver dishes without giving it more than a passing glance.

Feeling almost as edgy as Henri, Doc glanced at Adam. Sprawled at his ease in an upholstered armchair, the director wore a thoughtful expression as he watched the boy pace. Earlier this afternoon, while Paige and Doc took Henri on an expedition to the Carlton's exclusive gift shops to accomplish the first item on her list, Adam had set Control to working on items two and three. Claire wasn't quite sure what the French authorities would come up with for the boy in terms of shelter and protection, but she'd promised to get back to them as soon as possible.

Doc slid back the cuff of his white dress shirt to check his watch. What in the hell were Maggie and Paige doing in there? Swanset's car would be here at any moment. Doc wanted to go over the contingency plan and the emergency codes with Paige one more time before they left.

As he stared at the closed doors, Doc found himself wondering if he'd recognize the woman who would step through them. Folding his arms across his chest, he considered just how much he'd learned about this incredible, complex woman in the past few days. Far more, he guessed, than she'd learned about him.

His sometimes timid, usually sweet, Paige was showing an inner resilience and stubborn courage that alternately irritated and amazed him.

She was as nervous as a cat about tonight, he knew. She'd all but worn a track in the carpet with her pacing during the mission brief. Her color had fluctuated with each mention of Swanset's name, and she'd stumbled more than once over the emergency codes. But she wasn't about to give up on her damned adventure.

If everything went as planned tonight, Paige would have her adventure. If not…

Doc felt his jaw tighten as the urge rose in him to call off this part of the operation. Now, before Paige stepped through those doors. Now, while they still had room to maneuver and time to activate an alternate plan.

In the past forty-eight hours, however, he'd learned to accept the fact that this wasn't the fifteenth century, when a man could shut his wife away in a stone tower to keep her from harm or chain her to his bed, if he wanted to.

Not that this Paige would have allowed him either option, in the fifteenth or the sixteenth or any other century. What was more, Doc acknowledged ruefully, he couldn't have loved a woman who would allow it.

Although his need to protect his mate was as natural to him as breathing, either consciously or otherwise he'd chosen one as strong as he in her own way. One who would not sit quietly on the sidelines while others acted. Despite his reservations about her involvement in this mission, Doc felt a reluctant pride and silent admiration for Paige's determination to see it through.

Still, he admitted, glancing at his watch once more, the idea of those chains did hold a lingering appeal as the minutes until their meeting with Swanset ticked steadily by.

When the bedroom doors finally opened and Maggie walked into the sitting room, Doc straightened. Smiling, she gave him a thumbs-up, then stood aside.

The woman who stepped through the double doors after her was not quite Meredith Ames and not quite Paige Lawrence, but a fascinating combination of both.

A skilled application of Meredith's makeup had heightened Paige's delicate features. Shadows deepened the tint of mossy green eyes and added thickness to the sweep of her lashes. Her full lips were melon ripe and glossy and altogether too alluring for Doc's peace of mind.

The sophisticated Meredith had drawn the wings of her hair back from her face and pinned them up in some kind of elaborate braid, but the rest of Paige's silky mane hung down her back in a shining curtain of pale gold.

The gown she wore could have been designed for either woman. It was elegant, elaborate, seemingly demure and totally erotic. Doc didn't quite understand how a long-sleeved, floor-length creation that, for once, concealed more skin than it showed could engender immediate fantasies in his mind about peeling the thing off, but this one did.

Maybe it was the color, a deep olive green that added a glowing luster to her smooth skin. Or the fitted bodice that hugged her slender form like a glove. Or the tiny crystal beads accenting the bold trim at the neckline and waist and wrist. The beads shimmered and sparkled with each breath she took, each small movement she made, drawing Doc's eyes like tiny beacons of light.

Her only jewelry was a magnificent pair of drop earrings, made from the finest Swarvoski crystal. Doc had purchased them this afternoon in one of the hotel's gift shops. Just an hour ago, the left earring had been fitted with a highly sensitive state-of-the-art wireless communications device. Paige had only to murmur the new emergency code words, and the earring would transmit them instantly to Maggie's receiver.

Between this miniaturized communications system and the electronic tracking device implanted under her skin, Paige wouldn't be out of contact for a moment. The knowledge should have reassured Doc, should have eased his knife-edged concern for her safety. But despite her dramatic appearance, this was Paige. *His* Paige. The small smile she'd plastered on her lips didn't disguise her nervousness. Not from him.

Fear was a healthy emotion for any field operative, Doc reminded himself as he walked across the room. It kept agents alert. Kept their senses tuned to the least fluctuation in the environment, the hidden nuances in a target's voice or behavior. Anyone who didn't experience fear was a fool.

Doc just didn't like seeing that particular emotion in Paige's eyes. He stopped in front of her and reached up to brush back a wispy tendril of hair with one knuckle.

"You take my breath away."

His quiet, confident tone seemed to reassure her far more than the compliment. Her shoulders relaxed a bit, and her mouth curved into a smile.

"You're having a very similar effect on my respiratory system."

In fact, Paige thought she'd never seen David look quite so devastating. It wasn't so much the crisp white dress shirt, or the stunning black tux that molded his wide shoulders. It was his assured air, his absolute mastery of the tension she knew must be gripping him as it was her. Paige could only marvel at the iron control she'd once resented and now drew strength from.

"You've got the microdot?" Maggie croaked from behind her.

"Yes, in my purse."

"And the mascara?"

Paige paled a little, but nodded. "Yes."

"Pah!" Henri snorted, coming across the room. "That toy! Here, Mademoiselle Paige. Take this."

Paige stared at the worn black knife handle resting on his upturned palm. She knew the deadly blade enclosed by that handle, and didn't want any part of it. But she also knew what it meant for Henri to offer the one possession he valued.

The knife was the only object he'd insisted on keeping after their excursion to the hotel shops this afternoon. He'd gleefully tossed everything else—his ratty sweater, the well-worn shorts, even his sandals and scruffy underwear—into the wastebasket. After a bath and a grooming session supervised by David, the boy had sauntered into the sitting room clothed in new Adidas, designer jeans, a jaunty blue-and-red-striped polo shirt with the Carlton's distinctive crest on the pocket, and a broad grin.

There wasn't any sign of the grin now, and his brown eyes carried a grim knowledge that made Paige's heart ache.

"You press the side of the handle, like so," he said with deadly seriousness. The blade slid out with a soft click. "Hold the knife low, *mademoiselle,* and go for the gut, like so."

He gripped the knife in one small fist to demonstrate, then bent the blade back into the handle, reversed it, and held it out to Paige.

Wetting her lips, she lifted it gingerly with a thumb and forefinger. "Thank you."

"Remember, *mademoiselle,* go for the gut."

"The gut," she repeated weakly, dropping the knife into her gold evening bag.

His freckled nose wrinkled. "I do not like this! Me, I should be with you."

The jangle of the telephone sent Paige's heart leaping into her throat and deepened Henri's fierce scowl. Fighting the sudden, craven impulse to slip back into the bedroom and lock the double doors behind her, she watched David move across the suite and lift the receiver.

"Yes?"

After a moment, he replaced the instrument in its old-fashioned cradle. His eyes met hers across the room, and then his cheeks creased in that slashing grin Paige was coming to both love and dread. The one that said she was his partner in what was to come.

"Ready?"

Paige swallowed. "As ready as I'll ever be."

Paige's secret, lingering hope that Victor Swanset was simply a charming, if eccentric, expatriate faded the moment David escorted her out the Carlton's columned main entrance.

As soon as she spotted the swarthy, dark-haired driver who stood beside the silver Rolls, she recognized him. She'd last seen him just before she tumbled off a gangplank into the oily waters of the marina. He'd been sent to pick up Meredith Ames, and had bundled Paige into the silver Rolls-Royce instead.

His face pleasantly blank, the chauffeur touched a gloved hand to his hat.

*"Bonsoir, mademoiselle, monsieur."*

David returned the greeting, which was just as well, since Paige's throat had closed completely. Her knees felt like unset Jell-O as the driver handed her into the back seat. She sank down with a grateful sigh and was immediately surrounded by soft gray leather and the heady scent of the white roses filling the silver vases attached to the frame on either side of the car.

Surreptitiously Paige wiped her palm on the green satin skirts of her gown. When David joined her, she inched her hand across the soft leather. His fingers folded around hers, warm and strong and infinitely reassuring.

"There is champagne and pâté, if you wish it," the driver informed them, sliding behind the wheel. "It will take perhaps an hour to reach the villa. Monsieur Swanset hopes you enjoy the ride and the view."

Paige did *not* enjoy either.

Her anxiety mounted with each whisper of the tires as the Rolls glided through the twilight traffic along the Croisette with silent, majestic grace. A few minutes later, it turned inland, and headed toward the mountains that rose behind Cannes like sleeping sentinels.

When they entered the foothills, the city gradually fell away. The road swirled and curved, backtracking on itself in an endless series of hairpin turns. Through gaps in the stands of fragrant eucalyptus and fir trees, Paige caught glimpses of a stunning panorama.

Far out on the bay, the last of the sun's rays painted a kaleidoscope of colors across the distant horizon. Brilliant pink, deep magenta and royal purple clouds all swirled together above an indigo sea. Lights strung from the masts of the yachts anchored in the bay bobbed slowly in the ebbing tide.

It was a scene she might have drunk in with wonder if she hadn't been clutching David's hand in a death grip and holding her breath each time the long, sleek vehicle swung around another of those impossible turns.

"This car is *not* designed for roads like this!" she gasped, staring into the stretch of dark, empty space just outside her window with the morbid fascination of a rabbit gazing into the wide-stretched mouth of a cobra.

David smiled a reassurance. "As a matter of fact, a car like this is much safer on these roads than a mini. With its heavy engine and armor plating, the Rolls has a center of gravity well forward of the driver's seat. It's not going to go over unless he loses control—or sends it over deliberately."

"Oh, that's comforting."

Paige closed her eyes as they swung around another curve and the vehicle's rear end seemed to hang suspended in thin air.

"Have a little champagne," David advised her. "It will help you relax."

Gently easing his hand from her clawlike hold, he poured a small amount into a gold-rimmed crystal flute. He poured some for himself, as well. Leaning back, he touched his glass to hers.

"To us."

He'd warned her that the Rolls would be wired with the latest in electronic listening and recording devices. In her role as Meredith Ames, his paid companion during his stay in Cannes, Paige couldn't answer his toast as she so desperately wanted to.

She couldn't tell him that she loved him with every corner of her heart and soul. That she knew all she ever needed to know about him. That when this night was over, she was marching him straight to the American consulate on the Croisette and forcing the first official they came across to marry them on the spot.

"To us," she replied, holding his eyes with hers. "And to tomorrow."

His teeth gleamed in the gathering darkness. "To tomorrow."

Paige took a sip of her champagne and willed herself not to do anything as unadventurous as stain the underarms of her shimmering ball gown with nervous perspiration.

Just when she was sure neither the champagne nor the lingering effects of David's rakish grin would protect her or her gown much longer, the car's headlights illuminated tall stone pillars and a pair of massive wrought iron gates. An ornate *S* in gleaming brass was entwined amid the iron grillwork on either side.

At their approach, the gates swung open and the Rolls swept through. Paige sagged in relief at leaving the narrow cliffside road behind, only to discover a moment later that she'd relaxed too soon. More hairpin turns followed as they climbed even higher. When they finally passed through the arch of what looked like a medieval gatehouse set into a high stone wall, her jaw sagged in sheer astonishment.

Victor Swanset's mountaintop villa looked like something right out of one of his movies. Which one, Paige didn't know, but it was too perfect, too stunningly beautiful, to be real.

A cluster of outbuildings roofed in red Mediterranean tiles circled a wide, cobbled courtyard. At the west end of the yard was a long building that had obviously been a stable in a previous century, but had been converted to a garage for Swanset's collection of vintage luxury automobiles. Another low building, connected to the central structure by a graceful arched walkway, housed the kitchens. That much Paige remembered from her study of the floor plan.

But it was the main residence that drew her awed gaze. Washed a pale yellow in the moonlight, the red-tiled villa boasted a central tower and two sweeping wings. Light spilled out of the many leaded-glass windows and illuminated a magnificent stone portico that might have been sculpted by Michelangelo himself. Muscular Roman gods stood with one arm upraised, supporting an arched pediment. Beneath the pediment was a set of massive timber doors that looked as though they could withstand any medieval battering ram ever constructed.

When the Rolls purred to a halt at the steps of the portico, the huge doors swung open, and more light cascaded onto the cobbles. A butler or majordomo or whatever the dignified individual in black tails was called came forward with a measured tread to open the Rolls's rear door.

Paige gripped her skirts in one damp palm and took his outstretched hand with the other.

"Good evening, Miss Ames. Mr. Swanset has been eagerly awaiting your arrival."

Paige wished she could say the same.

She mumbled something she hoped was appropriate and gave David a grateful smile when he tucked her hand into the crook of his arm to escort her inside.

How in the world could he appear so calm? she wondered. As though he were looking forward to nothing more than a pleasant evening with a gracious host.

Paige could only marvel at this David, so handsome in his white shirt and dinner jacket, so sophisticated and self-assured. Drawing in a deep breath, she strolled beside him as he followed the butler into a paneled library.

The huge, barrel-vaulted room took her breath away. Floor-to-ceiling bookcases lined the length of one long wall and were filled with leather-bound volumes. A fire blazed in a marble hearth at one end of the library, and a larger-than-life portrait of

Victor Swanset dominated the other. Paige's fingers clenched spasmodically on David's arm when she saw the painting.

This one portrayed the film star in perhaps his most famous role, as a swashbuckling Elizabethan pirate who single-handedly sank most of the treasure-laden Spanish galleons plying the seas. One hand rested on his sword hilt with unconscious arrogance, the other held a white rose. He'd presented the rose to a beautiful, titled Spanish captive he'd plucked from one captured ship, Paige recalled, just before he ravished her.

"If Victor Swanset steps out of that portrait, I'm going to embarrass myself and ruin this dress," she whispered to David, uncaring what listening devices might pick up her comment.

He smiled down at her. "You can't embarrass yourself. Not with me."

That showed what *he* knew!

To Paige's infinite relief, Victor Swanset's appearance on the scene this time was far more conventional than the last. Leaning heavily on his cane, he entered the paneled library wearing his own body and a gracious smile. Crossing the polished parquet floor, he took her hand and raised it to his papery lips with a courtly flourish.

"Miss Ames! How elegant you look this evening." His trained, melodious voice rolled over Paige like smooth, dark velvet.

"Thank you," she murmured, impressed by his charm in spite of herself.

He relinquished her hand with a show of real regret and turned to David.

"I must tell you, Dr. Jensen, that I reread the paper you presented to the symposium earlier this week. I was impressed, most impressed, with your research into improved digital imaging techniques."

"Thank you. That paper was written some months ago, however," David commented casually. "We've gone well beyond the research stage, and are now into concept demonstration."

Swanset paused in the act of directing the butler to the crystal decanters arrayed on a massive sideboard. He turned back to David, his dark eyes filled with interest.

"You have?"

"We have. In fact, I developed an unclassified version of the concept to demonstrate at the symposium. It's quite simple, really. Basically a variation of the imaging process you yourself introduced a few years ago."

Swanset folded one hand atop the other on his cane. "My lab downstairs is rather well equipped. Perhaps you might demonstrate this variation after we dine?"

"I'd be delighted."

The distinguished gray-haired butler, or whatever he was, appeared at Paige's elbow, a gold tray in hand.

"Would you care for a glass of sherry?"

Normally she hated sherry. The few sips she'd tried in the past had been too sweet for her palate and coated her throat with a smoky almond flavor. At this point, however, Paige didn't trust her voice to request anything else. She grasped the fragile crystal stemware in one hand and listened to the increasingly technical exchange between David and Victor Swanset with a growing sense of wonder.

She hadn't expected it to be this easy.

Despite the rehearsals, despite David's endless lists of possible scenarios and Maggie's careful coaching and Adam's quiet observations, Paige really hadn't expected their plan to work so smoothly. Yet they'd been in the villa less than ten minutes, and David had already laid the groundwork for his part of the operation.

Now she had to do hers.

She gulped down a healthy swallow of the sherry, trying not to grimace at the taste, and waited for a lull in the conversation.

"Mr. Swanset..."

"Victor, my dear. You must call me Victor."

Paige returned his smile. "Victor. Would you and David excuse me for a few moments? I'd like to freshen up before dinner."

"But of course. How thoughtless of me to keep you standing

here after that long ride. Please, let me show you to the first-floor retiring room. It's outfitted with the exact furniture and fixtures we used in *The Rogue of Versailles*. I think you'll find it quite delightful.''

''I'm sure I will,'' Paige returned faintly.

He crooked an arm, inviting her to accompany him.

Clutching her evening bag, with its deadly mascara wand, well-worn switchblade and neatly folded gold halter in one hand, Paige placed the other on his bent arm.

Her heavy satin skirts swished in a hushed counterpoint to the tap of his walking stick on the parquet floor as he escorted her out of the library.

# Chapter 15

"It doesn't feel right."

Maggie's raspy whisper hung on the cool night air that permeated the small operations hut. One by one, the black-clad team seated at the table turned their attention from the receiver nestled amid a litter of blueprints and scribbled diagrams and focused on their leader.

Maggie shook her head and repeated her murmured worry. "It just doesn't feel right."

Adam stood in the shadows at the rear of the hut, his arms folded, his expression neutral, as he watched the interplay between Maggie and her team. They were all pros, all highly trained and experienced, the best operatives France and the U.S. had to offer. Several of them had worked together in the past. All of them had volunteered for this mission. They'd assembled at this isolated airstrip outside Cannes earlier this afternoon, bringing with them their individually tailored equipment and their governments' full sanction for whatever action they deemed necessary.

During the long wait for Doc and Jezebel to move into position, they'd reviewed the villa's floor plans, studied ingress and egress points, and confirmed team assignments. Just moments ago, they'd presented their individual plans for Maggie's throaty concurrence.

They were ready.

Adam felt the steady thrum of adrenaline in his veins. It had been a long time, too long, since he'd been in the field, but he understood how this team felt. Controlled. Intent. Edgy with anticipation. Eager to swing into action.

Now Maggie's raspy whisper had given that anticipation a sharper edge.

A small, wiry man with a ginger mustache leaned forward into the light, his eyes narrowed on her face. "What doesn't feel right?"

Brows furrowed, she thrust a hand through hair that gleamed a pale silver.

"It's too easy," she muttered.

A silence descended, to be broken a few moments later by a gasp. All eyes turned to the receiver.

Her face taut, Maggie planted both palms on the table and leaned toward the source of the sound.

"Is that a throne?" The sensitive device magnified a hundredfold the stunned surprise in Jezebel's voice. "I mean, a real one?"

Victor Swanset's chuckle floated on the still air. "A foolish whim, is it not? But what better use for a discarded movie prop than to grace a bathroom?"

"I can't imagine."

The dazed reply brought a grim smile to Adam's lips. For all her delicate appearance and thinly disguised nervousness, Paige Lawrence had impressed him with her determination to see this operation through. He'd expected the woman who'd captivated Doc to be special. Paige, he'd decided, was several cuts above special.

A slight movement to his right caught Adam's attention. Henri shifted on the rickety straight chair he'd been banished to earlier and propped his elbows on the knees of his new jeans. His freckled face scrunched into a scowl as he listened to Jezebel's exclamations over Swanset's majestic retiring room.

The boy still hadn't forgiven Doc for not taking him along tonight. His fertile imagination had come up with a wide assortment of reasons why an engineer out for an evening with his very expensive hired companion would have a small redheaded boy in tow, none of which Doc would listen to. Adam had been forced to bring Henri with him to the team's rendezvous point tonight, sure that he'd slip away and find his own way up to the villa if he wasn't kept under close watch.

"I believe you have something which interests me, my dear."

Swanset's soft, cultured tones caused a ripple of immediate reactions.

Maggie sucked in a swift breath.

Adam's eyes narrowed to icy blue slits.

Henri hunched his thin shoulders and scowled ferociously.

The rest of the team froze.

Several miles away, and several hundred feet up in the rarefied elevations above Cannes, Paige stared at Victor Swanset's wrinkled face with the fascination a mouse might give a patient gray cat. His eyes met hers, as dark as obsidian, as inscrutable as death.

"The microdot? You have it with you, do you not?"

Paige nodded. The movement was reflected a hundred, or perhaps a thousand, times in the tall, gilded mirrors lining this wide antechamber. It was, Victor had told her, an exact, if somewhat smaller, version of Versailles's famed hall of mirrors.

At one end of the corridor was the most sumptuous bedroom Paige had ever seen, furnished as it had been for Louis XVI. At the other was a vast bathroom featuring an eighteenth-century throne with twentieth-century plumbing. Victor had graciously demonstrated the flush mechanism before returning with her to this hall of mirrors.

So nervous she could barely keep from shaking, Paige wanted desperately to banish Victor immediately and retreat to that throne. The knowledge that Maggie and Adam and half a dozen other assorted individuals were listening to every word of this conversation through the tiny transmitter in her earring held her in place. She couldn't chicken out now and let them all down. She wouldn't disappoint David. Or herself.

"Yes, I have the microdot."

Resting both gnarled hands on his ivory-headed cane, he regarded her benignly. "May I have it, my dear?"

"Of...of course."

Paige fumbled with the clasp of her evening bag. Her fingers shaking, she withdrew the slithery halter and passed it to him.

"Ah."

Intense satisfaction gave his voice a vibrant depth as he lifted the sparkling collar up. The shimmering gold sequins caught the bright glow of the lamps that marched at regular intervals along the hall. Flickering, dancing light swirled around and around in the endless mirrors, until Paige felt dizzy and a little sick. She swallowed hard against the nausea that gripped her stomach.

Just when she thought she might have to beat an undignified retreat to the throne and toss up the thimbleful of sherry she'd allowed herself, Victor lowered the collar. He folded the halter carefully and slipped it into his pocket.

"You will be suitably recompensed, of course," he murmured absently, as if such mundane matters as money were of little interest to either of them. "Please, take your time, my dear. We'll go in to dinner when you rejoin us."

The moment the mirrored door closed behind his stoop-shouldered form, Paige slumped against the opposite wall. Her heart was hammering so hard and so fast it hurt. She gulped in several deep breaths and willed her lungs to pump the air to the rest of her body. She was sure they hadn't operated at full capacity since Victor had led her from the library.

Slowly her eyes focused on the image in the opposite mirror. A pale, slender woman in a green-and-gold designer gown and crystal drop earrings stared back at her. A stranger. A sort of secret agent. An almost call girl. An honest-to-goodness, full-fledged adventuress.

She'd done it!

She'd passed the microdot to Victor Swanset!

The heady realization gave Paige the spurt of energy she needed to dash to the throne. Just in time, she rid her heaving, swirling stomach of the damned sherry.

Paige passed the next few hours in a blur of unimaginable, unabashedly sybaritic luxury. The butler seated her next to her host and across from David at a polished table half a mile long. She gazed at the forest of sparkling crystal stems in front of her with some consternation. After suffering from the combined effects of the champagne and sherry, she wasn't about to court any more trips to the throne room by working her way through that maze of wineglasses.

A small army of servants set course after course before her, each nestled on a baroque gold charger emblazoned with a scrolled *S*. Paige nibbled at each dish, contributed her share to the wide-ranging conversation, and resolutely stuck to sparkling water. To all intents and purposes, her part in this mission was over, but she didn't intend to start celebrating until she and David were safely back at the Carlton.

Later, she promised herself. They'd celebrate later.

A mental image of a scrap of lemon lace sent a sudden spear of heat through her belly. Half startled, half embarrassed by its intensity, she studied the man opposite her from beneath lowered lids.

If David was the least bit nervous about pulling off his part of this mission, Paige couldn't detect it. He lounged against the high back of his chair, one big hand loosely wrapped around a fragile crystal stem as he conversed with their host. The candlelight hid the subtle red tints in his dark brown hair, but Paige knew they were there. She'd seen them often enough in the bright light of day. She curled her fingers into fists, wishing with all her heart that this dinner was over and she could reach up to disturb the disciplined order of his hair.

She wanted to feel its springy softness. To taste his mouth on hers. To forget these nerve-racking hours and lose herself in the solid, soaring passion that David brought her.

Later, she promised herself.

After what seemed like two dozen courses, the parade of servers bearing new dishes finally dwindled to a trickle, then slowed to a halt. At the butler's murmured query, Victor gave his guests a choice.

"Shall we take coffee in the library, or would you like to see my laboratory first?"

David rose. "Your laboratory, by all means."

Victor's pleased smile softened as he turned to Paige. "Would you care to wait for us in the library, my dear? My little demonstration at the Palais yesterday was a bit unsettling for you, I'm afraid."

"A bit," Paige admitted dryly.

"I wouldn't want to startle you again."

"Now that I'm familiar with your propensity for stepping through walls, I think I can handle another demonstration."

He chuckled in delight. "Good. Good. Come with me, please."

His cane clicking on the black-and-white tiles, Victor led them through the central hallway, toward the rear of the main tower, and ushered them into a paneled elevator. In contrast to the Carlton's clanking wrought-iron cage, the doors to this one slid shut with silent efficiency and the elevator plunged downward.

Victor rested his hands on his cane. "We're descending to what used to be the dungeons. They were quite primitive, originally, as you might expect." His dark eyes glinted. "I've done some rather extensive modifications."

Without realizing that she did so, Paige nudged closer to David. For some unexplained reason, her euphoria at having completed her part of the mission dissipated with every foot they dropped downward.

"We're descend…what used…to…dungeons."

Swanset's voice fuzzed.

Maggie shot up out of her chair. "We're losing them!" she said, her voice a rasp.

"Done...mod..."

The entire team stared at the receiver as the broken transmissions degenerated into an indistinct hiss. A second or two later, even the hiss disappeared.

"Dammit, we've lost them."

Maggie yanked a folded blueprint out of the pile on the table and spread it out in front of her.

"According to these floor plans, the dungeons are approximately forty feet below the villa's ground floor. The communications folks swore that we'd be able to hear all transmissions from them."

Frowning, she shoved a hand through her hair. "Santorelli, get hold of the technician who inserted that device in Jezebel's earring. I want to know why that transmission failed, and fast!"

Paige held her breath as the elevator door hissed open at last. She expected another fantastic scene from one of Swanset's movies. An early version of *Frankenstein,* perhaps, or *The Prisoner of Zenda.*

But Victor's subterranean lair held little resemblance to either a mad scientist's habitat or a medieval dungeon. Bright fluorescent light bathed a large environmentally controlled chamber that contained only a few scattered armchairs with a table between them, a single computer workstation and a bank of small, innocuous-looking white boxes.

Paige had worked for a major defense firm long enough to recognize the logo on those boxes instantly. They were components of the most powerful, most sophisticated supercomputer in the world, one whose sale was rigidly restricted by the United States government and whose price hovered at about a hundred million dollars.

Her disbelieving eyes met David's. She could tell by the set to his jaw that Swanset's acquisition of this computer for private use was an unwelcome surprise to him, too.

"Please," Victor said, gesturing toward the armchairs, "make yourself comfortable while I access my latest program. I think you might find the application interesting.''

*Interesting* wasn't the word for it.

*Frightening* came close.

*Terrifying* even closer.

But by the time Paige could recover her power of speech, it was too late to even try to categorize what she'd seen.

At Victor's invitation, Doc seated Paige and then himself in an armchair. For long moments, nothing happened. No walls moved. No swashbuckling pirates materialized before them. No sounds disturbed the stillness except the subdued clatter of the keyboard and the discreet whirring of the small white boxes.

When Swanset finished, he swiveled around on his chair and gave them a charming, apologetic smile.

''It takes a few moments to activate. Why don't I ring for coffee while we wait? Or cognac, perhaps?''

Doc eased the slight pressure on his gold cuff link. The tiny device implanted in it had recorded the audible clicks of Swanset's keyboard and translated them into digital impulses. With that translation, Doc could duplicate Swanset's computer access code at will.

''Coffee would be fine,'' he replied, his relaxed tone giving no hint of his gathering tension.

This was too easy.

It didn't feel right.

Swanset was playing with them. Had been playing with them all night. Doc knew it with a gut-deep instinct honed by years in the field. What he didn't know was why.

He found out moments later.

Both he and Paige turned as the elevator door hummed open once more. The stately gray-haired butler stepped out, the handles of a footed silver tray gripped in both hands.

''Put the tray on the table by Miss Ames, if you would, Peters.''

The butler inclined his head and moved forward with a measured tread.

His every instinct on full alert, Doc heard the faint click of the keyboard. He turned his head and caught Swanset's bland smile.

Beside him, Paige gave a small gasp. Eyes narrowed, Doc swung his gaze to the butler.

It was Peters. And it wasn't. Before Doc's eyes, the man's features blurred.

He heard another soft click of the keyboard.

The butler's gray hair darkened imperceptibly at first, then with deeper and deeper shading. His bushy eyebrows followed suit. A shadow appeared along his chin, then sharpened into a pointed beard.

Swanset pressed the keyboard once more.

Peters's faded blue eyes took on a dark hue.

"Oh, my God!" Paige shrank back in her chair as the Dark Baron approached her, silver coffee service in hand.

"Will you…"

The keyboard clicked, and Peters's pleasant tenor changed pitch, dropping with each syllable until it became Swanset's deliberate, dramatic baritone.

"…take milk and sugar with your coffee, Miss Ames?"

Her hands pushing against the chair's armrests, Paige strained away from the hovering butler and stammered an incoherent reply.

Doc rose and moved to stand between her and the attentive server.

"I don't think she cares for anything right now."

"Very good, sir."

Peters, in the living, breathing guise of a young Victor Swanset, turned aside to set the tray on the nearby table.

Even Doc, who understood the limitless, as yet untapped, power of virtual reality and image projection, had never seen anything like this. A cold sweat trickled down his spine, but the face he turned to Swanset held only professional approval and admiration.

"Remarkable."

Victor—the older, white-haired, liver-spotted Victor—chuckled in genuine delight.

"It is, isn't it? Quite remarkable."

Doc turned to the eerie image standing quietly, his hands tucked behind his back.

"I assume you ingested some kind of material that reflects the digitized images?"

Peters nodded. "Mr. Swanset assures me it's entirely harmless, quite like the dye a patient ingests before an MRI or CAT scan or similar procedure."

Doc searched the man's eyes. The pupils were the slightest bit out of focus, like a TV screen that needed a fine adjustment. "Why would you consent to an experimental procedure like this?" he asked slowly.

"For the money, of course. Even butlers need retirement funds. I shall exist quite comfortably on what I've put by these past few months."

"Assuming you exist at all," Doc murmured, turning back to his host. "Do you really believe he'll experience no ill effects from this transformation?"

Swanset waved a thin, veined hand. "None at all. The process is all but perfected."

Doc raised a brow. "*All* but perfected?"

The film star's brilliant smile dimmed a bit. "The ingested material is quite safe, I assure you."

"But?"

Swanset gave a small shrug. "But, as you can see from Peters's eyes, I've encountered annoying difficulties in the image transfer software. I must break the visual images down into minuscule particles, small enough to be projected from the lining of living cells. I've developed a scanner that does that. All I need now is a conveyor with sufficient capacity to handle the transfer of the millions of data bits involved."

The man's voice gained in dramatic fervor. "Think, Dr. Jensen! Just think what this imaging technique can mean! No more unsightly deformities. No pathetic wrinkles and sagging jowls. At least none that the eye can perceive. We can all look like—'' he nodded toward the Dark Baron ''—like that.''

Good Lord! Swanset had just confirmed Doc's worst fears. This insane man had been experimenting with unproved technology in an attempt to project images onto living cells. No wonder the medical examiners had puzzled over the poor dead cook's tissue damage. And no wonder the aging film star had been so eager to acquire the fiber-optic technology.

He wasn't interested in the high-speed transfer of information via the burgeoning Internet. He didn't intend to tap into or divert military command-and-control networks. He wasn't out to expand his own communications empire.

He wanted the increased data transfer capacity to project his own image at will. To surround himself with himself. To relive his past glory every day of his life.

The implications of his process were staggering, even to Doc's trained mind. This was genetic engineering taken to its highest plane. Why wait for medicine or selective breeding to perfect the species? With Swanset's imaging technique, a click of a keyboard could change hair texture or skin tone or even speech intonation to more ''acceptable'' patterns.

Paige grasped the implications only moments after Doc. Her eyes wide and unbelieving, she pushed herself out of the armchair.

''You…you want to populate the world with dashing, youthful Victor Swansets?''

His smile encompassed her from head to foot. ''My dear Miss Ames, not only with Victor Swansets. The world will also need women with your fresh, luminous beauty.''

''Forget it.'' Doc rapped the words out. ''You're not experimenting with her.''

The star gave him a pained look. ''I'm well past the experimental stage, I assure you.''

''And I'm well past the diplomatic stage. Listen, and listen good, Swanset. You try any of your imaging techniques on her, and you won't live long enough to see yourself projected on anything.''

"I was afraid that might be your attitude, Dr. Jensen. I can understand why you're taken with her. She's really quite lovely, isn't she?"

"She is, and she's going to stay that way."

Swanset folded his hands across his cane and heaved a dramatic sigh. "I had so hoped a man of your brilliant vision would be more receptive to my program, Dr. Jensen. In fact, I thought to persuade you to assist me."

"You thought wrong."

"I'm afraid I must insist," the older man said softly. "I haven't much time left. My heart, you understand, among other disgustingly feeble organs, is failing me."

His gaze shifted to Peters, to the image of himself in his prime. His eyes took on a glitter that raised the hairs on the back of Doc's neck.

"With your assistance, I can perfect this program. Then I will live forever. As I once was."

At that moment, the missing piece of the puzzle fell into place. Doc finally grasped the tiny bit of illogic that had nagged at his subconscious all afternoon.

Swanset hadn't invited them up here to retrieve the microdot from Paige. If that had been his sole objective, he would have found a way to accomplish it at the Palais des Festivals. He'd invited them to his villa because he wanted Dr. David Jensen's help in eliminating the last annoying bugs from the program that would ensure his immortality.

With sudden, chilling certainty Doc understood Paige's role here tonight. She was the leverage Swanset needed, the means to guarantee Doc's cooperation. Somehow, some way, the film star must have discovered her true identity and her relationship with David Jensen.

Her purse! Damn, the purse she lost when she fell off the gangplank! It had held her passport, her wallet. Swanset must have recovered the damned thing from the bay. With his vast communications empire, it would have taken him only a few moments to verify who she really was.

The man's next words confirmed Doc's gut-wrenching certainty.

"I'm afraid I must ask Peters to escort Miss Lawrence next door for a little while."

Miss Lawrence, Doc noted. Not Miss Ames. The wily bastard had known all along.

"Peters can give her a tour of the real dungeons," Swanset said, with a smile Doc ached to wipe off his face. "They're quite interesting from an historical perspective. You and I have work to do, Dr. Jensen."

Doc didn't need to turn around to know that Peters had a weapon trained on Paige. With the speed of Swanset's supercomputer, he composed a mental list of all possible options.

A—he could cooperate and wait for Maggie to bring in the extraction team. Without a second thought, he nixed that option. Paige wasn't going into any dungeon. Not while he was alive to prevent it.

B—he could try to talk Swanset out of his mad scheme, which wasn't really a viable option at all.

Or C—he could terminate the mission now and get Paige the hell out of here.

# Chapter 16

The next few minutes contained enough excitement and adventure to last Paige through several lifetimes.

She was never quite sure what happened first. It might have been the sudden blow from David that knocked her sideways. Or Swanset's shout. Or the gunshot that exploded somewhere behind her and plowed into one of the white boxes with a sickening *splat*.

Whatever it was, Paige went flying. Her heel caught in her long skirt, and she went down on all fours. The chain of her evening bag twisted around her wrist as she reached behind her and wrenched frantically at the snagged material.

The skirt came free, and she pushed herself upright just as David sent Peters crashing to the floor. Across the room, Victor raised the tip of his cane.

Too late, Paige remembered a scene from *The Baron of The Night,* the one in which a dark, brooding hero brought down an attacker with the rapier hidden in his walking stick. Although the ivory-handled instrument Swanset held clutched in both hands was similar to the cane in the movie, Paige suspected it now housed something far more lethal than a rapier.

"David!" she screamed as she lunged toward the console. "Look out!"

She didn't have time to dig either her mascara or the switchblade out of her bag. Instead, she used the small gold purse itself as a weapon. Swinging it by the chain, she slammed it into Swanset's outstretched arm with every ounce of strength she possessed.

The walking stick bucked in his hands a split second before Paige's purse connected. She glanced over her shoulder and gave a terrified sob as David crumpled to the floor.

"You bastard! You damned bastard!"

Raging with fury, she swung the bag once more. Swanset threw up an arm to block the blow to his head and jerked backward. He toppled over, just as Paige had during her first encounter with him, taking the console chair and the keyboard with him. The monitor teetered unsteadily on the console table for a second, then settled back with a thud.

Paige kicked the cane out of the fallen man's grasp, then whirled and raced across the lab. Ignoring the semiconscious, twitching Peters, sprawled a few yards away, she dropped to her knees and dragged David into her arms.

"Are you all right? Where were you hit?"

She knew the answer as soon as her palm made contact with his shoulder. A sticky warmth smeared across her hand and oozed through her fingers. Her arms convulsed around David, who grunted and gave a little jerk.

"Stay still!" Paige panted. "Let me take a look at the wound."

"I'm—I'm all right."

"No, you're not! You're bleeding!"

Cradling him in her right arm, Paige stretched out her left to unbutton the black dinner jacket and peel it back. The spreading blossom of red on David's shoulder sent terror streaking through her every vein.

"Don't move!" she sobbed, clutching him even tighter while

she grabbed at the hem of her gown and wadded it against his shoulders.

"I'm all right." He twisted upright in her arms, his voice slowly gaining in strength. "It's just a flesh wound. I'm all—Jesus!"

At the startled exclamation, Paige threw both arms around David and crushed his head against her breasts. She was determined to shield him at all costs from this new threat, whatever it was. Shoulders rigid, nerves screaming, she waited for the attack.

None came.

"Paige." His voice was muffled against her breasts. "Sweetheart. Let me go."

Reaching up, he pried loose her stranglehold and eased himself out of her arms. With another small grunt, he pushed himself up on one knee. The effort sent a ripple of pain across his face, and he paused, panting a little. Paige watched him, her heart in her throat.

Only then did she absorb the unnatural stillness in the lab. There was no sound but her rasping sobs and David's breath whistling through his clenched teeth. No movement other than the lift of his body as he forced himself to stand upright.

She twisted around on her knees, searching for the other two men. Peters she saw immediately. He was lying only a few yards away. His limbs were grotesquely rigid and outflung, as though he'd suffered some sort of electrical shock. A trickle of blood had traced a path from the corner of his mouth and pooled on the floor.

His jaw tight, David knelt beside the butler and searched for a pulse. After a moment, he reached up to close the eyes that would remain forever blurred.

"He's dead."

"How—?" Paige gasped. "What—?"

In answer, David swiveled on his knee and looked toward Swanset.

The aging film star lay sprawled where he'd fallen, his eyes fixed sightlessly on the ceiling, his lips blue. One bony hip rested squarely on the keyboard, depressing half its keys. On the console above him, a steady stream of electronic messages raced across the computer screen.

"Evidently his program wasn't as far past the experimental stage as he thought," David said grimly. "When he fell on the keyboard, he sent several million bits of visual imaging data pouring into Peters's cells. The poor bastard must have exploded internally."

While Paige watched, stunned, David crossed to the unmoving Swanset. Hunkering down in a stiff, awkward movement, he felt for a pulse. After a few seconds, he shook his head. Easing the keyboard from under the man's body, he set it on the console. The screen flickered, then went blank.

"Oh, my God," Paige moaned, burying her face in her hands. "I killed him. I killed them both."

David covered the short distance between them in a few strides. "No, you didn't."

"I did!" she cried, rocking back and forth on her knees. "I hit Victor in the head with my purse. I knocked him out, and he fell on the keyboard. I killed them both."

Using his good arm, David reached down and pulled her to her feet. It took some doing, but he finally managed to pry her hands from her face.

"Paige, listen to me. You didn't kill him. You didn't kill either one of them. Swanset had a heart attack. He was probably dead before he hit the floor."

She turned her tear-streaked face up to his. "What?"

"His lips are blue. He had a heart attack. A massive coronary, by the looks of it."

"Are you sure?"

Doc folded her into his arms. This wasn't the time to remind her that he was an engineer, not a medical examiner.

"Yes, I'm sure."

He held her until her sobs dwindled to watery hiccups. She lay against his chest for a moment longer, then jerked out of his arms.

"Oh, David, your shoulder! Let me look at it."

Doc stood quietly while she fumbled with the studs on his shirt and lifted the edge to peer at the wound. He'd had enough experience in the field to know that the hit wasn't fatal, although white-hot pain ripped through his shoulder with his every movement and bright red blood seeped from the wound. Paige's face whitened when she saw the ragged hole in his flesh, but she swallowed a couple of times and glanced around the sterile lab. Her gaze fell on the footed silver tray.

Shuddering, she stepped around Peters's rigid body and snatched up a handful of white linen napkins. Within moments, she had eased off Doc's dinner jacket and shirt and pressed the folded napkins against the bullet hole. While he held the compress in place, Paige dug Henri's switchblade out of her evening bag and sawed a long, ragged strip of green satin from her full skirt. Her brows knitted in fierce concentration as she brought the makeshift bandage under his armpit and wrapped it around his shoulder.

Doc gritted his teeth against the lancing pain and focused his concentration on Paige. This frowning, intent woman held little resemblance to the Paige he'd kissed and left behind in L.A. less than a week ago. This one looked as though she'd been through a small war. Which she had.

Her hair had tumbled free from its elaborate braid and hung in wisps about her face. Her brief bout of tears had left smudges of mascara under her eyes. When she buried her face in her hands, she'd smeared his blood across her cheeks, and one of her gown's tight sleeves had ripped at the shoulder seam when she swung her lethal little purse. Yet her hands were steady as she tied the edges of the green strip, and her eyes intent as she surveyed her handiwork.

"You're pretty handy to have around in a tricky situation, Jezebel," he told her, his lips curving into a smile.

"Yes, well, I'd prefer to avoid tricky situations in the future, if you don't mind. And don't grin at me like that! I know I insisted on being part of this team, but I do *not* want any more excitement like this. Not in this lifetime. Or the next! Or the one after that!"

Doc curled a knuckle under her chin and tilted her face to his. "As soon as we get out of here, my darling, we'll generate a whole different kind of excitement. Enough to last us through this lifetime. And the next. And the one after that."

When he bent to brush a quick kiss across her mouth, Paige almost forgot his bleeding shoulder and her slowly receding terror and the two still forms just yards away. His mouth was warm and hard and tasted of David. *Her* David.

She closed her eyes, savoring that brief kiss. An image of the man she loved imprinted itself on her every sense. She felt the strength and the gentleness in his touch. She heard his rasping, indrawn breath. She drew in the salty tang of his sweat, or perhaps it was his blood.

She didn't need any visual imaging wizardry to see him in the mirror of her mind. Tall and broad-shouldered and incredibly handsome, his brown hair disordered for once, his steel blue eyes filled with an emotion that set her heart thumping painfully. She ached with the need to hold him, to feel his body against hers, to arch her hips into his and take him into her.

She stepped back, breathing heavily.

"I was wrong," she admitted, with a ragged sigh. "I'm ready for whatever excitement you care to generate."

She couldn't know, of course, that she'd regret those rash words not two minutes later.

David planted another hard kiss on her lips, then strode to the console. "Let's insert that bug, then get the hell out of here. Swanset's too smart not to have at least one, perhaps more, backup systems. We don't want anyone accessing them before we can locate them and shut them down."

Still shivering from the force of her own reaction, Paige blinked at his swift transition from lover to secret agent. Half-naked, his bare upper torso streaked with blood and bound by a ragged strip of green satin, he looked like a character out of one of Victor Swanset's movies. The muscles in his shoulders rippled as he leaned over the console and punched one of the keys. The screen flickered back to life.

"Good. The program's still active. I recorded his access code, but it looks like I won't need it."

With swift, sure confidence, he keystroked in a series of commands. A few moments later, he straightened.

"There," he murmured in satisfaction. "Anyone who tries to—"

He broke off, his dark brows snapping together, as he studied the monitor. From where she stood a few feet away, Paige could see some kind of a message flicker across the screen.

"What?" she asked. "What's wrong?"

"There's a posthumous message here from Swanset."

"There is?" she squeaked.

"The bastard knew he was just a heartbeat away from a coronary. He must have coded in this message months ago and triggered it somehow just before he died."

David's eyes scanned the print that painted across the screen. "Damn it all to hell!"

"I don't think I want to hear this," Paige said in a faint voice.

He whirled and grabbed her hand. "Good—because there isn't time to explain. We've got to get out of here. Fast!"

Yanking her along behind him, he raced to the elevator. He stabbed the button, his breath harsh as he waited for the door to open. When nothing happened, he stabbed it again. And again.

When the door refused to open, David slammed the heel of his hand against the wood panel, listening intently.

"It's reinforced with some kind of alloy," he snarled. "The damn thing's sealed tighter than a drum. The whole lab probably is."

Spinning on one heel, he scanned the room. "Look for another exit. There has to be one."

"How do you know?"

"Swanset told Peters to escort you 'next door.' For a historical tour of the dungeons, remember?"

"Oh, God! Yes!"

His eyes met hers. "We have approximately ninety seconds to find that door and get the hell out of here."

They found it in less than sixty.

Actually, Paige found it. By the simple expedient of scraping her nails along the far wall as she ran the length of the lab. When she encountered a slight depression, she screamed for David. He was at her side in seconds. Endless heartbeats later, he uncovered a concealed latch. Yanking the handle upward, he slammed his shoulder against the panel.

Paige could imagine the pain that must have caused him. The green bandage darkened with a fresh spurt of blood as David turned and shoved her through the opening ahead of him.

Darkness and cold, dank air surrounded them like a smothering shroud.

These were definitely the dungeons. As they raced down the narrow corridor, Paige caught a glimpse of barred cells cut from solid rock. A rusted implement of some kind dangled from a hook on the wall. She almost tripped over a discarded tool, the use of which she didn't even want to *guess* at.

Panting with fear and exertion, Paige thought she caught a faint glow of moonlight ahead. She twisted around, intending to tell David, when an ominous rumbling sounded in the laboratory behind them.

''Run!'' David shouted.

Paige ran.

The rumbling grew to a roar, then exploded in a blinding wave of light and noise. David threw himself against her, knocking her to the stone floor and covering her body with his. Her head smashed against the stone, and she must have lost consciousness for a few seconds or minutes or hours.

When her eyes opened, she was trapped between David's weight and the unyielding stone. Paige couldn't breathe, couldn't move.

Neither could David, she discovered.

He was unconscious. His breath rasped in her ear, and his body lay sprawled over hers. Paige felt his warm blood soaking through the back of her gown and wanted to scream with terror. Instead, she wriggled and scratched and snaked her way forward until she'd cleared enough of his weight to twist free.

With the last of her strength, she dragged at his good arm

until she had him turned over on his back. She refused to cry, refused to let the blood seeping down his chest reduce her to the quivering mass of hysteria she knew she was.

Dragging the gold bag still chained to her wrist into her lap, she fumbled for the switchblade and sawed another ragged strip from her skirt. If—*when!*—they got out of here, she'd find some way to thank Henri for the gift he'd pressed on her. The knife had been his most valued possession. At this moment, it was hers.

Hands shaking, she folded the heavy satin over and over again, then pressed the pad against David's wound with both hands. She held it there for what seemed like hours, murmuring his name, pouring out her love.

When he stirred, she wanted to cry in relief.

When his eyes fluttered open, she did.

"Paige!"

She barely heard his raspy whisper over the sound of her own gulping sobs.

"Paige, send…signal."

"What?"

"Send…signal."

"To Maggie?" Paige wiped the back of her sleeve across her nose. "Can't she hear us?"

"Alloy…seal…lab. No emissions."

"You mean she couldn't hear us the whole time we were in the lab? She doesn't know what's happened?"

"Send…"

"David!"

His muscles slackened under her hand, and he slumped unconscious once more.

Moaning, Paige pressed the pad against his shoulder with one hand and reached for the crystal eardrop with her other. To her horror, it was missing.

Trying not to jar David more than she had to, she dragged him a few inches to the side. Frantically she brushed her fingers across the stone where she'd hit her head, sweeping the area over and over again.

She found the earring. Or what was left of it. The crystal drop had shattered upon impact with the stone, as had the tiny device it concealed.

Paige stared at the bits of glass and plastic in her hand in disbelief.

She wouldn't panic! She wouldn't!

She pushed herself to her feet. One glance told her she couldn't go back to the lab. It wasn't there. The explosion, or implosion, had dumped tons of stone into the subterranean chamber.

Her feet dragging, Paige turned and stumbled toward the opposite end of the dark tunnel. Toward the faint glow that she hoped, prayed, was moonlight.

It was.

"Thank God!" she whispered.

She wondered fleetingly why the small, square window wasn't barred, as the cells were. As soon as she leaned over the sill, she understood why.

Given her difficulty with numbers, Paige couldn't have said whether the cliff dropped for two hundred, or two thousand feet straight down. She only knew that it was a long, long way to where the sea crashed against the cliff's base.

She twisted in the small opening, scanning the sheer rock on either side. There was no path, no ledge, no outcropping of stone of any kind. Nothing but a perpendicular wall of granite.

Her heart sinking, Paige realized that this tiny opening wasn't a window at all, but rather a ventilation hole. It didn't need bars. No one was going out through that opening. Not alive, anyway.

Slumping back against the wall, Paige felt her knees buckle. She sank to the floor in a dejected heap.

David seemed to think Maggie didn't know what had happened. Even if the OMEGA team stormed the villa, it would be days, maybe weeks, before they cleared the lab and found this narrow subterranean tunnel.

She couldn't wait, not for a day, not for hours. David needed medical attention. Now.

What was she going to do? Paige asked herself in desperation. What could she do?

She could send a signal, as David had instructed. But how? A fire, maybe. Or a flash of light from the other earring, when the sun came up. Or…

Paige's heart leaped into her throat. Scrambling to her feet, she ran back to where she'd discarded her little gold evening bag. Tearing at the clasp, she dumped the contents on the stone. The mascara. A lipstick. And the compact! The diamond-studded compact!

With the introduction of the crystal earrings, the compact had been retired from active service as a communications device, but Paige had kept it for its more mundane and utilitarian purpose. She'd powdered her nose with it only an hour or so ago in the throne room.

She snatched it up and raced back to the opening, fumbling for the square stone in the center.

Dear Lord, how did the thing work? Once to transmit, twice to receive? Or was it once to receive, twice to transmit?

And what was the damn emergency signal? One-one-three? Three-one-one? Three-two-two?

Paige swallowed a groan and reminded herself this was for David. *Her* David.

She could remember the code! She had to! All she had to do was concentrate. Think of the alley behind the tobacco shop, she told herself, emptying her mind of everything else. Think of David's instructions as he'd cradled an unconscious Maggie in his arms. Think of Henri hopping up and down on one foot in impatience as he repeated the instructions in a near shout.

Not a half a mile away, a fleet of five black-painted helicopters skimmed the surface of the bay. Rotor blades whirring, they raced without lights or directional signals toward the high peak that housed Victor Swanset's aerie.

Maggie hunched forward in the copilot's seat of the lead aircraft, scanning the darkness through high-powered starlight-vision goggles. Beside her, Adam worked the controls with a skill that had astounded her when they first took off. She'd had no idea he could pilot a craft like this, but she hadn't wasted time arguing with him.

Maggie had made the decision to launch immediately after losing contact. Her instincts had told her that the broken transmission wasn't the result of any equipment malfunction. Wherever that elevator had taken Doc and Paige to had been shielded to prevent emissions. Although Doc hadn't signaled for help, hadn't called for backup, Maggie intended to be within range if and when he did.

They were only minutes away from the target area. Sheer cliffs loomed in front of them, looking much like a wall of chalk through the night-vision goggles. Adam pulled back on the stick and began a smooth climb to the central, highest peak.

Maggie spun the dial on the aircraft's digital radio, hoping, praying, for a signal. She'd tried every emergency frequency, every satellite channel, on the system at least a dozen times during the short flight.

She had just reached for the dial to spin to another frequency when static cackled through her headset. She froze, her hand in midair.

More static filled the earphones, then a voice filled with quiet desperation.

"…can't remember the code, but we need help."

"It's Paige!" Maggie shouted over the helo's intercom.

Adam lifted a hand from the controls to give her thumbs-up.

Maggie pressed the radio mike to her throat to activate it. "Jezebel, can you hear me?"

Evidently not.

"…dead, and David's hurt," Paige continued, in the same desperate tone. "He said the wound wasn't bad, but he's bleeding heavily and unconscious. Uh, we're in a tunnel beneath the villa. It ends at the cliff face, in a small hole that overlooks the sea."

Maggie's heart sank as she peered through the helo's Plexiglas windshield at the endless stretch of chalky white cliffs below.

Even with the goggles, it was going to be tough to locate a small opening in that indented, snaking wall.

Paige's voice faltered, then resumed. "I hope this is transmitting. I pressed the stone once, but I may have the sequence wrong, so I'm going to press it twice and try again."

"She's using the compact," Maggie breathed. "Do it, Paige. Do it! Press the stone twice, so I can talk to you."

A staticky silence hummed through the earphones. Maggie spoke slowly, clearly, into the mike.

"Jezebel, this is Chameleon. If you pressed the diamond twice, you should be hearing me. Now press it once, and acknowledge my transmission."

The helicopter swerved to one side, caught in a sudden updraft. Maggie ignored the violent movement and Adam's smooth corrective action. Her entire being was turned inward, focused on the mike pressed to her throat.

"Press the stone once," she repeated calmly. "Acknowledge my transmission."

"This is Jezebel. I can hear you!"

"Yes!"

Reining in her wild elation, Maggie jammed the mike against her throat.

"Search Doc's pockets, Jezebel. See if he has the receiver on him. The one that homes in on the tracking chip you were fitted with. It looks like a small flat calculator with a liquid crystal display."

Maggie held her breath until Paige replied.

"I've got it."

"Good! There's a small switch in the upper left-hand corner. Push it to the right, then read me the coordinates. Slowly!"

"Do you mean these numbers in the display? I—I can barely see them."

"Yes, those numbers. We need those coordinates to find you. Read them to me. Slowly!"

She did. Slowly and accurately, repeating them over and over until Maggie locked them into the helicopter's global positioning unit.

Within moments, Adam had the aircraft hovering two hundred feet above the crashing sea and a powerful searchlight trained on a small square opening in a sheer rock wall. With a skill learned long ago and kept finely honed, he held the platform steady while one of Maggie's team members fired a titanium-tipped steel anchor dart from a shoulder-held launcher. The dart shot through the night, trailing a snakelike nylon line, and buried itself in the rock just a few feet above the opening.

Adam kept one eye on the instruments while Maggie and the wiry Santorelli strapped body harnesses on over their black jumpsuits. Rushing wind whipped through the belly of the helo as they pulled open the side hatch.

"Have you used this rig before?" Santorelli shouted to her over the noise from the chopping rotor blades.

"No, not this one!" Maggie yelled back. "One similar to it, though!"

"Roger! Let's go!"

Adam made no comment as they rigged a lifeline to the specially designed lift that swung out over the open hatch. But his jaw was so tight it ached as Maggie snapped the lifeline to her harness and stepped toward the hatch.

"Okay, Jezebel," she said into the mike, her hoarse voice filled with a breezy confidence that made Adam's fist clench on the control stick. "We're coming in. And once we get back to Cannes, we'll have to hit the boutiques. Don't you have a wedding dress to shop for? I saw just the thing. All white silk and silver sequins."

Paige's shaky laughter floated over the headset. "No sequins. Please, no sequins."

# Chapter 17

Paige sat at the ornate rosewood dressing table and towel-dried her hair. While she rubbed the squeaky-clean strands through the thick cotton, she went over the arrangement she'd made for the ceremony scheduled to take place thirty minutes from now.

As weddings went, theirs would be a relatively small affair. Only a handful of people would attend—just the immediate wedding party, the deputy from the American consulate who'd act as an official witness, and the French magistrate hurriedly contacted to perform the ceremony.

Paige had refused to wait until more of their friends and family could gather in Cannes. She was determined to join her life to David's today, scant hours after swinging out of a dark tunnel and dangling hundreds of feet above the sea while she was winched aboard a hovering helicopter. Today, before Maggie and Adam got called back to OMEGA for some crisis or another. Before she and David flew to Paris with Henri to arrange his passport and visa for an extended stay in the United States. Before any of them began any new adventures!

It had taken most of the night to sort through the aftermath of their mission. Luckily, Maggie's extraction team had included a skilled paramedic who patched David up so neatly that he was able to conduct a detailed debrief on-site with Maggie and Adam and the rest of the team. That done, they'd evacuated the servants, sealed off the villa and left guards in place until the French authorities arrived to excavate the laboratory.

Dawn had feathered the skies with gold and painted the sea a deep wine red by the time they returned to the hotel. Too wired from the night's events to sleep, they'd all feasted on the breakfast Henri ordered from his friend the head chef.

After that, Paige had taken charge. With a ruthless assumption of authority, she'd directed an amused but compliant Adam to use whatever influence was necessary to take care of the legalities. Henri was put in charge of the wedding supper. David was told to rest and recuperate. And Maggie... Maggie had gleefully accompanied her on the promised shopping expedition. They'd found exactly what Paige wanted in the first shop they entered.

Her senses tingling with delicious feminine anticipation, she swiveled on the dressing stool to gaze at the two-piece dress that hung on the wardrobe door. It met her stringent requirement of no sequins, but even without any glittery trim, it was an outfit Meredith herself might have purchased. The snowy watered silk shimmered with a luster all its own, and the exquisite beading on the three buttons and the low square-cut neckline of the short-sleeved jacket was handworked. The straight skirt stopped just above Paige's knees, but was slit high on one side to allow ease of movement.

In thirty minutes or so, she'd slip on that deceptively demure skirt and fasten those tiny beaded buttons. She'd walk out of this sumptuous bedroom for the last time to join David in the suite across the hall, then leave immediately for the honeymoon Adam had arranged aboard a luxurious yacht owned by a friend of his. Paige made a silent vow not to fall off the gangplank this time.

Now, though, she had thirty minutes to get ready. Thirty minutes to blend the best of Paige Lawrence and the worst of Meredith Ames.

Grinning wickedly, she tossed the towel aside and walked over to the bed. With unabashed eagerness, she plucked the lemon-colored lace teddy off the coverlet and held it up by its thin straps. She'd been waiting far too long for the opportunity to put this little baby to use. When they hit that yacht, both she and David would be ready—more than ready!—for immediate carnal copulation.

Shrugging out of her robe, Paige stepped into the flimsy scrap of lace and shimmied it up her thighs. She wiggled to adjust the divided strip of fabric that ran between her legs, a little shocked in spite of herself at the intimacy of the garment. She'd just slipped her arms through the narrow shoulder straps and was tucking the underwire lift beneath her breasts when the sound of the door opening made her spin around, both hands plastered against the front of her chest.

David stepped inside, still dressed in the tan slacks and blue knit shirt he'd changed into as soon as they returned to the hotel last night. This morning. Whenever. The bandage on his left shoulder bulged a bit under the shirt, but he showed no other signs of his recent wound.

"You can't come in here," Paige protested. "It's bad luck to see the bride before the ceremony. You're supposed to get changed in the suite across the hall."

"I'm going to," he said slowly, his eyes skimming her body. "I just came in to give you— Jesus, Paige, what *is* that thing?"

"It's called a teddy. I think. I've never seen one, um, constructed quite like this."

"Neither have I," he muttered. "It doesn't have any back."

"Not much of a front, either," she admitted. With a little spurt of daring, she dropped her hands. The stunned expression that crossed David's face sent a dart of pure delight through her.

"Good grief! Is that what you bought when you went shopping today?"

"No. This is—was—Meredith's. I've been saving it for a special occasion." Her shining, fresh-washed hair swept her bare shoulders as she tilted her head and smiled at him. "I think our wedding night qualifies as special, don't you?"

David stared at her for long moments. Then he returned her smile with a slow, crooked one of his own.

"Very special. But I don't think I can wait until tonight."

He turned, and the sound of the key snicking the tumblers in the lock thundered in her ears.

The old Paige, the shy, timorous one who had driven through the French Alps with an aching heart because she believed she wasn't woman enough for this man, might have protested. She might have reminded David that Maggie and Adam were waiting just across the hall. That Henri would be pacing the floor, all puffed up with importance over the fact that Paige had asked him to give her away. That the American consul might arrive at any minute, or the French magistrate.

This Paige simply shivered in delicious anticipation. They had thirty minutes, after all.

As David crossed the room, she wet her lips in an unconscious invitation. He stopped in front of her, his fingers reaching to brush the tip of one breast. She drew her shoulders back, and the underwire lifted her soft flesh even higher. The scalloped edge of the lace cup barely covered her nipples as it was. Paige's instinctive little movement exposed them completely.

David drew in a sharp breath. His eyes darkening with pleasure, he shaped her breasts, fondling them, worshiping them. Then he bent and brushed the soft mounds with his mouth. The sight of his dark head against her flesh sent a shaft of savagely primitive possessiveness slicing through Paige.

She wanted to wrap her arms around him, cradle him against her breasts as she had last night, keep him safe and secure from all harm. She now understood David's urge to protect her, to shield her. She felt the same, exactly the same.

His breath was ragged when he lifted his head. Paige saw the hot, urgent need flaring in his eyes, and her own rose in waves. His hands less than gentle, he searched her front for a hook or a fastening on the one-piece teddy.

"How the hell does this thing open?"

"It doesn't. It doesn't have to."

"What?"

"You're an engineer," Paige purred. "You figure it out."

With a half laugh, half growl, he drew her into his arms. Paige went willingly, eagerly. Her hands slid up the broad planes of his chest—then stopped abruptly when her fingers encountered the bulge of the bandage.

"Oh, David! We can't! Your wound!"

He drew her closer, nuzzling the side of her neck. "What wound?"

"You lost a lot of blood," she reminded him, hunching a shoulder against the tickle of his moist breath in her ear.

"I had a steak for lunch."

Despite her own fiery need, Paige stepped back. The memory of those desperate moments when she'd tried to stanch his bleeding was too fresh to ignore.

"David…"

"I'm here, sweetheart."

The look in his eyes almost melted her resistance, but she took another step backward, until her bottom bumped against the dressing table. She gestured helplessly toward his shirtfront.

"Doesn't it hurt?"

He nodded. "Like hell."

"Oh, David!"

Her heart aching in sympathy, Paige reached out to brush her fingertips gently over his poor, injured shoulder. He caught her hand.

"Not there." He redirected her hand to a spot considerably below his shoulder. "There."

"Oh!"

Paige had hoped this sinful little garment would have an instantaneous, erotic impact on David. It had. Her fingers pressed against the bulge in his slacks, and the hot, liquid desire in her own belly flowed into her loins.

Still, she was careful to avoid touching his shoulder when he swept her into his arms once more and brought his mouth crushing down on hers. He held her hard against him, his palms spearing down the small of her back to cup the bare, rounded flesh of her bottom.

When his fingers found the narrow strip that traced between her legs, he stiffened. The old David, the one who had always held himself rigidly in control for fear he'd hurt her with the violence of his passion, might have drawn back at this point. He might have undressed her gently and laid her on the bed, supporting himself on his arms as he surged into her.

This David took full advantage of the teddy's ingenious construction. Holding her mouth with his, he arched her against him and explored the moist dampness between her legs. Paige gasped as his fingers found the opening in the fabric and parted it. One, then two, blunt fingers slipped along her slick, wet channel.

She strained upward, her belly clenching as he stretched her, entered her, impaled her. She moaned far back in her throat. Or David did. She wasn't sure.

Sensation after sensation rippled through her body. She was sure she couldn't take much more when her brilliant engineer figured out just how to put that narrow strip of lace to even greater effect.

He twisted one thumb around the fabric and tugged on it, sawing it gently back and forth, creating a friction that had Paige squirming frantically. Wave after wave of heat shot out of her belly to her thighs, her breasts, her throat.

"David," she panted, dragging her mouth from his. "I can't... I won't..."

"You can. You will."

He reached behind her and swept the various bottles and brushes and combs on the dressing table to one side. Wrapping his good arm around her waist, he lifted her and set her on its smooth, satiny surface. The cool wood only heightened by contrast the fevered heat of her skin.

While Paige worked frantically at his belt buckle, he snagged his shirt and drew it, one-armed, over his head. In seconds, he stood before her, hard and rampant and hungry.

The old Paige might have waited for him to make the next move.

This one planted her hands on the smooth surface behind her, spread her legs wide and tipped her hips to receive him.

David surged into her with a power and a strength that took her breath away. The bottles rattled. A brush tumbled off the table. Paige arched her neck, throwing her head back as she wrapped her legs around his waist.

The savage thrusts slowed, then stilled.

Surprised, she opened her eyes.

He planted both hands beside hers, his chest heaving as he leaned over her.

"Who do you see, Paige?"

She struggled for breath. "What?"

Eyes as stormy as a winter sky bored into hers. "I warned you that we might not recognize each other by the time this mission was over. Who do you see now?"

"I see you," she panted, lifting a hand that shook with the force of her love to cup his cheek. "*My* David."

"Me, I do not like this!"

Red hair slicked down, scrubbed face scrunched up in a scowl, Henri folded his arms across his shiny new suit coat, with its jaunty red carnation in the lapel, and stared at the foyer.

"It is past the time they were to be here. Well past the time. The magistrate, he comes. The consul, he comes. But Mademoiselle Paige and David, they do not come." His scowl deepened. "The champagne goes flat."

Maggie twisted her half-empty flute in one hand and nodded sympathetically. "So it does."

She knew very well what had delayed the errant couple. She'd gone across the hall some time ago to check on them. It hadn't required any exercise of her linguistic skills to interpret the rough, urgent intonation in Doc's voice when he told her they'd be there shortly.

*Shortly,* of course, had stretched into *longly.*

Grinning, Maggie took another sip of the new sparkleless champagne. She'd known when she met Paige Lawrence in the boutique on the Croisette that there was more to the younger woman than met the eye. But the Paige who'd emerged these past few days had surprised everyone, herself included.

That once shy, demure young woman was now late for her own wedding because she was unabashedly enjoying her honeymoon.

A few moments later, the door to the suite flew open and a glowing Paige dashed in, followed more slowly by Doc. The bride wore the two-piece Saint-Laurent suit she'd purchased earlier today, but the side slit was twisted to the back and the jacket buttons were fastened crookedly. Instead of the white heels she'd chosen to go with the dress, she'd pulled on the same gold sandals she'd worn last night. She hadn't bothered or hadn't had time to put on any makeup, but this Paige certainly didn't need any. Her green eyes were huge, her lips red and ripe, and her cheeks were flushed with what Maggie guessed was whisker burn.

"I'm so sorry we're late," she said in a breathless rush. "David stopped by the suite to…to…"

"To give Paige her engagement ring," he finished smoothly for her.

Maggie turned to Doc in surprise. "Her engagement ring? Did someone fish her purse out of the bay, after all?"

"No. The emerald's gone, but I had another stone set for her this afternoon."

Shyly Paige held out her hand for general inspection.

Henri whistled, tilting her hand this way and that. "The stone is of a fine quality. If we are in need of money, I can get a good sum for this, I think."

David rested a hand on his shoulder. "Forget it. Paige and I will make sure you're not in need of money."

"I couldn't ever pawn this, anyway," she told the boy. "It's the diamond from the compact."

"No kidding," Maggie exclaimed.

"It was a wedding gift from Adam," she added, glancing at the tall, dark-haired man watching the proceedings with his usual cool air.

"From OMEGA," he said easily, strolling over to admire the square-cut diamond solitaire.

Maggie grinned at Paige. "So anytime you want to call Doc home, all you have to do is…"

"Press once to transmit, twice to receive," she finished, laughing. Her eyes sparkled as she grinned up at the man beside her. "Now who's got whom on a leash?"

"Before anyone does any more pressing," Adam suggested dryly, "I suggest we proceed with the ceremony."

Henri seconded his suggestion with a quelling look at Doc. "*Oui!* The champagne goes flat."

The civil service was simple and poignant.

Paige gripped the bouquet of white roses Adam had presented to her, somehow managing to look radiant and confident and shy, all at the same time.

Doc stood beside her, his eyes never leaving her face as he repeated his vows.

The maid of honor, positioned at Paige's left, translated the magistrate's stuttering half English, half Provençal phrasing for her whenever necessary. Maggie's throat closed at the look that passed between Paige and Doc when they joined hands.

Adam, at Doc's right, handed him the white-gold ring at the appropriate time, then stepped back. Paige passed roses to Maggie, who stepped back, as well.

Maggie tried not to stare at the tall, immaculately groomed man at Doc's side, concentrating on the service instead. But during each slight pause, she felt her gaze straying to Adam.

He hadn't purchased that charcoal gray suit in any boutique, she knew, or that red silk tie. They were hand-tailored in Boston, she suspected. Or New York. Or Paris. He looked so aristocratic. And so damned handsome, she thought with a small sigh.

No one would believe this wealthy, jet-setting politician had expertly worked the controls of a hovering helicopter just hours ago, his whipcord-lean body encased in black and his jaw darkened with stubble.

And no one would believe this calm, distinguished individual had icily torn a strip a half-mile wide off Maggie during the mission debrief. She buried her nose in the white roses to hide her grin, wondering if he'd *really* skin her alive if she ever swung out of a helicopter without prior jump certification again.

"And so, *madame* and *monsieur,* I pronounce you husband and wife."

Tucking the laminated card with the words of the service into his pocket, the portly magistrate beamed at the couple before him.

"You may kiss your bride."

Doc didn't need his permission. He swept Paige into his arms with a hungry, masculine fervor that made the magistrate blink, Adam smile and Maggie suppress a twinge of envy. Of their own volition, her eyes strayed to Adam.

When Doc raised his head, Paige laughed up at him, her face glowing.

The wedding supper was cheerful, noisy, and a tribute to Henri's taste. The head chef himself presented the last course himself, bowing regally when the small crowd applauded his spectacular flaming crepes suzette. Looking more like a royal duke than a head cook, the distinguished gentleman smiled benignly while his minions served the dessert.

"It was here, in Cannes, that the Prince of Wales first tasted flambéed crepes," he informed them importantly. "The dish was named for his companion of the night. A most ravishing woman, or so we're told."

He kissed his fingertips in a tribute to the glorious Suzette, a long-ago counterpart of Meredith Ames. Paige slanted David a private smile.

When the last crepe was consumed and the last toast offered, the newly wedded couple rose to leave. A shower of rose petals tossed by Maggie and a gleeful Henri followed them to the door.

At the foyer entrance, David shook Adam's hand. "Thanks for coming to Cannes. And for staying a few more days, to look after Henri for us. We'll take him off your hands when we get back."

"No problem."

"Just keep an eye on your wallet."

"Roger."

Henri's innocent brown eyes reproached him. "*Monsieur!* I have retired from the business. *That* business," he added scrupulously.

David ruffled his red hair. "We'll talk about your next business ventures when we return. See you in a couple days."

"You will watch Mademoiselle Paige?" the boy asked, trailing them to the door. "Me, I do not like this idea of the boat."

"I'll make sure she doesn't go overboard unless I'm with her."

Paige didn't take offense at the assumption by these two males that she still needed looking after, since she knew very well they needed it, also. And she intended to provide it. For the rest of their natural lives. Smiling, she took David's arm.

Halfway out the door, she suddenly stopped and slipped her hand free. "Wait! I almost forgot."

She spun around and tossed the bouquet. The roses sailed across the room, heading right toward the tall, platinum-haired woman.

Laughing, Maggie caught them with both hands. She buried her nose once again in the soft, velvety roses, breathing in the heady scent of love.

When she glanced up, the laughter died in her throat. Adam was watching her, with an expression in his blue eyes that she'd never seen before. Maggie's heart slammed sideways against her ribs. Her fingers crushed the white roses.

"I have something for you, too," Paige told Adam with a shy smile. She came back to him, holding out her hand. His dark brows rose when she laid a small rectangular box on his palm.

"You're going to need this far more than David will."

A slashing grin creased his cheeks as he slipped the receiver into his pocket.

"I'm sure I will."

Paige wasn't sure just how or when Adam Ridgeway would manage to fit the laughing, fiercely independent Maggie Sinclair with a leash, electronic or otherwise. But from the look that flared in his blue eyes as they rested on the long-legged blonde, she suspected it wouldn't be long until he tried.

\* \* \* \* \*

# PERFECT DOUBLE

To Dee and Betty—friends, treasured in-laws
and two people who know what romance is all about!
With bunches of love...

# *Prologue*

*She had to die.*

*That was the best solution.*

*The only solution.*

*He stood at the window and stared, unseeing, at the winter-grayed streets. The thought of killing her, of snuffing out her vibrant essence, twisted his gut. But there wasn't any other way. She didn't know she held a tiny scrap of information that could bring him and his world tumbling down. She had no idea she possessed the power to destroy him.*

*She had to die before she discovered she held that power.*

*And a part of him would die with her.*

# Chapter 1

Softly falling snow blanketed Washington, D.C., adding a touch of lacy white trim to the elegant town houses lining a quiet side street just off Massachusetts Avenue. The few residents of the capital who weren't glued to their TV sets this Superbowl Sunday scurried by, chins down and collars turned up against the cold. Intent on getting out of the elements, they didn't give the town house set midway down the block a second glance. If they had, they might have noticed the discreet bronze plaque set beside the entrance that identified the offices of the president's special envoy.

Most Washington insiders believed the special envoy's position had been created several administrations ago to give a wealthy campaign contributor a fancy title and an important-sounding but meaningless title. Only a handful of the most senior cabinet officials knew that the special envoy secretly served in another, far more vital capacity.

From a specially shielded high-tech control center on the third floor of the town house, he directed a covert agency. An agency whose initials comprised the last letter of the Greek alphabet,

OMEGA. An agency that, as its name implied, sprang into action as a last resort when other, more established organizations, such as the CIA, the State Department or the military, couldn't respond.

Less than an hour ago, a call from the president had activated an OMEGA response. From various corners of the capital, a small cadre of dedicated professionals battled the snow-clogged streets to converge on the scene.

Maggie Sinclair unwrapped the wool scarf muffling her mouth and nose and stomped her calf-high boots to remove the last of the clinging snow. Stuffing the scarf in her pocket, she hurried through the tunnel that led to OMEGA's secret underground entrance. At the end of the passageway, she pressed a hand to a hidden sensor and waited impatiently for the computers to verify her palmprint. Seconds later, the titanium-shielded door hummed open. She took the stairs to the second floor and scanned the monitors set into the wall. Satisfied that only the special envoy's receptionist occupied the spacious outer area, she activated the sensors.

Gray-haired, grandmotherly Elizabeth Wells glanced up in surprise. "My goodness, Chameleon, you got here fast."

"I took the subway. I wasn't about to try driving through this mess." Shrugging out of her down jacket, Maggie hooked it on a bentwood coat tree. "Besides, I wanted to leave my car for Red. Just in case."

Elizabeth's kind face folded into sympathetic lines. "What a shame you were called in right in the middle of your father's visit. He doesn't get back to the States all that often, does he?"

"No, he doesn't."

Actually, Red Sinclair was lucky if he managed a quick trip stateside once a year. As superintendent of an oil-field exploration rig, the crusty widower traveled continually from one overseas job to the next. He might be drilling in Malaysia one week, Saudi Arabia the next.

"And when he does come home," Maggie added with a grin, "he usually times his visits to coincide with the Superbowl. I left him and Terence ensconced in front of the TV, alternately cheering the Cowboys and cursing the Redskins.''

"You left the poor man with Terence?" A ripple of distaste crossed Elizabeth's face. Like most of the OMEGA team, she actively disliked the bug-eyed blue-and-orange-striped iguana a certain Central American colonel had given Maggie. The one time the receptionist had been pressed into lizard-sitting, the German shepherd-size creature had devoured her prized water lilies.

"Honestly, dear, I don't understand how you can keep that…that creature as a house pet. I find him utterly repulsive."

"Dad does, too," Maggie replied, laughing. "Unfortunately, the reverse doesn't hold true. Terence hates this cold weather. He's been trying to climb into Red's lap to share his warmth, not to mention his beer, all afternoon long. I left them just before halftime, tussling for possession of a bottle of Coors."

"Perhaps I should give your father a call," Elizabeth mused. "If you're going out of town, he might like to get away from that disgusting reptile for a while. Maybe have dinner with me."

Maggie's brows rose. "*Am* I going out of town?"

Elizabeth gave a little cluck of disgust at her uncharacteristic slip. Having served as personal assistant to OMEGA's director since the agency was founded, she knew when and how to keep secrets. She also knew how to use the Sig Sauer 9 mm pistol she kept in her upper-right-hand desk drawer. She'd fired the weapon only once in the line of duty, to deadly effect.

Maggie grinned to herself. This kind, lethal woman had a background and a personality as intriguing as her father's.

"I wish you would give Dad a call, Elizabeth. I'm sure he'd enjoy having dinner with someone who doesn't prefer bugs as an appetizer."

The receptionist grimaced and reached for the intercom phone. "I will, I promise. Right now, though, I'd better tell the chief you're here. He's waiting for you."

While Elizabeth announced her arrival, Maggie raked a hand through her snow-dampened, shoulder-length brown hair. A quick tug settled her faded maroon-and-gold Washington Redskins sweatshirt around her jeans-clad hips. This wasn't quite her standard professional attire, but the coded message summoning her to headquarters had signaled a matter of national importance, and she hadn't taken the time to change. Oh, well, OMEGA's director had seen her in worse rigs than this. Much worse.

Now all brisk efficiency, Elizabeth nodded. "Go on in, dear."

As Maggie walked down the short corridor leading to the director's private office, a flicker of anticipation skipped through her, like a tiny electrical impulse darting across a circuit board. She tried to tell herself that her suddenly erratic pulse was due to her imminent mission, whatever it might be. Herself wasn't buying it. She knew darn well what was causing the shimmer of excitement in her blood.

He was waiting a few steps away.

Maggie paused outside the door to draw in a deep, steadying breath. The extra supply of air didn't do her any good. As soon as she walked into his office and caught her first glimpse of the tall, dark-haired man standing at the window, her lungs forgot to function.

After almost three years, Maggie thought wryly, she ought to be used to Adam Ridgeway's effect on her respiratory system. The sad fact was that each contact with this cool, authoritative, often irritating man left her more breathless than the last.

He turned and gave her one of his rare smiles. "Hello, Maggie. Sorry I had to drag you away from the game."

She forced the air trapped in her chest cavity to circulate. Okay, the man looked like an ad for *GQ* in knife-pleated tan wool slacks, a white oxford shirt and a V-necked cashmere sweater in a deep indigo blue that matched his eyes. And, yes, the light from his desk lamp picked up a few delicious traces of silver in his black hair, traces he claimed she herself had put there.

But he was her boss, for heaven's sake, and she was too mature, too professional, to allow her growing fascination with Adam Ridgeway to complicate her relationship with the director of OMEGA. Unfortunately.

"Hi, Adam," she replied, moving to her favorite perch on one corner of his massive mahogany conference table. "I don't mind the weather, but if the Skins lose this game because I'm not there to cheer them on, Red's going to gloat for the rest of his visit. He still can't believe I've transferred my allegiance from the Cowboys."

"That is a pretty radical switch for an Oklahoman," the Boston-bred Adam concurred gravely.

"No kidding! A lot of folks back home think it ranks right up there with abandoning your firstborn or setting fire to the flag."

Actually, Maggie's move to Washington three years ago had resulted in far more than a shift in allegiance in football teams. Until that time, she'd chaired the foreign language department at a small Midwestern college. An easy mastery of her work and a broken engagement had led to a growing restlessness. So when she received a late-night call from the strange little man Red Sinclair had once helped smuggle out of a war-torn oil sheikhdom, she'd been intrigued. That call had resulted in a secret trip to D.C. and, ultimately, her recruitment as an operative.

From the day she joined OMEGA, Maggie had never considered going back to sleepy little Yarnell College. What woman could be content teaching languages after leading a strike team into the jungles of Central America to take down a drug lord? Or after being trapped in a Soviet nuclear-missile silo with a brilliant, if incredibly clumsy, scientist? Or dangling hundreds of feet above the dark, crashing Mediterranean to extract a wounded agent from the subterranean lair of a megalomaniacal film star? Not this woman, at any rate.

Although...

If pressed, Maggie would have admitted that the life of a secret agent had its drawbacks. Like the fact that most of the men she associated with in her line of work were either drug dealers or thieves or general all-around sleazebags.

Oh, there were a few interesting prospects. A certain drop-dead-gorgeous Latin American colonel still called her whenever he was in D.C. And one or two operatives from other agencies she'd worked with had thrown out hints about wanting to know the woman behind the code name Chameleon. But none of these men possessed quite the right combination of qualities Maggie was looking for in a potential mate. Like a keen, incisive mind. A sense of adventure. A hint of danger in his smile. A great bod wasn't one of her absolute requirements, but it certainly wouldn't hurt.

So far Maggie had only met one man who came close to measuring up in all categories, and he was standing a few feet away from her right now. The problem was, whenever they came face-to-face, it was generally just before he sent her off to some far corner of the world.

As he was about to do now, apparently.

"So what's up, Adam?" she asked. "Why are we here?"

"I'm here because I got a call from the president an hour ago," he said slowly, his eyes on her face.

"And?" Maggie prompted.

The tingling tension that always gripped her at the start of a mission added to the fluttering in her veins that Adam's presence generated. Anticipation coursed through her, and her fingers gripped the smooth wood as she focused her full attention on his next words.

"And you're here because you're going to impersonate the vice president for the next two weeks."

Maggie's jaw dropped. "The vice president? Of the United States?"

"Of the United States."

"Taylor Grant?"

"Taylor Grant."

Maggie's astonishment exploded into shimmering, leaping excitement. In her varied career with OMEGA, she'd passed herself off as everything from a nun to a call girl. But this would be the first time she'd gone undercover in the topmost echelons of the executive branch.

"Now *this* is my kind of assignment! The vice president of the United States!" She shoved a hand through the thick sweep of her brown hair. "What's the story, Adam?"

"For the last three months, the vice president has been working secretly on an international accord in response to terrorism. According to the president, the parties involved are close, very close, to hammering out the final details of an agreement. One that will send shock waves through the terrorist community. When this treaty is approved, all signatories will respond as one to any hostile act."

"It's about time!"

In the past few years, Maggie had seen firsthand the results of differing government approaches to terrorism. Depending on the personality of the people in high office, the response could be swift or maddeningly slow, strong or fatally indecisive.

"The key players involved in crafting the treaty are gathering at Camp David to hammer out the final details," Adam continued. "No one—I repeat, no one—outside of the president, the VP herself and a few trusted advisors know about this meeting."

Maggie eyed him shrewdly. "So I'm to deflect the world's attention while this secret meeting takes place?"

"Exactly."

She chewed on her lower lip for a moment. "Why me?"

"Why not?" he countered, watching her face.

"Mrs. Grant has at least half a dozen women assigned to her Secret Service detail," Maggie said bluntly. "They know her personal habits and routine intimately. They wouldn't need the coaching I will to double for her."

"True, but none of them matches her height and general physical characteristics as well as you do."

Maggie composed a swift mental image of the attractive young widow. Tall. Auburn-haired. Slightly more slender than Maggie herself. A full mouth that quirked in a distinctive way when she was amused, which was often. Stunning violet eyes that sparkled with a lively intelligence.

Far more important than any physical characteristics, however, were the vice president's personality traits. Taylor Grant was totally self-assured. Gracious, yet tenacious as a pit bull when it came to the political issues she championed. And she carried herself with an easy confidence that Maggie knew she projected, as well. With a flash of insight, she sensed that was the key to this assignment.

She'd earned her code name, Chameleon, because of her ability to dramatically alter her physical appearance when going undercover. But she'd survived in the field because she knew that a successful impersonation came from within, not from without. The trick was to believe you were the person you pretended to be—if you did, you could convince others. This mission would take intense concentration and all of Maggie's skills, but she could do it. She would do it.

"Imagine," she murmured, her brown eyes gleaming. "I'll be presiding over joint sessions of Congress. Just think of the bills I can push through in the next couple of weeks. The bloated bureaucratic budgets I can slash."

"I'm afraid you won't have much opportunity to exercise your political clout," Adam said dryly. "To cover her absence, the vice president has announced that she's taking a long-overdue two-week vacation to her home in the California Sierras."

With real regret, Maggie abandoned her plans to ruthlessly streamline the entire federal government.

"Okay, what's the catch?"

One of Adam's dark brows rose.

"A two-week vacation in the High Sierras is too easy. I've got this tingly little feeling there's more to this role than what you've told me so far."

The ghost of a smile curved Adam's lips. "Your tingles are on target."

"They usually are," she said with a trace of smugness.

His smile faded as he studied her face. "Early this morning, Taylor Grant received a death threat. Your mission while you're undercover will be to discover the source of this threat."

The fact that Mrs. Grant had received a death threat didn't particularly surprise Maggie. A Secret Service contact she'd once worked with had mentioned that the White House switchboard screened upward of fifty thousand calls a day. A battery of skilled operators separated disgruntled voters from dangerous malcontents and forwarded the "sinisters" for investigation. Maggie had been amazed at both the number and the content of the wacko calls that came over the switchboard. One, she'd been told, had ended with a long-drawn-out shriek and the sound of the caller blowing out his brains.

But in addition to outright kooks and psychotics who might target Taylor Grant, Maggie could name at least half dozen ultraright-wing groups the vice president had outraged. An intelligent, outspoken woman with strong liberal leanings, she'd been chosen as the president's running mate to balance his more conservative platform and to guarantee California's huge block of electoral votes. No, Maggie wasn't surprised Mrs. Grant had received a death threat.

Still, the Secret Service was charged with investigating such threats. Once again, Maggie puzzled over the reason for her involvement in this mission. She knew Adam too well to suppose that he'd called her in just because she resembled Taylor Grant in general size and shape.

"So what was different about this threat, that it activated an OMEGA response?" she asked.

"The call came in over the VP's personal line. Whoever made it knew how to bypass the filters that protect her from such calls, and how to electronically synthesize his voice."

"His voice? If it was electronically disguised, how do we know the caller was a he?"

Adam regarded her steadily across the half acre of polished mahogany that constituted his desk. "Because the nature of the call suggests it was made by someone who knows Mrs. Grant well. *Very* well. Well enough to mention her husky little gasp at moments of extreme passion."

"Extreme passion?" Maggie's jaw sagged once more. "Good grief, are you saying the vice president of the United States is being threatened by…by a former lover?"

"So it appears."

While Maggie struggled to absorb this astounding information, Adam rose, a sheet of notepaper in his hand.

"This is a list the VP supplied of the men she's known intimately."

Eyes wide, Maggie glanced down at the list he handed her. To her surprise, she saw that it was very short. *Amazingly* short, for a charismatic, dynamic woman who'd been a widow for over ten years. A woman who kept the press and the public titillated with a string of very handsome and very eligible escorts.

There were only four names on the list:

Harold Grant, the vice president's husband. The California sculptor had died from a rare form of bone cancer more than a decade ago.

Peter Donovan. Maggie couldn't place him, but the notation beside the name indicated that he had managed the VP's first campaign for governor.

Stoney Armstrong. That name she recognized immediately! The handsome, square-jawed movie star had escorted then-Governor Grant one whole, tempestuous spring. Their pictures had been splashed across every tabloid and every glossy magazine on several continents.

And...

Maggie's eyes widened. "James Elliot?" she gasped. "The secretary of the treasury?"

Adam nodded. "Elliot met Mrs. Grant after the president named him to head Treasury. Their liaison was reportedly short, but passionate."

"So that's why OMEGA's running this show instead of the Secret Service!" Maggie exclaimed.

In addition to his responsibilities for the fiscal policies of the United States, the secretary of the treasury also directed the Secret Service. The idea that the supervisor of the very agency charged with protecting the vice president was one of three men suspected of threatening to kill her boggled Maggie's mind.

"Elliot himself suggested OMEGA take the lead in this case," Adam said slowly. "He recognized that his liaison with Mrs. Grant, as brief as it was, compromised him in this case."

"No kidding!"

Her forehead wrinkling, Maggie studied the short list once

again. Four names, three suspects—one of whom was a close personal friend of the president, and a member of his cabinet. Whew!

"There's another name that should be included on the list," Adam added in a neutral tone.

"Really?" she murmured, still absorbing the implications of James Elliot's involvement. "Whose?"

"Mine."

With infinite care, Maggie raised her eyes from the paper in her hand. As she searched Adam's face, a wave of conflicting emotions crashed through her.

Instinctive denial.

Instant awareness of the staggering impact this had on her mission.

And jealousy. Sheer, unadulterated jealousy. The old-fashioned green-eyed kind that was embarrassing to own up to but impossible to deny.

Taylor Grant was just the kind of woman who would attract Adam, Maggie admitted with painful honesty.

Polished. Sophisticated. At ease with politicians and princes. She moved in the same circles Adam did. Circles that Maggie, content with herself and her world, had never aspired to…until recently.

Summoning every ounce of professionalism she possessed, she sent him a cool look. "Well, that certainly puts a new twist on this mission. Suppose you tell me why the vice president didn't include your name on her list."

A glimmer of emotion flickered through his eyes at her tart rejoinder. It might have been amusement or irritation, but it disappeared so quickly, Maggie couldn't tell. With Adam, she rarely could.

"Because I'm her future, not her past, lover," he replied evenly.

For the space of several heartbeats, silence blanketed the spacious office. Maggie fabricated and rejected a dozen possible interpretations of his statement. Only one of them made any sense, and she wouldn't let herself believe that one.

"Come again?" she asked.

Navy cashmere contoured Adam's well-defined shoulders as he crossed his arms. "Until this point, I've enjoyed only a casual friendship with Taylor Grant."

Maggie fought down a ridiculous rush of relief.

"That friendship is about to deepen."

"It is?"

"It is."

She cleared her throat. "Just how deep do you intend to take it?"

"As deep as necessary."

She refused to acknowledge the slow curl of heat his words generated. "I think you'd better give me something more specific."

"For the duration of the time you're undercover, I'll be your sole contact. We'll be together night and day for the next two weeks. As far as the rest of the world is concerned, we're in love. Or at least in lust."

Right. As far as the rest of the world was concerned. Maggie bit down on the inside of her lower lip and forced herself to concentrate as Adam continued.

"We'll debut this new relationship at the VP's last official Washington function before she leaves for California."

"Which is?"

"A special benefit performance at the Kennedy Center tomorrow night."

"Tomorrow night?"

Maggie jumped off the corner of the conference table, her mind racing. She had less than twenty-four hours to transform herself into the person of the vice president of the United States. And into Adam Ridgeway's latest companion/lover.

At that moment, she wasn't sure which role daunted her—or thrilled her—more.

# Chapter 2

The next hours were the most intense Maggie had ever spent preparing for a mission.

A quick call to her father glossed over the reason for extended absence. Although she'd never told Red Sinclair about her work for OMEGA, he knew his daughter too well to believe that her civilian cover as an adjunct professor at D.C.'s Georgetown University occupied all her time.

Grumbling something about making clear to a certain reptile who was in charge during Maggie's absence, Red hung up and went back to the Superbowl.

After that, the OMEGA team moved at the speed of light.

Jake MacKenzie, code name Jaguar, arrived to act as headquarters controller for this operation. Since his marriage last year to a woman he'd rescued from a band of Central American rebels, Jake hadn't spent much time in the field, but he was one of OMEGA's most experienced agents. There wasn't anyone Maggie trusted more to orchestrate the behind-the-scenes support for this mission than the steely-eyed Jaguar.

With Jake beside her, she listened to the chilling tape of the early-morning phone call.

*"You were so good,"* the eerie, electronic voice whispered, *"so beautiful. I can still hear your soft, sweet moan, that little sound you make when…"*

Disgust twisted Maggie's mouth. That someone could speak of love in one breath, and death the next, sickened her.

*"I must kill you. I don't want to, but I must. Try to understand…."*

The call ended with a click, and Taylor Grant's swift, indrawn gasp.

"All right," Jake said, his mouth grim. "Let's go over these dossiers on the three suspects one more time. Intel is champing at the bit to start your political indoctrination."

The dossiers didn't give her any more insight into which of the three prominent men might want to assassinate the vice president, but Maggie studied their backgrounds in minute detail. Then she spent hours in briefings on the political personalities and issues the vice president dealt with daily.

Finally she closeted herself in a small room to study videotapes of Taylor Grant's speech patterns and gestures. Given her background in linguistics, Maggie soon had the vice president's voice down pat. Copying her gestures and facial expressions took a bit more work, but after hours in front of the mirror and a video camera, Maggie passed even Jake's and Adam's critical review.

At that point, the wizards of the wardrobe, as she termed OMEGA's field dress unit, whipped into action. A gel-like adhesive "bone" shaped her chin and nose to match Mrs. Grant's profile. A quick dye job and an expert cut resulted in the well-known stylish auburn shag. Tinted contacts duplicated the vice president's distinctive violet eyes.

Reducing Maggie's more generous figure to the vice president's exact proportions, however, required a bit more ingenuity. After taking some rather intimate measurements and stewing over the matter for a while, the pudgy, frizzy-haired genius who headed Field Dress produced a nineties version of a corset that also, he proclaimed proudly, doubled as protective body armor. The thin Kevlar wraparound vest flattened Maggie's bust and trimmed several inches off her waist. The vice president's well-known preference for pleated pants and long tunic-style jackets would disguise her slightly fuller hips.

"Suck it in, Chameleon," the chief wizard ordered sternly, yanking on the adjustable straps at the waist of the bodysuit-corset.

Maggie clutched at the edge of a table. "Hey! Go easy there," she said over one shoulder. "I've got to be able to breathe for the next few weeks, you know."

"Don't panic," he replied, grunting a little with effort. "This baby should fit more easily in a day or so."

"It should?" she gasped. "Why?"

He backed away, surveying his handiwork. "A couple of days on the VP's diet will shave a few pounds off you."

Maggie straightened and took a few shallow, experimental breaths. "The vice president is on a diet?"

"Uh-oh. You didn't know?"

"Intelligence is going to cover her personal habits as soon as we're through here. What kind of a diet?"

"You'd better let intel brief you," the chief replied evasively. Not meeting her eyes, he held out a cobalt blue St. John knit tunic with a double row of gold buttons.

Maggie poked her head through the square-cut neck of the tunic and eyed the pudgy chief suspiciously.

"What kind of diet?" she repeated. "Come on, spill it."

"She's, uh, a vegetarian."

"You've got to be kidding!"

"It's true, I swear. It's not public knowledge because Mrs. Grant doesn't want to get the beef and poultry lobby groups up in arms."

"Wonderful," Maggie muttered.

While she wouldn't exactly classify herself as a junk food junkie—after all, she did enjoy sampling Washington's wonderful diversity of restaurants—Maggie preferred hamburgers and pizzas to vegetables any day. In fact, she'd recently discovered that she was violently allergic to a distant relative of the carrot family.

"It's only for two weeks," the frizzy-haired wizard reminded her.

"Oh, sure. What's a mere two weeks without real food?"

Sucking in her tummy to ease the bite of the constrictive corset, Maggie headed for the laboratory in the basement of the town house to check out her equipment for this mission.

A spear of regret lanced through her when she surrendered her faithful Smith & Wesson .22 automatic. Although small, when loaded with hollow-point long-rifle stingers, the weapon could cause as much tissue damage as a .38 Police Special. But not even the high-tech masterminds in the Special Devices Lab could figure out how to shield her Smith & Wesson from the sophisticated security screens that surrounded the vice president. In its place, Maggie was issued a palm-size, .22-caliber derringer.

"This is the same model Mrs. Grant keeps in her California home," the chief of Special Devices told her. "It's single-action, with a spur trigger, and carries five rounds."

After a few practice rounds at the firing range, Maggie felt comfortable with the derringer. But she felt decidedly uncomfortable with the fact that she wouldn't have a weapon in her possession until she reached California. For the first time, she was going out on a mission naked. All she had to protect her from a potential assassin was her training, her instincts and her wits.

And Adam.

He joined her at the range a few moments later. The acrid scent of cordite filled the air as Maggie watched him test fire the small, rapid-fire Heckler & Koch 9 mm Special Devices had issued him. Legs spread, arms lifted, he pumped round after round into the targets. His tight expression underscored the grim reality of her mission.

Back in the lab, Special Devices fitted Maggie with the combination directional beeper and body bug they'd hurriedly devised for this mission. To her amazement, she discovered that they'd soldered a state-of-the-art miniaturized radio transmitter/receiver to the inside of a wide gold wedding band.

"It's identical to the one Mrs. Grant wears," the technician explained.

Maggie turned the heavy gold band over and over in the palm of her hand, but couldn't find any trace of the tiny embedded device. She did, however, see the inscription engraved on the inside. Her heart thumped painfully as she read the words *Now, and forever.*

How tragic, she thought. The woman who wore this ring, or one identical to it, hadn't had much of a forever with her husband. Some years older than his attractive young wife, Harold Grant had died while still in his mid-thirties. They'd had only a few good years together, yet his widow had never remarried, and still wore her wedding band.

"Because the bug is so small," the head of Special Devices explained, "its range is more limited than we'd like. You'll be able to communicate only with the chief, who'll relay the necessary information to OMEGA headquarters via his own, more powerful device."

"Which is why we won't be more than a few miles apart during this entire operation," Adam said, coming to stand beside her. He took the ring from her unresisting fingers to examine it himself.

Maggie frowned, not entirely sure she liked this turn of events. She was used to operating independently in the field. Very independently. The idea of passing all her communications through Adam was a little unsettling.

She slanted him a quick speculative look as he hefted the gold band in his palm. She'd worked for and with Adam Ridgeway for three years now. In the process, she'd learned to respect his sharp, incisive knowledge of field operations. Like the other OMEGA operatives, she trusted him with her life every time he sent her into the field.

Still, for all her personal and very private admiration of Adam, Maggie had to admit they sometimes clashed professionally. They'd had more than a few disagreements in the past over her occasionally unorthodox methods in the field. In fact, the only times any of the OMEGA agents had ever seen Adam come close to losing his legendary cool were during Maggie's mission debriefs.

Well, the next few weeks would no doubt provide a severe test of his restraint, she thought. She was the field operative on this mission, and she fully intended to follow her instincts, just as she always had. Her generous mouth curved in a private smile. She'd always hoped to be on the scene when the iron-spined Adam Ridgeway's control finally slipped its leash.

Maybe, just maybe, she would be.

He caught her sideways glance. "Let's see how well this works," he said, holding out his hand.

A funny little quiver darted through her stomach as she placed her left hand in Adam's right. His palm felt warm and smooth beneath her fingertips, like supple, well-tanned leather. Nibbling on her lower lip, she watched him slide the gold band over the knuckle of her ring finger. When it slipped into place, his hand closed over hers.

Startled by both the tensile strength of his hold and the intimacy of the gesture, Maggie glanced up at the face so close to her own. His blue eyes locked with hers.

A voice at her shoulder jerked her attention back to the hovering technicians. "How does it feel?"

Her hand slipped from Adam's hold. "Fine."

Actually, the heavy circle felt odd. Unfamiliar. Maggie rarely wore jewelry, and when she did, it was more the funky, fun kind. This solid ounce of precious metal weighting her hand was a new experience for her. Using her thumb, she twisted the ring around her finger. It fit perfectly. Not too tight, not too loose. Yet when she tried to remove it, the thing balked at her knuckle.

"The inside of the band is curved to slide on easily, but that sucker won't ever come off," the team chief told her with a smug grin.

Her newly dyed dark red brows snapped together. "What?"

"Not without a special lubricant."

"Wait a minute. This special lubricant isn't another one of

your no-fail formulas, is it? Like the solvent that was supposed to instantly remove the tattoo you put on my chin? It took three months for the thing to fade completely.''

The technician waved a hand to dismiss that minor inconvenience. ''The lubricant will work, I'm sure.''

''You're *sure?* You mean you haven't tested it yet?''

''As a matter of fact, we haven't quite developed it yet. But we will by the time this mission is over. Besides, the chief suggested we size the ring like that.''

''Oh, he did?'' She turned to the man at her side, her brows arching.

''So you won't have to worry about losing it,'' Adam said easily. ''And I don't have to worry about losing you.''

After another round with intelligence and a final mission prebrief with Jake and Adam, Maggie pulled on the cobalt blue pea jacket that matched her designer knit outfit and slid into the back seat of a limo. A slow, simmering excitement percolated through her veins during the ride to the target point. She locked her gloved hands in her lap to keep from beating a nervous tattoo on the leather armrest and stared out at a capital still blanketed by a layer of white, now more slush than snow.

They'd decided to make the switch at the vice president's official residence. The old executive office building, where the VP's office and staff were located, swarmed with people all day and far into the night. By contrast, the pillared, three-story residence tucked away on the wooded grounds of the naval observatory in northwest Washington had limited access and much less traffic.

Outside of OMEGA, only three people knew exactly when and how the switch would take place. The vice president, of course. Lillian Roth, Mrs. Grant's personal assistant and dresser. And the SAIC—the special agent in charge of her personal security detail—William ''Buck'' Evans.

Maggie, Adam and Jake had debated strenuously whether or not to read Buck Evans into the script. With the treasury secretary himself under suspicion, they hesitated to include anyone in his chain of command in this deep-cover operation. But Mrs. Grant had insisted, and the president himself had concurred.

Evans had been assigned to the vice president's detail since the early days of the campaign. At one whistle-stop, he'd thrown himself in front of a two-hundred-and-fifty-pound crazy who objected to her stand in favor of government subsidies for AIDS research and treatment. In the ensuing brawl, the protester had chewed off the tip of Buck's ear. The agent had declined cosmetic surgery, claiming that the mangled ear added to his character. From that day on, he'd been permanently assigned to Taylor Grant's detail, and she trusted him with her life.

Besides, the vice president had said tartly, without Buck's assistance, it would be impossible to pull off this masquerade. As SAIC, he screened the agents assigned to her protective detail, approved all security procedures and set the duty schedules. He could ensure that the people accompanying the VP on her long-planned vacation were the ones least familiar with the twists and turns of her personality. He would also provide the real Mrs. Grant with protection during her secret treaty negotiations at Camp David.

So when Maggie's limo drove around to the back of the turreted turn-of-the-century mansion that served as the vice president's official residence, it was Buck Evans who stepped out of the shadows and yanked open the rear door. Digging a hand into her arm, he half helped, half hauled her out of the back seat.

"I've diverted the surveillance cameras. Let's get you upstairs, fast."

He hustled her through a side door, past a darkened room and up a set of narrow stairs. After scanning the wide hallway that ran the length of the second floor, he tugged her after him, toward a door set halfway down the hall.

"Go on inside. I'll reset the cameras, then come back for Mrs. Grant when she calls."

Maggie had barely stepped into a small foyer before the door shut behind her. She stood still for a moment, trying to slow her pounding heart. From her breathless state, she guessed that the total elapsed time from the moment Buck Evans pulled open the limo's door until he shut this one behind her had been less than a minute.

"Harrumph!"

At the sudden sound, Maggie spun to the left and dropped into an instinctive crouch. Her hand reached for her weapon before she remembered she wasn't armed.

"So you're the one!"

A diminutive figure in a severely cut navy blue suit, thick-soled lace-up shoes, and an unruly mass of steel gray curls stood framed in a set of glass-paned French doors. She held herself ramrod straight, her chin tilted at a belligerent angle and her mouth thinned to a tight line as she surveyed the newcomer from the tip of her auburn head to the toes of her black leather boots.

Maggie straightened slowly. From her intelligence briefings, she recognized the other woman instantly. Lillian Roth, the vice president's personal confidante and assistant for almost twenty years. The sixty-three-year-old woman had appeared rather formidable in the few photographs intel had dug up of her. Maggie now discovered that the photos hadn't really captured the full force of Lillian's character. In person, she radiated all the warmth and charm of a Marine Corps drill sergeant on a bad hair day.

"Well, I must say you've achieved a startling resemblance," the dresser said with a small sniff. "But it takes more than mere physical presence to emulate someone of Mrs. Grant's stature."

"I agree completely."

Maggie's cool reply duplicated exactly the vice president's voice and intonation. Lillian's gray brows rose, but she obviously couldn't bring herself to unbend enough to praise what Maggie considered a rather impressive performance.

"I'll take your coat. The vice president is waiting for you in her sitting room."

Having memorized the floor plans of the residence, Maggie walked confidently through the double doors into a tall-ceilinged, airy room. She paused just past the threshold, visually cataloging the fixtures and furniture in her mind. Although an attack on the VP was unlikely in this secure environment, Maggie wasn't about to take any chances. She'd spend only one night here, but she wanted to be able to find her way around these rooms in total darkness if she had to.

The furnishings in the spacious sitting room were a tribute to Taylor Grant's exquisite taste and vibrant personality. A framed print of Monet's famous water lilies of Giverny hung in a lighted alcove between tall curtained windows. Accent pieces scattered throughout the room took their cue from this masterpiece of swirling blues and greens and purples. A magnificent green jade Chinese temple dog, one paw resting imperiously on a round ball, dominated the huge coffee table set between two facing sofas, which were covered in a shimmering blue-and-purple plaid. A collection of crystal candlesticks in varying shapes and sizes decorated the white-painted wood mantel, reflecting the light from the fire in a rainbow of glowing colors.

But it was the woman standing beside the fireplace who drew Maggie's attention. For an eerie moment, she felt as though she were looking at her own reflection through a large invisible mirror.

The vice president wore royal blue pleated slacks and tunic exactly like the one Field Dress had procured for Maggie. Overhead spots highlighted the subtle gold tints in her wine-colored hair, which was styled in the simple, elegant shag the OMEGA agent now sported. Her eyes, deepened to a dusky violet by the bold color of her outfit, stared at Maggie with the same unwavering scrutiny.

For a long moment, neither woman spoke. Then Mrs. Grant's full mouth twisted.

"It's kind of a shock, isn't it? Every woman wants to think she's unique. Special in her own way. Yet here we are, two identical clones."

"Not quite identical," Maggie replied, smiling. "Underneath this very flattering outfit, I'm trussed up like a Christmas turkey."

The vice president's lips quirked in response. Without thinking, Maggie duplicated the small smile.

Mrs. Grant's eyes widened. "Good grief, you *are* real, aren't you?"

"Yes, ma'am."

"Adam said you were good," the vice president murmured, "but I see now that was somewhat of an understatement."

Adam, Maggie noted. Not the special envoy. Not even Adam Ridgeway. Just that casual, familiar *Adam*. A little too familiar, in her opinion.

Taylor Grant gestured toward one of the sofas, then took the other. "You go by the code name Chameleon, don't you?"

Maggie nodded. No one, not even the president, knew the OMEGA operatives' real names or civilian covers. That simple but rigid policy protected the president in the event anything should go wrong on a mission. It protected the agents, as well. With OMEGA maintaining absolute control over such privileged information, they didn't have to worry about the inevitable leaks that plagued the CIA or FBI.

"Well, I can certainly understand how you earned that particular designation," the vice president said. She eyed Maggie for a moment, her expression uncompromising. "You understand that I'm not happy about this charade? At all?"

"So I was told."

"If my presence at these secret treaty negotiations wasn't so necessary, I wouldn't allow you to be used as a decoy like this. I've never backed away from a challenge…or a threat…in my life."

"I know that, Mrs. Grant."

For all her refined appearance and well-known sense of humor, this woman was as tough and as resilient as they came. She'd battled her way up through the political ranks on her own, without a prominent family name or fortune to ease her way. Obviously, she didn't like someone else taking the heat for her. Her deep brown eyes speared Maggie.

"I understand I have approximately twenty minutes to fill you in on the more intimate details of my life."

"Yes, ma'am."

The vice president's jaw tightened. "I'm not used to sharing this kind of information," she said after a moment. "With any-one. Politics doesn't encourage a person to reveal her innermost secrets."

"Whatever you tell me doesn't go beyond this room," Maggie said with quiet assurance.

She and Adam had agreed that this half hour with the vice president would be private, unrecorded. The little bug in her ring wouldn't activate until Mrs. Grant left the compound. Maggie's innate honesty compelled her to add a kicker, however.

"Unless you tell me something that will help identify the man who called you this morning."

An emotion that wasn't quite fear, but was something pretty close to it, rippled across the vice president's face as she glanced at the phone on a table beside the sofa. Maggie could only admire the vice president's courage as she mastered that brief, unguarded emotion and turned away from the telephone with a contemptuous look.

"I don't like being threatened any more than I like revealing the details of my private life."

Realizing that they weren't making much headway, Maggie sat up straight, tucked her hands into her sleeves and assumed a soulful expression.

"I once went underground in a convent. If it helps any, just think of me as a *religiosa*, a sort of female father confessor."

Some of the stiffness went out of Mrs. Grant's slender frame. "Somehow I can't see you as a nun," she drawled.

"It wasn't my favorite assignment," Maggie admitted with a grin, abandoning her postulant's pose. "Those wool habits itch like the dickens."

The vice president chuckled. "I believe you. All right, where do you want me to start?"

"Let's start with Stoney Armstrong, since I'll be meeting him in L.A. tomorrow. You dated for almost six months, didn't you, Mrs. Grant?"

"Taylor."

At Maggie's surprised glance, she smiled. "I can't bring myself to share the most intimate details of my love life with someone who addresses me as 'ma'am' or 'Mrs. Grant.' Please, just call me Taylor.''

No wonder Adam had developed such a close friendship with this woman, Maggie thought. The power of her office hadn't diminished her charm or charismatic personality.

''What do you want to know about Stoney?''

''For starters, what's behind his studio image of a muscle-bound, over-sexed, gorgeous hunk of beefcake?''

''A muscle-bound, oversexed, gorgeous hunk of beefcake,'' Taylor responded dryly.

''So it wasn't his, ah, intellectual prowess that attracted you to him?''

Absently the vice president plucked at the fringe on one of the sofa pillows. ''No, it wasn't. But at that point in my life, I didn't need the challenge of a rousing debate on domestic politics or international affairs. I needed, or thought I needed, Stoney Armstrong.''

She stopped playing with the fringe and glanced across the coffee table at Maggie. Her remarkable eyes filled with the gleam of laughter that had made her the darling of the international press corps.

''Every woman should have a man like Stoney in her life at some point or another, if only to remind her that great sex is highly overrated as the foundation for a permanent relationship.''

''True,'' Maggie replied with an answering laugh. ''But it's certainly not a bad place to start.''

Twenty minutes later, Lillian Roth knocked on the sitting room door, then poked her head inside. She glanced from Maggie to the vice president for a moment in startled confusion.

''Yes, Lillian?'' Maggie asked, testing her skills.

The dresser's birdlike black eyes narrowed. She studied Maggie for long, silent moments, then switched her focus to Taylor. Giving a little sniff, she spoke slowly, as if not quite sure of herself.

"Buck just called on your private line. They're just starting the shift change. You have to go, Mrs. Grant."

Pleased with the fact that she'd managed to fool the dresser, at least for a few seconds, Maggie rose.

The two auburn-haired women faced each other. Mrs. Grant—Taylor—held out her hand.

"Good luck, Chameleon."

"Thanks. I'll need it! I just hope I don't do something stupid and totally ruin your image in the next couple of weeks."

"You won't. Besides, I don't worry about my image when I'm in the Sierras. That cabin is the only place in the world where I go without makeup, don't bother with my hair, and bundle up in layers of flannel and wool. You just have to make it through a couple of brief public appearances, then you're home free."

"Right." Maggie laughed. "One huge benefit at the Kennedy Center tonight, and a dinner for two hundred of your closest friends in L.A. tomorrow."

"Don't worry. Stoney will make sure all the media focuses on him tomorrow. And tonight...well, tonight you'll have Adam at your side."

There it was again, that easy, familiar *Adam.* Maggie's grin slipped a bit.

As Taylor eased into her coat, her amethyst eyes took on a distant, almost dreamy expression. "I've been wanting to invite Adam up to the cabin for some time. If it weren't for these treaty negotiations..."

"Yes?"

The cool note in Maggie's voice drew the vice president's gaze.

"Well," she finished after a moment, "let's just say that Adam's the kind of man any woman would want to have around whenever she was in the mood for a stimulating intellectual debate...or anything else."

At that moment, the foyer door opened and Buck Evans slipped inside. His rusty brown hair, worn a little long on the sides, didn't quite cover his half-chewed ear.

"You ready to go, Mrs. Grant?"

"I'm ready."

He paused with one hand on the knob and gave Maggie a hard look. "Officially, I'm on leave while Mrs. Grant is in California."

"I know."

"I'll be with her every moment at Camp David. Have your people contact me there if you need me."

"Roger."

The Secret Service agent's eyes narrowed. "Just for the record, I think this subterfuge is ridiculous. Every man and woman on this detail has sworn to protect the vice president with their lives."

Maggie didn't answer. The decision to keep the switch secret from everyone but Buck Evans had been made by the president himself. She wasn't about to engage in a debate, public or private, about it. But she saw the total dedication in this man's fierce, protective stance toward Mrs. Grant, and understood the depth of his anger.

"Let's go, Buck," the vice president said quietly. "We've only got an hour before the others begin arriving at Camp David."

With a final nod to Maggie, she followed the agent out the door.

Lillian closed it behind them. Clearly unhappy at being left behind, she scowled at Maggie, then reluctantly assumed her duties.

"Have you had dinner?"

"No, there wasn't time."

Her small mouth pursed into a tight bud. "I'll call down to the kitchens for a tray, then run your bath."

"Fine. In the meantime, I'll look around the suite."

"Humph."

The dresser turned and marched out, her back rigid. Lillian Roth possessed not only the disposition of a drill sergeant, Maggie decided, but the carriage, as well.

* * *

A short time later, a scrubbed and powdered Maggie tightened the belt of a fluffy terry-cloth robe. Wandering into the sitting room, she sat down at a small table pulled up to an armchair. Her stomach rumbled in anticipation as she lifted a domed silver cover.

In some consternation, she stared at the four stalks of an unidentifiable yellow vegetable. They were arranged in solitary splendor on a gold-rimmed plate bearing the vice-presidential seal. Swallowing, Maggie poked at the stalks with the tip of her fork, then cut off an experimental bite.

At the taste, her face scrunched up in a disgusted grimace. Laying down the fork, she pushed the tray to one side. Maybe she could sneak a bag of peanuts or a candy bar at the Kennedy Center during intermission, she thought hopefully.

She soon discovered that the role of vice president of the United States didn't include any intermissions.

# Chapter 3

"Lillian, have a heart! Not so tight!"

As Maggie's protest pierced the well-engineered quiet of his sleek black Porsche, Adam glanced down at the gold watch on his wrist. The faint pattern of her voice had grown stronger and stronger as he neared the naval observatory. Now, less than half a mile away, it came through the receiver built into his watch with startling clarity. As did Lillian Roth's tart reply.

"Suck it in. Mrs. Grant is a perfect size eight, you know."

"Well, I'm not a perfect anything. Loosen the straps a bit."

"Humph."

Adam smiled to himself as he swung the leather-wrapped steering wheel, following the curve of Massachusetts Avenue. He had to agree with Maggie on that one. She was far from perfect.

Of all the agents he directed, Maggie Sinclair, code name Chameleon, was the most independent and the least predictable. There was no denying her fierce dedication to her job. Yet she approached it with a breezy self-confidence and an irrepressible sparkle in her brown eyes that had alternately fascinated and irritated Adam greatly at various times in the past three years. What was more, she possessed her own inimitable style of operating in the field.

His hands clenched on the steering wheel as he remembered a few of the impossible situations Chameleon had extricated herself from. Adam knew he would never forget the way she'd blown her way out of a Soviet nuclear-missile silo with the aid of a terminally klutzy physicist. He'd noticed the first streaks of gray in his hair when Maggie returned from that particular mission.

She hadn't been any more repentant over that incident than any of the others he'd taken her to task for. Although respectful—most of the time—Maggie Sinclair was by turns cheeky, irrepressible and so damned irresistible, that Adam didn't know how he'd managed to keep his hands off her as long as he had.

If he wasn't OMEGA's director… If he didn't have to maintain the distance, the objectivity, necessary to send her into danger…

The thought of touching Maggie, of tasting her, of burying his hands in that sweep of glossy, shoulder-length brown hair and kissing her laughing, generous mouth, sent a spear of hot, heavy desire lancing through Adam.

"Lillian! For Pete's sake!"

Willing himself back under control, Adam pressed the stem on his watch, cutting off Maggie's indignant protest. His jaw tight, he turned off Massachusetts Avenue onto the approach to the U.S. naval observatory.

Sited on what had once been a hilly farm well outside the capital, the sprawling complex still functioned as an active military installation. A battery of scientists manned the round-domed observatory, which tracked celestial movements and produced navigational aids. More experts maintained the master clock of the United States, accurate to within thirty billionths of a second.

In addition to its military mission, however, the complex also served as home to the vice president. Since 1976, the occupant of that office had also occupied the fanciful Victorian mansion built at the turn of the century for the superintendent of the observatory.

The entire facility was guarded by an elite branch of the marine guard, one of whom stepped out of a white-painted guard post at Adam's approach. The granite-jawed gunnery sergeant bent to shine a high-powered beam into the Porsche's interior.

"Evening, sir. May I help you?"

"Good evening, Gunny. I'm Adam Ridgeway. Mrs. Grant is expecting me."

He handed over the pass issued by the vice president's office. The plastic card looked ordinary enough but concealed several lines of scrambled code. After running a handheld scanner over it, the marine squinted through the window to compare Adam's face to the digitized image on the scanner's small screen. He returned the pass, then punched a button on his belt. Heavy iron gates swung open.

"Go on up, Mr. Ridgeway."

"Thanks."

As he drove the tree-lined drive, Adam searched for signs of the highly sophisticated defensive security system that supplemented the military guards. He saw none, but knew that canine patrols roamed the area and electronic eyes swept the grounds continuously, particularly along the approach to the vice president's residence. The mansion itself was wired from attic to subbasement. Even the food, purchased from a list of carefully vetted suppliers, went through chemical and infrared screening before cooking. The security surrounding the woman who stood only a heartbeat away from the Oval Office was almost as heavy as that around the president himself.

For that reason, Adam believed that whoever had called Taylor Grant in the early hours of yesterday morning wouldn't try to make good on his threat here. The attack, when it came, would occur when she was most vulnerable. At a public appearance. Or on the road. Or in that isolated cabin of hers high in the Sierras.

Whenever and wherever it came, Adam intended to be there. Another guard stopped him at the gate in the wrought-iron fence surrounding the residence. After scrutinizing his pass once again, the marine stood back.

Adam drove up a sloping drive toward the Victorian structure, complete with wraparound verandah and a distinctive round tower. White-painted and green-shuttered, the mansion rose majestically above a rolling blanket of snow, a picture postcard of white on white.

Adam pulled up under the pillared drive-through and shifted into park, but left the motor running. Having escorted Taylor to several functions in the past, he knew the drill. A valet would park his car around back, a safe distance from the house in the unlikely event it had been tampered with and now carried explosives. He and the vice president would ride to the Kennedy Center in her armor-plated limousine, preceded and followed by Secret Service vehicles. The agent in charge would sit beside the driver in the limo and remain a only few steps away after they arrived at their destination.

Adam and Maggie wouldn't have a private moment the entire evening. Theoretically.

He pulled his overcoat from the front seat, nodded to the valet and strolled up the wide front steps. A navy steward showed him into a paneled sitting room and offered a choice of drinks while he waited.

"Hello, Adam."

He turned at the low greeting. The heat that spiraled through his stomach had nothing to do with the swallow of Scotch he'd just downed. This was a Maggie he'd never seen before.

In the past three years, she'd gone undercover in everything from a nun's habit to a slinky gold mesh halter that barely covered the tips of her breasts. That particular article of clothing had cost Adam a number of hours of lost sleep. Yet it hadn't carried half as much kick as this elegant, deceptively demure black velvet gown.

On second observation, Adam decided it wasn't the floor-length skirt, slit to the knee, that caused his knuckles to whiten around the heavy crystal tumbler of Scotch. Or the tunic studded with jet beads that shimmered seductively with her every step.

Or the feathery cut of her auburn hair, framing a face that bore an uncanny resemblence to Taylor Grant's.

It was the gleam in her violet-tinted eyes. That sparkling glint of excitement, of shared adventure. And the conspiratorial grin that vanished before the cameras in the downstairs rooms could record it—but not before Adam had felt its impact in every part of his body. Carefully, very carefully, he set the tumbler down.

Stepping forward, he brushed a light kiss across her lips. "Hello, Taylor. You look ravishing tonight."

She stared up at him, startled by the intimate greeting, but then her mouth quirked upward in the vice president's distinctive smile.

"Thank you. You look rather delectable yourself."

Actually, when she recovered from the surprise of that brief kiss, Maggie had to admit that Adam looked more than delectable. He looked delicious. Good enough to eat. Which was, she realized immediately, an unfortunate metaphor. The mere thought of digesting anything, Adam included, made her stomach growl. Loudly. Embarrassingly.

He lifted a dark brow.

"It's getting late," she said, her cheeks warming. "Shall we go?"

As if on cue, the woman designated to serve as agent in charge during Buck Evans's absence stepped into the reception room. Promoted only a week ago from her position as head of the Secret Service's Chicago field office, the sandy-haired Denise Kowalski was brisk, efficient and still very new to vice president's detail. Buck Evans had vouched for her personally.

In keeping with the occasion, she wore a chic red plaid evening jacket that disguised the weapon holstered at the small of her back. Her black satin skirt was full enough to allow her complete ease of movement if she had to throw her body across the vice president's. Which, Maggie sincerely hoped, she wouldn't have to do tonight. Or any other night.

"Your car is at the front entrance, Mrs. Grant."

"Thank you, Denise. We'll be right out."

The agent nodded and went to get the rest of the team into

position. The heavy oak front door swung open behind her, its leaded glass panels refracting the light of the brass lanterns mounted on either side of the porte cochere. Golden light flooded the covered drive, but beyond that, blackness beckoned. Beyond that, a possible assassin waited.

Maggie stared at the open door, pysching herself for her first public appearance as Taylor Grant. She drew in a slow breath, and suddenly the Kevlar body shield didn't seem to bite into her flesh quite as much as it had before.

Moving to her side, Adam lifted the silk-lined black angora cloak she carried over one arm. He held it out, and when she'd wrapped herself in its sybaritic warmth, he rested his hands on her shoulders for a moment.

"I'm glad you invited me to join you tonight," he murmured.

Maggie gave him her best Taylor-made smile. "Me too."

"Ready to go?"

"As ready as I'll ever be."

Maggie had been to the Kennedy Center several times before. In fact, she'd taken her father to a performance of Andrew Lloyd Webber's *Phantom of the Opera* just last week. Red Sinclair had thoroughly enjoyed both the lavish production and the spectacle of jeans-clad students and camera-snapping tourists rubbing elbows with socialites dripping mink and diamonds.

But this was the first time Maggie had driven to a private performance in an armor-plated limousine. Or stepped out of the car into a barrage of TV cameras and bright lights.

Adam turned to help her alight, shielding her with his broad back while the Secret Service agents fanned out to open a corridor through the crowd. The smile he gave her caused a ripple of murmured comment among the onlookers and a shock of sensual pleasure in Maggie. Her fingers curled in his before she reminded herself that they were playing to the audience.

The elegantly dressed crowd parted before them like the Red Sea rolling back for Moses. With Agent Kowalski a few steps ahead, Maggie and Adam made their way toward the grand foyer at the rear of the marble-walled structure.

Since tonight's concert was a special benefit to raise funds for a flood-ravaged province in India, the guests had been invited by that country's ambassador. The Secret Service's Office of Protective Research had run all two thousand names through its computerized list of "lookouts." Reportedly, none of the persons present tonight had triggered a flag that would identify a potential threat to the vice president. Nevertheless, by the time Maggie and Adam reached the short flight of stairs leading down to the red-carpeted grand foyer, her heart was thumping painfully against her body armor.

The ambassador and his wife awaited them beneath the striking seven-foot-high bronze bust of John F. Kennedy that dominated the wide hall. Brilliant light from eighteen massive chandeliers overhead made the colorful decorations pinned to the sash across the ambassador's chest sparkle like precious gems. The same glowing light illuminated the rich green and purple jewel tones of his wife's sari.

The diplomat bowed over Maggie's hand with polished charm. "Madam Vice President. We are most honored that you join us this evening."

"It's my pleasure, Ambassador Awani, Madam Awani. Do you know my escort, Special Envoy Adam Ridgeway?"

The tips of the ambassador's luxuriant mustache lifted in a wide smile. "But of course," he replied, pumping Adam's hand. "I have played both with and against this rogue on the polo field."

"Have you?"

Maggie arched an inquiring eyebrow at Adam, not really surprised that a man who sculled the Potomac in gray Harvard sweats to keep in shape also played a little polo on the side. Maggie herself was more the tag-football-and-long-lazy-walks type.

"Did he not tell you that he scored the winning goal for my team the last time he was in Bombay?"

"No, he didn't."

"It was a lucky shot," Adam said, with a small shrug of his

black-clad shoulders. "I couldn't have done it without Sulim's fantastic pass."

The ambassador preened visibly at the compliment. With the fervor of a true enthusiast, he plunged into a recap of that memorable game. To Maggie's amusement, the ensuing conversation was soon peppered with terms like *chukker* and *grass penalty*. A spirited argument broke out over a controversial call in the last challenge for the Cup of the Americas. Even the ambassador's wife joined in, denouncing the officiating in a soft, melodic voice. Polo was a passion in India, she confided to Maggie in a smiling aside. It had been played in her country for over a thousand years.

As Maggie listened to the lively exchange, a sense of unreality gripped her. She'd been so keyed up for this first appearance as vice president. So intent on maintaining the fierce concentration necessary to stay in character. So determined to dodge any protocol gaffes—not to mention any stray bullets. Yet here she was, chuckling at the increasingly improbable tales of polo games won and lost, as though she moved in these sophisticated circles every day.

She gave most of the credit for her smooth insertion into this glittering world to Adam. This was his world, she thought, slanting him a quick glance. He moved comfortably among ambassadors and artists, Greek shipping magnates and the high-priced gunmen who guarded them. With his cool air of authority and commanding blue eyes, he appeared every bit as regal as any king or prince she could imagine. Although he wore no jewelry except the small gold studs in his white dress shirt and a thin gold watch, he didn't need to advertise either his background or his breeding. It showed in his understated, casual elegance and the ease with which he kept both the ambassador and his wife entertained.

And in the ways he displayed his interest in the woman at his side.

Adam Ridgeway didn't resort to any sort of this-is-my-woman caveman tactics to advertise his budding relationship with the vice president. The signals he sent out were subtle, but unmistakable. There was that small, private smile when Maggie laughingly asked if he'd *really* fallen off his pony in full view of India's prime minister. The glance that lingered on her face a few seconds longer than necessary. The relaxed stance at her side, not quite touching her, yet close enough for her to catch the clean scent of his after-shave with every small movement.

He was playing a role, Maggie reminded herself sternly. The same role he'd been playing when he kissed her earlier. When he'd taken her hand to help her out of the limo.

But then the foyer lights flashed, and Adam's hand moved to the small of her back to guide her toward the opera house. The gesture was at once courteous and possessive. Comforting and strangely disturbing. Maggie felt it right through her layers of Kevlar and velvet. Tiny ripples of awareness undulated through her middle.

Of course, she thought ruefully, those rippling sensations might well be hunger pangs. As their party mounted the wide, red-carpeted stairs to the opera house, she gave a silent prayer that her stomach wouldn't drown out the guest artist's performance.

Once they were inside the opera house, a black-suited usher escorted them up a short ramp to the box tier. Denise Kowalski halted the party just outside the entrance to the presidential box.

"If you'll wait here, please, I'll do a final visual."

Maggie knew that the Secret Service had swept the entire theater for hidden explosive devices earlier this afternoon. According to Denise, they'd done another sweep just prior to the vice president's arrival. Now the senior agent made personal eye contact with each of the other agents stationed around the three-tiered red-and-gold auditorium.

Watching Denise Kowalski in operation, Maggie felt a mounting respect for her cool professionalism. She also tried very hard to ignore the fact that President Lincoln had been assassinated as he sat in a theater box only a few miles from this one.

At Denise's nod, Maggie pasted a smile on her face and stepped into the box.

Heads twisted.

Necks craned.

Murmurs snaked through the opera house.

A seat cushion thumped against a chairback as a lone figure rose. As if in slow motion, he twisted around to face their box.

Adam stepped to her side, and Maggie felt her nails dig into her palms.

Then another man rose, and the woman beside him. Within moments, the entire audience was standing. The orchestra broke into "Ruffles and Flourishes," then played the Indian and American national anthems.

Unclenching her fist, Maggie placed her palm over her heart. She wasn't surprised to feel it drumming wildly against its velvet-covered shield. She'd had some interesting moments in her OMEGA career, but for sheer hair-raising, knee-knocking excitement, that second or so when she and the man in the center section had faced each other ranked right up there with the best—or worst—of them. By the time she sank into the plush red seat, her smile was so stiff, it could have been cut from cardboard.

Immediately, the lights dimmed. The featured artist, a slender, dark-haired flutist of Indian birth and growing international fame, walked out to center stage. Maggie was certain she wouldn't hear a note over the pounding in her ears, yet the haunting woodwind call gradually pierced the drumming in her ears. The music soothed. Soared. Evoked images of the flowing Ganges and the moonlit Taj Mahal. Beat by beat, her heart picked up the flute's rhythm. Her spine slowly relaxed. When the last notes of the first half of the program died away, she joined in the thunderous applause.

During the brief intermission, the ambassador relinquished his place at her side to circulate among his other guests and to allow them access to the vice president. Maggie cast a quick glance at the buffet table, loaded with platters of lobster pastries and succulent slices of smoked ham. Suppressing a sigh, she turned her back on the forbidden feast and forced herself to concentrate on the steady stream of people vying for her attention.

With Adam at her side, she got through the nerve-racking interval relatively unscathed.

She soon discovered that most of the politicians who elbowed their way into her circle were more interested in hearing themselves speak than in anything the VP might say. The only near-disaster occurred when the chairman of the senate fiduciary committee groused that the peso's steep nosedive was going to wreak havoc on international markets.

Maggie nodded in agreement.

"Given today's unrestrained markets, that's a real possibility," Adam interjected smoothly. "Of course, the president's Pan-American Monetary Stabilization Plan, which you helped draft, will help prevent future disasters like that."

Right. The president's Pan-American Monetary Stabilization Plan.

On behalf of Taylor Grant, Maggie smiled and accepted Adam's accolade. The senator immediately launched into a long and incredibly boring explanation of his own strategy to single-handedly save third-world economies. Thankfully, the grand foyer's lights dimmed before he wound down, saving Maggie from having to formulate a reply.

By this time, she was feeling the combined effects of her few sips of champagne and her taut nerves, not to mention the pressure of Lillian's determination to make her a perfect size eight.

"Do I have time to powder my nose?" she murmured to Adam.

His mouth lifted. "You have time to powder anything you want. They won't start the second half of the program until you're seated."

The belated realization that several thousand people would have to wait while she went to the bathroom effectively eliminated Maggie's need. Before she could tell Adam she'd changed her mind, however, he had steered her toward the ladies' room on the second-floor landing.

Denise Kowalski quickly grasped the situation and stepped ahead of them. Signaling to Maggie to wait, she threaded her way through the women standing patiently in line and checked out the facility.

Good grief, it hadn't occurred to Maggie that the vice president of the United States couldn't even tinkle without a security check. She was discovering that this job wasn't quite as glamorous and exciting as it appeared to the rest of the world.

Evidently no assassins lurked in the stalls. Denise returned in less than a minute to escort Maggie to the head of the line. The other women graciously yielded their places, but Maggie, now thoroughly embarrassed by the whole affair, paused with one hand on the stall door.

"This is ridiculous," she commented. "I'll bet there isn't a line like this in the men's room."

The other woman gaped at her for a moment, then broke into laughter.

"Maybe it's time the government took a look at the distribution of public toilets by gender," one of them suggested.

"Maybe it is," Maggie agreed. "I'll put it on the agenda as soon I get back from California."

To a chorus of cheers and applause, she sailed into a stall. One way or another, she'd convince Taylor Grant to follow through on her rash promise to look into public potties.

"What was that all about?" Adam asked when she and the grinning agent in charge emerged a few moments later.

Tucking her hand in his arm, Maggie smiled demurely. "It's a woman thing."


The presence of the driver and the Secret Service agent prevented Maggie discussing the evening's events with Adam during the drive back to the naval observatory. Still wired, and reluctant to see their time together end, Maggie forced herself not to fidget, but her fingers tapped an uneven beat on the leather armrest.

When Adam's hand closed over hers, she wasn't sure whether his intent was to still the nervous movement or to further their supposed relationship. Whatever the reason, she obligingly turned her palm up and entwined her fingers with his.

"Did you enjoy the concert?" he asked conversationally.

"Very much." She gave him a quick grin. "Although I enjoyed hearing about your exploits on the polo field even more. Especially the part where you fell off your horse."

"I hope that tale didn't totally destroy my credibility with you."

"Well," she murmured provocatively, "your romantic image is a bit tarnished around the edges. You'll have to apply some polish to restore it to its former state."

He lifted their entwined hands and brushed his mouth across the back of her hand. "I'll see what I can do."

Ruthlessly ignoring the streaks of fire that shot from her hand to her elbow to her heart, Maggie followed Adam's lead and fell into an easy bantering dialogue for the rest of the ride. All the while, she was blazingly conscious of the warm, strong fingers nesting hers.

A part of her thrilled to his touch.

To her considerable surprise, a small part of her also resented it.

She'd always kept her relationship with her boss strictly professional, which hadn't been difficult at first. Adam Ridgeway could be somewhat daunting when he chose to. If Maggie had been the dauntable kind, she might have wilted like a limp lettuce leaf the first time he turned that icy stare on her. Or rocked back on her heels the first time those chiseled features had relaxed into a genuine smile.

Adam's smile could cause a less sensible, less professional woman than Maggie to weave all kinds of ridiculous fantasies.

Okay, she admitted, so she'd done some weaving. And some fantasizing. So she'd imagined the feel of his hand in hers more and more often lately, and the memory of his after-shave would tease her at the most unexpected moments. In unguarded moments like this, she found herself wondering just when, or if, they'd tear down the barriers that kept them from acknowledging the attraction simmering between them.

Because it wasn't all one-sided. Despite the elegant, sophisticated women Adam escorted to various diplomatic functions, despite the unshakable air of authority he always displayed on the job, Maggie had sensed his growing awareness of her as a woman.

But being aware of her as a woman and doing something about it were two entirely different matters. Maggie had no idea if he'd felt the same leap of excitement she had at the thought of their spending two weeks together. If his pulse hammered from the feel of her hand in his. Or if he was simply playing his assigned role.

As they sped north along Rock Creek Parkway under a pale winter moon, she reminded herself that she, too, was playing a part. Still, she couldn't help wondering just how far they'd take their respective roles when the limo pulled up at the vice-presidential residence.

After her experience in the ladies' room, she was just beginning to realize just how little privacy the vice president enjoyed. Conducting a romance, even a fake one, under the watchful eyes of half a dozen agents and those all-pervasive cameras was going to take a bit more savoir faire than she'd realized.

So when they stepped out of the limo under the sheltering overhang of the porte cochere and Adam suggested a walk in the moonlight to stretch their legs, Maggie readily agreed. Unless she invited him up to the vice president's bedroom, which she couldn't quite bring herself to do, the only place they could talk privately was the open air.

"Are you sure you'll be warm enough?" he asked, lifting the collar of her angora cloak to frame her cheeks.

With her face cradled in his hands and his blue eyes gazing down at her like that, Maggie discovered that warm was *not* a problem.

"I'm fine."

"Good."

He pulled on the black wool overcoat he hadn't bothered with in the limo and tucked her gloved hand in his arm. As he led the way toward the rose garden at the west side of the house, Maggie saw Denise Kowalski nod to another agent who'd stepped out of the chase car. The man bundled his collar up

against his ears and trudged after them, staying far enough behind to remain out of earshot.

Wonderful. Just what she needed, the first time she was alone
with Adam Ridgeway on a star-studded, moonlit night. A chap-
eron.

# Chapter 4

With the Secret Service agent trudging some distance behind them, Maggie and Adam walked side by side through the dappled moonlight. Snow-laden trees shielded them from the distant murmur of traffic still moving along Massachusetts Avenue. Their footsteps echoed softly on the wet pavement, almost lost in the pounding of Maggie's pulse.

She was vividly, stunningly aware of Adam's nearness. Of the way he slowed his long stride to match hers. Of the warmth of his body where he kept her hand tucked against his side.

"You did well tonight," Adam said quietly. "Very well."

Her small laugh puffed out in a cloud of white vapor. "I almost blew it on the Pan-American Monetary Stabilization Plan. Thanks for rescuing me."

"My pleasure, Madam Vice President."

With a confidence that told Maggie he knew his way around, Adam led her to a brick path cutting through a winter white garden. Concentric rings of severely pruned rosebushes poked through the blanket of snow, like ghostly dwarfs standing sentinel around the small arched arbor at the center of the garden.

Despite the bright moonlight streaming through the latticework, Maggie soon discovered that the airy bower provided an illusion of privacy. She ran a gloved finger along a wooden slat, causing a soft shower of white, and tried not to wonder just how many times Adam had escorted Taylor Grant to this same little arbor.

Their Secret Service escort halted at the perimeter of the garden. Hunching his shoulders against the cold, he stomped his feet once or twice and turned slowly to survey the surrounding area. As if to take advantage of their privacy, Adam's shadow merged with Maggie's from behind, and then his arms slid around her waist. He pulled her back against his chest, and she promptly forgot all about their escort.

They were playing a role, Maggie reminded herself once more. This intimate contact with Adam was integral to their mission. Despite her stern reminder, however, she was finding it more and more difficult to separate reality from this enactment of her secret, half-formed fantasies. With a little sigh, she laid her head against his shoulder.

"Did Taylor pass you any information we need to check out?" he asked, his warm breath fanning her ear.

Taylor, Maggie noted. Not the vice president, or even Mrs. Grant.

"She thinks Stoney Armstrong was motivated by something other than a desire to see an old friend when he asked to escort her to the fund-raiser in L.A. tomorrow night. He wasn't particularly pleased when she told him no."

Adam tightened his arms, drawing her closer into his warmth. "What does she think was behind his call?"

"She wasn't sure, but suggested we talk to his agent and his hairstylist."

"His hairstylist?"

Maggie turned in his arms. Mindful of the cameras that swept the grounds continuously, she flattened her palms against the fine wool worsted of his lapels. The steamy vapor of her breath mingled intimately with his as she tilted her head back to look up at him.

"Evidently Stoney's stylist has more input into his career than his agent."

Adam's hand tunneled under the collar of her cape to cradle her neck. "We'll check it out."

His caressing smile made Maggie's heart thump painfully against her bodysuit. When it came to role-playing, she thought, Adam Ridgeway could give Stoney Armstrong a run for his money at the box office.

"Anything else?"

Maggie stared up at the face just inches from her own. The bright moonlight reflecting off the snow cast his lean, aristocratic features into sharp relief. Cameras or no cameras, she felt the impact of his presence to the tips of her toes. Forcing herself to concentrate on her mission, she relayed what the vice president had told her about the other men who'd appeared so briefly in her personal life.

"Mrs. Grant hasn't seen Peter Donovan, her former campaign manager, in over three years. He and his new wife received invitations to the inaugural ball but didn't make it. Donovan had just had surgery, I think."

"An emergency appendectomy," Adam confirmed. "What about the treasury secretary?"

"Mrs. Grant meets frequently with James Elliot. Whenever the president calls a cabinet meeting. Or when Elliot needs to talk to her separately on Treasury business."

The hand cradling her head brought her mouth to within inches of his. Anyone watching would see two people in an intimate embrace, but only Maggie knew just how intimate it was. She'd never realized how well she and Adam would fit together.

"And?" he prompted, his warm breath feathering her cheeks.

She could do this. She could keep her voice calm and her mind focused on the mission with her hips nestled against his and his mouth a whisper from hers.

"She can't believe the secretary is behind this threat. Besides being one of the president's closest friends, he's a good man, according to Mrs. Grant. The crazy weekend they spent together was just that—a moment out of time that neither one expected to happen and neither wants to repeat. James reconciled with his wife shortly after that, and they seem—''

She broke off as his lips traced across her cheek.

''Keep talking,'' he murmured.

Right. Uh-huh. She was supposed to talk while Adam planted explosive little kisses on her face and her heart was jackhammering in her chest.

''You said my romantic image needed polishing, remember?'' he said, angling her face up for a slow, sensual exploration. ''I'll polish while you tell me what else Taylor had to say.''

There it was again. That friendly little *Taylor*.

''That's about it,'' Maggie got out. ''Anything new from your end?''

''Not much. Jake's checking out a classified program Donovan's company, Digicon, is trying to sell the Pentagon. He's heard rumors that the program is a last-ditch effort to keep the company from going under.''

''Mmm?''

Carefully filing away that bit of information for future reference, Maggie focused on more immediate aspects of her mission. Like the heat that burned just under her skin when Adam trailed a soft kiss toward the corner of her mouth. And the cold that was creeping up under the back hem of her cloak.

''Adam?''

He raised his head. ''Yes?''

''Just how much polishing are you planning to do tonight?''

''Quite a bit.''

''Then you'd better do it quickly.'' Her lips curved into a quicksilver grin. ''My front is all toasty from snuggling up to you like this, but my backside is freezing.''

His blue eyes glinted. ''Let's see what we can do to warm you up.''

Maggie had been kissed by a respectable number of men in her thirty-two years. Some had exhibited more enthusiasm than finesse. A few had demonstrated very skilled techniques. More than one had raised her body temperature by a number of degrees. But none had ignited the instantaneous combustion that Adam did.

At the crush of his mouth on hers, heat speared through Maggie's stomach. Tiny white-hot flickers of desire darted along her nerves, setting them on fire. In those first, explosive seconds, she decided that Adam's kiss was all she had dreamed it would be. Hard. Demanding. Consuming.

Then she stopped thinking altogether. Wrapping her arms around his neck, she did some polishing of her own.

When they finally broke contact, Adam's image had been restored to its full glory and Maggie could barely find the strength to drag air into her starved lungs.

His eyes raked her face, their blue depths gleaming with a fierce light that thrilled her for all of the two or three seconds he allowed it to show.

"Warm enough now?"

"Roasting," she answered truthfully.

He started to reply, but at that moment a loud, reverberating thump shattered the stillness of the night.

They sprang apart.

Adam whirled toward the sound, his hand diving under the flap of his overcoat.

Maggie jumped to one side to get an unobstructed view around him. She reached instinctively for her weapon, then grimaced when she remembered she wasn't armed. Muttering a rather un-vice-presidential oath under her breath, she peered across the moonlit rose garden.

Pinned by their combined glares, the Secret Service agent standing guard at the entrance to the rose garden paused, one foot lifted high in the air.

"Er, sorry..."

Shamefaced, he lowered his foot to the ground.

Guilt flooded through Maggie as she straightened. The poor man had obviously been trying to stomp some warmth into his chilled feet. While she and Adam were polishing away, he must have been freezing.

"We'd better go inside," she murmured.

"I'll take you back to the house, but I won't come in. Not tonight."

Try as she might, Maggie couldn't tell whether the reluctance in Adam's voice was real, or part of this charade of theirs. Her reluctance, on the other hand, was very real. "I'll see you at the airport tomorrow, then."

He brushed a thumb across her mouth, which was still tender from his kiss. Although his touch and his posture were those of an attentive lover, his message held a hint of grim reality.

"You'll see me before that, if you need me. We've rigged a communications center in the British embassy, right across the street. It's well within range of the transmitter in your ring. I'll hear every sound, every breath you take throughout the night."

Maggie swallowed as an unforeseen aspect of this tight communications net suddenly occurred to her. Good Lord, what if she snored in her sleep?

If the memory of Adam's searing kiss wasn't enough to keep her tossing and turning, that daunting thought was. Her own romantic image might need serious polishing come morning, if she treated Adam to a chorus of snores and snuffles.

Tucking her hand in his arm, they strolled back toward the house. Just before they stepped into the pool of light cast by the glowing brass lanterns, Adam pulled her to a halt.

"Here, you'd better take this."

Keeping her body between his and the watchful eyes of the Secret Service man, he slipped a small, handkerchief-wrapped package into the pocket of her cloak.

"What is it? Something from Special Devices?"

Maybe they'd come up with some kind of a weapon for her, after all.

"No," Adam replied, escorting her to the front door. "Something from me."

As she watched the taillights of his car disappear down the long, winding driveway, Maggie felt strangely bereft. She folded her right hand over her left, taking comfort from the feel of the heavy band under her glove.

When the last crunch of tires on snowy pavement faded, she said good-night to her foot-stomping watchdog, went inside and climbed the curving staircase to the second floor.

The soft click of the bedroom door brought Lillian Roth awake. Jerking upright in a chintz-covered armchair, the dresser ran a hand through her fuzzy gray hair. Fatigue etched her face before it settled into its habitual severe lines.

"You shouldn't have waited up," Maggie protested, shrugging out of the cape.

Lillian pushed herself to her feet. "I always wait up for Mrs. Grant. Well, how did it go?"

"It went…"

A kaleidoscope of colorful images flashed through Maggie's mind. The Kennedy Center's brilliant red-and-gold opera house. The huge ruby winking in the decoration pinned to the Indian ambassador's sash. A moonlit, winter white garden, and Adam's face hovering inches from hers.

"…very well," she finished softly.

"Humph." Lillian reached for the cape lying across the back of a chair.

"I'll take care of that," Maggie said. Whatever Adam had tucked in her pocket, she wanted to check it out herself. "Why don't you go to bed? I can undress myself."

"Mrs. Grant always—"

"Lillian."

The small woman squared her shoulders. In the quiet of the sitting room, two strong wills collided.

"Perhaps you intend to sleep in that corset you're strapped into?"

Maggie conceded defeat. "No, I don't."

"I'll get your gown and robe."

The expression in Lillian's black eyes as she sailed toward the huge walk-in closet wasn't exactly smug, but it was pretty darn close to it.

By the time she returned with a lemony silk nightdress and robe, Maggie had stashed Adam's package under her pillow and loosened as many of the back buttons on the velvet tunic as she could reach. Turning, she waited while Lillian undid the rest. When the Velcro fastening on the bodysuit gave way, she heaved a sigh of relief.

Only later, when the big house had settled down to an uneven, creaking slumber and Maggie was finally alone, did she pull the package from its hiding place under the pillow. With infinite care, she unwrapped the folds of Adam's crisp, starched handkerchief.

Two bags of cashews and a souvenir box of Godiva chocolates stamped with the seal of the Indian embassy tumbled onto the sheet.

Maggie gave a gasp of delight. Lifting her hand, she murmured into the ring, "Thunder, this is Chameleon. Do you read me?"

"Loud and clear."

"You doll! Thanks for the emergency rations. I owe you one."

After a pause so slight Maggie thought she might have imagined it, his reply drifted through the stillness. "I'll let you know when I'm ready to collect."


"Time to get up."

Maggie opened one eye. She peered at Lillian, then squinted past her at the curtained windows.

"It's still dark out," she protested, pulling the covers up around her ears.

"Mrs. Grant always runs early."

"This early?"

"This early," Lillian confirmed unsympathetically.

Intel had briefed Maggie about the vice president's morning jog, of course, but they'd left out one or two key points. Like the fact that it was apparently accomplished in cold, dank darkness.

"I've laid out some running clothes in the bathroom. Breakfast will be ready by the time you get back."

Breakfast!

The thought of food gave Maggie the impetus she needed to crawl out of her warm cocoon. Frigid air washed over her body, raising goose bumps on every patch of exposed skin. She shivered as the silk of her nightdress cooled and new bumps rose. Although she'd much admired this frothy confection of pale yellow silk and gossamer lace last night, Maggie now heartily wished the vice president's tastes ran to warm flannel pajamas. Pulling on the matching lemon robe, she glanced at the small gold carriage clock on the bedside table.

Five-twenty—a.m.

If she'd slept a full hour last night, she'd be surprised. The knot of tension caused by concentrating so fiercely on her role had taken forever to seep out of Maggie's system. The tension generated by a certain dark-haired special envoy had refused to seep, however. Instead, her inner agitation had coiled tighter and tighter every time she felt the weight of the ring on her finger. It was as though Adam were with her in the darkness. Which he was.

With every restless toss, she remembered the touch of his mouth on hers. Every turn brought back the scent of his expensive after-shave. And every time her stomach grumbled about its less-than-satisfied state, she snuck another chocolate from the foil-covered box.

As she hurried to the bathroom, Maggie smiled at the memory of those luscious vanilla creams and melt-in-your-mouth caramels. Somehow, that little box of candies symbolized more than anything else the subtle shift that had occurred last night in her relationship with Adam Ridgeway.

Over the past three years, they'd shared some desperate hours and days and weeks. They'd grown close, as only members of a small, tightly knit organization can. But until last night, they hadn't allowed themselves to step through the invisible wall that separated OMEGA's cool, authoritative director from his operatives. Maggie had always maintained her independence, and Adam had always kept his distance.

Right now, that wall didn't seem quite as high. Or as impenetrable. And after last night, the distance between them had shortened considerably. Twisting the gold ring around on her finger, she smiled and turned on the taps full blast.

She returned to the bedroom a short while later dressed in blue metallic spandex thermal leggings, a matching long-sleeved top, and comfortable Reeboks. Lillian eyed her critically, then held up an oversize gold-and-blue UCLA sweatshirt.

"I found this in the closet. It should be long enough to disguise your hips."

"Thanks," Maggie said dryly.

"Remember, Mrs. Grant usually does ten minutes of warm-up exercises before her run. Leg bends, calf stretches and twists. Then it's twice around Observatory Circle and back through the grounds."

As she tugged the sweatshirt over her head, Maggie did a rapid mental calculation of the circumference of the seventy-three acres that comprised the observatory grounds. She multiplied that by two, translated the distance into miles, and bit back a groan at the result.

Six miles. At least. Good grief!

Of necessity, OMEGA agents kept in top physical shape, but they had all developed their own individualized conditioning programs. Given a choice, Maggie would have far preferred her own regime of high-impact aerobics in a nice warm spa to slogging six miles in the icy, predawn air.

"By the way," Lillian let drop as she headed for the door, "the agent who usually jogs with Mrs. Grant won the Boston Marathon a couple of years ago."

This time Maggie didn't even try to hold back her groan.

Lillian's mouth softened into something suspiciously close to a smile.

"But that particular individual is in L.A.," she continued, "working the advance for her—for your trip. The other agents drew straws to see who has to run with you this morning. The loser's waiting downstairs. He's a few pounds overweight, and very slow."

Giving silent thanks for small blessings, Maggie made her way down the curving staircase. Okay, she told herself, it was only six miles. She could do this. She could run six miles in the service of her country.

Four and a half miles later, she was seriously questioning both her sanity and her dedication to her country.

Frigid air lanced into her lungs with every labored breath. Her heart slammed painfully against her ribs. Her legs felt like over-cooked spaghetti and threatened to collapse with every step.

The slap of her sneakers against the wet pavement grew more and more erratic as Maggie struggled to pump her way up yet another damned incline. The rolling hills that had appeared so picturesque when she drove through the naval observatory complex yesterday afternoon now loomed in front of her like mountain peaks. Her only consolation was that the poor agent chugging along behind her couldn't hear the sound of her labored breath over his own heaving gasps.

At least the gloomy darkness had given way to a drizzly dawn. Headlights sliced through a soupy gray mist as military and civilian workers arrived for work at the various scientific facilities scattered around the extensive grounds. The civilians gave a cheerful wave, obviously used to seeing the vice president on her early-morning run. The military snapped to attention and saluted. Hoping her grimace would pass for a smile, Maggie returned their greetings.

When the two-story building that housed the nautical almanac office loomed out of the mist, Maggie sagged with relief. Thank God. Only a half circuit of the perimeter to go! Dragging in another lungful of cold air, she concentrated fiercely on placing one foot in front of the other once. Twice. Three times. Counting seemed to help, she discovered.

Sixty-two steps took her across the broad expanse of parking lot beside the almanac office.

Another thirty-seven brought her to the path that paralleled Massachusetts Avenue.

Five more paces, and she was shielded from the wind by the tall pines, thick on her right, thinner on her left, where the path edged almost to the wrought-iron fence. Her lungs on fire, her calves cramping, Maggie following the curving asphalt trail.

At one hundred and three steps past the west gate, the distinctive conical turret of the vice president's mansion poked into view above the tops of the snow-laden pines. She almost sobbed in relief.

At exactly one hundred and twenty-six paces, the shot rang out.

With a startled "Umph," Maggie hit the ground.

# Chapter 5

In a small room on the fourth floor of the British embassy, less than a half block away, Adam froze.

He tore his gaze from the bank of flickering monitors and stared down at the face of his watch, as if expecting an instant replay of the single sharp report—and of Maggie's surprised grunt. Then he exploded into action.

Racing for the door, he snarled an order at the stunned communications technician. "Call Jaguar! Tell him Chameleon's down."

He ripped open the door and raced into the deserted hallway, cursing himself every step of the way. How could he have underestimated the threat? How could he have been so damned cold, so analytical, about the security on the grounds of the naval observatory? He shouldn't have trusted that abstract analysis. Not with Maggie.

His heart battering against his ribs, he crashed through the door to the stairs. The stairwell was empty, as Adam had known it would be. He'd pulled a few strings for this mission. Without a single question, the British ambassador had cleared the entire fourth floor of the embassy for OMEGA's use. It had proven an ideal site for an observation post. Only the broad expanse of Massachusetts Avenue, a screen of pines and a rolling lawn separated it from the vice-presidential mansion and the surrounding grounds.

Even more to the point, the embassy was close enough for OMEGA to tap into the Secret Service's own surveillance system. Adam had tracked Maggie from the moment she emerged from her bedroom this morning. Infrared cameras so sensitive that they picked up even the trickle of sweat rolling down her cheek had recorded her jog through the predawn gloom. With the aid of the concealed transmitter in her ring, Adam had heard her every gasp—and every increasingly acerbic comment she muttered under her breath as she jogged up yet another hill.

As he barreled down the stairs, Adam replayed over and over in his mind those moments when she'd entered the home stretch. There, in those few yards where the pines branched over the path and obscured the camera's angle, she'd disappeared from view for a few seconds. Christ! A few seconds, and he—

"Get…off…me! Puh-leez!"

Maggie's voice jerked Adam to a halt. His chest heaving, he stared down at his watch.

"Are you…all right?"

He didn't recognize the panting male voice, but guessed immediately it was the agent who'd trailed Maggie during her run.

"I'm…fine."

"Are…you…sure, ma'am?"

She sucked in a rasping breath. "I'm sure."

"But you…went down!" The man was still huffing. "That bus, when it backfired…I thought it was a shot. And you went down."

"I thought…it was a shot, too. That's why I went down." Chagrin, and the faintest trace of rueful laughter, crept into her voice. "I guess I'm a little jumpy this morning."

Alone in the empty stairwell, Adam closed his eyes. His throat was so damn tight he couldn't breathe, cold sweat was running down his back, and Maggie was laughing. Laughing! With great physical effort, Adam unclenched his jaw and headed back to the control room.

Joe Samuels, OMEGA's senior communications technician, stood with one big hand fisted around a radio mike.

"She okay?"

"She's okay. It wasn't a gunshot. A bus backfired."

The grim expression on Joe's face eased, and his brown eyes lost their fierce glitter. "A bus!"

"A bus."

The black man shook his head as tension drained visibly from his big body. "Well, with Chameleon, you never know."

"No, you don't," Adam replied, an edge to his voice that he couldn't quite suppress.

Joe's brows lifted in surprise at the director's acid tone, but he refrained from commenting.

"Get Jaguar on the net, would you? I'll give him a quick update before I go upstairs to the heliport."

Nodding, Joe reseated himself at the communications console. An acknowledged expert in satellite transmissions, he'd been actively recruited by half a dozen major corporations when he left military service a few years ago. He could have named his own salary, strolled into work wearing tailored suits and vests and jetted across continents in sleek corporate aircraft. Instead, he'd joined the OMEGA team at about the same time Maggie had.

Adam was well aware of the bond between them. During long, tense days and nights in the control center, the technician worked his electronic magic to keep her plugged into whichever field agent she was controlling at the time. When Chameleon was in the field, Joe always arranged the duty schedules so that he manned the control center himself.

Adam suspected that their friendship might have been tested a bit lately, however. To Joe's disgust, his twins had developed a passion for Maggie's repulsive house pet. The boys begged to keep the reptile whenever she left town. They delighted in Terence's unique repertoire of tricks, particularly his ability to take out a fly halfway across a room with his yard-long tongue. Joe had been visibly relieved when Maggie informed him she'd drafted her father for iguana duty this time.

While he waited for Jaguar to come on-line, Adam forced himself to relax his rigid muscles. Gradually the tension gripping his gut eased. In its place came a different and even more unsettling sensation.

For the first time in a long, long time, he'd reacted without thinking. Sheer animal instinct had sent him crashing out into the hallway. The last time he reacted like that had been in a dark alley outside a Hong Kong hotel. Eight years ago. Just before the night had erupted in a blinding explosion, and he'd dived for cover.

When he'd heard Maggie's surpised cry a few moments ago, Adam had felt the same as he had when the world blew up all around him.

With a wry grimace, he acknowledged that her cry had irrevocably, irretrievably shattered the detachment he'd forced himself to maintain all these years as OMEGA's director. The distance he'd kept between himself and Maggie Sinclair had narrowed to a single heartbeat. To the sound of a bus backfiring.

Adam refused to deny the truth any longer. He wanted her. With a need so fierce, so raw, it consumed him.

Thirty minutes, he thought, dragging in a slow breath. Thirty minutes until he met her at Andrews Air Force Base for the flight to California. Thirty minutes, and Adam wouldn't have to watch her from a half block away over these damned monitors. When they met at the airport, he promised himself, the ''relationship'' between the vice president of the United States and the president's special envoy would enter a new and very intimate stage.


''Thirty minutes!''

Sweat-drenched, her lungs on fire and her legs wobbling like overstretched rubber bands, Maggie stared at Lillian in disbelief.

''I thought our plane wasn't scheduled to leave until nine!''

''The White House command post called a few moments ago. There's another snowstorm moving in. The pilot would like to get off before the front hits, if you can make it. I told them you could.''

The dresser jerked her mop of frizzy gray curls toward the bathroom. ''You have seven minutes to shower and do your makeup. Your breakfast tray and travel clothes will be waiting for you when you get out. We leave the house at exactly oh-seven-twenty.''

''Were you ever in the Marines, by any chance?'' Maggie tossed over her shoulder as she forced her vociferously protesting legs to carry her toward the bathroom.

Lillian snorted. ''Before I came to work for Mrs. Grant, I ran a preschool. I'd like to see any platoon of Marines handle that. You'd better get it in gear.''

Maggie got it in gear.

She sagged against the shower tiles for two precious minutes, letting the steaming-hot water soak into her aching muscles, then soaped and shampooed with record-breaking speed. Thankfully, the vice president's short, stylish shag took all of ninety seconds to blow-dry. A slather of concealing foundation, a quick application of mascara and mauve eye shadow, a slash of lipstick, and she was out of the bathroom.

The sight of the VP's breakfast tray, with its single granola bar on a gold-rimmed china plate and its crystal goblet filled with a greenish liquid, stopped Maggie in her tracks.

''What's in that glass?'' she asked suspiciously.

''Guava juice,'' Lillian replied, bustling forward with a creamy wool pantsuit over one arm.

''*Guava* juice?'' Maggie groaned. ''Why couldn't your boss be a grease-loving biscuits-and-gravy Texan instead of a California health nut?''

Her mouth pursing, the older woman laid the pantsuit on the bed. She lifted the Kevlar bodysuit and dangled it in one hand.

''Maybe if you drank more guava juice and ate fewer biscuits,'' she said, with patently false sweetness, ''you wouldn't need this.''

Grinning, Maggie acknowledged the hit. That would teach her

to criticize Mrs. Grant to Lillian Roth! Intelligence hadn't understated the bond of affection between the two women.

"Drink your juice," Lillian instructed. "We have exactly fifteen minutes to get you suited up and out of here."

Fourteen minutes later, Maggie and Lillian descended the curving central staircase. After a hurried last-minute update by a staffer on the short speech she was to give tonight in L.A., she said goodbye to the various members of the staff who drifted out to wish the vice president an enjoyable vacation.

A car waited under the portico to take her and her small party to the naval observatory helipad. Gray, drizzly mist closed around the vehicle, almost obscuring the grounds, as they drove the short distance. Like an impatient mosquito, a navy-and-white-painted helicopter squatted on its circular pad, its rotor blades whirring.

Maggie, Lillian and Denise Kowalski, who would accompany the vice president to California, had no sooner strapped themselves in than the chopper lifted off, banked sharply and headed east. Maggie had flown out of Andrews Air Force Base in Maryland, just across the Potomac from Washington, many times. She settled back against the padded seat to enjoy the short flight and grab the first few moments of relative calm since Lillian had rousted her out of bed two hours ago.

"Have you seen this morning's *Post?*" the sandy-haired agent asked, raising her voice to be heard over the thump of the rotor blades.

"No."

Denise held out a folded section of Washington's leading newspaper. "They did a whole center spread on your appearance at last night's benefit."

"Really?"

Just in time, Maggie bit back the observation that she'd never thought of herself as centerfold material.

"The special envoy looks rather distinguished in black and white, doesn't he?" the agent commented mildly.

He looked more than distinguished, Maggie thought. He

looked devastating. Her stomach gave a little lurch when she saw the enlarged close-up shot of her and Adam. Or rather Taylor Grant and Adam. The photographer had caught them just as she emerged from the limo. Adam was holding his out his hand to help her out. Her face was in profile, but his was captured in precise detail. If Maggie hadn't remembered just in time that he was playing a role, the expression in his eyes as he looked down at her, or at Taylor—whoever!—would have caused a total melt-down of her synthetic corset. She stared at the picture, mesmerized, for several long minutes before studying the accompanying article.

The reporter covering the glittering gala had evidently found the VP and her escort far more titillating than the event itself. The story included several more shots of Maggie/Taylor and Adam, as well as a gossipy little side note about the fact that the wealthy, sophisticated special envoy was accompanying the vice president to her private retreat for two weeks. Judging by the way his eyes devoured the lovely Mrs. Grant, the reporter oozed, it should be a most enjoyable vacation for all parties involved.

Maggie might have agreed with her, but for the fact that some-time during this supposed vacation she hoped to lure a killer into the open.

She spent the rest of the short trip leafing through the thick *Post*, although she couldn't help sneaking repeated glances at the folded section in her lap. As she studied the shot of them getting out of the limo, the curious niggle of resentment she'd felt when Adam first took her hand last night returned.

Her lips twisted as she identified the feeling for what it was. Jealousy. Weirdly enough, she was jealous of herself.

She'd wanted Adam to look at *her* like that, to touch *her*, for so long. Almost as much as she'd wanted to touch him. But he'd held himself back, just as she had. Neither of them had been ready to acknowledge the attraction that sizzled between them, as electric and charged as a sultry summer night just before a storm. Neither had wanted to upset the delicate balance between their professional responsibilities and their personal needs.

Now they hovered in some kind of in-between state. That shattering kiss in the snow-swept garden, not to mention those sinful chocolates, had destroyed that balance forever. When this mission was over, when they stopped playing these assigned roles, they'd have to find a new level, a new balance. What that balance would be, she had no idea, but for the first time since joining OMEGA she was more excited about concluding an operation than about conducting it.

Adam's helicopter landed at Andrews Air Force Base a few moments before the vice president's.

Home to the fleet of presidential aircraft and the crews who flew and maintained them, Andrews was well equipped to handle the entourages that normally traveled with their distinguished passengers. Although the various craft used by the chief executive and his deputy were always parked in a secure area a safe distance from the rest of the flight-line activity, a well-appointed VIP lounge was only a short drive away.

Yanking open the helo's door, a blue-suited crew chief gestured toward a waiting sedan. "There's hot coffee in the lounge, sir, if you'd like to wait there. The driver will take you over."

Ducking under the whirring rotor blades, Adam shook his head. "I'm fine. I'll wait by the plane." Turning up the collar of his tan camel-hair overcoat, he walked to the Gulfstream jet warming up on the parking apron.

When discharging the duties of her office, the vice president usually traveled aboard Air Force Two, a huge, specially equipped 747 crammed with communications gear and fitted with several compartments for the media and assorted staff members who traveled with their boss. For this trip—a combination of party business and personal pleasure that didn't require her normal entourage—she'd fly aboard a smaller, more economical plane.

Cold wind whipped Adam's hair as he waited beside the sleek white-painted Gulfstream. Around him, crew members performed a last-minute visual check of the aircraft while a portable power cart slowly revved up the twin Rolls-Royce turbofan engines. Having flown jet fighters during his long-ago stint in the navy, Adam had maintained his flight proficiency over the years. At any other time, he would have observed the takeoff preparations with a keen eye, and his hands would have itched to take the stick. Today, the fists he'd shoved into the pockets of his overcoat remained tightly clenched.

During the short flight to Andrews, reality had set in. The raw male need that had surged through him when he finally admitted that he wanted Maggie had given way to an even fiercer need. The need to protect her.

She was at risk, as she'd never been before. Like a sacrificial goat staked out at the end of a tether, she was offering herself as a target for an assassin. Adam couldn't believe he'd allowed himself to consider, even for a moment, unleashing his desire. He couldn't allow himself or her to be distracted from their deadly mission during the days ahead.

But when this mission was over...

By the time he heard the distant *whump* of rotor blades, he had himself well in control again. Narrowing his eyes against the drizzle, he searched the dense gray haze. A few seconds later, a blue-and-white chopper broke through the mist and hovered above the runway. It drifted down until its skids touched lightly. Then the copilot jumped out to open the passenger-compartment door.

Maggie climbed out first. She smiled her thanks at the helmeted copilot and darted out from under the turning rotor blades. The downwash from the blades ruffled her auburn hair and whirled the skirts of her cream-colored wool coat around her calves.

Although Adam was expecting it, her likeness to Taylor Grant still generated a small shock. The resemblance didn't have anything to do with the wine-colored hair or the jawline that Field Dress had molded so exactly, he decided as he watched her cross the wet tarmac. It was a matter of style. An inner vitality. A shimmering essence that the two women had in common.

But the mischievous gleam that filled Maggie's eyes as she returned the greetings of the crew members who snapped to attention was hers alone. She knew very well that her less-than-precise rendition of a military salute would make Adam grimace inwardly. Which it did. After this mission, he promised himself, he'd teach her just how to bend that elbow. Among other things.

"Good morning."

Taylor's voice carried over the whine of the Gulfstream's engines and the whir of the helo's blades. This was Chameleon at her finest, Adam thought in silent admiration. No one in OMEGA could come close to matching Maggie's skill at pulling a deep-cover identity around her like an invisible cloak.

"Good morning," he replied, taking her outstretched hands in both of his.

In the periphery of his vision, he saw the news team from the White House pool who'd braved the cold to cover the VP's departure recording their greeting.

So did Maggie. Suddenly ridiculously self-conscious, she smiled up at Adam. She felt like a teenager about to go out on a closely chaperoned date, for Pete's sake!

"Are you sure you want to exchange two weeks of Washington's cold, snowy weather for California's cold, snowy weather?" she asked, tilting her head in a coquettish gesture while the cameras whirred.

"I'm sure. Come on, let's get you aboard before your…nose freezes."

She bit back a grin as he passed her hand to the steward who was waiting to help her aboard.

Shrugging out of her wool coat, Maggie handed it to the hovering attendant. She could get used to this pampering, she thought, if not to the idea of being constantly under surveillance. The interior of the plane was like none she'd ever seen before, all gleaming oak, polished brass and plush blue upholstery.

She had no trouble identifying her seat. A slipcover embroidered with the vice president's seal draped a huge armchair, one of two in a private forward compartment. While she strapped herself in, Adam took the seat opposite her. She shifted her feet under the smooth oak table to make room for his long legs.

Lillian and Denise settled themselves in the rear compartment, along with several other Secret Service agents, who'd coordinated the final details of the L.A. visit. Even before the hatch had closed, Denise had bent over an outspread map and begun a review of the security along the route from the airport to the hotel.

Within moments, the pilot's voice came over the intercom, welcoming them aboard and detailing the flight times and refueling stop. After a smooth, swift roll down the runway, they were airborne. Immediately dense, impenetrable mist surrounded the plane and cut off any view of the capital. The aircraft climbed steeply, and eventually leveled out at twenty thousand feet.

"Would you care for juice, Mrs. Grant?"

Maggie repressed a shudder at the sight of the grayish liquid filling the decanter on the steward's tray. It wasn't guava juice, obviously, and that had been bad enough.

"No, thank you. I'm fine."

"And you, sir?"

"Coffee, please. Black."

Maggie's mouth watered as the aroma of fresh-brewed coffee filled the compartment.

"Mrs. Grant doesn't care for them, sir, but I have an assortment of rolls and Danish for the other passengers. Or I can prepare eggs and bacon in the galley, if you'd like."

Carefully avoiding Maggie's eyes, Adam shook his head. "No, in deference to Mrs. Grant, I'll skip the bacon and eggs. Just bring me a Danish."

Maggie kicked him under the table.

"And some rolls."

"Very good, sir."

As soon as the door closed behind the steward, Maggie fiddled with the intercom switch on the communications console beside her seat. The low hum of voices from the cockpit was cut off.

"Can we talk?" she asked, couching her question in a playful tone, in case the cabin contained listening systems she wasn't aware of.

"We can," he replied, relaxing. "Joe went over the communications wiring diagram of the plane last night, and our people did a sweep this morning. This cabin is secure.''

Maggie sagged back against her seat. "Thank God. I never realized how nerve-racking it is to live in an electronic fishbowl every day of your life." She eyed the steaming mug in front of him. "Are you going to drink that coffee?"

"No, you are. Go ahead. I'll listen for the steward."

Cradling the cup in both hands, she inhaled the fragrant aroma before taking a hearty gulp. Her eyes closed in sheer delight as she savored the hot, rich brew.

"Ahh…"

"Better than guava juice?"

She opened one eye to find Adam watching her. "You heard that, did you?"

"I did."

Maggie refused to ask what else he'd heard. Sometime during her restless night, she'd decided that if she snored, she didn't want to know about it.

His voice took on an edge. "I also heard the bus backfire this morning."

She took another sip of coffee. "Talk about your basic motivational techniques! I wasn't sure I could get up that last hill, but after a near-miss by a killer bus, I didn't have any difficulty making it to cover."

"I'm glad you find the incident so amusing."

The acid in his words surprised her. "Didn't you?"

"Not particularly. It just demonstrated how vulnerable you are. How vulnerable the vice president is."

Maggie set the mug down carefully. "So do we have anything more on our list of potential assassins?"

"Nothing on the treasury secretary. Other than his one brief fling with Mrs. Grant during a rocky period in his marriage, Elliot's squeaky-clean. Before being confirmed by the Senate, he went through a background screening that revealed everything from his personal finances to his taste in food."

"Let's not talk about food! What about his finances?"

"He built a personal fortune speculating on the market, but over the years converted his riskier ventures to T-bonds."

She frowned. "T-bonds? Isn't it a conflict of interest for him to hold treasury bonds in his current position?"

"It would be, if he hadn't placed them in a blind trust, administered by his lawyers and the board of directors of First Bank."

"First Bank?" Something nagged at the back of Maggie's mind, but she couldn't quite place it. "Isn't that the one headquartered in Miami?"

"With branches all through Central and South America."

She frowned, searching her memory. "I've heard something about First Bank recently."

Adam waited for her to continue. When she didn't, a smile tugged at his mouth. "First Bank helped draft the president's Pan-American Monetary Stabilization Plan."

"Oh. Right."

She was going to have to read up on that darn plan, Maggie thought. Stretching out her legs, she leaned back in the buttery-soft leather armchair. Her feet bumped Adam's under the oak table, then found a nest between them.

"Well, so much for James Elliot. What about the others?"

"Jaguar's digging into the contract Digicon, Donovan's firm, is pressing on the Pentagon. He should have something today."

"That leaves the gorgeous hunk of muscle-bound beefcake," she murmured, then caught Adam's cool look. "According to Mrs. Grant. And just about every female over the age of thirty," she added under her breath.

"Evidently Stoney Armstrong's public doesn't consider him quite as gorgeous as it used to. His last five movies were box-office bombs. The word is that he's washed-up in the industry. The exact phrasing, I believe, was that his sex appeal has gone south."

"Did we get that from his agent?"

"His agent's en route to Poland to consult with an international starlet he's just taken on as a client." Adam paused, his eyes gleaming. "This information came from Armstrong's hair-stylist."

"Someone got to him already? That was quick work."

"It took a near act of God, but Doc managed a late-evening appointment with the man."

Maggie choked back a laugh. "Doc? Our Doc had his hair styled?"

Dr. David Jensen was one of OMEGA's most skilled agents. In his civilian cover, he headed the engineering department of a major L.A. defense firm. Brilliant, analytical and cool under fire, he was also as conservative as they came. Maggie would give anything to see him with his short brown locks dressed by an avant-garde Hollywood hair designer.

"The things we do in service to our country," she commented, shaking her head.

"In this case, Doc's sacrifice paid off. Armstrong's stylist also let drop that the star attributes the downward spiral in his career to the fact that Taylor dumped him. As long as he was in her orbit, they shared the limelight. When she moved on, the spot-light followed her, and left him standing in the shadows."

A knock on the door heralded the arrival of the steward with more coffee and a basket of sweet rolls.

Maggie eyed the basket greedily and could barely wait for the steward to pour Adam's coffee and leave. This bundle of yum-mies would have to hold her until the banquet this evening. She needed all the calories she could ingest to maintain the intense concentration necessary for her various roles as vice president, former lover of an over-the-hill sex symbol, and present com-panion to the special envoy.

When Stoney Armstrong stepped out of the crowd gathered in the hotel lobby to greet the vice president a few hours later, Maggie realized immediately that Doc had received some faulty information. Whatever else had gone south, it wasn't the star's sex appeal.

Tanned, tawny-haired, and in possession of an incredible assortment of bulging muscles under a red knit shirt that stretched across massive shoulders, he grinned at Maggie.

"Hiya, Taylor—uh, Madam Vice President."

Since he carried no weapon in his hands and there was no way he could conceal anything under his body-hugging knit shirt, she responded with a cautious smile.

"Hello, Stoney."

At which point he sidestepped the ever-present Denise, brushed past Adam and swept an astonished Maggie into a back-bending, bone-crushing embrace.

A barrage of flashes exploded throughout the lobby. Dimly Maggie heard waves of astonished titters sweep through the crowd. Cameras whirred, and news crews climbed over each other for a better shot.

When he set her upright some moments later, Maggie was breathless, flushed, and almost as shaken as when the bus had backfired this morning.

# Chapter 6

$A$ million-dollar smile beamed down at her. "You're looking great, Taylor. Really great."

"You too, Stoney," Maggie returned, easing out of his hold.

"I like you with a little flesh on your bones."

"Thanks."

At her dry response, Stoney flashed another one of his trademark grins, all white teeth and crinkly eyes.

"What say I sneak you away from all this political hoopla for a few hours tonight? Like I used to, when you were governor?"

"What say you don't?" Adam's cool voice cut through the babble of the crowd. "The lady will be with me tonight."

Another barrage of blinding flashes went off as the two men faced each other. Talk about your basic headline-grabber, Maggie thought wryly. The vice president's former and current romantic interests squaring off in the lobby of L.A.'s Century Plaza Hotel. The media were going to play this one for all it was worth. With a flash of insight, she realized that Adam had once more stepped into the breach and diverted attention from her.

Stoney's sun-bleached brows lifted. "Who are you?"

"Adam Ridgeway. Who are you?"

The onetime movie idol blinked, clearly taken aback at the question. "Me? Hey, I'm—"

He caught himself, then gave a bark of laughter. "You almost got me there, Ridgeway."

Grinning good-naturedly, he stuck out a paw the size of a catcher's mitt. Adam took it, a sardonic gleam in his blue eyes.

The media went wild.

The scene had all the drama of a daytime soap, and then some. Two men shook hands in a glare of flashing lights. When this shot hit the newspapers, Maggie thought, every woman in the country would envy Taylor Grant. Imagine being forced to choose between your basic sun-bronzed, superbly muscled Greek god and a dark-haired aristocrat whose eyes held a glint of danger.

When Stoney had milked the scene for all it was worth, Maggie knew it was time to move on.

"Will I see you at the banquet tonight?" she asked.

"Sure. But—" he glanced at Adam "—I kind of hoped we'd have a chance to talk. Privately."

"Maybe after the banquet," she suggested easily. "I'll be tied up until then."

"Yeah. Okay. After dinner."


Maggie spent a long afternoon listening to the California Council of Mayors present their list of grievances against the heavy-handed federal bureaucracy. Fortunately, all she was required to do was nod occasionally and, at the end of the session, promise that their complaints about programs mandated by Congress without accompanying funds to implement them would be looked into.

By the time she and Adam and the ever-vigilant Denise took the elevator to the penthouse suite, the long night, the transcontinental flight and the packed day had drained even Maggie's

considerable store of energy. Or maybe it was the lack of sustenance, she thought, collapsing onto one of the sleek white leather
couches scattered about the suite.

Sunlight streamed through the two-story wall of glass that
overlooked the city, for once miraculously clear of smog, and
bathed Maggie in a warm glow. After Washington's snowy cold,
L.A.'s balmy, unseasonable seventy degrees felt heavenly. Feeling an uncharacteristic lassitude, she slipped off her shoes,
propped her stockinged feet on a glass coffee table the size of
a football field and heaved a huge sigh.

"We've got an hour until the banquet," Adam replied, his
eyes on her face. "Why don't you relax for a while? I'll go next
door to check in with my office, then shower and change. Shall
I join you for a drink before we go downstairs?"

"That would be nice," Maggie replied.

"The hotel left a basket of delicacies in my suite. Shall I bring
it with me, and we can explore it together?"

"By all means."

The hotel had left a basket in the vice president's suite, as
well. To Maggie's infinite disappointment, it had contained only
fruit and fancy glass jars of what looked and tasted like dry oats.

Buoyed by the thought of both food and time alone with
Adam, Maggie pushed herself off the sofa and headed for the
bedroom.

A half hour later, Lillian zipped up the back of a stunning
flame-colored gown in floating layers of chiffon, then stood back
to survey her charge. Her keen black eyes took in every detail,
from the dramatic upsweep of her short hair to the tips of her
strappy sandals, dyed to match the gown.

"You'll do."

Coming from Lillian, that was high praise indeed. Maggie
smiled as she peered into the mirror to make sure her matte
makeup fully covered the gel-like adhesive bone on her nose
and chin.

"Thanks, Lillian. I couldn't pull this off without you."

"After twenty-four hours in your company, I'm beginning to

suspect you could pull off this or any number of other improbable capers.''

Maggie grinned. ''Capers? We refer to them as missions.''

''Whatever. I'll be right across the hall. Call me when you get back from the banquet.''

''Don't wait up. I can manage. Besides,'' she added to forestall the inevitable protest, ''I may have a visitor after the banquet, remember?''

If things got tense when Stoney Armstrong showed up, Maggie didn't want the older woman in the line of fire.

Lillian gave one of her patented sniffs. ''You're going to have more than one visitor tonight, missy. I don't imagine the special envoy is going to leave you alone with Stoney.''

Maggie lifted a brow. ''We'll see how the situation develops. I'm used to operating independently on a mission, you know.''

''Who's talking about your mission?''

Lillian gave the bedroom a final inspection, then left Maggie to mull that one over. She was still thinking about it when she walked into the huge, white-carpeted living room some time later.

Denise Kowalski rose at her entry. Attired in the full-length black satin skirt that Maggie recognized as her uniform for formal functions, the sandy-haired agent was all brisk efficiency as she ran through the security arrangements for the banquet. When Denise finished, she stood and moved to the door.

''I've got to go downstairs for the final walk-though. We're using locals to help screen the guests as they arrive. I want to make sure they know how to operate the hand scanners.''

''Fine.''

''This entire floor's secure,'' Denise stated earnestly, as if needing to justify her brief absence. ''There are two post-standers at the elevators, and one at each of the stairwells. If you need them, just call.'' She nodded toward the hot line that linked the vice president's suite with the command post across the hall. ''Or hit the panic button beside the bed.''

''I know the routine,'' Maggie said, smiling.

The other woman grinned sheepishly. "Yes, ma'am, I guess you do."

Maggie studied the agent thoughtfully as she gathered her things and left. She was good. Darn good. From the moment their plane touched down at Los Angeles International, she'd been the vice president's second shadow. During the trip in from the airport, she'd directed the motorcade via the radio strapped to the inside of her wrist like a general marshaling his forces. What was more, she'd been prepared to take Stoney Armstrong down when he stepped out of the crowd in the lobby, and no doubt would have done so if Maggie hadn't acknowledged him.

According to the background brief OMEGA had prepared on Denise Kowalski, the woman had almost fifteen years with the Secret Service. She had joined the service at a time when female agents were a rarity, and had worked her way up the ranks. One divorce along the way. No children. Who could manage children and a career that demanded months on the road? Maggie wondered. Or the eighteen-hour days? Or a job that required instant willingness to take a bullet intended for someone else?

Denise would be one hell of an addition to the OMEGA team, Maggie decided. She made a mental note to speak to Adam about it when he joined her.

At the thought of their coming tête-à-tête, Maggie wrapped her arms across her chest. A shiver of anticipation whispered down her spine. They hadn't had a moment alone together since stepping off the plane. In his position as the president's special envoy, Adam commanded almost as much attention as the vice president had. Lobbyists and party hopefuls had clustered around him at every opportunity, bending his ear, asking his advice.

For the next thirty minutes, at least, Maggie would have his complete and undivided attention.

They needed to strategize, she reminded herself. To coordinate their plans for an evening that would include an intimate dinner with two hundred party faithful and a possible assassin in the person of a tanned, handsome movie star.

Although...

After her admittedly brief meeting with Stoney Armstrong this afternoon, Maggie found it difficult to believe he was the one who'd made that call. She'd met her share of desperate men, and a few whose utter lack of remorse for their assorted crimes chilled her. But when she looked up into Stoney's eyes after that mind-bending, back-bending kiss this afternoon, she hadn't seen a killer.

Then again, she reminded herself, Stoney Armstrong was an actor. A good one.

Her brow furrowed in thought, Maggie wandered through the living room toward the wide flagstone terrace outside the glass wall. A balmy breeze warmed by the offshore Japanese currents lifted her layers of chiffon and rustled the palms scattered around the terrace. Drawn by the glow of lights, she crossed to the waist-high stone balustrade that circled the terrace.

The sight that greeted her made her gasp in stunned delight. Far below her, adorned in glittering gold diamonds, was the city of angels. Los Angeles by day might consist of palm trees and smog, towering skyscrapers and crumbling, thirties-era stucco cottages. But by night, from the perspective of the fortieth floor, it was a dreamscape of sparkling, iridescent lights. Thoroughly enchanted, Maggie leaned her elbows on the wide stone railing and drank in the incredible sight.

The buzz of the telephone sent a rush of pleasure though her veins. That had to be Adam. With his basket of goodies. She went back inside and caught the phone on the third ring.

"Yes?"

"This is Special Agent Harrison, Mrs. Grant. A Mr. Stoney Armstrong just stepped off the elevator. He'd like to speak to you."

Maggie didn't hesitate. "Of course."

In the blink of an eye, her excitement sharpened, changed focus. The woman whose senses had tingled at the thought of a private tête-à-tête with Adam transitioned instantly into the skilled, highly trained agent. Her mind racing with various ways to handle this unexpected contact with a prime suspect, Maggie lifted her left hand.

"Thunder? Thunder, do you read me?"

When he didn't respond, Maggie guessed Adam was still in the shower. As soon as he got out, he'd pick up on her conversation with Stoney and join her—if the circumstances required it. Actually, she thought, it might be better if Adam didn't appear on the scene. She'd be able to draw Stoney out far more easily without another man present, especially one he might consider a rival.

Quickly she dimmed the lights and retrieved the small gold lipstick Special Devices had included in her bag of tricks for this mission. As she tucked the tiny stun gun in the bodice of her gown, she wondered briefly if it was powerful enough to take down a man of Stoney Armstrong's massive proportions, as Special Devices had claimed.

If not, and if necessary, she'd bring Stoney down herself. He'd be unarmed, she knew. He couldn't have passed through the highly sophisticated security screens with a weapon on his person. She'd handled bigger men than him in the past.

When a knock sounded on the door to her suite a few moments later, she was ready, both mentally and physically, to face a possible killer.

If Stoney Armstrong harbored any deadly intent toward Taylor Grant, he didn't show it. His tanned cheeks creased in his famous studio grin that, for all its beefcake quality, was guaranteed to stir any woman's hormones. Perfect white teeth gleamed, and his Armani tux gaped open to reveal a broad expanse of muscled, white-shirted chest as he leaned one arm negligently against the doorjamb.

"Hello, Taylor."

"Hello, Stoney."

"I'm a little early."

"So I noticed. Come in."

He strolled into the penthouse, looking around with unabashed interest. The glass wall drew him like a magnet. Shoving his hands in his pockets, he strolled out onto the terrace.

"It's something, isn't it?" he murmured, his eyes on the endless sweep of lights against a now-velvet sky.

"It is," Maggie agreed.

His mouth twisted. "Hard to believe a thin crust is all that separates the glitter and glamour from the tar pits underneath."

His subtle reference to the La Brea tar pit, the famous archaeological site in the center of the city, wasn't lost on Maggie.

"You sound as though a few saber-toothed tigers might have crawled out of the sludge," she commented softly.

If OMEGA's information was correct, those predators were circling Stoney Armstrong even now, about to close in for the kill.

His broad shoulders lifted. "Hey, this is Tinseltown. Saber-toothed tigers do power lunches every Tuesday and Friday at Campanile."

Turning his back on the dazzling vista, he leaned his hips against the rail.

"God, you look great, Taylor. Sort of sleek and well fed, like a cat or a horse or something."

Stoney did a lot better in a tender scene when he used a script, Maggie thought sardonically.

He leaned against the railing, ankles crossed, hands in his pockets. With the breeze ruffling his gold hair and his tux gaping open to reveal a couple of acres of broad chest, he looked pretty well fed himself.

He cocked his head, studying her face. "It can't be all those raisins and sunflower seeds you put away that gave you such a glow. Is it this guy Ridgeway?"

When Maggie didn't answer, his smile twisted a bit.

"I saw some pictures of you two in the afternoon edition of the *Times*. Christ, I wish I had your publicist. Those were great shots. Especially the one where you were getting out of the limo."

Maggie had rather liked that one herself.

"I thought maybe they were posed," he said, "like the ones you used to do for me, but..."

"But?"

"But after seeing you two together, I guess not." He paused, his eyes on her face. "You used to look at me like that, Taylor, and not just for the cameras. What happened to us? We used to be so good together.''

Maggie gave silent thanks for Taylor Grant's frankness about her relationship with this man. ''What we had was good, Stoney. Very good. But it wasn't enough for either one of us.''

''I know, I know. But, hey, we've both changed a lot since then. Our needs have changed. I mean, when we were together, you were governor and I was being courted by all the big studios.''

''It wasn't our professional life that got in the way.''

He raked a hand through his hair, destroying its casual artistry. ''Yeah, I know. You were still hurting from your husband's death, and I was paying alimony to two ex-wives. You didn't want emotional ties, any more than I did. But that was then.''

''And now?''

The tanned skin at the corners of his eyes crinkled as he gave her a rueful grin. ''And now you've got this guy Ridgeway prowling around you like a hungry panther, and I'm paying alimony to three ex-wives.''

No wonder Taylor had enjoyed this man's company so much during their brief time together, Maggie thought. For all his absorption with himself, Stoney had a disarming charm when he chose to exert it.

''We could be good together again, Taylor.''

''What we had was right for that moment, that time,'' Maggie said softly, echoing the vice president's own words. ''But not for now. Not for the future.''

''Why not? Just think about it. You might decide to go for top billing in the next election. You'd make a hell of a president. Together we'd make an unbeatable team. Just think of the publicity if I hit the campaign trail with you. Hey, look at the press Barbra Streisand got when she campaigned for Clinton.''

Maggie bit the inside of her lower lip, not wanting to be the one to break it to Stoney that he possessed neither the star power nor the political acumen of a Barbra Streisand.

''Taylor…''

He closed the small distance between them. Maggie kept her

smile in place as he leaned forward, planting both hands on the balustrade on either side of her, but her mind coldly registered his vulnerabilities. With his legs spread like that, he'd left himself wide open to a quick knee to the groin. His outstretched arms gave her room to swing her hand at the side of his neck or to shove a fisted thumb into the bridge of his nose.

When she looked up into his eyes, however, Maggie knew she wouldn't need to exploit those vulnerabilities. In three years of living on the knife-edge of danger, she'd learned to trust her instincts, and every one of those instincts told her this man was no killer.

"Stoney..." she began.

"I want you, Taylor."

Water dripped from Adam's hair and rolled down his back as he yanked a pair of black dress pants off the hanger on the back of the bathroom door.

"It won't work for us, Stoney. Not now."

Maggie's voice, soft and too damned sympathetic, drifted out of the watch on the marble counter. His jaw working, Adam tugged the slacks up over still-wet flanks.

"I need you."

Stoney delivered the line with a husky, melodramatic passion that set Adam's teeth on edge. Christ! No wonder the man couldn't get a part in anything except B-grade action flicks.

"Give me another chance. Give us a chance."

"It's too late."

"No. I don't believe that. I'll prove it!"

"Stoney, for Pete's sake!"

Maggie hadn't requested backup, Adam reminded himself. She obviously wanted to play this one alone. But her muffled exclamation propelled him out of the bathroom, bare chested and still dripping.

He was halfway to the door connecting their suites when a note of panic entered her voice.

"Stoney! You're too heavy! You're— Watch out!"

Her shrill yelp of terror sent Adam racing for the glass doors leading to the terrace. A knife blade of fear sliced through his gut when he saw Armstrong bent over the stone rail. A single sweep of the terrace showed no sign of Maggie anywhere.

"I...I can't...hold...you!"

Armstrong's agonized cry seared Adam's soul.

He didn't stop to think, didn't allow himself to feel. In a blinding burst of speed, he tore across the terrace and reached over the railing to grab the wrist Stoney held in one huge paw. The instant Adam's right hand clamped around Maggie's wrist, his left swung in a vicious arc. His fist smashed into Armstrong's jaw with the force of a pile driver.

The brawny movie star crumpled without a sound, but Adam didn't even flick him a glance. All his attention, every ounce of his concentration, was focused on the woman who dangled forty stories above the Avenue of the Stars, held only by his bruising lock on her wrist.

"I've got you," he grunted, his neck muscles cording.

Maggie twisted at the end of his arm, her bloodred gown billowing around her flailing legs.

"I...can't...get a foothold!" she gasped.

"You don't need one! Dammit, don't twist like that!" Bent double, Adam kept his left arm anchored around the railing. The rough stone took a strip of flesh off his bare chest as he leaned farther out. "Just grab my arm with your other hand. I'll pull you up."

Maggie's fingers clawed at his, then crept up to fasten around his forearm. With a surge of strength, Adam dragged her up and over the railing. Holding her upright with an iron grip, he raked her with a fierce, searching look.

"Are you all right?"

"I..." She sucked in a huge gulp of air. "I will be. As soon as you...stop crunching my bones."

His adrenaline raging, Adam ignored her attempt to shake loose of his hold. "What in hell happened? Didn't you anticipate his attack?"

"Attack? He didn't attack me."

"He pushed you off a rooftop!"

"Adam, he didn't push me! He was just trying to make love to me. We sort of…overbalanced."

She stopped tugging at his iron hold on her wrist and managed a shaky grin. "I guess you could say he swept me off my feet."

It was the grin that did it. That exasperating, infuriating lift of her lips. For the second time in less than twenty-four hours, Maggie was laughing while fear pumped through Adam's veins.

With a low sound that in anyone else might have been mistaken for a snarl, he wrapped her manacled wrist behind her back. A single flex of his muscles brought her body slamming against his. His other hand buried itself in her hair.

"You're forgetting your role. I'm the only man who's going to make love to you during this mission."

Maggie's eyes widened. She stared up at Adam, stunned as much by his unexpected force as by the way he held her banded against his chest. His black hair fell across his forehead, damp and tangled and untamed. His eyes glittered with a savage intensity. The muscles of his neck and shoulders gleamed wet and naked and powerful in the dim light.

He was close, so close, to unleashing the power she'd always sensed behind the steel curtain of his discipline. The realization sent a thrill through every fiber of Maggie's being. But at that moment, she wasn't quite sure whether the thrill she felt was one of triumph, or anticipation, or uncertainty.

"Adam…" she began, her voice husky.

She stopped, not knowing whether she wanted to soothe this potent, powerful, unfamiliar male or push him past his last restraint.

They hovered on the edge, each knowing that the next word, the next breath, could send them over.

To Maggie's intense disappointment, the next breath was Stoney's.

Groaning, the star pushed himself up on all fours, then lifted a hand to flex his jaw.

"Damn, Ridgeway," he muttered. "I hope to hell you didn't break my caps."

# Chapter 7

Still banded against Adam's body, Maggie didn't see the look he sent the aggrieved star. But it was enough to keep the man on his knees.

"If you touch her again, Armstrong, I'll break more than your caps."

Stoney blinked, as startled by the controlled savagery in his voice as Maggie herself had been a moment ago.

"Hey, man, I get the picture."

"You'd better."

When Adam stepped away, Maggie felt the loss in every inch of her body. She also saw the blood smearing his bare chest for the first time.

"Adam, you're hurt!"

"It's just a scrape," he replied brusquely, yanking the star to his feet. "Go call Kowalski. I'll entertain your friend here until she arrives."

Denise and two other security agents came rushing into the suite a few moments later. The senior agent turned ashen when she saw the front of Maggie's gown.

"Are you all right, Mrs. Grant?"

Glancing down, Maggie discovered that Adam's blood had darkened the flame red chiffon to a deep wine. "I'm fine. I just fell on the terrace. Well, off the terrace, but..."

Denise paled even more. "You fell off the terrace?"

"Stoney, er, got a little carried away. We overbalanced, and Adam came to the rescue." She gestured toward the glass wall, and the two figures on the terrace.

Denise turned, her eyes rounding at the sight of the president's special envoy, his naked chest streaked with blood, his slacks riding low on lean hips.

With a less-than-gentle shove, Adam propelled Stoney through the open sliding glass doors, into the suite. The two agents with Denise leaped forward to grab the star's arms.

Indignant, he tried to shake them off. "Hey, watch it!"

"Get him out of here," Adam ordered.

"Take Mr. Armstrong downstairs to interrogation," Denise instructed the others. "I want a full statement in my hands as soon as you get it out of him. And, Harrison—"

"Yes, ma'am?"

"Keep him away from the media."

"Yes, ma'am."

The senior agent pulled herself together as she swept the room. Her keen gaze took in the open connecting door between the suites before returning to Adam. Maggie caught a flicker of something that might have been feminine awareness or even admiration in Denise's eyes as they skimmed his lean torso, but it disappeared immediately when she caught the icy expression on his face.

"Where were you?"

Both women stiffened at the whipcrack in Adam's voice. Denise because she'd never heard it before, Maggie because she'd heard it several times. The furious man who'd slammed her up against his chest was gone. In his place was the Adam Ridgeway Maggie knew all too well.

"Downstairs," the agent responded tightly. "Conducting a final walk-through."

"Just what kind of security screens have you set up, Kowalski? How did Armstrong get past your men?"

Maggie stepped into the fray. "Hold it, Adam. Stoney didn't get past them. I told them to send him up."

Two equally accusing faces swung toward her. Adam's could have been chiseled from ice, but Denise's was folded into a frown.

"Was that wise, Mrs. Grant? After Armstrong's stunt in the lobby this afternoon?"

"I thought so," she replied coolly.

Adam didn't say a word, but Maggie could see he was *not* pleased. She fought back a small surge of irritation. She wasn't used to justifying or explaining her actions in the middle of an operation. To anyone.

As quickly as the irritation flared, Maggie suppressed it. Adam was her partner on this mission. She owed him an explanation of Stoney's presence in her suite, but she couldn't give it in front of Denise.

"We'll conduct a postmortem after the banquet," she told the agent with crisp authority. "Right now, I need you to go across the hall and get Lillian."

Denise firmed her lips, then reached for the phone. "I'll call her."

"I'd prefer you go get her. I don't want her hearing about this over the phone and becoming all upset. You know how overprotective she is."

It was a feeble excuse, and they all knew it, but Denise dropped the receiver back into its cradle.

"Fine. I'll go get Lillian. And we'll conduct a *thorough* postmortem after the banquet."

The door shut behind her, and a small, tense silence descended.

Adam was the first to break it, his tone frigid. "I think we need to review our mission parameters."

"I agree."

"This is supposed to be a team effort, remember?"

Maggie's jaw tightened, but she kept her voice level. "I tried to contact you after I told Security to send Stoney up."

"After? It didn't occur to you to contact me before you told them to send him up?"

"No, it didn't. I saw a target of opportunity, and I took it."

"Try coordinating your targets with me next time."

The stinging rejoinder lifted Maggie's chin. "I don't operate that way. I won't operate that way."

His eyes narrowed dangerously. Maggie had never seen that particular expression in them before—not directed at her, anyway. But she didn't back down. Her gaze locked with his, unwavering, determined. There was more at stake here than operating procedures, or even her job. Far more. She knew it. Adam knew it.

"You shouldn't have tried to handle this situation alone," he said, spacing his words. "It was too dangerous."

"I'm trained to handle dangerous situations. You trained me yourself. You and Jaguar."

A muscle ticked in the side of his jaw. "As best I recall, your training didn't include rappelling down a forty-story building without a rope."

"No," she tossed back, "but it included damn near everything else."

Which was true. As the first OMEGA operative recruited from outside the ranks of the government, Maggie had run the gamut of a battery of field tests and survival courses. She'd come through them all, disgruntled on occasion and cursing a blue streak after a memorable encounter with a snake Jaguar had slipped inside her boot, but she'd come through.

"Look, Adam, you know as well as I do, this job isn't just a matter of training. I follow my instincts in the field. I always have."

"I wondered when we were going to come around to that sixth sense of yours." He stepped toward her, his mouth hard. "I'll admit it's gotten you out of more tight spots than I care to think about, but—"

"But what?" she asked him challengingly.

"But even instincts can fail in certain situations."

He was so close, she could scent the tincture of blood and sweat that pearled his body. So still, she could see the pinpoints of blue steel in his eyes. So coiled, she could feel the tension escalating between them with every breath.

The heady, frightening feeling of hovering on the edge returned full force. Maggie had caught a brief glimpse of another Adam behind the all-but-impenetrable wall of his discipline. A part of her wanted to poke and probe and test that discipline further, to take him over the edge, and herself with him. Another part held her back. She knew this wasn't the time or the place. Denise would return with Lillian at any moment.

The time would come, though. Soon. She sensed it with everything that was female in her. With instincts more powerful, more primitive, than any she brought to her job.

Something of what she was thinking must have shown on her face. Adam took another step closer, his eyes locked with hers.

"What does your sixth sense tell you now, Maggie? About *this* situation?"

She hesitated a moment too long. The sound of a door slamming across the hall cut through the heavy stillness between them.

"It tells me we'll have to finish our discussion later," she said, torn between relief and regret.

"We'll finish it," Adam promised. "We'll definitely finish it."

The murmur of voices in the hall grew louder. With a last glance at her face, he started to turn away.

"Thunder?"

"Yes?"

She chewed on her lower lip for a second. "I'm sorry you were wounded in the line of duty."

Driven as much by the overwhelming need to touch him as by the urge to dull the hard edge of anger between them, Maggie reached out to brush her fingertips over the swirl of dark hair that arrowed his chest. Avoiding the raw, reddened patch of scraped flesh, she stroked his skin. Lightly. Soothingly.

He'd been wounded before, she discovered. Her fingers traced the ridge of an old, jagged scar that followed the line of his collarbone and passed over a puckered circle on his shoulder that could only have been caused by a bullet.

"Thank you," she said, dragging her gaze back to his face. "For hauling me back onto the terrace."

His hand closed over hers, capturing it against his heated skin. Under her flattened palm, Maggie felt the steady drumming of his heart.

"You're welcome." The sharp lines bracketing his mouth eased. "Just try to keep both feet on the ground from here on out."

It was too late for that, she thought. Far too late for that.

He'd almost lost her.

Adam stood unmoving while a shocked Lillian painted his chest with iodine, then covered the scrape with a white bandage. She brushed aside his quiet thanks and left to hurry Maggie into a fresh gown, tut-tutting all the while, in her own inimitable fashion.

With a damp cloth, Adam removed the ravages the stone railing had done to his dress pants. His hands were steady as he slipped on his white shirt, but the damned gold studs just wouldn't seem to fit the tiny openings. Clenching his jaw, Adam forced the last stud into place. Throughout it all, his mind followed a single narrow track.

He'd almost lost her.

This morning he'd finally admitted to himself how much he wanted Maggie, and tonight he'd almost lost her.

Before he possessed her—as much as it would be possible to possess someone like Chameleon—he'd almost lost her.

The raw need he'd acknowledged less than ten hours ago didn't begin to compare with the ache that sliced through him now. Seeing Maggie half a breath away from death had effectively stripped him of any illusion that he could control his need for her.

Two weeks, and this mission would be complete, he reminded

himself. Two weeks until he could satisfy the gnawing hunger he didn't, couldn't, deny any longer. For the first time, Adam doubted his own endurance.

Grimacing at the tug of the bandage on his chest hair, he pulled on his black dinner jacket and left the bathroom. He stopped short at the sight of the towering, beribboned basket resting majestically on a glass-topped sofa table.

He'd take it to Maggie after the banquet. At least one of them wouldn't go to bed hungry tonight.

He was halfway to the door when his watch began to vibrate gently against his wrist.

"Thunder here."

"This is Jaguar, Chief. Thought you might want to know we finally cornered Stoney Armstrong's agent."

"And?"

"And he passed on the interesting information that his client floated an eight-figure 'loan' just a week ago. Seems Armstrong decided to produce and star in his own film. The funds went through half a dozen holding companies, but we finally traced them to First Bank."

Adam went still. "First Bank?"

"Yeah. Ready for the kicker?"

"I'm ready."

"Armstrong refused the loan when he discovered that First Bank was putting up the cash. Seems he'd heard some rumors about the institution and didn't want his name connected to it."

"What kind of rumors?"

"Nothing specific, but the agent hinted strongly that it might be doing business with some questionable characters in Central America. Said Armstrong didn't want anything to do with it."

The fact that the brawny star had a few scruples buried under those bulging muscles didn't particularly impress Adam.

"Put a team on First Bank, Jaguar. I want to know the source of every dollar it takes in, and every possible connection between the bank and the vice president."

"I've already got it working. Will get back to you as soon as I have anything."

"Fine. Anything else?"

"No."

Adam flicked a glance at the dial of his watch. "I'd better sign off. The vice president is waiting."

Jaguar chuckled. "How's Chameleon holding up in this role?"

The memory of Maggie's shaky grin after her brush with oblivion filled Adam's mind.

"Better than I am," he replied grimly.

The banquet went off without a hitch.

Stoney Armstrong failed to make an appearance, which didn't surprise Adam. From the determined set to Denise Kowalski's chin, he guessed the agent wasn't about to release the star until she was fully satisfied with his statement.

Maggie, stunning in a two-piece turquoise silk sheath beaded in silver, charmed the men seated on either side of her. From his place across the round table, Adam watched as she picked at the elaborate chef's salad she'd been served. Every so often, her eyes strayed to the succulent rack of lamb on her neighbor's plate.

Remembering the cellophane-wrapped basket in his suite, Adam smiled. The thought of feeding Maggie, bite by bite, the various delicacies snaked through his mind. Sudden, erotic images of what could be done with red beluga caviar and soft Brie made his hand clench around the stem of his wineglass. He kept his smile easy and his conversation with the women seated on either side of him lively, but he couldn't keep his body from tightening whenever he looked at the woman separated from him by a wide expanse of white linen. Adam knew that each lingering glance he gave Maggie added more grist to the rumor mills about the vice president's latest romantic interest.

He also knew that he'd long since stopped playing a role.

When the banquet finally ended, they made their way slowly through the crowded ballroom. Denise and her squad cleared the way, and Adam followed a step or two behind Maggie as they both greeted various guests. As much as it was possible in this press, he kept her body between his and the agent in front of her.

She was incredible, he thought, watching her work the crowd. The people who caught her ear didn't notice that she listened far more than she spoke, or that she waited for them to drop clues about their personal agendas before she gave a noncommittal response.

His gaze traveled from the auburn curls feathering her neck, down the slender back now encased in turquoise silk, to the swell of her hips. The modest slit in the back of her long skirt parted with each step, revealing a tantalizing glimpse of shapely calf. Maintaining her role had to be a tremendous physical and emotional strain, but she didn't allow any sign of it to show in her demeanor or her carriage.

Until they reached the elevator.

When Denise turned to issue a last-minute instruction to the task force leader, Maggie slumped back against the brass rail for a second or two. Adam caught the way her shoulders sagged and her eyelids fluttered shut. With a wry inner smile, Adam abandoned his plans to feed her in erotic, exotic ways.

As it turned out, Denise Kowalski had her own plans for them for the rest of the evening. After a quick but thorough security check, she joined Maggie and Adam in the sitting room.

"We still have to do that postmortem, Mrs. Grant."

Maggie glanced at the clock on the white-painted mantel. "It's almost 3:00 a.m., Washington time. Why don't we get together in the morning, before we leave for the cabin?"

"It's best if we go over what happened while the details are still fresh in your mind," the agent insisted politely but firmly. "Mr. Armstrong's statement, and his subsequent polygraph, substantiate your belief that he didn't intend you bodily harm, but I need to hear exactly what happened. You could have been killed."

"I know," Maggie replied, with a gleam in her eyes that Adam recognized instantly. "I was the one about to add a new, indelible splash of color to the Avenue of the Stars, remember?"

She realized her mistake almost as soon as the words were

out of her mouth. The flippant tone and gallows humor were far more characteristic of Maggie Sinclair than of Taylor Grant.

Denise frowned, and Maggie recovered without missing a beat. Curving her mouth into Taylor's distinctive smile, she tossed her beaded bag down on the sofa.

"Look, I know you're just trying to do your job. I guess I'm a little tired."

A touch of reserve entered the agent's voice. "I'm sorry to badger you this late, but I'm charged with protecting you. I can't do it without your cooperation."

With one hand tucked casually in his pants pocket, Adam eyed the two women. Denise Kowalski was every bit as strong willed and determined as Maggie when it came to her job. She wasn't about to back down, any more than Chameleon had earlier.

Maggie gave in with good grace, recognizing a pro when she saw one. "You're right, of course. Why don't we sit down?"

"Would you join us, please?" Denise asked Adam. "I'd like your input, as well."

"I didn't intend to leave. Mrs. Grant and I have a few matters of our own to discuss when you're though."

Ignoring Maggie's quick sideways glance, he joined her on the buttery-soft sofa.

The Secret Service officer was too well trained to allow any expression to cross her face. But as she moved forward to take the seat opposite them, she slanted a quick look at the open connecting door.

The brass carriage clock on the mantel had chimed twice by the time Agent Kowalski finally called a halt to the questions.

"Well, I guess that's it." She rubbed a hand across her forehead, then rose. "I'll tell the folks downstairs to release Armstrong. We'll keep someone on him for a while, with orders to get real nasty, real quick, if he tries to, uh, approach you again."

"He won't," Maggie asserted.

"No, he won't," Adam promised.

The agent glanced from Maggie's confident face to Adam's implacable one. "I guess not. I'll see you in the morning."

When the door closed behind her, Maggie heaved a sigh. Letting her head loll back against the leather, she plopped her stockinged feet on the brass-and-glass table.

"That's one tough woman."

"She reminds me of someone else I know," Adam commented dryly.

"She does, doesn't she?" Maggie's hair made a bright splash of color against the white leather as she turned to face him. "I think we should recruit her for OMEGA after this mission."

"I may have to consider it. If you pull any more stunts like you did with Armstrong, I'll have an opening for an agent."

A gleam of reluctant laughter entered her violet-tinted eyes. "Okay, so maybe dangling above the Avenue of the Stars was a bit extreme," she conceded.

"It was. Even for you."

"Even for me. But at least it convinced me that Armstrong's not our man. I don't have anything to base it on, except the fact that Stoney didn't let go—and the sixth sense you took me to task for earlier."

"As much as it pains me to admit it, your instincts were right. Again."

She sat up straight. "Really?"

"Jaguar called just before we went downstairs to the banquet."

With a succinct economy of detail, Adam filled her in on the details of Jake's call.

"First Bank, huh? Stoney turned down a loan from First Bank because he thinks they might be laundering dirty money?"

"Evidently he was afraid a connection with them might…tarnish his image."

She grinned. "There's a lot of that going around lately."

A small silence settled between them. Reluctant to break it, Maggie slumped back against the soft leather. She and Adam still had matters left to resolve, not the least of which was exactly how she would operate for the next two weeks. But she couldn't seem to summon up the energy or the intensity that had driven her earlier.

"If we eliminate Armstrong, that leaves only two names on the list of possible suspects," Adam said after a moment.

"Digicon's CEO, and the president's best buddy."

"Peter Donovan, and James Elliot."

"Jaguar hasn't dug up anything on either?"

He shook his head. "Not yet."

The clock on the mantel ticked off a few measures of companionable silence, broken only when Maggie gave a huge, hastily smothered yawn.

"Sorry," she murmured.

Adam's gaze rested on her face for a long moment, and then he pushed himself to his feet and held out one hand to pull her up beside him.

Maggie put her hand in his. Despite the weariness that had dragged over her like a net, a sensual awareness feathered along her nerves at the firmness of his hold. She'd felt Adam's strength twice tonight. Once when he'd hauled her up to the terrace. Once when he'd hauled her up against his chest.

"You'd better get some sleep," he told her.

She hesitated, knowing she was playing with fire. "We didn't finish what we started, out there on the terrace."

"We'll finish tomorrow," he said slowly. "When we get to the cabin."

Tomorrow, she told herself. Tomorrow, they'd be at Taylor's isolated mountain retreat. Tomorrow, Maggie would be rested, in control of herself once more. There wouldn't be as many people hovering around her. Only Denise and a small Secret Service team. Lillian. The caretaker who lived at the ranch. And Adam.

Tomorrow, she and Adam would sort through roles and missions. Tomorrow, they'd finish what they'd started tonight.

"Good night," she said softly.

"Good night, Chameleon."

Leaving the door open behind him, Adam walked through the sitting room of his own suite. With every step, his body issued a fierce, unrelenting protest. But as much as he wanted to, he wouldn't allow himself to turn around, walk back through the door and tumble Maggie down onto that soft white leather.

She needed sleep. That much was obvious from the faint shadows under her eyes. From the droop of her shoulders under the beaded silk. She needed rest. A few hours' relief from the strain of her role.

And Adam needed to keep the promise of tomorrow in proper perspective. If he could.

Halfway across the sitting room, the glint of cellophane caught his eye. He halted with one hand lifted to tug at the ends of his black tie, and surveyed the towering collection of champagne, caviar, imported biscuits and cheeses. Somehow he suspected that those damned cheeses were going to figure in his dreams tonight.

Scooping up the basket, he walked back into the adjoining suite. The thick white carpet muffled his footsteps as he approached the bedroom door.

"You'd better eat something before—"

He stopped short on the threshold, transfixed by the sight of Maggie twisted sideways, struggling with the straps of her body shield.

She'd shed the beaded gown, and she wore only the thin Kevlar corset, a lacy garter belt that held up sheer nylon stockings, and the skimpiest pair of panties Adam had ever seen. No more than a thin strip of aqua silk, they brushed the tops of her full, rounded bottom and narrowed to a thin strip between her legs. In the process, they exposed far more flesh than they covered.

When she glanced up, Adam saw that she'd removed her violet-tinted contacts. Those were Maggie's brown eyes, he saw with a rush of fierce satisfaction. That was her body that beckoned to him.

Another woman might have flushed or stammered or at least acknowledged the sudden, leaping tension of the moment. Maggie gave him a wry grin.

"Remind me to tell Field Dress what I think of this blasted contraption when we get back. It was supposedly designed for easy removal, but I'm stuck."

"So I see. Need some help?"

"Yes, I…"

She straightened, and the last Velcro fastening gave with a snicker of sound. The body shield slipped downward, exposing a half bra of aqua and lace. Maggie bit her lip.

"No, I guess I don't."

Across the broad expanse of white carpet, their eyes met. For a long moment, neither moved. Neither spoke. Then her gaze dropped to the cellophane-covered basket in his arms, and she gave a whoop of delight.

"Adam! Is that food? Real food?"

"It is."

Snatching up a robe, she threw it on. "Thank God! I'm starving! I didn't know how I was going to get any sleep with my stomach rumbling like this."

Her forehead furrowed as she crossed the room, yanking at the sash of the robe.

"I got sloppy with Denise tonight, and I know it's just because I'm tired. And hungry. What's in the basket?"

"Caviar."

"Yecch!"

"And Brie."

Her face brightened, and she reached for the bundle of goodies. "Great! I love Brie. Especially warm, when it's so soft and creamy, you can spread it on all kinds of stuff."

Adam's jaw clenched. He'd spent over a decade in service to his country. He'd done some things he might have been decorated for if they hadn't been cloaked in secrecy. Some things he might have been shot for if the wrong people had caught up with him. But handing that basket over to Maggie was the toughest act he'd ever had to perform in his personal or professional life.

"Eat up," he told her, "then get some sleep. You can't afford to get sloppy. With anyone."

"Mmm..." she mumbled, busy delving into the assorted treasures.

Tomorrow, Adam promised himself as he walked back to his suite. Tomorrow, this hard, pounding ache would ease. They'd be at the cabin. There'd be fewer people around. He could put a little distance between himself and Maggie, yet still keep her under close surveillance.

By tomorrow, he'd have himself under control.

## Chapter 8

The vice-presidential party arrived at the white-painted twenties-era frame house tucked high in the Sierra Nevada late the next evening.

Too late for Maggie and Adam to finish the "discussion" they'd begun on the terrace of the Century Plaza's penthouse suite. Too late for more than a cursory look around the rustic hideaway. Too late for anything other than a quick cup of hot soup in front of a low, banked fire and a weary good-night. The trip that shouldn't have taken more than a few hours had spun out for more than twelve.

The short flight from L.A. to Sacramento had gone smoothly enough. They landed in the capital city in time for a late lunch at one of Taylor's favorite restaurants. Maggie basked in the reflection of the former governor's popularity with the restaurant staff and managed a cheerful smile when she was served a glutinous green mass in the shape of a crescent with unidentifiable objects jiggling inside it. She was still too stuffed from her late-night raid on Adam's treasure trove of goodies to give his ham and cheese on sourdough more than a passing glance.

It was only after they lifted off in the specially configured twin-engine Sikorsky helicopter for the final leg of their trip that the problems began. The pilot, a veteran of the Gulf War, countered most of the sudden up-and downdrafts over the foothills with unerring skill. But when the aircraft approached the higher peaks, the ride took on a roller-coaster character.

At one violent thrust to the right, Maggie grabbed the armrests with both hands. Behind her, Denise sucked in a quick breath. Even the redoubtable Lillian gasped.

"Feels like we've run into some convective air turbulence," Adam commented.

"We've certainly run into something," Maggie muttered.

He stretched his long legs out beside hers, unperturbed by the violent pitch and yaw of the craft. Having seen him at the controls of various aircraft a number of times, Maggie wasn't surprised at his calm. Adam could handle a stick with the best of them. He knew what to expect. She, on the other hand, was bitterly regretting even the few bites of green stuff she'd managed to swallow at lunch.

"This kind of turbulence is common when flying at low levels over mountains." He scanned the tilting horizon outside the window. "From the looks of those clouds up ahead, we're going to lose visibility soon."

"Great."

He smiled at her drawled comment. "I suspect we'll have to turn back."

Sure enough, a few moments later the pilot came back to inform her that regulations required him to return to base. He couldn't risk flying blind, with only instruments to guide him through the mountains, while ferrying a code-level VIP.

On the ground in Sacramento, they waited over an hour for the front to clear. When the weather reports grew increasingly grim, Maggie was given the choice between remaining overnight in the capital city and driving up to the cabin in a convoy of four-wheel-drive vehicles. In blessed ignorance of the state of the roads leading to Taylor Grant's mountain retreat, she chose the drive.

At first, she thoroughly enjoyed her first journey into the High Sierras. Despite the lowering clouds, the scenery consisted of spectacular displays of light and shadow. White snow and gray, misty lakes provided dramatic backdrops for dark green ponderosa pine and blue-tinted Douglas firs.

When the convoy of vehicles turned off the interstate onto a narrow two-lane state road, Maggie spied deer tracks in the snow. Chipmunks darted along the branches arching over the road and scattered showers of white on the passing vehicles. Every so often the woods thinned, and she'd catch a glimpse of an ice-covered waterfall hanging like a silvery tassel in the distance.

As they climbed to the higher elevations, however, the two-lane highway gave way to a corkscrew gravel road that twisted and turned back on itself repeatedly. Fog and swirling snow slowed their progress even more, until the four-vehicle convoy was creeping along at barely five miles per hour.

It occurred to Maggie that one of those blind curves would make an excellent spot for an ambush. With the vehicles slowed to a crawl, a sniper perched in a nearby tree would have no difficulty picking off his target. As a result, she spent most of the endless trip alternately searching the gray snowscape ahead and wondering why in hell Taylor Grant would choose such an inaccessible spot for her personal retreat.

As soon as she saw the cabin, she understood. The small white frame structure nestled on the side of a steep slope in a Christmas-card-perfect setting. Surrounded by snow-draped pines and a split-rail fence, its windows spilled golden, welcoming light into the night. The scent of a wood fire greeted Maggie as soon as she stepped out of the Land Rover. While Adam went back to help sort and unload the bags, she stood for a moment in the crisp air. The profound quiet of the night surrounded her. Deliberately she willed the knotted muscles in the back of her neck to relax.

Boots crunched the path behind her. Lillian appeared at her elbow, looking much like a pint-size snowman in a puffy down-filled coat, with a fuzzy beret pulled over her springy curls.

"Feels good to be home," she said, sniffing the air.

"Mmm…"

"Too bad it's too late for you to jog down to the lake."

"Yes, isn't it?"

Maggie was *not* looking forward to running anywhere in this thin mountain air, much less down a steep mountain path to the tiny lake she knew crouched in the valley below, then back up again. Running was bad enough at sea level. At an elevation of nine thousand feet, a jog like that would be sheer torture. She had several excuses in mind to justify a change in the vice president's routine, including a desire for long, *slow* walks with a certain special envoy.

Mindful of the agents milling around behind them, Lillian shot her a look heavy with significance.

"You'll just have to wait until morning to trek down to the lake, even though you say you never feel at home until you've seen your tree. The one with the initials."

Biting back a sigh, Maggie resigned herself to the inevitable. "I don't. If the snow doesn't obscure the path, I'll go down in the—"

"Grrr-oo-of!"

She broke off with a startled gasp as the mounded snowbank on her left suddenly erupted. In a blur of white, a shaggy creature sprang out of the snow and planted itself in front of her. Its shaggy coat hung in thick, uncombed ropes, and only the upright stub of a tail told Maggie which end was which. The thing looked like a well-used floor mop, only this mop had to weigh at least a hundred pounds and was making very unfriendly noises.

"Radizwell! Get back, you idiot!" Lillian swatted the woolly head with her purse. "It's too late to play games tonight. Go on! Shoo!"

The creature stood its ground, growling deep in its throat at the woman garbed in its mistress's clothes.

Maggie had been briefed that the livestock kept on Taylor's small ranch included several horses, a flock of sheep that grazed the high alpine meadows in spring, and a breed of sheepdog she'd never heard of before. According to intelligence, the komondor had been introduced into Europe by the Magyars when they invaded Hungary in the ninth century. The animal was ideal for the rugged Hungarian mountains. Its huge size and thick, corded coat enabled it to withstand the harshest winter climates, and at the same time protected it from the fangs of the predators that preyed on the flocks.

Maggie could understand how the creature in front of her would intimidate a bear or a wolf or a fox. It certainly intimidated her. Unfortunately, intel had stressed that Taylor Grant never went anywhere around the ranch without this beast at her side. Maggie knew she had to win him over, and fast.

Dragging in a deep breath, she crouched down on one heel and held out a hand. "Come here, Radizwell. Come here, boy."

Another growl issued from deep under those layers of ropelike wool.

Maggie set her jaw. If she could convince a bug-eyed iguana to respond—occasionally—to her commands, she could win over this escapee from a mattress factory.

"Here, Radizwell. Come here."

A warning rumble sounded deep in its throat.

Despite the almost overpowering urge to draw her arm back, Maggie kept her hand extended. "Here, boy."

One huge paw inched forward. A black nose poked out of the shaggy layers. The creature sniffed, growled again, then edged closer.

From the corner of one eye, Maggie saw the front door open and a jacketed figure step out onto the porch. She guessed it was Hank McGowan, the caretaker. Of all the dossiers she'd studied for this mission, his had fascinated her the most. An ex-con who owed Taylor both his life and his livelihood, he'd made this isolated ranch his home.

Before Maggie could give her full attention to McGowan, however, the showdown between her and Radizwell had to be decided. One way or another.

"Come here, boy."

A cold nose nudged her palm. Understanding his confusion,

she let the dog sniff her for a few moments. When he didn't amputate any of her fingers, she lifted her hand and gave his feltlike coat a cautious pat. That proved to be a mistake.

Radizwell instantly moved forward to make a closer inspection. His massive head butted into her chest with the force of a Mack truck. Maggie lost her precarious balance and toppled backward.

Adam and the caretaker arrived at the same moment from opposite directions to find her on her back in the snow, with a hundred pounds of dog straddling her body. Thankfully, its growls had given way to a low rumble as his wet nose moved over her cheeks and chin. She managed a laughing protest to cover what she knew was the dog's uncharacteristic behavior.

"Radizwell, you idiot. Get off me!"

Shaking his head in disgust, the caretaker burrowed a hand under layers of wool to find a collar.

"I penned him up when they radioed that you were on the last mile stretch. Guess I should have put a lock on the shed."

He bent forward to haul the dog back, and Maggie saw his face clearly for the first time. Although the dossier she'd studied had prepared her somewhat, his battered features shocked her nonetheless. They added grim emphasis to his checkered past.

Henry "Hank" McGowan. Forty-three. Divorced. Onetime foreman of a huge commercial sheep ranch outside Sacramento. Convicted murderer, whose death sentence had been commuted to life imprisonment by the then-governor, Taylor Grant.

His conviction had been overturned when new evidence proved he hadn't tracked down and shot the drunk who'd battered him senseless with a tire jack after an argument over a game of pool. McGowan had drifted after that, unable to find work despite his exoneration, until Taylor hired him to act as stockman and caretaker.

In his last security review, McGowan had stated flatly that he owed Taylor Grant his life. He'd give it willingly to shield the vice president from any hurt, any harm.

Right now, that consisted of hauling a hundred pounds of suspicious sheepdog off her prone body.

"For heaven's sake, lock him in the shearing shed tonight," Lillian said tartly. "You know how excited the idiot gets whenever we come home. The last time he just about stripped the paint off the porch, marking his territory for the new agents who came with Mrs. Grant."

To Maggie's relief, the dog allowed himself to be led away before he felt compelled to mark anything for this stranger in Taylor's clothes.

"There's a pot of vegetable stew on the stove," McGowan tossed over one shoulder. "If anyone's hungry."

*If* anyone was hungry! At this point, even veggies simmering in a rich, hearty broth sounded good to Maggie. She grabbed the hand Adam extended and scrambled up. Dusting the snow from her bottom, she gave him a grin.

"I certainly seem to be taking more than my share of falls lately."

"So I've noticed. Do you think you can make it to the cabin upright, or shall I carry you?"

Now there was an intriguing invitation.

"I can make it," she said, regret and laughter threading her voice. "Come on, let me show you the homestead, such as it is."

The vice president's home had been featured in a five-page spread in *Western Living* magazine, but not even that glossy layout had prepared Maggie for the stunning interior. Only a woman of Taylor Grant's style and confidence could pull off this blend of rustic and antique, polished mahogany and shining oak, plank floors and scattered floral rugs.

Most of the cabin's downstairs interior walls had been demolished, leaving only an open living-dining area, a small kitchen, and the bedroom Lillian occupied. A huge stone fireplace in the living room was the focus of a collection of comfortable dude-ranch-style furniture. A magnificent Chippendale dining room table with eight chairs dominated the dining area. Interspersed throughout were bronze pieces sculpted by Taylor's deceased husband, Oriental vases filled with dried flowers, framed Western art, and the occasional mounted trophy, including a huge moose head beside the door that served as a hat rack.

While Maggie showed Adam around, using the impromptu tour as an excuse to familiarize herself with the downstairs, Lillian went upstairs to direct the placement of the luggage. Denise dragged off her gloves and conferred with the agent who'd been sent to the cabin several days ago as part of the advance team. After a thorough walk-through of the entire cabin, she joined Maggie and Adam at the stone fireplace. Politely declining a mug of the steaming stew, she gave a brief report.

"The cabin and the grounds are secure, Mrs. Grant. We've activated the command center in the barn."

According to intelligence, the Secret Service had converted the barn behind the cabin into a well-equipped bunkhouse and a high-tech command-and-control center—at a cost of several million dollars. Idly Maggie wondered whether the horses were going to enjoy the central heat and exercise room when the Secret Service finally vacated the premises.

"If you don't need me any more tonight, I'll get the team settled. Dunliff will stand the first shift."

"All right. It's been a long day. Get some rest, Denise."

"You too," the agent responded.

Although Denise kept her face carefully neutral when she wished Adam a courteous good-night, Maggie caught the quick speculative look the other woman gave him.

A few moments later, Lillian came downstairs. "You're all unpacked, Mrs. Grant."

"Thank you."

"I think I'll turn in, too. It takes me a while to reacclimate to the altitude."

"Don't you want some stew? It's delicious."

Surprisingly, it was. Maggie might have awarded the rich stew her own personal blue ribbon, if it had contained just a chunk or two of beef or lamb or even chicken.

"No, thank you."

When Lillian retired to her room, the agent on duty discreetly left Maggie and Adam alone. More or less. Hidden cameras swept the downstairs continuously, allowing the occupants only the illusion of privacy.

Upstairs, Maggie knew, was a different matter. Upstairs there were only two small rooms, each with its own bath. Upstairs, Mrs. Grant had insisted on privacy for herself and her guests. Which meant Maggie and Adam didn't have to take their assigned roles as lovers any farther than the first stair. At this moment, Maggie wasn't sure whether she was more relieved or disappointed.

This complex role they were playing had become so confused, so blurred, she'd stopped trying to sort out what was real and what wasn't. Since last night, when she'd felt Adam's arms locked around her and his naked chest beneath her splayed hands, she'd hungered for a repeat performance.

Not that she'd either experience it or allow it. The rational part of her mind told her they wouldn't, couldn't, complicate their mission further by setting a spark to the fire building between them. But when she thought of that small, private nest upstairs, her fingers itched for a match.

Not an hour later, she tiptoed across the darkened hall and ignited a flame that almost consumed them both.

The soft scratching on the wooden door to his room brought Adam instantly awake. He didn't move, didn't alter the rhythm of his breathing, but his every sense went on full alert.

The door creaked open.

"Adam? It's me. Taylor. Are you awake?"

Maggie's use of her assumed identity in this supposedly secure part of the house tripped warning alarms in every part of Adam's nervous system. He rolled over, the sheets rustling beneath him, and followed her lead.

"I'm awake."

She stepped out of the shadows and moved toward the wide double bed that took up most of the floor space. Bright moonlight streamed through the windows, illuminating the fluid lines of her body. She wore only a silky gown, and without the constraining Kevlar her breasts were lush and full. Nipples peaked from the cold pushed at the thin gown.

Adam felt his stomach muscles go washboard-stiff. Forcing himself to focus on the reason behind her unexpected visit, he rose up on one elbow. The old-fashioned hickory-rail bedstead bit into his bare back as he propped a shoulder against it.

"I couldn't sleep," she whispered, her feet gliding across the oak plank floor.

She stopped beside the bed, so near that Adam could see the tiny beads of moisture pearled on her shoulders. Her hair was spiked with water, as though she'd hurriedly passed a towel over it once or twice.

As if in answer to his unspoken question, she ran a hand through her damp waves. "I took a hot bath. To help me relax. It didn't work."

His mouth curved. "I tried a cold shower. It didn't work for me, either." He raised an arm, lifting the covers, not sure where this was going, but following her lead. "Maybe we can help each other relax."

She hesitated, shifting from one bare foot to the other. "I know we promised to take this slow and easy, to use these two weeks to get to know each other, but…"

"Come to bed, Taylor."

"I need you to hold me, Adam. Please, just hold me for a little while."

She slid in beside him, her gown a slither of damp silk against his skin. He dragged the covers over them both.

Her body felt clammy through the gown where it touched his, which was just about everywhere. Wrapping an arm around her waist, Adam brought her closer into his heat. She burrowed against him and tucked her icy feet between his. Her head rested on his shoulder. Her mouth was only an inch from his.

They fit together as if cast from molds. Male and female. Man and woman. Adam and Maggie. Thunder and Chameleon, he amended immediately.

"I was thinking about what happened last night," she said softly, "and I started to shake."

That didn't help him much. A lot had happened last night. He didn't know if she was referring to Stoney's unexpected appearance, her near-fall, or the sharp difference of opinion they'd had over procedures. A difference that had yet to be resolved.

"I guess I experienced a delayed reaction to the fall," she murmured, her breath feathering his cheek. "It happened so fast, I didn't have time to be frightened last night. But now…now I shake every time I remember how…how…"

She shivered and pressed closer. Adam pulled the downy covers up higher around her shoulders, almost burying her head in their warmth.

*"There's a bug in my room."* The words were hardly more than a flutter of air against his ear. "I was so terrified, so helpless," she continued, a shade more loudly. "And then you reached for me and pulled me to safety."

The covers shook as she shuddered again.

"It's okay, Taylor. It's okay." His lips moved against her cheek. *"I thought you swept the room yourself."*

*"I did. Either I missed this one, or someone planted it while I was downstairs scarfing up vegetable stew."* She gave a tremulous sigh. "Oh, Adam, I could have pulled you over that railing with me. I could have killed us both."

"No way. I wasn't about to let go of either you or that stone rail. *Where did you find it?"*

*"Above the bathtub."* Her hand inched up to rest lightly on the bandage on his chest. "I'm so sorry you were hurt. You should have had a doctor take a look at this."

"It's only a scrape. *Where above the tub?"*

*"Behind the wallpaper. When I ran hot water into the tub, steam dampened the paper. All but this one small patch.* Are you sure you're all right?"

"I'm fine, darling. *Did you neutralize it?"*

*"No. I didn't want to tip off whoever was listening. There's probably one in here, too."* She nuzzled his neck. "I'm glad you're here, Adam. I'm glad you came with me."

"I'm glad, too. We both have too many pressures on us in Washington. *I'm sure there is.*"

The knowledge that someone had planted devices in these supposedly secure rooms churned in Adam's mind, vying for precedence with the signals his skin was telegraphing to his brain at each touch of Maggie's body against his.

No one could have gotten into the cabin undetected. Despite its isolated location, the ranch bristled with the latest in security systems. Which meant that whoever had planted the bug had ready access to the grounds.

The caretaker, Hank McGowan? He certainly had access, although his loyalty and devotion to Taylor Grant supposedly went soul-deep.

Lillian Roth?

A member of the Secret Service advance team?

Denise Kowalski herself, when she'd done her walk-through of the cabin?

Which one of them, if any, was in league with the man who'd made that chilling call to Taylor? And why?

Suddenly the threat to Maggie became staggeringly immediate. Instead of narrowing, their short list of suspects had exploded. The sense of danger closing in rushed through Adam, and his arms tightened reflexively around her waist.

She took the gesture as a continuation of their roles, and snuggled into him. "Just think," she murmured. "Two weeks to learn about each other. Two weeks for each of us to discover what pleasures the other."

Her movement ground her hip against his groin. In spite of himself, Adam hardened. The dappled moonlight and soft shadows in the room blurred, merged into a swirling, red-tinted mist.

"I don't think it's going to take two weeks for us to get to know each other," he said, his voice low.

She tilted her head back to glance up at him from her nest of covers, a question in her shadowed eyes. "Why not?"

"Now that I have you in my arms, I don't think I can let you go."

He angled his body, allowing it to press hers deeper into the sheets. His hands tunneled into her still-damp hair. The muscles in his upper arms corded as he angled her face up to his.

He shouldn't do this. His mind posted a last, desperate caution. Deliberately Adam ignored the warning. Lowering his head, he covered her mouth with his. It was warm and full and made for his kiss.

After a moment of startled surprise, Maggie pushed her arms out of the enfolding covers and wrapped them around his neck, returning his kiss with a sensual explosion of passion. Her mouth opened under his, inviting, welcoming, discovering.

With an inarticulate sound, Adam plunged inside, tasting her, claiming her. Teeth and tongues and chins met. Exploration became exploitation.

Maggie couldn't be a passive player, in this or in any part of life. Her arms tightened around his neck, and she arched under him, lifting her body to his in a glory of need. She felt his rock hardness against her stomach, and a shaft of heat shot from her belly to her loins. Without conscious thought, she wiggled, rubbing her breasts against his chest. The tips stiffened to aching points. She shifted again, wanting friction. Wanting his touch.

As though he'd read her mind, Adam dragged a hand down and shaped her breast. His fingers kneaded her flesh. His thumb brushed over the taut nipple. Maggie gave a small, involuntary gasp.

"Adam!"

The breathless passion in her voice drew him back from the precipice. The very real possibility that someone else had heard her gasp his name acted on Adam like a sluice of cold water. He dragged his mouth from hers, his breath harsh and ragged. Resolve coiled like cold steel in his gut.

When he made love to Maggie, which he now intended to do as soon as he got her away from this cabin, it sure as hell wouldn't be with anyone listening or watching. There would be just the two of them, their bodies as tight with desire as they were now. But he'd be the only one to hear her groans of pleasure. No one else would see the splendor of her body. Would observe her responses to his kiss and his touch and his possession. Would watch while he drowned in the river of passion flowing in this vital woman.

He eased his lower body away from hers. "I'm sorry, Taylor."

The sound of another woman's name on Adam's lips slowly penetrated the haze of desire that heated Maggie's mind and body. Like a cold mist seeping under the door, reality crept back. It swirled around her feet and, inch by inch, worked its way along her raw, burning nerves, dousing their fires.

His body was heavy on hers. Hard and heavy. Yet when he looked down at her, she wondered who he saw—her, or Taylor Grant.

"I shouldn't have done that," he said softly. "I'm sorry. We both agreed to take this slow and easy."

Adam's withdrawal stunned Maggie...and shamed her. For the first time since joining OMEGA, she'd lost sight of her mission. In his arms, she'd forgotten her role. When it came to cool detachment in the performance of duty, she wasn't anywhere near Adam's league.

It took everything she had to slip back into Taylor's skin. "You don't have to take all the blame," she murmured throatily. "Or the credit. I was the one who asked to be held, remember?"

She pushed herself out of his arms. One bare foot hit the icy floor, and then the other.

"We've got time. Time to savor each other. Time to get to know each other." She struggled to pull herself together and grasped at the straw Lillian had offered earlier. "Why don't you come with me in the morning? We'll walk down to the lake, see the sunrise together."

"Taylor..."

"I want whatever it is that's between us to be right, Adam."

His eyes met hers. His seeming detachment was gone, and in its place was a blazing certainty that went a long way toward soothing Maggie's confused emotions.

"It's right," he growled. "Whatever it is, it's right."

# *Chapter 9*

A distinctive aroma jerked Maggie out of a restless doze. She lifted her head, sniffing the cold air like a curious raccoon.

Bacon! Someone was cooking bacon!

She squinted at the dim light filtering through the closed shutters. Not even dawn yet, and someone was cooking bacon!

A crazy hope surged through her. Maybe Adam hadn't been able to sleep, any more than she had. Maybe he'd decided to take her up on her offer to see the sunrise, and was cooking himself breakfast while he waited for her. Maybe she could snatch a bite before the tantalizing scent lured everyone else out of bed, as well.

The thought of food, real food, galvanized Maggie into action. Throwing off the covers, she dashed into the bathroom and ran water into the old-fashioned porcelain sink. She washed quickly and, remembering Taylor's comment that she'd didn't bother with makeup in the mountains, slathered on only enough foundation needed to cover the artificial bone.

Returning to the bedroom, she tugged on a pair of thin thermal long johns. The lightweight silky fabric molded to her body like a second skin. Maggie wished she'd been issued subzero-tested undergarments like these for the hellish winter survival course OMEGA had put her through. They would have been far more comfortable for a trek over the Rockies than the bulky garments she'd had to wear.

Twisting and bending, she managed to strap the Kevlar body-suit in place, then pulled on a white turtleneck and pleated brown flannel slacks. The palm-size derringer and spare ammunition clip Maggie had found in the bedside table fit nicely in the roomy pants pocket. Relieved to be armed again, if only with this small .22, she rummaged in the chest of drawers for an extra pair of wool socks. The thick socks warmed her toes and made the boots she found in the closet fit more comfortably.

The vice president might wear a smaller dress size, Maggie thought with a dart of satisfaction, but her feet were bigger. As ridiculous as it was, the realization that Taylor wasn't quite perfect helped restore Maggie's balance—a balance that had been badly shaken by those few moments in Adam's arms last night.

Grinning, she paused with her hand on the cut-glass doorknob. Okay, so she'd almost lost it for those breathless, endless, glorious moments. So she'd come within a hair of jumping the man's bones. So he'd been the one to pull back, not her.

It was right. He'd said it. She felt it. Whatever this was between them, it was right.

His parting words had lessened the shock of her loss of control, but they'd also kept her tossing all night. His words, and the utter conviction that she and Adam would make love. Soon. Maggie felt it in every bone in her body.

But they wouldn't do it in another woman's bed. What was more, she darn well wasn't going to be wearing another woman's skin. She wanted to hear Adam murmur *her* name in his deep, husky voice. She wanted to feel his hands in her hair. Dammit, she wanted him. Fiercely. Urgently. With a hunger that defied all logic, all caution, all concerns over their respective positions in OMEGA.

All she had to do was stay alive long enough to discover who among the various people at the cabin had planted that bug.

Learn if that person was in league with a possible assassin. And track said assassin down. Then she could satisfy her hunger.

Another succulent aroma wafted through the thin wood, and Maggie twisted the doorknob. If she couldn't satisfy one hunger for a while longer, maybe, just maybe, she could satisfy another. Chasing the mouth-watering scent, she went downstairs.

A tired-eyed agent pushed himself out of an armchair beside the fire in the living room. In her rush to get to the kitchen, Maggie had forgotten all about the post-stander. No doubt the agent had heard her tiptoe across the hall to Adam's room last night. In spite of herself, heat crept up her neck. Good grief, she felt like a coed who'd been caught sneaking out of a boy's dorm room. No wonder Taylor's list of romantic liaisons had been so brief! The woman had no privacy at all. Bugs in her bathroom. Agents standing guard in her living room. Armed escorts on all her evenings out.

Summoning a smile, Maggie nodded to the man. "Good morning."

"Good morning, Mrs. Grant. You're up early."

"Yes, I wanted to catch the sunrise."

"Should be a gorgeous one." He lifted an arm to work at a kink in his neck. "The snow stopped around midnight, just after I came on shift."

"Mmm…"

Maggie was trying to think of some excuse to keep him from accompanying her into the kitchen when he supplied it himself.

"If you're going out, I'd better get suited up and let Agent Kowalski know."

"Fine."

He moved toward the front door, snagging a ski jacket from the convenient moose-antler rack. "Just buzz when you're ready to go."

Maggie hurried toward the kitchen, praying fervently that the person rattling pans on the top of the stove was Adam.

It wasn't.

Years of field experience enabled her to mask her intense disappointment when the figure at the stove turned. Resolutely

Maggie ignored the thick slabs of bacon sizzling in a sea of grease and smiled a greeting.

"Good morning, Hank."

"Mornin', Taylor."

She barely kept herself from lifting a brow at his casual use of the vice president's first name. Either Mrs. Grant didn't bother any more with protocol than with makeup while in the mountains, or this was a test.

Maggie had nothing to fall back on in this moment but her instincts. And the memory of the charismatic smile Taylor had given her when she invited Maggie to call her by her first name. She guessed that the vice president didn't stand on ceremony with the man she'd rescued from death row. Nor was he likely to be intimidated by a position or a title.

In the well-lit kitchen, his rugged features appeared even more startling than they had when Maggie first glimpsed them last night. The drunk who'd wielded that tire jack had done so with a vengeance.

McGowan jerked his head toward a carafe sitting on the oak plank table that took up most of the small kitchen. "Coffee's on the warmer. Hotcakes are just about done."

He turned back to the stove, and Maggie pulled out one of the ridgepole chairs. Pouring the rich black brew into an enameled mug, she propped her elbows on the table and studied McGowan. He looked almost as formidable from the rear as he did from the front.

Brown hair, long and shaggy and obviously cut by his own hand, brushed the collar of his blue work shirt. The well-washed fabric stretched tight across wiry shoulders. Rolled-up sleeves revealed thick hair matting his forearms, one of which bore a tattoo of a snarling, upright bear. His scuffed boots had been scraped clean of all dirt, but looking at their stained surface, Maggie didn't doubt he wore them for every chore, including cleaning out the stables.

He walked over to the table and placed a heaping platter in front of her.

"Buckwheat hotcakes. Like you like them. No butter. No syrup."

"Thank you." She managed to infuse a creditable touch of enthusiasm into her tone. "They look wonderful."

"Figured your…friend might want something more substantial. Biscuits and bacon do for him?"

The hesitation was so slight, most people might have missed it, but Maggie's training as a linguist had sensitized her to the slightest nuances of speech.

"Biscuits and bacon will be fine," she replied casually.

McGowan nodded and returned to the stove. Her eyes thoughtful, Maggie forked a bite of the heavy pancake.

Did the caretaker resent Adam Ridgeway's presence in Taylor's cabin, not to mention her life? Had his supposed devotion ripened into something deeper? And darker? Had he been corrupted into planting that bug in her room, or had he done it for his own purposes? His closed face gave her no clue.

After a moment, he tossed the spatula into the sink and leaned his hips against it. Folding his arms, he raised a brow in query.

"You want the snowmobiles?"

Maggie chewed slowly to cover her sudden uncertainty. Did she want the snowmobiles? Would Taylor want them?

"You don't need them," he added on a gruff note, watching her. "I cleared the path down to the lake with the snowblower before I started breakfast. Knew you'd want to go down there first thing."

The lake. Evidently everyone was aware of Taylor's little ritual of walking down to the lake to find her tree, whatever and wherever that was.

Before Maggie could reply, the kitchen door opened. The lump of buckwheat lodged halfway down her throat.

After last night, she should have anticipated Adam's impact on her traitorous body. She should have expected her empty stomach to do a close approximation of a triple flip. Her thighs to clench under the table. Her palms to dampen. But she darn well hadn't expected her throat to close around a clump of dough and almost choke her to death. She took a hasty swallow of coffee to ease its passage.

Damn! Adam Ridgeway in black tie and tails was enough to make any woman whip around for a second, or even third, look. But Adam in well-worn jeans and a green plaid shirt that hugged his broad shoulders was something else again.

He wore the clothes with a casual familiarity that said they were old friends and not just trotted out for a weekend in the woods. He hadn't shaved, and a dark stubble shadowed his chin and cheeks. Seeing him like this, Maggie felt her mental image of this man alter subtly, like a house shifting on its foundations—until she caught the expression in his blue eyes as he returned the caretaker's look. That was vintage Thunder. Cool. Assessing. In control.

"We didn't get a chance to meet last night," he said, crossing the small kitchen. "I'm Adam Ridgeway."

A scarred hand took his. "Hank McGowan."

Their hands dropped, and the two men measured each other.

"I understand from Taylor you run the place."

A wiry shoulder lifted. "She runs it. I keep it together while she's away."

"It's a big place for one man to handle."

"A crew comes up in the spring. To help with lambing, then later with the shearing. The rest of the time, we manage." He flicked Maggie a sideways glance. "Me and the hound."

"You met him last night," Maggie interjected, although she knew Adam wouldn't need a reminder. Even if they hadn't been briefed on what to expect at the cabin, the first encounter with that strange-looking creature would have stayed in anyone's mind.

"So I did. Radizwell, isn't it?"

"Actually," she replied, dredging through her memory for details, "his registered name is Radizwell, Marioffski's Silver Stand."

McGowan's lips twisted. "Damnedest name for a sheepdog I ever heard. You going to take him down to the lake with you?"

"Of course. You know very well that I couldn't get away without him, even if I wanted to."

His battered features relaxed into what was probably meant as a smile. "True. Biscuits and bacon are on the stove, Ridge-way."

Politeness demanded that Taylor share the table with her guest while he ate. Adam, bless him, took pity on Maggie.

"I'm not hungry right now. I'll just have a cup of coffee and tuck a couple of those biscuits in my pocket for later. A walk down to the lake should help me work up an appetite."

"Suit yourself."

"You'd better take more than a couple," Maggie suggested blandly. "It's a long walk."

When the huge, shaggy sheepdog bounded through the snow toward her, Maggie saw at once that he was still suspicious of her. Her hands froze on the zipper of her hot-pink ski jacket as he circled her a few times, sniffing warily.

Before he issued any of the rumbling growls that had raised the hairs on the back of her neck last night, however, Adam dug into the pocket of his blue ski jacket and offered the dog a bacon-stuffed biscuit.

"Here, boy."

Maggie bit back her instinctive protest as she watched, and the delicacy disappeared in a single gulp. The animal, now Adam's friend for life, cavorted like an animated overgrown dust mop, then took off for the trees.

Muttering under her breath, Maggie zipped up her jacket, tugged a matching knit band over her ears and trudged after him. Adam followed her, and the ever-present Secret Service agent trailed behind.

The path to the lake was steep, snow-covered in spots, and treacherous. It pitched downward from the side of the cabin, wound around tall oaks and silver-barked poplars, then twisted through a stand of Douglas fir. On her own, Maggie would have been lost within minutes. Luckily, the komondor knew exactly where they were headed. Every so often he stopped and looked back, his massive head tilted. At least Maggie assumed it was his head. With that impenetrable, shaggy coat, he could very well have been treating her to a calculated display of doggy disdain. Or waiting for Adam to offer another biscuit as an incentive. Ha! There was no way the creature was getting any more of those biscuits, Maggie vowed.

Although cold, the air was dry and incredibly sharp. The snow, a foot or more deep along the slopes, thinned as they descended to the tiny lake set in its nest of trees. Maggie was huffing from the strenuous walk by the time they left the path to circle the shoreline. Her silky thermal undershirt stuck to her shoulder blades, and the Kevlar shield trapped a nasty little trickle of perspiration in the small of her back.

Well aware that wet clothes led to hypothermia, which could kill far more swiftly than exposure or starvation, she slowed her pace and strolled along the shore beside Adam as though they were, in fact, just out to enjoy the spectacular sight of the sun burnishing the surrounding peaks. In the process, she searched the trees ringing the lake.

Maggie had no idea which was Taylor's special tree—until a lone twisted oak on a narrow spit of land snared her gaze. Lightning had split its trunk nearly in half, but the tree had defied the elements. Alone and proud, it lifted its bare branches to the golden light now spilling over the snowcapped peaks. Sure enough, Radizwell raced out onto the narrow strip and bounded around the twisted oak. His earsplitting barks echoed in the early-morning stillness like booming cannon fire.

"He probably thinks he's going to get another treat," Maggie muttered.

"Isn't he?"

"If you give away another one of those biscuits, that shaggy Hungarian won't be the only one howling."

He sent her an amused look. "You get a little testy when you're hungry, don't you?"

"Very!" she warned. "Remember that."

"I will," he promised, his eyes glinting.

The agent patrolled the shore while Maggie and Adam walked

out onto the spit for a few moments of much-needed privacy. They had to contact headquarters. Relay the latest developments to Jaguar. Formulate a game plan for communicating in an insecure environment. None of which could be done in a house wired from rooftop to wood-plank floor.

Despite the urgency of their mission, however, the initials carved into the weathered trunk tugged at Maggie's concentration. Pulling off a glove, she traced the deep grooves.

"*T* and *H.* Taylor and Harold."

"Hal," Adam reminded her, leaning a forearm against the tree. His breath mingled with hers, soft clouds of white vapor in the sharp mountain air. "She called him Hal."

Maggie nodded. "Hal."

With the tip of one finger, she followed the smooth cut. It had been blunted a bit over the years, but had withstood the test of time.

"Did you know him?" she asked.

"I met him once, just before he died. He was a good man, and a gifted sculptor. I have a bronze of his at home."

The glint of gold on Maggie's finger caught her gaze. "They must have loved each other very much," she said softly. "The words inside this ring make me want to cry. *Now, and forever.*"

When Adam didn't reply, she squinted up at him, her eyes narrowed against the now-dazzling sunlight reflected off the lake's frozen surface.

"Don't you believe in forever?"

Unaware that she was doing so, Maggie held her breath as she waited for his answer. There was so much she didn't know about this man, she acknowledged with a stab of uncertainty. He kept his thoughts to himself. His past was shrouded in mystery. Their only contact was through OMEGA and their work together.

Only recently had she finally acknowledged how much she wanted him. Yet now, staring into eyes deepened to midnight by the dark blue of his ski jacket, she realized with shattering clarity that wanting wasn't enough. Physical gratification wouldn't begin to satisfy the need this man generated in her.

In that moment, with the sun cutting through the distant peaks and their breath entwined on the cold, clear air, Maggie knew she wanted more. She wanted the forever Taylor had never had. With this man. With Adam.

"I believe in a lot of things, Maggie, my own," he said softly, in answer to her question. "Several of which I intend to discuss with you very soon."

*My own.*

She liked the sound of that. A lot. Suddenly very soon couldn't come fast enough for Maggie.

"It seems as though the list of things we have to discuss with each other is getting longer by the hour," she replied, her smile answering the promise in his eyes. "Right now, though, I guess we'd better contact Jaguar."

They moved to a boulder at the end of the spit. While Maggie brushed the snow off its flat surface, Adam punched the necessary codes into the transceiver built into his watch.

To the agent on the shore behind them, it must have appeared as though they were enjoying the panoramic vista of an ice-crusted lake skirted by towering dark green firs. Shoulder to shoulder, Maggie and Adam shared the rock and waited for headquarters to acknowledge the signal. He kept his arm tucked against her body to muffle the sound of Jake's voice.

"Jaguar here. Been wondering where you were."

"I couldn't check in this morning. Chameleon discovered a hidden device in her room. We had to assume there was one in mine, as well."

Through the crystal-clear transmission, Maggie could hear the frown in Jaguar's voice. "What kind of device?"

"One that our scanners didn't pick up when we swept the rooms last night. Or someone planted while we were downstairs."

"Can you describe it?"

Maggie bent her elbows across her knees and leaned forward. Keeping her voice low, she spoke into the transmitter. "About an inch square. Wafer-thin. Blue-gray in color, made of a composite material I've never seen before. It looks like plastic, but it's a lot more porous, almost like a honeycomb.''

''That doesn't fit any of the designs I know. I'll have the lab check it out.''

''Tell them to dig deep. This might be the first break we've had on this mission.''

A hint of excitement had crept into her voice. She'd had plenty of time to think through this unexpected turn of events during the long hours of the night…after she'd left Adam's bed.

''Tell the lab to talk to the Secret Service's technical division. Those guys have access to the latest materials.''

''You think the Secret Service planted a bug in the vice president's bedroom without her knowledge or approval?''

''I don't know,'' Maggie confessed. ''But if they did, the order had to come from high up in their chain.''

''Like from the secretary of the treasury himself,'' Jaguar drawled.

''Exactly.''

''Slip someone into Digicon's labs, as well,'' Adam instructed. ''I'm willing to bet they're using this composite material in the work they're doing for NASA.''

''I'd say that's a pretty good bet,'' Jaguar commented. ''By the way, you might want to know that we've confirmed Stoney Armstrong's suspicions about First Bank.''

''First Bank is laundering drug money?''

''Laundering it, dry-cleaning it, and serving it up starched and folded. It took our auditors some time, but they finally uncovered a blind account that traced back to a dummy corporation fronted by a major cartel.''

''Tell them they did good work.''

''They didn't do it all on their own. We got some inside information. From a source tracking it from the other end.''

''Is the source reliable?''

''Ask Chameleon,'' Jake drawled. ''She had dinner with him when he was in Washington a few weeks ago.''

''Luis!'' Maggie exclaimed. ''*That's* where I heard about First

Bank! I knew it was in connection with something other than the president's inter-monetary whatever.''

Adam's black brows snapped together. The idea of Maggie having dinner with the smooth, oversexed Colonel Luis Esteban, chief of Cartozan security, didn't sit particularly well with him.

"What's Esteban's interest in First Bank?"

"His government's trying to unfreeze the assets of the drug lord Jaguar and I helped take down last year. Evidently First was holding some."

"And?"

Maggie shrugged. "Cartoza's a small country. They were getting the runaround from some bureaucrat or another. I made a few calls to one or two of my contacts and hinted at high-level government interest on our side."

"How high?"

Her eyes gleamed. "I more or less left it to their imagination."

Adam frowned. There were too many references to First Bank cropping up for simple coincidence. First, there was the president's plan for stabilizing the Latin-American economies, which the bank had helped draft. Then Stoney Armstrong. Now Maggie and her smarmy Latin colonel. There was a connection. There had to be.

"Is that team of auditors still in place?" he asked Jaguar sharply.

"I was going to pull them out today."

"Keep them there. Have them examine every transaction, every wire transfer, for the last two years. See if Digicon does any business with them."

"Roger."

"And have them look into any blind trusts that may have been set up to handle accounts for persons currently in public office."

"Like the secretary of the treasury?"

"Like the secretary of the treasury. Get back to me immediately if they turn anything up. Anything at all. There's a link here that we're missing. Something that ties it all together."

"Will do."

Adam signed off. Rising, he shoved his hands into his back pockets and frowned at the lake.

"What do you think it could be?" Maggie asked. "This link?"

"I don't know. But it's there. I'm sure of it."

She regarded him with a solemn air. "Careful, Thunder. Your sixth sense is showing."

Adam turned, and felt his heart twist.

Maggie shone through the facade of her disguise. His Maggie. Irrepressible. Irresistible. Her eyes alight with the mischievous glow that snared his soul.

Surrendering to the inevitable, he reached for her. At that moment, he didn't care who was watching. Who was listening. He had to kiss her.

"Mmm..." she murmured a few moments later. "Nice. See what happens when you let yourself go and operate solely on instinct?"

"I've been operating on instincts where you're concerned for a long time," he said dryly. "You defy all logic or rational approach."

Laughter filled her eyes. "I'll take that as a compliment."

Adam caught her chin in his hand. Tilting her face to his, he warmed himself in her vibrant glow. "It was intended as one."

"Hmm... I think this is something else we have to add to our list of topics to discuss. Soon."

"*Very* soon."

Her breath caught. "Adam..."

He would always remember that moment beside the lake and wonder what she might have said—if the distant throb of an engine hadn't snagged her attention. If the agent on the shore hadn't turned, his head cocked toward the humming sound. If the dog hadn't risen up off its haunches and swung its massive body around.

Adam lifted his head and searched the tree line.

"It sounds like a snowmobile," Maggie murmured, a frown

sketching her forehead. She listened for a moment, then stiffened in his arms. "It's not coming from the direction of the cabin."

"No, it's not. Come on, let's get off this unprotected spit."

Tension, sudden and electric, arced between them. The dog picked up on it immediately, or perhaps sensed the danger on his own. He growled, deep in his throat, and pushed ahead of them onto the pebbled shore. His huge paws had just hit the snow when the first snowmobile burst out of the screen of trees.

It darted forward, a blue beetle whizzing across the snow on short skis. A second followed, then a third. The white-suited driver in the lead vehicle lifted his arm, and a burst of automatic gunfire cut the Secret Service agent down where he stood.

Maggie and Adam dived for cover. In a movement so ingrained, so instinctive, that they could have been synchronized swimmers, they rolled across the snow. On the first roll, Maggie had freed Taylor's puny little weapon from her pants pocket. On the second, Adam's far heavier and more powerful gun was blazing.

The first attacker came at them, spewing bullets and snow as he swerved to avoid the counterfire. Maggie left him to Adam and concentrated on the second, who was circling behind them. She got off one shot, and then a shaggy white shape hurtled through the air.

An agonized scream rose over the sound of gunfire and roaring engines, only to be cut off by a savage snarl.

# *Chapter 10*

Adam saw at once that they were outgunned and outmaneuvered.

Their Secret Service escort lay writhing in the snow, blood pumping from a hit to the stomach. They couldn't reach him without running along a stretch of open, exposed shoreline. The downed man's only hope of survival was for them to keep the attackers focused on their primary target. And her only hope was escape.

Obviously Maggie reached the same conclusion at exactly the same moment. She thrust herself upward, leaving the shelter of the shallow depression her body had made in the snow.

"Cover me!"

"No! Get down! Dammit, Maggie—"

Since she was already plowing across the snow, Adam had no choice. Cursing viciously, he rose on one knee. His blue steel Heckler & Koch spit a stream of fire at a white-suited figure zigzagging through the trees on a gleaming blue snowmobile. The driver jerked, and a sudden blotch of red blossomed on his shoulder. The hit was too high, only a flesh wound, but the assailant fell back, out of range, before Adam could get another clear shot.

Cursing again, he swung around.

Radizwell had knocked the second figure sideways, out of his seat. The riderless vehicle had skidded forward for another fifty or so yards before running up a high drift at an angle and tilting over. Screaming and thrashing, the driver flailed his arms in an effort to protect his face from the dog's savage assault. Adam didn't dare risk a shot from where he knelt. The sheepdog's massive body all but covered the downed man.

The third attacker circled through the Douglas firs, spraying automatic rifle fire in wild arcs as he tried to handle both his vehicle and his weapon. Adam couldn't get a clear line of fire through the screen of trees. In frustration, he raised his arm and squeezed off a shot. An overhanging branch snapped, dumping a shower of white just as the figure passed under it. For a few precious seconds, the automatic went silent.

Those seconds were all Maggie needed. Plunging through the knee-high snow, she reached the overturned snowmobile. At that point, she had to choose between charging forward another fifty yards to retrieve the Uzi the driver had lost when Radizwell hit him and snatching at their only chance of escape. The sound of rifle fire behind her decided the matter. She couldn't hope to reach the weapon before the other two attackers cut her—or Adam—down.

Grunting with effort, she heaved the sputtering snowmobile upright. Bullets stitched a line in the snowbank just above her head as she threw herself onto the seat and grappled frantically with the controls. The vehicle jerked forward, almost tumbling her backward. She grabbed at the handles for balance, then leaned low and gunned the engine.

The few moments it took her to reach Adam would repeat themselves in her nightmares for the rest of her life. He knelt on one knee, arm extended, pistol sited at a target darting through the trees. His black hair and blue ski jacket stood out against the dazzling whiteness of the snow and made him a perfect target. He was trying to draw the attackers' fire, Maggie knew. Away from her.

At the sound of the snowmobile coming at him from an angle, Adam swung around. For a heart-stopping moment, his weapon was trained directly on Maggie. It jerked in his hand. A sharp crack split the air.

Glancing over her shoulder, she saw that the figure struggling to escape Radizwell had made it to his knees. Adam's shot sent him diving facedown in the snow for cover. The dog promptly landed on his back.

Maggie reached Adam half a heartbeat later. Throttling back on the controls, she slowed a fraction. As soon as she felt his weight hit the seat behind her, she rammed the machine into full power. His arm wrapped around her waist like an iron band, cutting off her air. She barely noticed. She hadn't drawn a full breath since the first shot. Opening the throttle all the way, she aimed for the tree line.

The chase that followed could have come right out of a movie. A horror movie. Using every evasive tactic she'd been taught, and a few she invented along the way, Maggie dodged under low-hanging boughs, swerved around granite outcroppings and sailed over snowbanks. At one point, she took a turn too close. Prickly pine needles lashed her face, momentarily blinding her. The snowmobile swerved, tilted, righted itself.

"There!" Adam shouted in her ear, pointing over her shoulder.

She squinted through the involuntary tears caused by the sting of the needles. Following the line of his arm, she saw a wall of serrated granite slabs thrusting out of the snow to their left. To her blurred eyes, the gray-blue mass looked impenetrable.

"Take it hard and fast! Right through the notch!"

"What notch? I can't see!"

He twisted on the seat behind her, shoving his weapon into his jacket. Then he reached forward, an arm on either side of her, and took the controls. Maggie felt a craven urge to close her streaming eyes completely as the sheet of granite loomed in front of their hurtling vehicle.

Just when it seemed they were about to hit the wall, Adam threw his weight to one side and took her with him. The vehicle tilted at an impossible angle. Its left ski lifted, scraped stone. The engine revved louder and louder as the right ski dug into the snow. The vehicle hung suspended for what seemed like two or three lifetimes, then shot through the narrow opening.

Maggie would have shouted in joyous relief, if her blurred vision hadn't cleared just enough to see what lay on the other side of the wall. A ravine. A big ravine. About the size of the Grand Canyon. At its widest point.

Adam's hands froze on the controls for half an instant, then twisted violently. The engine screamed into full power.

"Hang on!"

As if she had any choice!

Maggie didn't hesitate at all this time. She scrunched her eyes shut and didn't open them until a bone-jarring jolt told her they'd landed on the far side. When she saw the steep, tree-covered slope ahead, she was sorry she'd opened them at all.

Branches slashed at their faces, tore at their bodies, as they whipped down the incline in a series of snaking turns. Her heart jackhammered against her ribs with each zig. Her kidneys slammed sideways on every zag. All the while she strained to hear behind her, listening for sounds of pursuit over the scream of their engine and the roar of her blood in her ears.

At the bottom of the slope, Adam yanked on the controls and slewed the machine to a halt. He shoved himself off, backward, and immediately sank to his knees in the snow.

"You take it from here."

"No way!"

"Get moving."

"No!"

Above his whiskered chin and cold-reddened cheeks, Adam's eyes flashed icy blue fire. "That's an order, Chameleon. Move!"

"I'm the field agent on this mission. I'm not dividing my forces, or what little firepower I have!"

"Dammit—"

"I'm not leaving you. Get on the vehicle!"

Every second wasted in argument could be their last. She knew it. He knew it.

His jaw working, Adam threw a leg over the rear of the snow-mobile.

They finally slowed to a stop at the crest of a wooded rise. Maggie kept the snowmobile idling, afraid to shut it off completely, in case they had to make a quick getaway. Eyes narrowed against the sun's glare, bodies tense, they listened and searched the woods below for signs of pursuit. Maggie was the first to pick up the rise and fall of engines in the distance.

"There's at least...two of them," she panted. "Maybe three...if...Radizwell didn't have the S.O.B. for lunch."

Adam angled his head, listening intently. "They're following the ravine. Looking for a place to cross."

He shoved back his sleeve. The flat gold watch nestled among the dark hairs of his wrist glinted in the morning sun.

"Jaguar, this is Thunder. Do you read me?"

Their breath puffed out in white clouds, rapid and ragged, while they waited for a response.

"I read you. Go ahead, Thunder."

"We've run into a little unfriendly fire. How close is the backup team?"

"Twenty minutes by helicopter," Jake snapped instantly. "Give me your coordinates."

Anticipating the need, Adam had already dug a small rectangular case out of his pocket. Not much bigger than a package of chewing gum, the digital compass received signals from the Navstar Global Positioning System. Navstar had proved its capabilities during the Gulf War by guiding tank commanders across the vast, featureless Saudi deserts. Its current constellation of twenty-four orbiting satellites could pinpoint time to within one-millionth of a second, velocity to within a fraction of a mile per hour, and location to within a few feet.

"Latitude, three-nine degrees, six—"

He broke off as the distant sounds died. Maggie inched the

throttles back as far as she dared to quiet the noise of their own engine and concentrated all her energies on listening.

"Six minutes," Adam continued. "Longitude, one-two-oh degrees—"

A sudden burst of horsepower cut him off once more. He stiffened, the tendons in his neck standing out like cords as he swiveled in the direction of the sounds.

"They got across!"

Engines revved. Grew louder.

"They're coming straight at us!" he snarled. "How the hell did they double back and find our tracks so quickly?"

Maggie turned a startled face to his, as stunned as he. Then her eyes dropped to the gold watch.

"Maybe they didn't find our tracks! Maybe they're homing in on the satellite signal!"

Adam didn't waste time in further speculation. The satellite signals were supposed to be secure. Scrambled. They'd never been broken or intercepted before. But an individual who knew how to bypass the sophisticated electronic filters in the White House switchboard might well have broken into a supposedly secure satellite system.

"Six-one, Jaguar! Six-one!"

With that emergency signal telling Jake to stand by until further contact, Adam abruptly terminated the transmission.

They managed to shake their pursuers once again.

The sounds of the distant motors fell away as Maggie steered an erratic course, up one slope, down another. Dodging fallen trees and low-hanging branches, she headed for a line of low, ragged peaks to her right. From the angle of the sun, she calculated they were headed due east, away from the cabin. Given the topography, however, she couldn't circle back. She had to follow where the mountains led.

Her face was stinging with cold and her numbed fingers were locked on the throttles when the machine under her began to sputter and miss. Maggie glanced down at the dash, trying to find the fuel gauge. She tore one gloved hand loose and rubbed it across the snow-covered indicator. Sure enough, the red bar danced at the bottom of the frost-encrusted gauge, almost out of sight.

Not two minutes later, the engine died. The snowmobile skidded a few feet farther up the slope, slowed to a crawl, stopped, then began a backward slide. Adam dug his boots in and brought them to a halt.

For a few seconds, neither of them moved. They remained silent. Listening. Searching the trees behind them.

Somewhere below them, their attackers were equally silent. Listening. Searching the trees above them.

"They're waiting," Adam said, his voice low. "For us to signal again."

"Bastards."

"They won't have used as much fuel as we did riding double. They'll catch us easily."

"Who?" Maggie muttered angrily. Her mission had just exploded in her face, and she was furious with herself for not having anticipated it. "Who are 'they'? How did we go from a narrow list of suspects to a whole damned strike team?"

"Whoever knew you were going to be at the lake this morning," Adam tossed back.

From the rigid set to his jaw, Maggie saw that he was no happier about this unexpected turn of events than she.

"Everyone knew," she snapped. "It was some kind of a ritual with Taylor."

"And if they didn't know, we told them," Adam added, disgust lacing his voice. "Last night, in my bedroom."

Maggie struggled to rein in her anger. "We're no longer dealing with a lone assassin here. This individual has a whole organization behind him. Obviously we need to reassess our mission parameters."

"Obviously." Adam pushed himself off the snowmobile and drew in a steadying breath. "Right now, though, our first priority has to be cover. If they don't pick us up soon, they'll call in air support and continue the search from the air."

"Denise and her people will have heard the shots and found

their downed man by now. They'll be searching, too—assuming one of them wasn't behind the attack in the first place," Maggie finished heavily.

"I don't think we can assume anything at this point. I suggest we burrow in until dark. The chances of them picking us up at night after we signal Jaguar will be slimmer. Marginally slimmer, admittedly, but slimmer."

Nodding, she clambered off the snowmobile and surveyed the now-useless vehicle.

"I guess we'd better see what we can salvage from this hummer."

While Adam used the butt of his pistol to break off pieces of one of the small mirrors mounted on the handles, Maggie pried open the storage compartment. Inside, she found a pitiful cache of survival equipment—one metallic solar blanket, so thin it folded into a plastic pouch the size of a candy bar, a small tool kit, and a spare pair of goggles. Evidently their attackers hadn't planned on a prolonged stay in the wilderness.

Adam knelt on one knee to bundle their small cache of equipment in a piece of fender he'd broken off. "You'd better take that off," he said, nodding to indicate her bright pink jacket. "I'll wrap it up with the rest of this gear."

Maggie didn't need to be told that the vivid color made too visible a target. Her shiver when she tugged off the thick layer of down wasn't due to the chill air.

Adam removed his own jacket, as well, but didn't offer it to her out of any misguided sense of male gallantry. He knew as well as she that the exertion of walking through the snow would work up a sweat, which had to be allowed to evaporate, or it would freeze their clothes to their bodies.

They left the vehicle buried under a nest of branches. As she trudged up the slope, trailing a screen of branches to cover their tracks, Maggie repeated to herself over and over the principle her instructors had drilled into her during survival training. Stay dry. In the jungle. In the Arctic. Stay dry. Foot rot from wet boots while slogging through swamps was as dangerous as frostbite from sweat-dampened undergarments in cold climates.

With that in mind, she tugged the hem of her turtleneck out of her waistband to let air circulate. Adam did the same with his plaid flannel shirt. Maggie saw that he wore the same style of high-tech long johns she did—under his shirt, at least. She didn't see how anything would fit under those snug jeans.

As they neared the crest, the trees thinned, as did the snow. Bare, windswept slabs of granite made the going easier, but also made Maggie feel far too vulnerable. The skin between her shoulder blades just above the bulletproof corset itched as though a big round circle had been painted on it.

Once over the top of the ridge, they scouted for a spot that would protect them from both the elements and searching eyes while they decided on their game plan.

"There," she panted, out of breath from the steep climb. "Under that tree."

The conifer she pointed to was at least sixty feet tall and shaped much like a pointed stake. Its branches grew wide at the bottom to catch the sun and narrowed dramatically toward the top. Laden with snow, the lower limbs drooped to the ground. They'd provide both concealment and natural insulation.

Maggie and Adam scrambled down the slope, brushing away their tracks as best they could. Squatting, he peered under the sagging branches.

"Perfect. I'll tunnel us in. You gather some branches."

She smiled wryly at his ingrained habit of assuming command, but decided not to take issue with it. In this instance, it didn't matter who dug and who gathered, as long as the tasks got done, and fast. Besides, she didn't have enough breath right now to argue.

Using the fender from the snowmobile, Adam knelt on one knee and set to work scooping a shallow trench in the snow under the drooping limbs. He worked quickly, but took great care not to disturb the thick layer of white coating the branches.

When Maggie came back with the first armload of pine branches, she stopped abruptly a few feet away. Adam had shed his plaid shirt to keep it dry. His thermal undershirt showed damp patches, attesting to the strenuous effort physical labor required at this elevation. It also attested to his superb physical condition. The silky white fabric clung to his body with a loving attention to detail that made Maggie's mouth go dry.

His upper torso might have been sculpted by Michelangelo. Broad and well toned at the shoulders, narrow and lean at the waist, he was basic, elemental male. When he bent forward, his jeans rode low on narrow hips. A curl of dark hair at the small of his back drew Maggie's fascinated gaze. With each scoop, his muscles rippled with a primitive, utterly beautiful poetry.

At the sight, something wrenched inside her, and she knew she'd never view Adam the same way again. The image of the cool aristocrat that she'd carried for so long in her mind and her heart shattered.

"Want me to dig the rest?" she asked, dumping the prickly pine branches beside the entrance.

"No, I'm all right. We'll need more branches to line the interior walls, though."

She nodded, stooping to check his progress. "Better not make the opening too narrow," she advised him with a wry smile. "As Lillian is so fond of pointing out, I'm not quite a perfect size eight."

Adam rested an arm on the bent fender and watched her retrace her footsteps in the snow. A tantalizing snatch of conversation he'd overheard between her and Lillian the night of the Kennedy Center benefit came back to him. Maggie had protested then that she wasn't a perfect anything, and he'd silently agreed. He hadn't changed his opinion. If anything, the past few days had reinforced it.

*Fiercely independent* didn't begin to describe this woman. Her adamant refusal to follow his orders today came as close to insubordination as he'd ever allowed an OMEGA operative. Only her acid reminder that she was the field commander on this mission had stopped him from shredding her to pieces on the spot. That, and the fact that Maggie Sinclair wasn't particularly shreddable.

But Adam knew he'd never erase from his mind his stunned fury when she'd sprung up out of the snow and dashed for the snowmobile. Or his sudden, swamping fear. He'd expected a bullet to slam into her body at any second. To see her thrown back by the force of a hit. He'd kept his mind focused and his hand steady as he provided covering fire, but a silent litany had reverberated through him with every step she took.

No more talk.

No more waiting.

No more denying the raw need that gripped him. And her.

That same refrain echoed in his mind now as he bent to scoop fenderful after fenderful of snow out of the shallow trench.

No more talk.

No more waiting.

If they lived through this day, neither of them would ever be the same. Soon had become now.

While he dug, Maggie rounded up enough pine branches to construct a thick, springy mat that would keep them off the snow. More feathery branches provided insulation for the walls Adam built up around the depression. Above these walls the sagging tree limbs formed a natural sloping ceiling.

Within a remarkably short time, their hidden lair was complete. While Adam crawled inside to spread the lightweight solar blanket over the springy mat, Maggie gathered their meager gear.

She handed him the items one by one, still panting a little from her foraging trips. Pine needles stuck to her white turtleneck, which in turn stuck to her back and shoulders.

Adam got to his feet and dusted the snow from his knees, frowning as he took in the damp hair curling around her face.

"You crawl inside. I'll brush the rest of the tracks and seal the entrance."

Maggie nodded and dropped to her knees.

"Strip off as much as you can. I'll help you with the body shield when I'm done here, so you can get out of those damp long johns."

She paused halfway through the narrow tunnel. Bottom wiggling, she backed out again.

"Let's just review the situation here. We're in the middle of nowhere. Two, possibly three stalkers are searching for us as we speak. We don't know who sent them, we can't contact headquarters for help, and we have no idea at this moment how long we're going to be stranded here.''

"That about sums it up."

"Not quite."

She eyed his chest, which was damp from exertion. Her fingers dug into her thighs with the need to stroke its broad planes. Dry them. Curl into their warmth.

Lifting her gaze to his face, she grinned. It wasn't much of a grin, more a grimace than an expression of mirth, but it was the best Maggie could do at the moment.

"If we crawl into that hole and get naked together, I'm not going to be held responsible for my actions."

He smiled at her then. Not the smooth, easy smile he'd given "Taylor" the past few days. Not the cool half smile he allowed himself on occasion at OMEGA headquarters. This was a slow, satisfied, devastatingly predatory twist of his lips.

"Maggie, my darling, when we get naked together, responsibility is the last thing I want from you."

At her start of surprise, his smile lost its razor's edge. "Go on, get inside. You know as well as I do that the next few minutes could make the difference between life and death."

# Chapter 11

Mind racing, heart pumping, Maggie crawled through the narrow tunnel.

Okay. All right. It was a matter of survival. Hers and his. They had to strip off. They had to stay dry. In the Arctic. In the jungle.

She was a professional. She'd been trained for situations like this. It was a matter of survival.

Yet when she entered the chamber Adam had carved for them under the spreading boughs of the majestic fir, her chaotic thoughts centered on a different kind of survival. The kind that had to do with the continuation of the species.

Her blood rushed through her veins, bringing with it a heat that added to the moisture dewing her neck. Breathing hard, she made herself sit back on her heels. While she waited for her pulse to slow, she admired the fruits of their labors.

Both the size and the warmth of this subterranean nest surprised her. The tree's massive trunk formed a solid, rounded back wall. Mounded snow defined the rest of the area. Overhead, drooping, snow-laden branches slanted down at an angle from the base of the tree to the outer walls. The fragrant pine boughs Maggie had gathered lined the interior walls and made a thick mat for the floor, adding an extra layer of insulation.

Amazing. They'd constructed a tight, neat lean-to using nature's own materials, with no tools or modern implements except a fiberglass fender scoop. Adam had spread the thin Mylar blanket over the mat, but Maggie knew they could have survived without it.

Survival.

The pulse that had slowed a fraction leaped into action again. It was a matter of survival.

And, as Adam had said, the next few minutes could make the difference between life and death.

Settling cross-legged on the shifting mat, she pulled off her gloves. Carefully she placed her weapon atop her folded pink ski jacket to keep it both dry and close at hand, then went to work on her bootlaces. Within moments, her brown pants hung from one of the overhead branches. She was just reaching for the hem of her white turtleneck when Adam backed into the chamber.

Suddenly the pine-scented nest didn't seem nearly as spacious as it had a moment ago.

Maggie edged over to make room for him. The springy mat shifted under her and tipped her sideways. Her elbow dug into his thigh. His shoulder thumped her chest. It took a bit of doing, but they finally maneuvered themselves back into sitting positions. He laid his weapon next to hers and glanced around the interior. A half smile curved his lips as he surveyed his work.

"The hole seemed a lot bigger when I was digging it. It's kind of tight in here."

"At least it'll be warm."

He nodded, eyeing the mounded walls. "When the snow sets, this cave will be as well insulated as any house. Better than most."

Maggie believed him. She already felt the extra heat his presence generated in the small chamber. He'd brought a musky warmth into the dim interior, which combined with hers to drive off the chill. The trapped air warmed perceptibly around them while he unlaced his boots. And when his hand went to the zipper of his jeans, Maggie could have sworn the temperature shot up another dozen degrees or so.

It was a matter of survival. It was...

Hastily she dragged her turtleneck over her head.

Matter-of-factly he shoved the well-worn denim down over his hips. He rose up on one knee to drape his pants over the limb beside her top.

To Maggie's intense relief and equally intense disappointment, he did wear high-tech long johns under those snug jeans. But where her bottoms covered her from waist to ankle, his came only to midthigh, like running or biking shorts. They might have been meant for his warmth, but they contributed greatly to hers.

If his upper torso had been sculpted by Michelangelo, his lower body was by the same unknown Greek artist who'd created the statue of Hercules she'd once seen in a museum in Athens. All long lines and corded sinews. Sleek. Powerful. Well muscled. And bulging in places that sent a shaft of heat spearing straight through Maggie.

"Are your socks wet?"

She dragged her gaze up to his face. "My socks?"

"Your socks. Are they wet?"

"No."

"Good. You'd better keep them on, along with the thermal underwear. But the body shield needs to come off. Bend over."

Maggie bit her lip.

"You're damp under the Kevlar. You need to dry off. It's a matter of—"

"I know. A matter of survival."

Pushing herself to her knees, she twisted to one side. The rasp of Velcro echoed through the nest. Once. Twice. When the corset fell away, she felt strangely naked. Without the constraining shield, her breasts regained their fuller, firmer shape. Beneath the thin covering of her undershirt, her nipples puckered with the cold. Or the heat. At this point, she couldn't have said which.

The damp, silky underwear molded to every line of her chest

as faithfully as it did to Adam's. Maggie felt an instinctive urge, as old as woman herself, to hunch her shoulders and hide herself.

Immediately, another, even older urge flowed through her. The need to claim her man. Her mate. Her forever.

They might have only this hour together. Only these few moments. Yet Maggie knew they would last her a lifetime. Slowly she straightened her shoulders. Sitting back on her heels, she met Adam's eyes. The blue fire in them ignited the flames licking at her blood.

His gaze drifted from her face to her throat. Her breasts. Her stomach. Involuntarily her thighs clenched.

A muscle ticked in the side of his jaw, shadowed with the night's growth.

"Do you have any idea how beautiful you are?"

A momentary doubt shivered through her as she remembered the artificial bone that shaped her nose and chin. The violet contacts. The auburn hair. Who did he see? Who did he find beautiful? She had to know.

"Who, Adam? Me, or Taylor? Who do you see?"

In answer, he smiled and lifted a hand to curve her cheek. "I see you, Maggie. A woman of incredible courage and vibrant, glowing life."

That pretty well satisfied her doubts, but she had no objection when Adam expanded a bit.

"I see the same woman who sailed out of my office swathed from head to foot in a black nun's habit. I see the high-class hooker who took off for France in a slithery shoestring halter that kept me awake for a solid week."

She tilted her head into his hand. "A week, huh?"

"At least."

"Who else? Who else do you see?"

His thumb brushed her lower lip. "I see the woman who infuriates me on occasion, and intrigues me at all times. Who makes me want to lock my office door and throw her down on that damned conference table she always perches on."

Maggie's brows shot up. "Really?"

"Really."

"Hmm..."

The idea that he'd harbored a few fantasies about her thrilled Maggie to her core. Almost as much as the thumb rubbing across her lip. Incredible, what a single touch could do.

"Adam?"

"Yes?"

"Do you have any idea how many times I've imagined...us? Together? Alone?"

His hand curled around the back of her neck, urging her closer. Branches shifted. Mylar crinkled. They were chest to chest. Mouth to mouth.

"No. Tell me."

"A few."

"Only a few?" He kissed her right eyelid.

"Okay, more than a few. A dozen."

"Only a dozen?" He kissed her left eyelid.

She smiled up at him. "A hundred or two."

"And?"

"And never, ever, in any one of those thousands of times, did I picture us making love underground. In a nest of pine needles. Fully clothed. Well, one of us fully clothed."

"Maggie, my darling, I've pictured us underground and aboveground and on the ground."

Laughter welled inside her. "All that was going on behind your Mr. In Control, always-so-cool exterior?"

"All that, and more."

"Well, well..."

He kissed her mouth then, and brought her down with him. Legs entangled, she sprawled across his chest. Hungrily she explored his mouth with her tongue and teeth. His unshaven chin rasped against hers. The tiny, stinging sensation sent a rush of liquid warmth to Maggie's belly. Her hand slithered down his chest, and she discovered that clothes were no impediment to a determined woman. He filled her fist, rock-hard, ridged, sheathed in satiny softness.

His hand tugged up the hem of her shirt and found her breast. It swelled in his hold, the nipple throbbing with an ache that matched the one between her legs. An ache that grew with every kiss, every thrust of his thigh between hers.

Time and space dissolved. Merged. Melted into two bodies and one need. When she couldn't bear their separateness any longer, she lifted slightly and arched her pelvis against his hardness.

His hands stilled her hips. "Wait, Maggie. Wait."

"No. No more waiting."

"Not this way."

"Why not?"

His eyes glinted with regret. "Because, sweetheart, even my vivid fantasies didn't include making love to you in the snow beside a frozen lake. I didn't bring any protection when I walked out to view the sunrise with you."

Nonplussed, Maggie stared at him helplessly.

With a surge of his powerful body, he rolled her over. "Let me love you in a way that's safe. In a way that will still give us pleasure."

His hand found the convenient opening in the bottoms of her long johns. The wayward thought shot through Maggie that the manufacturers of winter survival wear knew what they were doing. A person didn't have to undress to perform any vital function. And taking Adam into her body was becoming more vital by the second.

He slid a finger inside her welcoming wetness, then another. His thumb pressed the hard core at her center. Gasping, she arched under him.

The scent of crushed pine needles, sharp and pungent, rose around her. Maggie knew she would never again walk through a forest or touch a Christmas wreath or open a bottle of kitchen cleaner without thinking of this man and this moment. Then his mouth came down on hers, and Maggie forgot about kitchen cleaners and walks and everything else.

Their breathing grew more labored. Their bodies hardened. As his hands and his mouth worked their magic, wave after wave of sensation washed through Maggie, drawing her closer to the edge.

With infinite skill, he primed her.

With infinite need, she caught his face between her hands. Panting, breathless, she could only gasp her desperate desire.

"Adam. Listen to me. We're in the middle of nowhere. On our own. We may never make it out of here alive. This could be the only moment we ever have."

"Maggie…"

"This could be our once. Our forever. I don't want protection. Not from you. I want you."

They fit together the way she'd always known they would. Female and male. Woman and man. Maggie and Adam.

He rose up and thrust into her. She lifted her hips and thrust against him.

He filled her, full and powerful and hard and urgent. She took him into her, wrapping her body and heart and soul around him.

Mylar twisted around their legs. Branches poked at backs and knees and elbows and bottoms. Maggie didn't feel any of it. Her entire being was focused on Adam.

When he reached down between their bodies and rubbed her tight, aching core, she climaxed in an explosion of white light and red, searing pleasure. She arched under him, groaning, flexing her muscles in an instinctive need to take him with her.

The violent movement dislodged a clump of snow from the branch overhead. It landed on Adam's shoulder, slid down to Maggie's chest.

Her eyes opened in shock, and she laughed.

Adam groaned at the sound and surged into her a final time.

Afterward, long afterward, they exchanged the clothes that clung to their slick bodies for the dry ones hanging over their heads. With a rustle of boughs, Adam propped his back against the tree trunk, stretched out his legs and brought Maggie into his lap. She laid her head against his shoulder, sighing.

"How much time do we have?"

Adam smiled at the reluctant question. He wasn't in any more of a hurry than Maggie to leave this small den. Resting his chin on the top of her head, he drew her closer into his warmth. The scaly bark of the tree trunk bit into his back through the flannel shirt, but he barely noticed. With one hand, he reached out to check his gold watch.

"It's not even ten. We have a long time to wait before we contact Jaguar and call in an extraction team."

She shifted a little. "Let's talk about that."

"What is there to talk about? As soon as the sun goes down, we go up on the net. We evade any searchers until the team arrives. They can have you—can have us out in fifteen minutes."

Adam cursed his slip, and Maggie didn't miss it. She twisted around in his arms.

"You're not going, are you?"

"No."

"Neither am I."

"The hell you're not."

One wine-colored brow arched, and Adam moderated his tone. "As you said yourself, our mission parameters have changed. Drastically. We're not trying to lure a lone assassin out in the open any longer. We're facing a strike team."

"And I'm their target."

Her words triggered a staggering suspicion in Adam. With great effort, he kept his face impassive. Before he said anything to Maggie, he needed to think this through.

She mistook his sudden silence for disagreement. Pushing herself out of his arms, she got to her knees. "I'm the only one who can bring them into the open, Adam. I'm the only one who can—"

A long, rolling growl filled the air, cutting Maggie off in midsentence. She clamped a hand across her stomach.

"Good grief. Sorry 'bout that."

Adam forced a smile. "Sounds like the natives are getting restless."

She sent him a sheepish grin. "Well, hungry, anyway."

Deliberately Adam decided to take advantage of the diversion her growling stomach offered. They had a few more hours. He needed the time to think. To absorb the gut-wrenching implications of her blithe comment. Maggie was right. He knew it with a cold, chilling certainty. She was the bait. She was the one they were after. Not Taylor Grant. Her.

Whoever had targeted the vice president could have hit without warning. Yet the assassin had signaled his intent with that anonymous phone call. He'd issued a threat he must have known would activate an elaborate screen of defenses.

Somehow, some way, that call had led to the attack on Maggie. Not Taylor. Maggie.

Adam didn't know why or who or how, and at this moment he didn't care. His only concern was to keep Maggie alive until they could unravel this increasingly bizarre situation.

They had a few more hours. A few precious hours. He needed to think.

"Maybe it's time to break out the emergency rations," he suggested evenly.

"Rations?" She swept their small pile of supplies with a quick glance. "What rations?"

He reached for his blue ski jacket.

"Adam!" She scrambled up on her knees, her face alight. "I forgot all about your stash of biscuits! And bacon!"

He fished around in the deep pocket, then withdrew his hand and flipped the jacket over to reach the other.

The eager anticipation in her eyes gave way to a look of comic dismay. "Oh, God, I hope they didn't fall out of your pocket when we did that wheelie through the pass. We were standing on our heads."

"No, here they are."

He drew out a napkin-wrapped bundle, and Maggie scuttled closer while he unwrapped the edges of the cloth. When the treasure was uncovered, it turned out to be little more than a handful of crumbled dough and bits of bacon, gray with cold, congealed grease.

The unappetizing sight didn't deter Maggie at all. She pinched a bite between thumb and forefinger and popped it into her mouth. Closing her eyes, she savored the tiny morsel.

He had to smile at her beatific expression. "Good?"

"Mmm...wonderful!"

Eyes closed, head back, she wiped her tongue around her lips in search of stray crumbs.

Adam's fist clenched on the napkin. Their small nest wasn't quite a penthouse suite, and the pile of crumbs in his hand hadn't come from a beribboned basket of imported delicacies. Yet the same primitive urge that had swept him in L.A. crashed through him once again. Now, as then, he wanted to feed her. Bit by bit. Bite by bite.

But here, in this tiny snow cave, with danger all around them, the swamping, driving urge intensified a hundredfold. Subtly, swiftly, it shifted from erotic to primordial.

It was a matter of survival. Of responding to the basic instincts that drove all species. This woman was his mate. Adam wanted to feed her, and protect her, and love her. The realization that he might be able to accomplish only two out of the three made his stomach twist. That, and the knowledge that Maggie didn't want protection.

Of any sort.

His gaze roamed her upturned face, and Adam knew he'd love her differently if she did. He'd still want her with a need so raw it consumed him. He'd still lose himself in her laughing eyes. Without the fierce independence that made her Maggie, however, he'd love her with a different need.

Somehow he suspected that need wouldn't be anywhere near as powerful as the one that drove him now.

Uncurling his fingers, he found a fair-size sliver of cold bacon. "Open your mouth."

Her eyes opened instead.

She glanced from his face to the morsel in his fingers, then back to his face.

"Aren't you going to have any?"

"No."

"You didn't have any breakfast. Aren't you hungry?"

"Yes. Very. But not for bacon. Let's feed you, and then we'll feed me."

The small stash of food and their clothes disappeared at approximately the same time.

With the passing hours, the light filtering through the snow-laden branches overhead grew brighter, then gradually dimmed.

They took turns dozing, and risked one trip outside the cave for a quick surveillance and an even quicker trip behind some bushes. After the warmth of the air trapped in the small cave, the outside seemed twice as cold. Maggie eyed the shadows drifting across the slopes as the sun played hide-and-seek among the tall peaks. They'd have to leave their small nest soon.

Her teeth were chattering by the time they'd blocked the entrance up again. She sat cross-legged on the Mylar mat and tucked her hands into her armpits to warm her fingertips.

"What time is it?"

Adam shoved back his sleeve. "Almost four. It should be dark in an hour."

"We'll have to leave then."

"We will."

She was silent for a moment, marshaling her thoughts. The muted growl that filled the small cavern took them both by surprise.

Maggie's red brows snapped together as she frowned down at her stomach.

"We cleaned out our entire supply of emergency rations," Adam reminded her. "You'll have to wait until we get back to—"

Another low growl rumbled through the air.

Maggie shook her head. "It's not me this time," she whispered.

Nodding, Adam reached for his pistol.

Maggie had hers in hand, as well, when they heard the scratching in the snow at the entrance to the tunnel.

Adam's jaw hardened. "Get dressed," he hissed. "Fast. Put on as many layers as you can."

As quickly and quietly as possible, Maggie scrambled into her clothes. Not for warmth. If a wild animal was digging at the entrance to their lair, she'd need the layers for protection against fangs and claws. And if the predator was of the two-legged variety, she didn't want to face him in her underwear.

Zipping her jacket up to her chin, she handed Adam his. While he pulled it on, she kept her pistol leveled at the entrance. Automatically they positioned themselves at either side of the tunnel entrance, out of the line of fire.

Another low, hair-raising growl convinced her their uninvited guest was close to gaining entry. Her finger tightened on the trigger.

The snow shifted. A black nose poked through the white. Sniffed. Pushed farther. More snow crumbled, and a muzzle covered in thick ropes of snowy fur appeared.

Radizwell!

Maggie sagged against the wall in relief, but had the presence of mind not to speak. The animal might not be alone out there. He might well have led a strike team right to them. Or a rescue team.

When he finally gained entrance, they discovered he hadn't led anyone to them at all. Apparently he'd come in search of Adam. And more bacon. The reproachful look the dog turned on Maggie when he discovered the empty, grease-stained napkin filled her with instant guilt.

# Chapter 12

With the komondor's arrival, the air in the small cave became suffocatingly warm and decidedly aromatic. Crushed pine needles couldn't begin to compete with the aroma drifting from his ropes of uncombed fur, or his doggy breath. Nor could Maggie or Adam move without crawling over or under or around the animal.

She nodded when Adam suggested that the dog's arrival necessitated a change in plans. With less than an hour of daylight left, they couldn't take the chance that someone might pick up the dog's tracks and follow them here. They should scout out a better defensive position until they could call in the extraction team.

Maggie crawled out of the snow cave with mixed emotions. As much as she hated to leave their private nest, she needed air. Adam followed a moment later. Keeping to the shelter of the towering conifer, they breathed in the sharp, clean scent of snow and pines. Radizwell hunkered down on Adam's other side, pointedly ignoring her. Maggie suspected that he still hadn't quite accepted this stranger in Taylor's clothes. Or forgiven her for the empty, bacon-scented napkin.

They stood still and silent for long moments, searching the slopes above and below. Nothing moved. No sounds disturbed the quiet except the distant, raucous call of a hawk wheeling overhead and Radizwell's steady panting. The sun slowly slipped toward the high peaks, deepening the shadows cast by the towering trees and bathing the snow in a soft purple light.

"We'll have to head farther east," Adam murmured after a few moments. "Just in case they picked up Radizwell's tracks and are heading this way."

He pointed toward a jagged ridge a short distance away. "Let's try for those rocks. Even if the wrong people lock on to our signal, it will be harder to see us up there at night. We can hold them off until the extraction team gets here."

Maggie drew in a deep breath. "I don't think we should hold them off. We should try to pull them in."

He swung around to face her. "We've already talked about this."

"We started to," she said evenly, "but my growling stomach interrupted us. As I recall, we got sidetracked by a few cold biscuits and bacon bits."

A small smile tugged at his mouth. "So we did."

As much as she wanted to, Maggie didn't let herself be drawn in by the softening in his face or the glint in his eyes. She'd known this confrontation with Adam would come, and she was ready for it.

Keeping her tone brisk and businesslike, she reiterated the conclusions they'd reached in the cave.

"Look, we both agree the scope of the mission has changed somewhat."

"Somewhat?"

"Okay, a lot. But my basic role in the operation hasn't changed at all. I'm still the bait."

"You were the bait when we thought we were dealing with a single assassin. Now we know that individual has a whole team backing him up."

"That's just it, Adam. I'm still the one they want. I'm still—"
She stopped abruptly, frowning.

"I'm still the one they want," she said slowly. "The one *he* wants."

Adam stiffened, and in his eyes Maggie saw an echo of the same suspicion that was forming in the pit of her stomach like a cold, heavy weight.

"He wants me." She articulated each word with careful precision, not wanting to believe them, even as she said them. "He wants me. Not Taylor Grant. Me."

He didn't answer. Didn't say a word, and his silence hammered at Maggie like a crowbar striking against a metal wall.

"You think so, too, don't you? Don't you?"

"I admit the idea occurred to me. But—"

"But nothing! This unknown assassin knew how to by-pass the White House phone system. Which meant he probably could have circumvented the personal security system and gotten to the vice president any time he wanted. But he didn't really want her, did he? He wanted me. I've been the target all along."

She stared at Adam, stunned. "That's it, isn't it, Adam? You know it as well as I do. He wants me."

A muscle ticked in his jaw. "All right, Maggie. Let's say you're right. Let's say he wants you. Who is *he?*"

She shook her head. "I don't know. Whoever made that call."

"Who? Who made it?"

"I don't know."

Snow crunched under his boot as he took a step toward her. "Think! Who wants you dead?"

"I don't know!"

Radizwell picked up on the tension arcing through the air between them. He whined far back in his throat and padded forward to nudge a jeans-clad hip. Adam ignored him, his attention focused on the woman before him.

"Who, Maggie? Who wants to get to you?"

She flung out a gloved hand. "Any one of a dozen men, and a few women, all of whom are behind bars now!"

"Why?" The single syllable had the force of a whip, sharp and stinging.

"Because they're behind bars!"

Adam's eyes were blue ice behind his black lashes. His breath came fast and hard on the cold air. "Not good enough. Try again. Think! Why would any of those people want you dead?"

"Because…" She wet her lips. "Because I know something I'm not supposed to know. Or I saw something I wasn't supposed to see. Or heard something I wasn't supposed to hear."

The shadows obscured his face now. Maggie couldn't see his eyes, but she felt them. Narrowed. Intent. Searing.

"What? What did you see or hear? What could you know that you're not supposed to?"

"I don't know, dammit! I don't know!"

The sharp frustration in her voice sliced through the tension-filled air like a blade. Radizwell gave a low growl, unsure of the source of their conflict, but obviously unhappy about it. He edged closer to Adam. If it came to choosing teams, Maggie thought in a wild aside, the dog had already chosen his.

"What I don't understand is, why here?" she said, bringing herself under control. "Why not in D.C.? Or anywhere else? Why set this trap, using me as bait? Luring me in like this. Or—" She stopped, her eyes widening. "Or out!"

"Out, how?"

"Out of my civilian cover. My God, Adam. Maybe that's it. Maybe someone staged this elaborate charade to draw me out, because he couldn't get to me any other way. He couldn't get to Chameleon."

The flat, hard expression on Adam's face might have signaled disbelief, or denial, or a combination of both.

"It's possible," she insisted. "No one outside OMEGA knows our real identities. Hell, only a handful within the agency have access to that information."

"You're saying someone set this whole thing up? Just on the chance you'd be tagged to double for the vice president?"

"It's possible," she repeated stubbornly.

''For God's sake, do you have any idea how remote that possibility is?''

''Not that remote,'' she snapped. ''I'm here, aren't I?''

That stopped him. He went completely still, his arms at his sides, his hands curled into fists. His face could have been carved out of ice.

''If that's the case,'' he said finally, ''this all boils down to a question of who knew you might double for the vice president. Who, Maggie?''

''No one,'' she protested. ''No one knew, except the president, and the vice president. Lillian. Jaguar. The OMEGA team. And—''

She stopped, swallowing hard.

''And the director of OMEGA,'' Adam said slowly.

She didn't breathe, didn't blink. It seemed to Maggie that her body had lost all capacity to move. Her brain had certainly lost all ability to function. It had gone numb and completely blank. The white, silent woods seemed to close in, until her world became a single, shadowed face.

''Why, Maggie?'' he asked softly, bringing them full circle. ''Why would any of those people want you dead?''

She struggled for an answer. Any answer. One that would satisfy him, and her. The silence spun out, second by cold, crystalline second.

A hundred chaotic thoughts tumbled through Maggie's numbed mind. A thousand shattering emotions fought for pre-eminence in her heart. Could Adam have brought her to this isolated spot for some desperate reason of his own? What did she know of him? What did any of the OMEGA agents know of him? His past was shrouded in secrecy. Even now, he led a double life that few knew about. He'd always kept himself so remote. His feelings so shuttered.

Until today. Until he'd held her in his arms and she'd taken him into her body. When he'd looked down into her eyes. There had been no shutters on his soul then.

Her riotous emotions stilled. The confusion dulling her mind faded. She didn't need to know the secrets in Adam's past. She didn't care about his present double life. If she was ever going to trust her instincts, it had to be now.

Adam didn't, couldn't, want her dead.

She'd stake her life on it.

Drawing on everything that was in her heart, she summoned a valiant grin. "Well, I think it's safe to cross the OMEGA team off our ever-expanding list of suspects. I put my life in their hands every time I walk out the door. And I know the director of OMEGA wouldn't set me up like this."

He didn't respond for long, agonizing moments. "Do you?" he said at last.

The cool, even tone was so quintessentially Adam that Maggie didn't know whether to laugh or to cry. She did neither. Instead, she folded her arms across her chest and nodded.

"I do. Although he's tried to take my head off on several memorable occasions in the past three years, he's in love with me. He hasn't admitted it yet. He may not even realize it yet. But he is. What's more, I love him. With all my heart and soul."

If anyone had told Maggie that she'd finally articulate her feelings to Adam while standing knee-deep in snow, with cold nipping at her nose and a team of killers searching for her, she would've checked their medication levels. Of all the times and all the places to have the "discussion" she and Adam had delayed for so long!

Not that it was much of a discussion, she realized belatedly. So far, the exchange had been entirely too one-sided.

"You can jump in here anytime," she invited sweetly.

With a sound that was half laugh, half groan, Adam swept her into his arms. He locked his fists behind her back, holding her against his chest. The deepening shadows didn't obscure his eyes now. Now they blazed down at her with a fierce emotion that warmed Maggie's nose and toes and all parts in between.

"I am. I do. I know."

"Come again?" she asked, breathless.

"I am in love with you. I do realize it. I know you love me, too."

"Well, well, well…"

Her smug, satisfied grin made Adam want to pick her up and carry her back to the snow cave. Hell, it made him want to throw her down in the snow right here, rip off her various layers and lose himself in her fire. He had to satisfy himself with a shattering kiss.

They were both breathing fast and hard when he pulled back. It took some effort, but Adam put her out of his arms.

"We'll finish this interesting discussion when we get out of here."

Her mischievous smile almost shattered the remnants of his control. "It's finished. At least as far as I'm concerned. You are. You do. You know. What more is there to say?"

"Maggie…"

"All we have to decide now is what to do about it."

"Correction. Right now we have to get you out of here. We can decide about it—about us—after we get you to a safe haven."

Her teasing smile faded a bit. "I can't operate out of a safe haven. I'm a field operative."

He bent to pick up their small store of supplies. "It's too dangerous in the field. I'm calling you in."

She winced at his use of the euphemism every OMEGA agent dreaded hearing. He was calling her in. Out of the cold. Ordering her to abandon her cover and her mission.

Maggie shook her head. "Not yet, Adam. You can't terminate this mission yet. We won't find the answer in a safe haven. The answer's here, in the field."

He didn't reply. He didn't have to. They both knew she was right. Maggie saw his jaw work. He wanted to find whoever was behind this scheme as much as, or more than, she.

"I can't go in," she said softly, firmly. "Not yet. You wouldn't have any respect for me if I did. You wouldn't…" She circled a hand in the air. "You wouldn't see me the same way, ever again. As an agent, or as a woman. You wouldn't love me the same way."

Her uncanny echo of his earlier thoughts pierced Adam's wall of resistance. He would love her. He would always love her. But he would love her differently if she wasn't the Maggie who stood nose to nose with him, in the middle of nowhere, with no food, little firepower, and a killer on her trail, yet refused point-blank to run for cover.

Still, he made one last effort. "Do you think I'll ever see you the same way again after those hours in the snow cave? As a woman, or as an agent?"

"Good Lord, I hope not!"

Her startled exclamation wrung a smile out of him. Maggie pounced on it like a cat after a ball of catnip.

"Whatever else happens," she said softly, "we'll always have those hours in the snow cave."

"Maggie…"

"And the memory of those bits of bacon."

She cocked her head, inviting him to capitulate, giving him the means to.

"And don't forget the feel of pine needles," she murmured wickedly. "Prickling us in places few people have ever felt pine needles prickle before. And the interesting way we found to melt that handful of snow. And…"

"All right, Maggie. All right." His jaw clenched. "Suppose you tell me how you think we should handle this situation."

She wasn't the type to crow. "We keep it simple," she said briskly. "I'm the lure. We use me to bait a trap, then spring it."

"We stake you out like a skinned rabbit and wait for the hungry predators to arrive, is that it?"

"That's not quite what I had in mind," she drawled.

"So tell me."

"We have to assume they'll lock on to our signal when we contact Jaguar, right?"

"Right."

"So instead of trying to evade them while we wait for the extraction team to arrive, we let them find us. Or think they have. We draw them in and pin them down until the team gets here."

Thankfully, Adam didn't point out the obvious. He knew as

well as Maggie that they didn't have enough firepower to keep attackers armed with automatic weapons and night-vision equipment pinned down. Which meant they had to use the terrain to their maximum advantage. And use their wits.

"We can do it, Adam."

"We can try it," he said slowly, reluctantly.

Yes! Maggie wanted to shout her relief, but one look at his face warned her he was not happy about this. At all. Wisely she kept silent while he scanned the darkening horizon.

"That ridge won't work. We'd lose them in the rocks and boulders."

"We'd better head down to lower ground." Shoving her hands in her pockets, she turned to scan the steep slope. "What we need is a canyon or crevice of some kind."

What they found was a shack.

Or rather Radizwell found it.

Maggie and Adam had only gone a few yards down the slope, angling through the trees to avoid detection and make the descent easier, when the komondor decided they were heading in the wrong direction. He stopped, and a low whine alerted Adam to the fact that the animal wasn't following.

"Come on, boy. Come on."

The dog backed up a few steps, rumbling a low sound deep in his throat.

"Heel!"

Even Radizwell recognized the voice of authority. Belly to the ground, he slunk across the snow, whining pitifully all the way.

Adam's dark brows slashed together. "What? What are you trying to tell us?"

Taking courage from the more moderate tone, the shaggy beast leaped up and bounded down the slope a few feet in the opposite direction. He skidded to a halt in the snow, turned back to face them, then let loose with a deep, rolling thunderclap bark.

"Good grief!" Maggie exclaimed. "Who needs a satellite

transmission? Anyone within a five-mile radius can lock on to that."

It was an exaggeration, but only a slight one.

Adam quieted the animal with a slicing gesture of command. Radizwell snapped his jaws shut and plopped back on his massive haunches, as if sitting at attention.

"Obviously he wants us to follow him," Adam commented. "Since he appears to know these mountains better than we do, I suggest we see where he leads us."

He led them on what Maggie suspected was a merry chase. The moment he saw them start in his direction, Radizwell whirled and raced down the slope at a steep angle. He dodged around trees and over snow-covered fallen logs with surprising agility. Just before they lost sight of him completely, he skidded to a halt and waited for them to catch up.

When they were almost up with him, he jumped up and took off again. After the third or fourth relay, Maggie was huffing from the exertion and Adam's breath was coming in short, sharp pants. The sun had slipped behind the peaks now, and the shadows had deepened to long purple streaks across the tree-covered hillside. Overhead, a few early stars glowed in an indigo sky. Maggie caught a glimpse of a pale moon floating between the tips of the pines.

Although it was difficult to judge distance with their visibility obscured by the towering trees, an occasional clearing gave them some idea of progress. Maggie guessed they were three-quarters of the way down the slope when she had to stop to catch her breath. The dog padded back, not even winded.

She eyed him with mounting suspicion. "You don't suppose...this is his way...of getting back at me, do you?"

Adam propped a foot up on a half-submerged boulder. Leaning an elbow across his knee, he drew in several long breaths. "For what?"

"For scarfing...up all the biscuits...and bacon."

"Could be."

Maggie groaned. "I knew it!"

"Come on. Let's keep moving. We're almost at the bottom of the slope."

The ground began to level out a little while later. To Maggie's relief, the trees thinned, then ended abruptly. A few more steps brought them to the edge of a flat expanse of snow, about the width of a football field and twice as long. A narrow, ice-encrusted stream cut a crooked path across the field, dividing it almost in half. On the far side of the field, tree-studded slopes rose to touch the dark sky.

As soon as he saw the open space, Radizwell charged forward. Just in time, Adam grabbed a fistful of his ropy fur and hauled him back. The dog growled a low protest, but stood beside Adam while he and Maggie surveyed the still, flat area.

"It's an alpine meadow," Adam murmured after a moment. "I would imagine some of Taylor's sheep graze here in the summer. Which means…"

He glanced down at the sheepdog at his side.

"Is there a shelter here, boy? A shepherd's hut? Is that where you're taking us?"

Maggie hunched her shoulders and huddled closer to Adam. Excitement shot through her.

"That would work. A hut would work. It would make a perfect trap."

"I'm only guessing there's anything here at all, Maggie."

"It's a good guess. Radizwell brought us here for a reason. Besides, my feet are freezing and we're both sweating. Before we set our trap, we should dry off and thaw out. Or thaw out and dry off."

She jerked her chin toward the eager animal. "Let him go. Let's see where he heads."

He headed straight across the meadow toward the trees on the other side. His white coat made him difficult to follow against the sea of snow. Maggie squinted, watching carefully to track the shadow flying with astounding speed across the open space. For a big, klutzy-looking guy, the Hungarian could sure move.

Weapon drawn, she crouched beside Adam in the shelter of

a dead pine and watched the dog's unerring progress. On the far side of the open space, Radizwell skidded to a stop, just short of the tree line. Lining up on a dark patch among the trees, he gave a deep, basso profundo bark.

The sound echoed from the surrounding peaks and rolled back at them. Maggie stayed absolutely still beside Adam's rigid form. Nothing moved on the other side of the meadow. No one answered Radizwell's call.

"Do you see anything?" she hissed.

"No."

They waited a while longer. The komondor padded back and forth in front of the dark tree line, then stretched out in the snow. He laid his head down on his paws, waiting.

A snicker of metal brought her head jerking around. Moonlight gleamed on the blue steel of the weapon in Adam's hand.

"Here, take my weapon."

"Why? What are you—?"

He grabbed her derringer and slapped the heavier, more powerful pistol into her hand.

"Cover me!"

"No! Adam, wait!"

It was Maggie's nightmare scene from this morning in reverse. This time it was Adam who plowed across an open, unprotected space and Maggie who dropped to one knee, weapon raised.

Her heart crashed against her ribs as she watched his progress, and the acrid taste of fear rose in her throat. At any moment, she expected to hear gunfire shatter the stillness. To see Adam's body jackknife through the air.

When he made it to the tree line on the far side, she almost sobbed in relief. Then reaction set in. By the time he returned, Radizwell plunging in circles at his side, she was so furious she was ready to shoot him herself.

## Chapter 13

Maggie stormed through the ankle-high snow, the P7 gripped in her gloved hand.

"Don't ever do that to me again!"

Her vehemence sent Adam's brows winging. "Do what?"

"Go charging off like that! Without coordinating with me first!"

"The way you did this morning at the lake, you mean?"

In the face of that piece of calm logic, Maggie fell back on an age-old, irrefutable argument. "That was different!"

"Of course."

She stomped up to him, still furious. "Listen to me, Thunder I love you. I do *not* want you dead. I do *not* want to see your body splattered across a snowy field. I have *plans* for that body!"

Evidently the dog did *not* like the threatening tone she directed toward Adam. With a deep warning growl, he placed himself between Maggie and his good buddy.

She glared at the huge lump of uncombed wool, then at the man surveying her with a cool glint in his eyes. The intensity of her fury surprised Maggie herself. In a back corner of her mind, she realized she'd just had a taste of what Adam must have gone through all these years as OMEGA's director. It was a hell of a lot harder to stand back and watch someone you loved run headlong toward danger and possible death than to make the charge yourself. For the first time, she understood his icy anger during the debriefs after some of her more... adventurous missions. Still, she wasn't quite ready to forgive him for the fear that had twisted through her body like barbed wire.

Adam handed her the derringer and took the P7 in exchange. "Remind me to ask about these plans of yours when we get out of here."

"They'll probably change—several times—before then," she muttered.

"I wouldn't be surprised. Mine are changing by the minute. Would you like to know what I found under the trees?"

She checked the safety on the .22 and shoved it into her pants pocket. "Yes."

"A small shack, just as we guessed."

"Good."

"Well stocked with blankets and fuel."

Maggie stomped over to pick up their small bundle of gear. "Good."

"And food," he added with a small smile.

She swung around. "Food?"

"I thought that might get your attention."

"What kind of food?"

"There's a whole metal locker full of canned goods. Pork and beans. Beef stew. Chicken and dumplings."

"Chicken and dumplings, huh?"

Adam's smile edged into one of his rare grins. It lifted his fine, chiseled mouth and crinkled the skin at the corners of his eyes. The last of Maggie's uncharacteristic anger melted as he stepped forward and brushed a knuckle down her cheek.

"I can see that one of my main tasks in the future will be keeping your stomach full."

"Among other things."

"First things first. Come on. Let's get you fed."

Hunching her shoulders, Maggie plowed through the snow beside him.

The shack was small and airless and dark. While Adam kept watch outside, Maggie explored its single room cautiously. She didn't dare use the matches she found in a waterproof tin container to light the oil lamp left on the single table, but then, she didn't really need to.

Adam left the door cracked just enough to let in a sliver of moonlight and allow him a clear view of the open meadow.

"The food and other supplies are in the metal locker in the corner," he told her.

When she opened the locker, the first items Maggie reached for were musty, folded blankets. Passing one to Adam, she pulled another one out for her own use and tossed it on the narrow cot built into one wall. Then she stacked half a dozen cans on the table and rooted for a can opener. She could open the cans without one, but she'd rather not trudge out in the snow to find a sharpened stick if she didn't have to. Luckily, the middle shelf yielded an old-fashioned, rusted opener and several large spoons.

As hungry as she was, Maggie was too well trained to attack the food without taking care of other, more urgent needs first. Perching on the narrow cot, she tugged off her boots. Her lightweight waterproof footgear had keep most of the moisture out, but her toes were numb with cold, and she didn't want to risk frostbite.

While she massaged warmth into her stockinged feet, Radiz well made himself right at home. He took a couple of circuit of the small room, sniffing out scents left by various visitor since the last time he'd been there. When he poked his nose into a stack of long-handled tools in one corner, sudden mayhem erupted. His stub of a tail shot straight up, he let loose with woof that made Maggie jump clear off the cot, and a half-doze tiny furry creatures darted out from among the tools. Squeakin and squealing, they scattered in all directions, with Radizwell pouncing joyfully after them. His resounding barks bounced off the hut's walls.

"For God's sake, shut him up!" Adam ordered from his post at the door.

"Right. Shut him up."

Maggie planted herself in the middle of the shack to wait for the dog's next pass and jumped half out of her skin when one of the tiny squeaking creatures ran across her foot. Praying it hadn't taken a detour up her pant leg, she braced herself as the dog skidded to a halt. Or tried to. His momentum carried him smack into her. Once again, Maggie found herself flat on her back, with a hundred or more pounds of belligerent komondor straddling her. Doggy breath bathed her face as he growled his displeasure.

"Look, pal," she growled back, "I don't like you any more than you appear to like me. But let's declare a truce, okay? I don't want to waste what little ammunition I have on you."

Adam deserted his post long enough to drag the dog off her. "Maybe if you offered to share the chicken and dumplings with him, you two might just strike up a friendship," he suggested dryly.

Maggie scrambled up. "Ha! What makes you think I want to be friends with an ugly, overgrown floor mop?"

"This from the woman who keeps a bug-eyed reptile for a pet?" Adam shook his head and resumed his post.

Holding out her pant leg, Maggie gave her foot a vigorous shake. When nothing more than a small clump of snow hit the floor, she sighed in relief.

Despite the glare she sent the unrepentant dog, she could no more let him go hungry than she could the frantic mama wood mouse who'd scurried back into the stack of tools after rounding up her tiny charges. Opening the different cans, Maggie dumped the contents of three of them into a metal bowl she'd scavenged from the locker.

"Come on, hound. You can eat this outside and pull guard duty at the same time."

Radizwell didn't move. Sitting on his haunches like an upright bale of unprocessed cotton, he looked from the bowl in her hand to Adam for guidance. Maggie shook her head. When males bonded, they bonded.

At Adam's signal, the dog graciously condescended to allow Maggie to feed him. Padding to the door, he stepped outside. She set the bowl down in the snow, took a quick glance around the serene moonscape, then ducked back inside. The knowledge that the moonscape wouldn't stay serene for long added impetus to her actions.

In short order, she handed Adam an open can and a spoon, dropped a cold, soggy dumpling behind the stack of tools and wrapped the blanket around her legs and feet to warm them. Shuffling across the hut, open can in hand, she joined Adam at the door.

"I'll stand watch. You go dry off."

"I'm not wet."

They shared a few moments of silent companionship while they ate, both wrapped in thought. Maggie tried to ignore the insidious, creeping realization that these quiet moments with Adam might be their last, but the cold reality of their situation intruded.

In a few minutes, they'd lure an unknown number of killers to this isolated spot and try to hold them off until the Jaguar's extraction team arrived. With a total of eight rounds of ammunition between them. Adam had expended all but two of the rounds in his nine-round Heckler & Koch during the firefight at the lake. Maggie had exactly six left for Taylor's .22, including the one in the chamber and five in the spare clip she'd tucked in her pocket this morning.

God, had it only been this morning? She tipped her head against the doorframe, thinking how much her life had changed since then. Her gaze slid to Adam's lean, shadowed face. Whatever happened, she'd have those hours in the snow cave. Whatever happened, she'd have the memory of his blue eyes smiling down at her when he'd taken her in his arms and said he was, he did, he knew.

"Adam?"

"Yes?"

"How long do you think we have?"

His eyes lingered on her lips, then lifted. In their depths, Maggie caught a glimpse of raw, masculine need, overlaid with regret.

"Not long enough."

She sighed. "That's what I thought you'd say."

"They could be following the dog's tracks and be heading this way right now. We have to contact Jaguar."

"I know."

He curled a hand under her chin, lifting her face. "Tomorrow, Maggie. We'll have tomorrow. And forever."

"If we don't...thank you for today."

His cheeks creased. "You're welcome."

Maggie dipped her chin to kiss the warm skin of his palm. Closing her eyes, she savored his taste and his touch and his scent. Then she sighed again and moved away. With the blanket swaddled around her lower body, she began to pace the small hut.

"Okay, let's review the situation here. We need to contact headquarters to let Jaguar know our coordinates. As soon as we do, there's a distinct possibility the unfriendlies, whoever they are, will glom on to the signal."

"If they haven't already picked up our tracks," Adam reminded her.

"When they arrive on the scene, it's up to us to make sure they don't leave until the counterstrike team can get here."

Maggie felt adrenaline begin to pump through her veins in anticipation of the action ahead. She'd been in tight situations before. Not quite as snug as this one, perhaps, but pretty darn close.

Blanket swishing at her ankles, she strode across the small room and yanked open the metal locker. The rectangular red container she pulled out was heavy and full.

"All right. We have eight rounds of ammunition and one gallon of gasoline to hold off a possible army of bad guys armed with automatic weapons, high-powered night scopes, and every destructive device known to man.'' She grinned at Adam. ''I've done more with less. How about you?''

He shoved his shoulders off the doorframe. ''A lot more with a lot less. Let's get to work.''

Pillaging the metal locker, they found the makings for crude flash bombs. While Maggie poured the gasoline into the bottles, Adam tore strips from his blanket to stuff in the neck as wicks. Carefully dividing the matches, he gave half to Maggie and tucked the other half in his pocket, along with the jagged pieces of mirror he'd smashed from the snowmobile.

Leaving Radizwell to stand sentry at the hut, they disappeared into the surrounding woods. Working silently, quickly, they gathered fallen limbs and dry timber. Within moments, they'd scattered the debris in a seemingly random pattern around the hut. After placing a few of the gasoline-filled bottles for maximium detonation, they doused the wood with the remaining fuel. A single careful shot could detonate the ring of fire.

After that they separated, Maggie going left, Adam right, searching for just the right tree to climb to put the hut in a cross fire and make the best use of their remaining flash bombs. The temperature had dropped significantly, but Maggie didn't notice. Her heart thumped with the realization that their time was running out. She zigzagged through the trees to find exactly the one she wanted.

Its thick trunk provided excellent cover and a full complement of stair-stepping branches. An easy climb took her a good thirty feet up. Using both hands and her body for leverage, she bent back a couple of obscuring limbs to give her a clear line of fire to the hut. With so few rounds of ammunition, she'd need it.

Her breath was coming in short, puffy gasps by the time she got back to the shack.

''You set?'' Adam asked tersely.

''As set as I'll ever be. Let's get Jaguar on the net.''

Maggie gave a small puff of surprise when he gripped her upper arms, his hands like steel cuffs.

''Listen to me, Chameleon. It's not too late. You can climb

the ridge behind the hut. Take cover in the rocks until the extraction team arrives."

"And just what do you plan to do while I'm taking cover?"

He gave her a small shake. "You're the one they're after, not me. I can stay here. Talk to them. Delay them."

"After that scene beside the lake, do you think they're going to stop for a friendly chat? You took at least one of them down, remember?"

"Dammit, Maggie…"

"Chameleon."

"What?"

"You called me Chameleon a moment ago. That's who I am, Thunder. That's who I have to be. I am not running for cover, and I'm sure as hell not leaving you to face the fire alone. Any more than you'd leave me."

His fingers bit into her arms. Maggie could feel their tensile strength through the thick down of her ski jacket. Under its day's growth of dark beard, his jaw worked.

"Thunder," she said softly, "kiss me. Hard. Then get Jaguar up on the net."

He kissed her. Hard.

Then he dug in his pocket for the handheld navigational device. While waiting for the readings to display on the liquid crystal screen, he shoved his sleeve back and activated the satellite transceiver.

"Jaguar, this is Thun—"

Jake's voice jumped out of the gold watch. "I read you! You okay?"

"We are."

"Both of you?"

"Both of us."

"Give me your coordinates."

Adam rapped out the reading from his GPS unit.

Jake was silent a moment, then came back on the net. "The extraction team's in the air. Twenty minutes away. Cowboy's leading them in."

"Cowboy?"

Maggie felt a rush of wild relief. She and the lanky Wyoming rancher had worked together before. The last time, they'd repelled an attack similar to this one, led by a scar-faced Soviet major. After Adam, Nate Sloan was Maggie's number one pick for a partner in a firefight. The knowledge that he was leading the counterstrike team gave her a surge of hope.

"Tell Cowboy to hover behind the ridge line due east of us," she instructed Jaguar. "I don't want him to scare away our game. We'll call him in when we've sprung the trap."

"Roger. You two sure took your time getting back to me. I've been having to hold off the entire Secret Service single-handedly."

"What do you mean?"

"Special Agent Kowalski's demanded half the federal government and most of the state of California to search the Sierras for you two. I convinced the president to hold her off until I heard from you, but she's mad. Hopping mad. Someone's attacked her charge, and she's taking it real personal. She doesn't understand why we've kept word of the attack quiet, and she doesn't like it." He paused. "Either that, or she's putting on one hell of an act."

"What do you mean?" Adam asked sharply.

"The lab confirmed that the listening device Chameleon found in the VP's bedroom is manufactured by Digicon—for the Secret Service. The Presidential Protective Unit personnel are the only ones using it."

Adam muttered a vicious curse. "Digicon and the Secret Service. Peter Donovan and James Elliot. Even if Kowalski planted the bug, we still don't know who the hell's behind this."

"We will soon," Maggie promised, her mouth grim.

Adam nodded. "Look, Jaguar, we've got to get into position. Tell Cowboy to wait for my signal. I'll bring him in."

"Roger. Good hunting, Chief."

"Thanks.

"And, Chameleon?"

"Yes?"

"When you catch that polecat you're baiting the trap for, I'll skin him and tan the hide for you. I remember how much you disliked gutting your catch during survival training.''

''I don't think I'll have a problem with this one,'' Maggie replied, grinning crookedly.

Adam dropped his sleeve down over the gold watch. For a few moments, the only sounds in the small shack were their rapid breathing and the faint thump of the sheepdog's paw on the snow as he scratched himself.

''You ready, Chameleon?''

''I'm ready.''

His gaze, blue and piercing, raked her face a final time. Maggie ached to touch him once more, to carry the feel of his bristly cheek with her into the night, but she didn't lift her hand. The time for touching was past.

He nodded, as if acknowledging her unspoken resolve. ''Let's get moving before our company arrives.''

''Too late. It's already here.''

Maggie and Adam spun around as a bulky figure in a sheepskin coat kicked the door back on its hinges.

''Don't!'' McGowan shouted. ''Don't reach for it! I'll shoot her, Ridgeway, I swear!''

Adam froze in a low crouch, his hand halfway to the weapon holstered at the small of his back.

For long seconds, no one moved. No one breathed. McGowan kept his rifle leveled squarely on the center of Maggie's chest. She didn't dare go for her gun, and she knew Adam wouldn't go for his. Not with the caretaker's weapon pointed at her.

''There's an oil lamp on the table, Ridgeway. Matches beside it. Light it. And keep your hands where I can see them, or she's dead.''

Adam straightened slowly. As though she were inside his head, Maggie could hear the thoughts that raced through his mind. With light, they could see McGowan's eyes. A person's eyes always signaled his intent before his body did. With light, they could anticipate. Coordinate. Take him down.

Moving with infinite care, Adam crossed to the small table. Metal rattled, a match scraped against the side of the box, a flame flared, low and flickering at first, and then steady as the wick caught.

In the lantern's glow, Maggie saw McGowan clearly for the first time. Above the rifle, his battered face was frightening in its implacable intensity. Not a single spark of life showed in his gray eyes. They were flat. Cold. A convicted murderer's eyes.

The click of claws on wood jerked Maggie's attention from the caretaker's face to the shape behind him. To her fury, Radizwell ambled into the hut and hunkered down, as if settling in to enjoy the show.

"Some guard dog you are, you stupid—"

With great effort, she bit back one of the more descriptive terms she'd learned from her father's roughneck crews. It was a mistake to let McGowan see how furious she was, and she knew damn well it was unfair to blame Radizwell. The sheepdog wouldn't view Hank McGowan as an enemy. Hell, the thumping they'd heard a few seconds ago was probably his stump of a tail whapping against the snow in an ecstatic welcome. Still, there were two hides she wouldn't have minded tanning at this moment.

"Who are you?"

McGowan's low snarl brought her eyes snapping back to his face.

"What?"

"Who the hell are you?"

The dog picked up the savagery of his tone and tilted his head, as if confused by this confrontation between humans he knew and trusted.

"Never mind," McGowan continued. "I don't care who you are. Just tell me what you've done with Taylor."

Maggie's mind raced with the possibility that this man wasn't the one they'd tried to bait the trap for. Slowly, carefully, she shook her head.

"I haven't done anything with the vice president."

His mouth curled. "I'd just as soon shoot you as look at you, lady. If Taylor's hurt, you're dead anyway. Where is she?"

"I can't tell you. You have to trust—"

"The first shot goes into her knee, Ridgeway." His eyes never left Maggie's face. "The second into her right lung. How many will it take? How many do I have to pump into her until you tell me?"

As it turned out, the first shot didn't go through Maggie's knee. It came through the open door and went right through McGowan's shoulder. Blood sprayed, splattering Adam as he leaped for the man.

It was the second shot that hit her. The rifle in McGowan's scarred hands bucked. A deafening crack split the air, and Maggie slammed into the back wall of the hut.

# Chapter 14

In the curious way time has, it always seems to move in the most infinitesimal increments at moments of greatest pain.

When Adam lunged forward to knock the rifle aside, he felt as though he were diving through a thick pool of sludge. Slowly. So slowly. Too slowly.

His mind recorded every minute sensation. He felt warm blood splatter his face. Saw McGowan's finger pull back on the trigger in an involuntary reaction to the bullet that ripped through him. Heard the roar as the rifle barrel jerked. Tasted the acrid tang of gunpowder and fear as Maggie crashed back against the wall.

Like a remote-controlled robot, Adam followed through with his actions. He shoved the barrel aside. Digging a shoulder into McGowan's middle, he took him down. He rolled sideways, away from the caretaker, and was on his feet again in a single motion. Through it all, every nerve, every fibrous filament, every neuron, screamed a single message in a thousand different variations.

Maggie was hit. Maggie was down. Maggie was shot.

Only after he'd yanked the rifle out of McGowan's slackened hold and spun around did another stream of messages begin to penetrate his mind.

She was down, but not dead. She was hit, but not bloodied. She was shot, but not wounded.

She'd been thrown against the wall and crumpled to the floor, but her eyes were wide and startled, not glazed with pain. A look of utter stupefaction crossed her face, then gave way to one of sputtering panic.

As Adam raced toward her, he heard a hiccuping wheeze and identified the sound instantly. He'd seen enough demonstrations of protective body armor to recognize that choking, sucking gasp. The force of the hit had knocked the air out of her lungs. She was so stunned that her paralyzed muscles couldn't draw more in.

He couldn't help her breathe. She had to force her lungs to work on her own. But he could sure as hell protect her from the two white-suited figures who came bursting through the open door at that precise moment.

Shoving Maggie flat on the floor, Adam covered her body with his. He twisted around, his finger curling on the rifle's trigger as he lined up on the lead attacker.

The figure in white arctic gear and goggles ignored him, however. Legs spread, arms extended in a classic law-enforcement stance, he covered the sprawled McGowan.

Or rather *she* did.

Adam recognized Denise Kowalski's voice the instant she belted out a fierce order to the downed man.

"Don't move! Don't even breathe!"

Keeping her eyes and her weapon trained on McGowan, she shouted over her shoulder, "Ridgeway! Is she hit? Is the vice president hit?"

Before Adam could answer, a savage snarl ripped through the hut. From the corner of his eye, he saw Radizwell rear back, his massive hindquarters bunching as he prepared to launch himself at this latest threat.

The second agent swung his weapon toward the dog.

"No! Don't shoot! Down, Radizwell! Down!"

At the lash of command in Adam's voice, the sheepdog halted in midthrust. Confused, uncertain, he quivered with the need to act. Under his mask of ropy fur, black gums curled back. Blood-curdling growls rolled out of his throat like waves, rising and falling in steady crescendos.

In the midst of all the clamor, Maggie's feeble cry almost went unheard.

"Adam! Get…off…me!"

At the sound of her voice, the two agents froze. Then Denise transferred her weapon to her right hand and shoved her goggles up with her left. Keeping the gun trained on McGowan, she risked a quick look at the far end of the hut.

Adam pushed himself onto one knee. With infinite care, he rolled the wheezing Maggie onto her side. She immediately drew up into a fetal position, her knees to her chin and her arms wrapped around her middle.

Relief crashed through Adam when he saw where she cradled herself. The bullet had struck low, below her breastbone. A higher hit might have broken her sternum or smashed a couple ribs.

"Herrera!" Denise snapped. "Get out your medical kit. The vice president's been hit."

"She's wearing a body shield," Adam said. "I think she's okay."

Maggie's awful wheezing eased. "Okay. I'm…okay."

Slowly, her face scrunched with pain, she straightened her legs. Adam slid an arm under her back and helped her to her feet. Her knees wobbled, involuntary tears streaked her cheeks, and she kept her arms crossed over her waist, but she was standing.

With everything in him, Adam fought the desperate urge to crush her against his chest. Added pressure was the last thing she wanted or needed now. She'd have a bruise the size of Rhode Island on her stomach as it was.

Incredibly, she gave a shaky grin and tapped a finger against her middle. "What do you know! It…worked."

After their hours together in the snow cave, Adam had been sure he couldn't love this woman more. He'd been wrong. Then, her passion and her laughter had fed his soul. Now, her courage stole it completely. As long as he lived, he would remember that small grin and the way she gathered herself together to shake off the effects of a bullet to the stomach.

A grunt of pain behind them brought both Maggie and Adam swinging around. The caretaker pushed against the floor with one boot, bright red blood staining his worn sheepskin jacket as he dragged himself upright.

"I told you not to move, McGowan," Denise warned.

He sagged against the wall, and he sent her a contemptuous look. "What are you going to do? Shoot me?"

"I'm considering it. And this time I won't shoot to wound."

"Too bad you took down the wrong man, Kowalski."

"I got the right one. The one holding a gun on the vice president."

His lips curled in a sneer. "Are you blind or just stupid, woman?"

"Neither. Nor am I lying in a pool of blood."

Pain added a rasp to McGowan's gravelly voice. "She's not the vice president."

"Sure. And I'm not—"

"That woman is not Taylor Grant."

His utter conviction got through to Denise. Adam saw the first flicker of doubt in her eyes as she threw a quick look at Maggie.

"Come on," McGowan jeered, wincing a little with the effort. "I know you're new to Taylor's detail. But even you must have picked up on the dog's reaction to her last night. She's good, whoever she is, damn good. But she's not Taylor Grant."

The agent's mouth thinned. "Herrera! Search this man for weapons."

She kept her gun leveled on the caretaker's head while the second agent opened the sheepskin and patted him down.

"He's clean."

"Keep him covered."

The agent swiveled on his heels to look up at her. "Shouldn't I patch that hole first?"

"In a minute."

"But—"

"He'll live!"

Her sharp retort wrung a half smile, half grimace from the wounded man. "You're one hard female, Kowalski."

"Remember that, the next time you pull a weapon on one of my—" She stopped abruptly. "On one of my charges," she finished slowly.

Maggie heard the hitch of uncertainty in Denise's voice. Well, the agent might have her doubts, but Maggie had a few of her own, as well. Hanging on to Adam's arm with one hand, she casually slipped the other into her pants pocket. Her palm curled around the derringer.

"Did you—?"

She had to stop and drag in a slow breath. Pain rippled through her at even that slight movement of her diaphragm, but Maggie gritted her teeth and finished. "Did you plant a listening device in my bedroom, Denise?"

The agent stiffened.

"Did you?"

Denise didn't respond for long moments. When she did, her brown eyes were flat and hard. "Yes."

Maggie felt Adam's muscles tense under her tight grip. "Why?" she asked sharply.

"Because it was ordered by the vice president," Denise replied with careful deliberation. "Who isn't you, apparently."

A sudden silence descended, broken a moment later by McGowan's snort of derision.

"Taylor wouldn't allow any bugs upstairs. She doesn't even like the cameras downstairs. That cabin is the only place in her whole crazy world she has any privacy. She'd never authorize you to peep into her bedroom."

"Well, she did." Denise bit the words out, her eyes on Maggie.

"Did she, Kowalski?" Quiet menace laced Adam's voice. "Did she personally order it?"

Denise dragged her gaze from Maggie to the man beside her. She frowned, obviously debating whether to reply. "The order came down through channels," she said at last.

"What channels?" Adam rapped out.

"Secret Service channels. What the hell's going—?"

"Who issued the order?"

Despite the ache in her middle, Maggie almost smiled at the stubborn, angry look that settled on Denise's face. She'd had the same reaction herself, on occasion, to being grilled by OMEGA's director.

"Dammit, what's—?"

"Who, Kowalski? I want an answer! Now!"

Denise responded through clenched teeth. "The order came from the secretary."

"The secretary of the treasury?"

"The secretary of the treasury. Personally. Direct to me. He told me…" Her jaw tightened. "He told me the vice president had authorized it."

"Bingo," Maggie whispered.

Adam's eyes met hers. A muscle twitched in one side of his jaw. The president's friend, he thought. The highest financial officer in the nation. The bastard.

"We may know who," he said, his jaw tight, "but we still don't know why."

"We will," Maggie swore. "We'll get the last piece of the puzzle if we have to…"

A coldly furious female intruded on their private exchange. "If one of you doesn't explain in the next ten seconds what this is all about, I'm going to take action. Very drastic action."

"Better tell her, Ridgeway," McGowan drawled. "If you don't, she'll shoot to wound, and get her rocks off watching you bleed to death."

"Oh, for—" Shoving her hood back, Denise raked a hand through her short sandy hair. "Stuff a bandage in his wound or in his mouth, Herrera. I don't care which. Now tell me—" she glared at Maggie "—just who you are and what the hell's going on here."

Maggie opened her mouth, then closed it with a snap. Slicing a hand through the air for quiet, she cocked her head and listened intently.

In the stillness that descended, she heard the echo of a faint, wavering roar. Her fingers dug into Adam's arm as she whipped around to face Denise.

"Is more—" She gasped as the violent movement wrenched at her middle, then shook her head, as if denying all pain. "Is more of your team on the way?"

Frowning, Denise responded to the urgency in Maggie's voice. "No. There's only Herrera and me. The president wouldn't authorize a full-scale search," she added stiffly.

"So you came on your own?"

Her chin jutted out. "So we came on our own. You are—you *were* my responsibility. We tracked McGowan from the moment he left the cabin."

"Hell," the caretaker muttered in profound disgust. "I'm getting sloppy. Tracked down and gunned down by a female."

Denise ignored him, her sharp gaze focused on Maggie's face. "What do you hear?"

"Snowmobiles," she murmured, moving closer to the door to listen.

"Do you think it's the team that hit you this morning and took down my man?"

"Probably."

"I owe them."

A ghost of a grin sketched across Maggie's mouth. "Me too."

"Listen to me, Kowalski," Adam cut in. "The vice president is safe. She's at Camp David, working on some highly sensitive treaty negotiations. But before she left, she received a death threat, a particularly nasty one, which is why my agent is doubling for her."

"Agent?"

"That's also why the president wouldn't authorize you to institute a search," Adam continued ruthlessly. "We told him not to."

Denise blinked once or twice at the news that the president apparently took orders from the tall, commanding man in front of her.

"Why no search?" she asked, doubt in her eyes, but still tenacious.

"Because we didn't want the wrong people walking into the trap we've set. We want the team that hit us and your man this morning. Badly. And the individual behind them. Are you with us?" Adam asked in a steely voice. "You have to decide. Now."

Maggie saw at once that she wasn't the only one who'd learned to trust her instincts. Denise flicked another look from her to Adam, then back again. Squaring her shoulders, she nodded.

"Tell me about this trap."

"I'll tell you as soon as I call in our reinforcements," Adam said, shoving back his sleeve. "From the sound of it, we're going to need them."

At Cowboy's laconic assurance that he was barely a good spit away and closing fast, the tension in the hut ratcheted up several more notches.

Working silently and swiftly, the small team readied for action. At Denise's terse order, Herrera divided up their extra weapons and ammunition. While Maggie showed the two agents the placement of their rudimentary defenses, Adam propped a shoulder under McGowan and took him into the shelter of the trees. Radizwell trotted at their heels, rumbling deep in his throat until Adam's low command stilled him.

"Christ," McGowan muttered. "He never obeys me like that. Or anyone else, Taylor included. Last time she was home, she threatened to skin him and use him for a throw rug."

"It's all in the tone."

"Yeah, I guess so."

His lips white with pain, McGowan was still for a moment.

The distant rise and fall of engines grew louder with each labored breath. "You'd better give me my rifle."

Without speaking, Adam eased his support from under the caretaker's shoulder.

"I didn't mean to pull that trigger," McGowan stated flatly. "Not when I did, anyway."

"I know."

"I would have, though. I would've shot you both if I thought you'd harmed Taylor."

The whine of the engines pulled at Adam. He needed to coordinate a final approach for Cowboy. To check the disposition of his meager forces. To make sure Maggie was secure. But the bleak expression in the caretaker's eyes held him for another second.

"You love her that much?"

A flicker of pain crossed McGowan's face, one that had nothing to do with his wound.

"About as much as you love that woman, I reckon," McGowan said quietly. His gaze drifted to Maggie, a slender shadow against the snow. "They're a lot alike, aren't they? Her and Taylor?"

"Many ways. And nothing alike in others." Adam started back to the hut. "I'll send Herrera out with your rifle."

"Ridgeway?"

"Yes?"

"Good luck. Take care of your woman."

A wry smile tugged at Adam's lips. "She prefers to take care of herself."

It was over almost before it began.

Scant moments after the hut's occupants took position in the trees surrounding the hut, a wave of dim shapes burst into the open meadow. They raced across the snow, throwing up waves of white behind their skis. The first few were halfway across when a Cobra gunship lifted above the dark peaks directly behind them.

Maggie couldn't see the chopper, since it flew without lights, but she heard it. The steady *whump-whump-whump* of its rotor blades drowned the sound of the approaching snowmobiles.

When they caught the sound of the chopper behind them, the attackers swerved crazily. Gunfire erupted, and streaming tracers lit the night sky. The cacophony of noise intensified with the appearance of a second gunship, then a third.

The choppers circled the swarming vehicles like heavenly herders trying to corral stampeding mechanized cattle. Blinding searchlights turned night into day. One of the 50 mm cannons bristling from the nose of the lead gunship boomed, and a fountain of snow arched into the sky.

One after another, the buzzing snowmobiles stopped. Their white-suited drivers jumped off, hands held high, while the giant black moths circled overhead.

Only two mounted attackers escaped the roundup. The first dodged across the snow and headed for the trees behind the hut. The second followed in his tracks, almost riding up the other's rear skis.

From her high perch, Maggie took careful aim. She wasn't about to let even one of these scum get away. As soon as the second vehicle entered the ring outlined in the snow by the scattered brush, neither one of them was coming out. No one in their right mind would drive a gasoline-powered snowmobile though the flames about to erupt.

Her finger tightened on the trigger just as a white shape flew out of the trees. Maggie's shot ignited a flash bomb at the same moment Radizwell crashed into the lead driver, knocking him off his churning vehicle.

Flames shot into the sky and raced around the ring of gasoline-soaked brush. Two drivers and one savage, snarling komondor were trapped inside a circle of fire. Horrified, Maggie saw the second driver jump off his snowmobile. Lifting his automatic rifle, he spun toward the dog and his thrashing victim.

In a smooth, lightning-fast movement, Maggie braced her wrist against the limb, took aim and fired. With a sharp crack, the driver's weapon flew out of his hand. When another warning shot threw up a clump of snow just in front of him, he dropped to his knees. Rocking back and forth, he clutched his injured hand to his chest.

Maggie had shimmied halfway down the tree when she caught sight of a dark figure running toward the wall of flames. Bending his arm in front of his face, he disappeared into the fire.

"Adam!" Her instinctive cry was lost in the fire's roar.

By the time Maggie leaped through the fiery wall and joined him, Adam had the injured driver covered, and Radizwell had terrorized and almost tenderized the other. Adam held the straining animal with one hand while the man scuttled backward, crab-like.

"I don't know!" he shouted.

"Talk, or I let him loose!" Adam snarled, as fearsome as the creature at his side.

"I told you, I don't know who hired us!"

Adam relaxed his grip enough for Radizwell to leap for the man's boot. Clamping his massive jaws around it, he shook his head. The driver screamed as his whole body lifted with each shake, then thumped back down in the snow.

"Call him off! I swear, I don't know!"

Maggie skidded to a halt beside Adam. She watched the man's frantic gyrations with great satisfaction.

"Have him chew on his face for a while," she suggested, loudly enough to be heard over the growls and cries. "It will improve his looks, if nothing else."

Evidently Radizwell had reached the same conclusion. He spit out the boot and lunged forward. The man screamed and threw up an arm. At the last moment, Adam buried a fist in the woolly ruff and hauled the dog back.

"You've got five seconds. Then I let him go."

"I don't know," the man sobbed. "Our instructions come to a post office box, unsigned. The money's deposited in an account at the bank."

Adam stiffened. "Which bank?"

"What?"

"Which bank?"

"First Bank. In Miami."

* * *

The three choppers settled on the snow like hens nesting for the night. In the blinding glare of their powerful searchlights, a heavily armed counterstrike team rounded up the band of attackers and stripped them down to search for weapons.

A tall, lanky figure left the circle of activity and plowed through the snow toward the ring of fire.

"Thunder? Chameleon?"

"Here!" Maggie shouted.

Leaping over dwindling flames, Cowboy came to an abrupt halt. He pushed his Denver Broncos ball cap to the back of his head, surveying the scene.

A white-suited figure with his hands behind his head stumbled forward in front of Maggie, who covered him with the puniest excuse for a weapon Cowboy had ever seen. Adam knelt in the snow to retrieve a semiautomatic. And a mound of shaggy white perched atop the stomach of a downed attacker, fangs bared. A series of spine-tingling growls rolled toward Cowboy, and he didn't make the mistake of moving any closer.

He shook his head in mingled amusement and relief. "Here I bring the cavalry chargin' to the rescue, and you didn't even need us. You've got your own..." He jerked his chin toward the still-growling creature. "What *is* that thing, anyway?"

"A Hungarian dust mop," Maggie said.

"A Hungarian sheepdog," Adam corrected.

The Hungarian in question snarled menacingly.

"Not exactly a hospitable sort, is he?"

Maggie shook her head emphatically. "No."

"Yes," Adam countered. "Once he gets acquainted with you."

"Well, we'll have to get acquainted some other time. My orders are to get you back to Sacramento immediately. Jaguar's got a plane standing by to fly us to D.C."

"Why the rush?" Maggie asked.

She was as anxious as he to bring down the final curtain on this mission, but she'd thought—hoped—she and Adam would have at least an hour or two at the cabin to clean up and finish one or more of the several interesting discussions they'd started in the past few days.

"Jaguar radioed just before we landed. The vice president's completed those treaty negotiations faster than she or anyone else thought possible. She's flying in from Camp David, and insists on resuming her public persona. Death threat or no death threat, she wants to be at the press conference tomorrow when the president announces the treaty. He's calling you in."

# Chapter 15

$A$s it turned out, the entire ragged band flew back to Sacramento with Maggie and Adam.

A grim-faced Denise Kowalski insisted on accompanying her "charge" back to D.C. Hank McGowan set his jaw and refused to be taken to a hospital. He wanted to see with his own eyes that Taylor was safe. A medic with the counter-strike team packed and patched his wound on the spot.

To Maggie's disgust, even the dog got into the act. He whined pathetically when Adam climbed aboard the chopper and refused to remove his massive body from a skid. Forced to choose between ordering the pilot to lift off with a hundred pounds of komondor on one track and taking the creature aboard, Adam had opened the side hatch. With a thunderous woof that had half a dozen well-armed counter-strike agents swinging around, weapons leveled, Radizwell leaped into the cabin.

With his odoriferous presence, the air in the helicopter took on a distinct aroma. After a day of strenuous physical activity followed by a night that had raised Maggie's nervous-tension levels well beyond the stage of a discreet, ladylike dew, she wanted nothing more than a bath, a good meal and Adam, not necessarily in that order. For a few more hours, though, she had to maintain her role.

With unerring skill, the chopper pilot put his craft down a few yards from the gleaming 747 that waited for them, engines whining. The media, alerted to the vice president's departure by the presence of Air Force Two, crowded at the edge of the ramp. Realizing that this might be her last public appearance as the vice president of the United States, Maggie gave them a grin and a wave as she walked to the aircraft. Luckily, the night was too dark and the photographers were too far away to record the precise details of Taylor Grant's less-than-immaculate appearance, much less the blackened hole in the front of her ski jacket left by a 44-40 rifle shell.

The diminutive martinet who waited for her inside the 747 saw it at once, however. Lillian's black eyes rounded as she gaped at Maggie's middle.

"Good heavens! Are you all right?"

"I'm fine."

Her face folding into lines of tight disapproval, the dresser scowled at Denise, who entered the plane behind Adam. "You told me she'd been attacked down at the lake. But you didn't tell me she was hit."

"She wasn't," Denise said wearily, dragging a hand through her sandy hair. "Not down at the lake. McGowan put a bullet through her, or tried to."

"Hank?" Lillian's gray eyebrows flew up. "Hank shot the vice president?"

The uniformed stewards ranged around the huge cabin listened with wide-eyed astonishment. All the crew knew was that a call from the president had cut short the vice president's scheduled vacation. And that an "accident" of some sort had occurred just prior to their departure from the cabin for Sacramento.

"It was a mistake," Denise said, confirming the story. "One McGowan's already paid for," she added. "I put a bullet through his shoulder."

"Good heavens!" Lillian repeated faintly.

"She's a damn hard woman," the caretaker stated, panting. He leaned a forearm against the bulkhead to catch his breath. The effort of climbing the stairs had pearled his face with sweat and darkened a spot on the shoulder of the jacket he'd borrowed from Herrera. He'd insisted on coming along, but it had obviously cost him.

The arrival of Cowboy, Herrera and an enthusiastically sniffing Radizwell snapped Lillian into action. In her best drill-sergeant manner, she took charge.

"I've laid out clean clothes in your stateroom, Mrs. Grant. I knew you'd want to shower and change as soon as we took off. Hank, you come with me. I'll look at that shoulder. Steward! Take this animal to the aft compartment. He stinks!"

"The understatement of the year," Maggie murmured.

Unfortunately, Radizwell refused to be separated from his pal, Adam. Maggie suspected the delicious aromas wafting from the galley had something to do with his fierce, growling stance. The hound wanted his share.

So did she. As her nose picked up the mouth-watering scents, her bruised stomach sent out a series of growls very close to Radizwell's in volume and intensity. Suddenly Maggie realized she could fulfill all three of her most immediate needs and still maintain her role.

"Why don't you come with me, Adam?" she suggested. Keeping her tone light, for the stewards' sake, she nodded toward the forward compartment. "You said you needed to contact your people to let them know about our change of plans. You can use my office while I shower and change. Then we can have a bite to eat."

"Fine."

"We'll serve as soon as we're airborne," the head steward added helpfully. "We've prepared a vegetable quiche for Mrs. Grant, but perhaps you'd prefer a steak, sir?"

"Steak," Adam replied, his eyes glinting. "Definitely the steak."

In the privacy of the well-appointed bathroom, Maggie made free use of various sundries kept on hand for the vice president.

It was amazing how much a toothbrush and the prospect of soothing, perfumed lotion after a hot shower could revitalize a woman.

The prospect of the hot shower itself was even more revitalizing. Eagerly Maggie shed her boots and socks, along with the turtleneck and brown pleated pants, now a great deal the worse for their wear. Her movements slowed a bit when it came to removing the bodysuit.

Wincing, she twisted to one side to reach the Velcro straps. Her stomach muscles screamed a protest as the supporting shield fell away. Using both hands, she lifted the hem of her thermal undershirt, then froze. Her jaw dropping, she surveyed the effects of the rifle shell in the bathroom mirror.

A bruise the size of a dinner plate painted her middle in various shades of green and purple, with touches of yellow and blue thrown in for dramatic emphasis. She gulped at the dramatic colorama, then tugged the shirt over her head and bent to push off the bottoms. An involuntary "Ooooch" escaped her when she tried to straighten up.

Realizing that she might have to adjust the scope of her plans for the next few hours or so, Maggie padded to the glass-enclosed shower. Under her bare feet, the floor vibrated with the power of the 747's huge engines. While she waited for the water to heat, Maggie let her appreciative gaze roam the wood-paneled bath.

Air Force Two was a model of efficient luxury. It had to be. It served as a second home for the vice president on her frequent trips around the globe. Just as her predecessors had, Taylor Grant represented the president at everything from weddings to funerals of various heads of state. This duty required extensive traveling, so much so that Mrs. Bush had once quipped that the vice president's seal should read Have Funeral, Will Travel.

Maggie smiled at the thought and stepped into the shower. With a groan of pleasure, she lifted her face to the pulsing jets and let the hot water sluice down her body. Sighing in sybaritic gratification, she dropped her arms to her sides while heat needled her shoulders and breasts.

She was still standing in a boneless, motionless lump when the shower door opened.

"The steward just served your dinner," Adam said, his face grave. "Having experienced firsthand how testy you get when you're hungry, I thought I'd better let you know immediately."

"Thank you," Maggie replied, equally grave, as though she weren't standing before him completely naked.

Through the mist of the escaping steam, she saw that he'd taken advantage of the selection of sundries in one of the other bathrooms, as well. The dark bristles shadowing his cheeks and chin were gone, and he'd made an attempt to tame his black hair. He'd scrounged up a clean white shirt, but wore the same snug jeans and ski boots.

Adam appeared just as interested in her state of dress, or undress, as she was in his. In a slow sweep, his gaze traveled from her face to neck to her breasts. Maggie felt her nipples harden under his intimate inspection, and a twist of love at the sudden pain in his eyes when he saw her stomach.

"Remind me to give the chief of Field Dress a superior performance bonus when this is over," he said fiercely. "A big one."

Maggie was too busy enjoying the blaze of emotion on his face to spare more than a passing thought for the pudgy, frizzy-haired genius who'd produced her torturous corset. A fiery warmth that had nothing to do with the water steaming up the shower enclosure coursed through her belly, and her muscles contracted involuntarily. Maggie ignored the stabbing ache in her middle and focused instead on the ache building a little lower.

Lifting his gaze to hers, he smiled. His eyes held a tender softness in their blue depths that Maggie had never seen before. One that intensified the liquid heat gathering low in her belly.

"Do you want to eat now, or later?"

"Now," she told him with a grin. "And later."

As she watched Adam strip off his clothes, Maggie thought

she'd melt from the sizzling combination of hot water and spiraling desire and disappear down the shower drain in a rivulet of need. From a snow cave to a 747, she thought. From under the ground to a mile above it. From an attack beside a frozen lake to a ring of fire beside a deserted shack. Out of all the missions she'd ever been on, she knew this one would always remain vividly emblazoned in her mind.

And when Adam stepped inside and closed the shower door behind him, Maggie knew the expression in his eyes would always—always!—remain imprinted in her heart.

Water streamed over his broad shoulders and down his chest as he buried his hands in her wet hair. Tilting her face to his, he smiled down at her.

"I love you, Chameleon. In all your guises. But I love you in this one most."

His use of her code name gave Maggie a little dart of pleasure, then one of pain. Her personal relationship with Adam was so inextricably bound to her professional one. Yet she knew in her heart that couldn't continue. They'd stepped through the barriers that separated them, and there was no stepping back. Not now. Not ever.

"I love you, too," she whispered, sliding her palms up the planes of his water-slick chest. "In all your guises. Special envoy. Director. Code name Thunder. Plain ol' Adam Ridgeway. But I love you in this one the most."

She wrapped her arms around his neck and brought his mouth down to hers. He tasted of warm, rich brandy. Of smoky fire. Of Adam.

Rising up on her toes, she brought her body into his. She managed to contain her startled gasp when her bruised tummy connected with his, but he didn't miss the tiny, involuntary flinch. Sliding his hands down the curve of her waist, he grasped her hips gently and pushed her away.

She murmured an inarticulate protest.

Guiding her gently, he rotated her slick body until she faced the wall. "Like this, my darling," he whispered in her ear. "Like this. I don't want to hurt you."

Maggie discovered that "this" wasn't bad, after all. In fact, she thought on a gasp of pure pleasure, "this" was wonderful. Adam's broad chest felt solid and strong and sleek against her back. The way he reached around to mold her breasts with both hands sent waves of sensation washing through her. The touch of her bare bottom against his belly was even more electrifying. Hard and rampant and fully erect, he pressed against her.

Bracing her palms on the shower tiles, Maggie arched her back. Her head twisted, and he bent to take her mouth. While his tongue and hers met in a slow, sensual dance, his hands played with her nipples. With each tug and twist, fire streaked from Maggie's breasts to her belly. With each nip of his teeth against her lower lip, she felt the sting of need in her loins.

When his hands left her breasts to brush with a feather-light touch down her middle, her pelvis arched to meet them. Her head fell back against his shoulder as he parted her folds and opened her to his touch and the pelting of the pulsing water. Maggie gasped at the exquisite sensation.

"Adam! I don't think— I can't hold— Oh!"

"Don't think," he growled in her ear. "Don't hold back. Let me love you, Maggie. Let me feed your soul, as you feed mine."

When her soul had been fed, twice, and Adam's at least once, they decided it was time to feed their bodies. While he used one of the fluffy towels monogrammed with the vice president's seal to dry himself, Maggie pulled on a thick, sinfully soft terry robe.

Plopping herself down on a vanity stool, she treated herself to a spectacular view of Adam's lean flanks and tight white buns as she towel-dried her hair.

"Mmm… Nice." Her fingers curled into the towel. "Maybe that steak could wait a few more minutes."

"The steak might, but Radizwell probably won't. I left him sniffing around the office. If we don't get back in there, he's liable to—"

"Adam!" Sheer panic sliced through Maggie. Throwing the towel aside, she jumped off the stool. "You didn't leave that animal in the same room with my steak, did you?"

The terry-cloth robe flapped against her legs as she rushed through the paneled bedroom and threw open the door to the office.

"I'm going to shoot him!"

Hands on hips, Maggie glared at the shaggy creature stretched out contentedly beside the litter of dishes he'd pushed off the table onto the floor, all of which were licked clean. Sublimely indifferent to her anger, Radizwell raised his head, thumped his tail at Adam a couple of times, then yawned and laid his head back down.

"I'll shoot him!" Maggie snarled again. "I'll skin him. I'll—"

"Strange," Adam murmured. "McGowan said Taylor threatened to do the same."

"It's not strange," Maggie fumed. "It's natural. It's possible. It's very likely, in fact, that someone will do so in the very near future. Why Taylor would keep this obnoxious, smelly, greedy beast is beyond me."

"Probably for the same reasons you keep a bug-eyed reptile with a yard-long tongue."

"Terence," Maggie pronounced with lofty dignity, "has class."

Adam laughed and lifted her in his arms. Taking care not to bump her stomach, he carried her to the wide leather sofa at the far end of the office.

"It's not funny," she muttered. "That...that Hungarian ate my steak!"

"My steak, remember? Don't pout, Maggie. I'll order another one. I seem to have worked up quite an appetite."

The head steward delivered Adam's second dinner some time later.

By then, Maggie had retreated once more to the bedroom to finish dressing. She couldn't bear the thought of strapping the body shield on over her sore stomach again, and she left it on the dressing stool.

To her surprise, the pantsuit Lillian had laid out fit perfectly even without the tight corset. A size eight, no less! She smoothed her hands over trim hips covered in a soft, pale yellow wool and admired her silhouette in the mirror. Biting her lip, Maggie debated whether she should forgo her half of Adam's second steak, after all.

Nah! Not this time!

She flipped off the lights, casting a last look over her shoulder at her reflection in the mirror.

Maybe next time, though.

They had just polished off their meal when Cowboy rapped on the door. Poking his sun-streaked blond head inside the office, Nate Sloan gave them a lazy grin.

"You two finished chowin' down yet?"

"We're finished," Adam replied.

"About time!"

Nate strolled into the office with his graceful, long-legged gait. Radizwell lifted his head lazily, issued a halfhearted growl, then thumped it back down again. A juicy steak appeared to have the same mellowing effect on his temperament as it did on hers, Maggie thought in amusement.

"Jaguar's been trying to raise you for the last half hour," Cowboy said casually. "Forget to put your transceiver back on, Chief?"

Adam glanced down at his wrist, which was bare except for its dusting of dark hair. "Apparently."

Maggie remembered last seeing the thin gold watch tossed on the bathroom carpet, along with Adam's clothes.

"Jaguar said he could wait, so I decided not to interrupt your…meal."

"I'll go get the transceiver," Adam said, unperturbed.

Maggie, on the other hand, wavered between a grin and a ridiculous blush at Nate's knowing look. She struggled with both while he sprawled with his customary loose-limbed ease in the leather chair opposite her and regarded her with a twinkle in his hazel eyes.

"We were all taking bets on which way this mission would go, you know."

"Is that right?"

"We figured you and the chief would find a way to patch up your differences or come back ready to use each other for target practice on the firing range. Looks like you did some patchin'."

Maggie tucked her legs under her and rested her hand on her ankle. The glint of gold on her ring finger caught her eye. She smiled, realizing that she and Adam would have their forever, after all.

"I'm not sure I'd call it patching," she said, her smile easing into the grin she'd struggled against the moment before. "And we still have a few significant differences to work out. But we will work them out, one way or another."

Nate's eyes gleamed. "He's a good man, Maggie. One of the best."

"*The* best," she replied.

"Hellfire, woman, it took you long enough to recognize that fact."

"I recognized it a long time ago. I just wasn't ready to do anything about it."

"Why not?"

Her smile slipped a bit, but she answered easily enough. "He's my boss, Nate. He's had to maintain a distance, an objectivity, just as I've had to keep my personal feelings separate from my professional ones."

"And now?"

"Now? Now I couldn't separate them if I tried."

"So what are you going to do about it?"

She hesitated, not quite ready to put into words the decision she'd come to in the shower, but Nate already knew the answer to his question.

"You're going to leave OMEGA."

Maggie nodded. "I have to. Wherever our relationship goes, I have to leave OMEGA. Neither one of us can operate the way we have been. Not anymore."

"Adam might have something to say about that."

A gleam of laughter crept into Maggie's eyes. "I'm sure he will. He usually has a long list of items to discuss with me when I return from a mission."

She stretched, feeling immeasurably relieved now that she'd taken the first step.

"There's nothing to discuss about this particular matter, though. You know Adam's needed more at OMEGA than I am. He has the president's ear. He moves in the kind of circles necessary to carry off his double role as special envoy and director of OMEGA. He's the best man for his job. The only man."

"So what will you do?"

"I don't know." She glanced around the wood-paneled compartment. "Maybe I'll run for office. I could get used to traveling like this. And there are a few issues I'd like to tackle."

"Such as?"

"Such as the distribution by gender of toilets in public places."

Nate gave her a look of blank astonishment. "Come again?"

"You don't think all those long lines outside women's rest rooms are a violation of the First Amendment? Or whichever amendment guarantees us life, liberty, and the pursuit of happiness?"

"Maggie, darlin', I can't say I've ever given women's rest rooms much thought."

"Neither has anyone else," she said sweetly. "That's going to change."

Nate was still chuckling when Adam came back into the office a few moments later. His blue eyes gleamed with a suppressed excitement that didn't fool Maggie for an instant. For once, Adam Ridgeway's cool control had slipped.

"What?" she asked, sitting up. "What is it?"

"I just talked to Jaguar. We've got it, Maggie. We've got the 'why.'"

"We do?"

She scrambled out of the leather chair.

Detouring around a half acre of prone sheepdog, she joined Adam at the vice president's desk. Her eyes widened as she scanned the notes he'd scribbled during his conversation with Jaguar.

"Adam! You were right! First Bank is managing James Elliot's blind trust during his term as secretary of the treasury. That might be the connection."

"They're managing more than a blind trust. Elliot has several accounts with them." Adam smiled grimly. "Accounts he failed to disclose during his background investigation and his Senate confirmation hearing. Accounts that received large electronic deposits from offshore banks."

"Good grief! Drug dollars?"

"It's possible, and very likely. We'll have to dig deeper for absolute proof. The mere fact that he failed to disclose the accounts will cost him his office, however."

Maggie shook her head. "But what does all this have to do with me? I don't have any involvement with First Bank. Why did he go to such desperate—?"

She broke off, her eyes widening. "Luis Esteban! Those phone calls I made for him, hinting at high-level government interest in First Bank! My God, Elliot must gotten wind of the calls and thought I was on to something."

"He thought a nameless, faceless special agent with the code name Chameleon was on to something. He had to flush her out. One way or another."

# Chapter 16

"We're here to see the president. I believe he's expecting us."

The White House usher looked a little startled at Adam's cool announcement. A dubious expression flitted across his face as he took in the gaggle of people ranged behind the special envoy.

Maggie couldn't blame the poor man. They constituted a pretty intimidating crew.

After flying through the night, Air Force Two had landed at Andrews Air Force Base just as a weak January sun washed D.C. in a gray dawn. The entire entourage had piled out of the plane and driven straight into the city. Adam couldn't have shaken any one of them if he tried.

Maggie, of course, wanted to be in on the kill.

Cowboy had come along for backup.

Denise Kowalski refused to abandon her post.

Hank McGowan wanted to make sure Taylor was all right.

Lillian insisted that the vice president, who was flying in from Camp David, would need her help to get ready for the news conference scheduled in less than a half hour to announce the historic treaty.

And no one could separate Radizwell from Adam without losing a hand or an arm in the process.

When faced with his newly appointed shadow, Adam had shrugged and stated calmly that the animal had taken down two of Maggie's attackers. He was as much a part of the team as any of them.

The usher swallowed as he looked the group over once more. "You're here to see the president, sir? All of you?"

"All of us."

Radizwell didn't seem to care for this unnecessary delay. He curled one black gum and issued a warning that made the man's face pale visibly.

"If you'll accompany me, sir."

With a measured pace, the usher led the small band through the corridor that connected the White House proper with the semidetached west wing. He stopped before a set of tall wooden doors, one gloved hand on the latch, and gave the uncombed, aromatic sheepdog another doubtful glance.

"All of us," Adam repeated firmly.

"Yes, sir."

The receptionist rose at their entrance. Giving Radizwell a wide berth, she took their coats and supplied them with coffee. Maggie had just taken a sip of delicious mocha laced with dark chocolate when the double doors opened once more. The vice president strode in, followed by the stony-faced senior agent with the half-chewed ear—Buck Evans.

"Adam! You're back!"

Taylor Grant strode across the patterned carpet, hands outstretched. Her broad smile encompassed the entire group, but her first greeting was for the special envoy.

"Buck briefed me on the attacks. Are you all right?"

Adam bent to brush a kiss across her cheek. "We're fine. Congratulations on the treaty, Madam Vice President. No one but you could have pulled it off. You're going to make history this morning."

She could handle this, Maggie told herself, swallowing a gulp of coffee that suddenly tasted like sludge. She could handle the sight of Adam's dark head bent over Taylor's sleek, beautiful one. She could handle it, but she didn't have to like it.

Beside her, Hank McGowan stiffened imperceptibly. Maggie caught the slight movement and darted him a quick look. His battered features showed no emotion, but below the rolled-up sleeve of McGowan's blue work shirt Maggie saw the snarling bear tattooed on his forearm twitch.

She wasn't the only one who caught the tiny ripple of movement. Across the room, Denise Kowalski's brown eyes narrowed as she glanced from McGowan to the vice president.

Her lips twisting, Taylor released Adam's hands. "I understand you're going to make history yourself this morning. You...and Chameleon."

She turned to Maggie, and a small shock of surprise widened her eyes when she looked at her alter ego fully for the first time.

Maggie's involuntary diet and rather strenuous activities during the past week had altered her face as subtly as her body. Her cheeks had small hollows under their prominent bones...like Taylor's. Her generous mouth had thinned a fraction...like Taylor's. She was far closer to a perfect double now than when she'd embarked on this masquerade.

The vice president quickly mastered her surprise and gave Maggie a sympathetic smile. "I understand I wasn't the target, after all. It was you all the time."

"We think so."

"Perhaps we should have reversed our roles. Instead of pouring out my most intimate secrets to a stranger, I could've spent a couple of weeks in the mountains with Adam, acting as your double."

"I *don't* think so."

Taylor blinked at the drawled response, and Maggie saw that her message had been received. No one, not even the vice president of the United States, was going to be spending any weeks with Adam Ridgeway. In the mountains or anywhere else.

Except Maggie.

Smiling, she took a sip of her mocha coffee while Taylor greeted the rest of the entourage. She gave Lillian a quick hug, then gasped aloud.

"Radizwell!"

Maggie swung around to see the sheepdog calmly lowering his leg. Having marked his territory to his satisfaction on the delicate hand-painted eighteenth-century wallpaper, he moved on to explore the rest of the office.

Taylor's violet eyes squeezed shut. "I'm going to skin that animal," she said through gritted teeth. "I'm going to skin him and tan him and use him as a throw rug."

Shaking her head in disgust, she summoned the dog. "Come here! Here, boy."

The komondor ignored her.

Adam snapped his fingers once.

Radizwell obediently plodded to Adam's side and settled back on his haunches with a satisfied air. He'd seen his duty, and he'd done it.

Taylor's auburn brows shot up, but before she could comment, the door to the inner office opened.

The chief of staff stepped out, his eyes widening as he looked from Taylor to Maggie, then back again.

"Madam Vice President...er, Madams Vice President, the president will see you now. And you, of course, Mr. Special Envoy. He's asked the secretary of the treasury to join you in a few moments, as you requested."

Adam stood aside to allow the women to precede him. Taylor took one step, then stopped and stood aside for Maggie. "This is your show. You have the honors."

Nodding graciously, Maggie sailed into the Oval Office.

After the gut-wrenching tension and chilling events of the past few days, Maggie would have expected the moment the perpetrator was finally unmasked to be one of high drama.

Instead, James Elliot's face turned ashen the moment he stepped into the Oval Office and saw her standing beside Taylor. When a shaken president confronted his longtime friend with evidence of his failure to disclose ties to a bank with links to a Central American drug cartel, Elliot seemed to collapse in on himself, like a hot-air balloon when the air inside the silk bag cools.

Under Adam's relentless questioning, Elliot admitted everything, including his desperate attempt to silence the woman known only as Chameleon.

Maggie's nails bit into her palms when the man who had wanted to kill her wouldn't even look at her.

"She had to die," he whispered, in a remorseless confession to the president. "That was the best solution. The only solution. I didn't know how much she knew. Just the tiny scrap of information linking First Bank to the frozen assets of the Cartozan drug lord was enough to bring my whole world tumbling down if she followed up on it. She had to die."

"Get him out of here," the president said in disgust.

A grim-faced Denise Kowalski was given the distinction of arresting her own boss. She walked into the Oval Office, flashed Elliot her badge and advised him of his rights. With Buck Evans on one side and Denise on the other, the former secretary of the treasury departed.

For long moments, no one moved. Then the president shoved a hand in the pocket of his charcoal gray slacks and walked over to the tall windows facing south. He stared at the stark obelisk of the Washington Monument rising out of the mists drifting off the tidal basin.

"Christ! Jimmy Elliot!"

His shoulders slumped, and the indefatigable energy that characterized both him and his administration seemed to evaporate.

Adam's eyes met those of the vice president. She gave a slight nod, then addressed the man at the window with remarkable calm.

"You have a press conference in ten minutes, Mr. President. Do you want to go over the treaty provisions a final time, or do you feel comfortable with them?"

The president squared his shoulders. Turning, he gave his deputy a tight smile.

"No, the brief you sent me from Camp David was excellent." He paused, and then his smile eased into one of genuine warmth. "I still can't believe you pulled this treaty off. Good work, Taylor. Whatever the hell bad choices I might have made, when I picked you, I picked a winner."

"I'll remind you of that when you get ready to announce your support for your successor," she replied, laughing.

"You do that!"

Walking across the room, he held out his hand to Maggie. "I'm sorry you had to go through this torturous charade."

"I'm not. The assignment had its finer moments. Besides," she continued smoothly, ignoring Adam's raised brows, "it was all in the line of duty.

"A duty I understand you do extremely well. The director has told me that you're good. Damn good. One of the best."

"*The* best," Adam said coolly.

Maggie flashed him a startled look. His eerie echo of her exact words to Cowboy surprised her, until she remembered the transmitter in her ring. Adam must have heard the entire conversation, including the part about her decision to leave OMEGA!

From the steely expression in his eyes, she knew that this mission's postbrief was going to make all her others seem tame by comparison.

"We'll have to talk about that later," the president said, with a smile for Maggie. "Right now, I have a press conference to conduct. Adam, if you'll stay just a moment, please?"

Some moments later, Maggie stood in the wings beside Adam and Taylor Grant as a composed and forceful chief executive strode to the podium in the White House briefing room. His back straight, he glanced around the packed auditorium. Ignoring the clear Plexiglas TelePrompTer in front of the podium, he addressed the assembled group directly.

"I called this press conference to announce a historic treaty, one that constitutes the first positive step toward eliminating a scourge that hangs over our world."

He paused, his jaw squaring. "But before I give you the details on this treaty, I have another, less pleasant duty to perform. I regret to say that a few moments ago I was forced to request the immediate resignation of James Elliot, my treasury secretary, for reasons I'm not yet at liberty to discuss.''

A wave of startled exclamations filled the room. The president waited for them to die down before continuing.

"I can tell you, however, that I've already selected his replacement. Ladies and gentlemen, it gives me great pleasure to introduce my nominee for secretary of the treasury, Adam Ridgeway.''

Stunned, Maggie lifted her eyes to the man beside her. She heard the spatter of applause that quickly rolled into thunder. And the hum of excited comments from the audience. And Taylor's warm congratulations. But none of them registered. All that penetrated her whirling mind was the glint in Adam's eyes as he tipped her chin.

"We'll talk about this, among other things, when we get back to headquarters,'' he promised.

"Our list of items to discuss is getting pretty long,'' she replied breathlessly.

He kissed her, hard and fast and thoroughly, then strode out to join the president at the podium.

Dazed, Maggie listened to his brief acceptance and the easy way he fielded the storm of questions from the media.

A welter of emotions coursed through her. She couldn't imagine OMEGA without Adam Ridgeway as director. He'd guided the organization and its tight cadre of agents and technicians for so long, with such unerring skill. In her mind, Adam *was* OMEGA.

At the same time, Maggie swelled with pride. She couldn't think of anyone more qualified for a cabinet post than this man.

And she wouldn't have been human if a thrill of excitement hadn't darted through her veins. Adam's promotion meant she didn't have to leave OMEGA. He wouldn't be her boss any longer. What he would be was something they would discuss as soon as they got back to the headquarters. Anticipation and joy leaped through her.

Knowing Adam would be mobbed by the media even after the treaty announcement to follow, Maggie decided to slip away. She wanted to be out of Taylor's skin and in her own when she and Adam met again. For once, Chameleon wanted no guises, no cover, nothing to hide her from the man she loved.

Her pulse thrumming, she turned to leave.

Taylor stopped her with a hand on her arm. "I didn't thank you. For being me when I was the target. Even though it was you... Well, you know what I mean."

Maggie's quicksilver grin blossomed. "It gets confusing, doesn't it? Half the time I wasn't even sure just who the heck I was."

The other woman's eyes gleamed. "It doesn't appear Adam had that problem."

"No, I guess he didn't."

"He'll make an excellent secretary of the treasury. And I think you'd make an excellent special envoy."

For the second time in less than ten minutes, Maggie was dumbfounded. "Me?"

"You. We don't have enough women with your rather unique qualifications in leadership positions. I'll talk to the president about it."

"While you're at it," Maggie replied, still astounded but regrouping fast, "you might mention establishing a commission to—"

She stopped, too anxious to get back to headquarters to take the time to explain the public potty proclamation she'd issued at the Kennedy Center.

"Never mind, I'll talk to you about it later. Right now I have to change back into me. I want to be wearing my own skin when I claim my forever."

A smile feathered Taylor's lips. "Your forever? That's nice."

"It's from your ring."

At her blank look, Maggie held up her hand. "The inscription in your wedding ring. *Now, and forever.*"

"What are you talking about? There's no inscription in my ring."

# Chapter 17

On the outside, the elegant Federal-style town house on a quiet side street just off Massachusetts Avenue appeared no different than its neighbors. Neatly banked snow edged the brick steps leading to its black-painted door. A brass knocker in the shape of an eagle gleamed in the cold afternoon sunlight. The bronze plaque that identified the structure as home to the offices of the president's special envoy was small and discreet, drawing the attention of few passersby.

Inside, however, the town house hummed with an activity level that would have astounded even the most jaded observer of the Washington political scene.

Raking fingers through hair newly restored to its original glossy chestnut color, Maggie stepped out of the third-floor crew room into a control center crackling with noise. Joe Samuels's banks of electronic boxes buzzed and beeped and blipped continually as the harried senior communications technician fielded a steady stream of transmissions from all corners of the globe. Word of the president's startling announcement had been beamed to OMEGA agents in the field, and they wanted to know the details. All the details.

"Roger, Cyrene," Joe said into the transmitter. "It's true. The confirmation hearings are scheduled for next week. There are going to be some changes around here."

His dark eyes caught Maggie's. "A lot of changes," he added, grinning.

Maggie shook her head at his knowing grin. She'd only been back from the White House a little over two hours. Most of that time had been spent with Jaguar in a closed-door mission debrief, the rest in a fever of anticipation in the crew room, working frantically to restore herself to her natural state.

She hadn't had time to discuss with anyone, let alone the still-absent Adam, any of the several urgent items on her list. Yet OMEGA's global network had already spread the word. There were going to be some changes around here. A lot of them.

Joe answered another beep, then nodded to Maggie over his bank of equipment. "Chief's on the way back from the White House, Chameleon. Be here in fifteen minutes. Think he'll have any news for us?"

Maggie sidestepped Joe's less-than-subtle probe to discover what she knew, if anything, about Adam's replacement. The idea that she might actually be named to head OMEGA was too fantastic to consider. Besides, she had more important matters to take care of right now.

"I don't know," she replied, heading for the elevator. "I'll let you know as soon as I hear anything for sure."

She took the specially shielded high-speed elevator to the underground lab and bearded the chief of Special Devices in his den.

"I need that special lubricant, Harry. Right away."

The scientist pushed his glasses to the top of his shining bald forehead. "Lubricant?"

She waggled her left hand in front of his face. "The one you developed so I can slide off this ring. I want to look at the inscription one more time before you guys remove the device soldered inside."

Maggie had no intention of surrendering the wide gold band permanently. In fact, she planned to put the ring to good use in the immediate future. But she wanted to see with her own eyes the words inscribed inside. Even with the pounds she'd shed, however, the band wouldn't fit over her knuckle.

"We didn't develop the lubricant."

"What? Why not?"

Blinking at her startled surprise, the senior technician hunched his shoulders and slid his hands into the pockets of his white coat. "The chief sent word through Jaguar that it wasn't necessary."

Maggie rocked back on her heels. "He did?"

"Didn't you know?"

She could only shake her head.

"The word came down the same day you left. No, the next morning. Jaguar said something about a bus backfiring and the chief swearing he wasn't going to ever let you out of range again."

"Well, well, well…" she said softly, twisting the ring around and around on her finger. "To think all that was going on behind his oh-so-cool, Mr. In Control exterior."

Maggie's mouth curved in a private smile as she recalled a few other revelations Adam had made during those hours in the snow cave about what went on in his mind. One of which, if she remembered correctly, had to do with locking his office door and throwing her down on the mahogany conference table she always perched on.

It was time to do a little perching.

"Gotta go," she told the still-confused lab chief as she whirled and raced for the elevator.

Her heart was thumping wildly when she stepped out onto the second-floor landing. A quick scan of the video monitors showed no one in the special envoy's reception area except the gray-haired Elizabeth Wells. Slapping her palm against the hidden sensors, Maggie shivered in impatience while she waited for the computers to verify her print.

The moment the titanium-shielded door hummed open, she dashed through the reception room.

"Is the chief back yet?" she flung at Elizabeth.

"No, but—Chameleon, wait!"

Maggie didn't have time for questions or explanations about all the changes coming down at OMEGA. Not now. Not with anticipation thrumming through her veins like heated wine. Not with a long list of urgent items to "discuss" with Adam.

"I'll catch you later, Elizabeth," she called over her shoulder. "I want to wait for the boss in his office."

Actually, she wanted to wait on a certain conference table, but she didn't think the matronly Elizabeth Wells would appreciate that bit of information.

"Wait, Chameleon, there are people in—"

Maggie stumbled to an abrupt halt on the threshold to Adam's office. Jaw sagging, she surveyed what looked like half the population of the nation's capital.

Apparently every OMEGA agent who wasn't in the field had gathered to hear firsthand the amazing news. With their wives. And children. And fathers-in-law.

Helplessly, Maggie looked from the dark-haired, steel-eyed Jaguar to a grinning Cowboy to the conservative, square-jawed Doc...who sported, she saw in stunned amazement, a mane of moussed hair that only Stoney Armstrong's Hollywood stylist could have sculpted.

Before any of them could comment, however, Senator Orwin Chandler strode forward, his unlit cigar clamped firmly in his mouth. "Is Ridgeway with you?" he boomed. "We have to start plotting our strategy for working his nomination through committee."

"Never mind that now, Dad."

Silvery-blond Sarah Chandler MacKenzie pushed through the crowd. Her aquamarine eyes alight, she took Maggie's hands in both of hers. "I can't believe Jake kept you in debrief for so long. We've all been waiting to hear about Adam's nomination. And when you two are going to announce your plans."

"Our plans?"

With a pang, Maggie realized she'd have to drastically revise her immediate plans. She cast a regretful glance at the huge mahogany conference table.

Three scrubbed, bright-eyed faces beamed back at her. Jaguar's adopted children were seated in the plush chairs pulled up to the table, being served a banquet of ice cream by a wiry preteen with a precocious air.

"We wish to know about your plans to wed, mademoiselle," the boy elaborated with Gallic savoir faire. "Did I not tell you when you lie so sick and green faced in Cannes that this Thunder, he has the eye for you?"

"Henri!"

Soft-spoken Paige Jensen admonished the pickpocket who had attached himself to her during her unexpected stint as a high-priced call girl.

"But it is true, Madame Paige! You said to Doc when we fly to this so-cold city last night that these two, they are made for each other."

"So I did, Henri." With a smile, Paige turned to Maggie. "Well?"

"We, uh, haven't quite finalized our plans yet. I was hoping to…discuss a few matters with Thunder when he got back."

The Russian-born, exotically beautiful Alexandra Danilova Sloan gave a low laugh. "Ah, Maggie. The women of my tribe have a saying about allowing men a say in such important matters."

"I'm not sure I want to hear this," Cowboy groaned.

Ignoring her husband, Alex smiled serenely. "At least once each year, it is wise to ask your man's advice about what should be done, but taking such advice is another kettle of potato soup entirely."

Maggie twisted the heavy gold ring with her thumb. "Well," she admitted with a grin, "I've already decided on one or two of the more important— Ack!"

She jumped straight into the air as a yard-long tongue shot out from under Adam's desk and planted a wet kiss on the back of her calf. Spinning around, Maggie saw a blue-and-orange-striped tail whip back and forth in lazy satisfaction. The rest of her pet iguana was firmly ensconced in the foot well of Adam's desk.

"Terence! What in the world are you doing here?"

"I brought him," Elizabeth said from the doorway. "The fool thing was pining away for you. It wouldn't even drink the Coors your father offered him last night before we went to dinner."

Maggie's brows soared. "You and Red went to dinner last night?"

The older woman patted her gray hair with a graceful, feminine gesture. "Actually, dear, we've had dinner together every night since you left. You suggested I call him, remember?"

"I...I think so."

The idea of crusty Red Sinclair connecting with this gracious, well-groomed woman who qualified every year at the expert level on a variety of lethal weapons both surprised and delighted Maggie. She started to tell her so, but just then a thunderous boom emanated from the outer office.

Half the people in the room reached for their weapons. The other half froze.

Maggie groaned. "Oh, no!"

A moment later, a shaggy white shape came bounding into the office. When he saw the assembled crowd, Radizwell dropped to his haunches and planted his front paws in an effort to skid to a halt, but his momentum carried him forward. Like a runaway bale of cotton, the sheepdog careened into Senator Chandler.

Arms windmilling, the dignified, silver-maned senator stumbled backward and landed on his duff. He glared at the unrepentant animal and clamped his jaw so tight the end of his unlit cigar broke off.

"Someone grab him before he decides to mark his territory," Maggie pleaded before she turned to face the man who stood in the doorway, surveying the scene with a look of unholy amusement on his face.

"Adam! What's that...that Hungarian doing here?"

With a nod to the various occupants of the room, the secretary of the treasury-designate strolled over to Maggie. When she saw the look in his eyes, dread washed through her in waves.

He confirmed her worst fears. "The vice president gave him to us as a wedding present."

"Oh, nooooo!"

Laughing, Adam gathered her into his arms. "Oh, yes, my darling."

"But—"

At that precise moment, Terence and Radizwell discovered each other. Total, uncontrolled pandemonium broke out.

Letting loose with a series of barks that had the resonance and earsplitting volume of an artillery barrage, the komondor danced around Adam's desk. Every time he got within striking distance of the foot well, a long pink tongue shot out and landed a stinging kiss on his face.

At least Maggie thought it was his face. With Radizwell, she was never quite sure.

Squealing with delight, the children jumped out of their chairs to join in the fun. Childish shrieks, adult laughter, and Senator Chandler's blustery admonitions to get that damned hound under control joined Radizwell's booming woofs.

In the midst of it all, Maggie stood cradled in Adam's arms. "What are my chances of convincing Taylor to take him back?" she shouted.

"About the same as convincing me to ever let you go."

Wrapping her arms around his neck, she grinned up at him. "In that case, I guess he's ours. Now, and forever."

\* \* \* \* \*

#1 *New York Times* bestselling author

# NORA ROBERTS

brings you two sizzling tales of
summer passion and unexpected love, in

## SUMMER PLEASURES

A special 2-in-1 edition containing
SECOND NATURE and ONE SUMMER

*And coming in November 2002*

**TABLE FOR TWO**

containing SUMMER DESSERTS
and LESSONS LEARNED

*Available at your favorite retail outlet.*

*Where love comes alive*™

Visit Silhouette at www.eHarlequin.com

PSSP

**Three bold, irresistible men.**
**Three brand-new romances by today's top authors...**
**Summer never seemed hotter!**

*Sheiks of Summer*

*Available in August
at your favorite
retail outlet!*

### "The Sheik's Virgin" by Susan Mallery

He was the brazen stranger who chaperoned innocent, beautiful
Phoebe Carson around his native land. But what would Phoebe do when
she discovered her suitor was none other than Prince Nasri Mazin—
and he had seduction on his mind?

### "Sheikh of Ice" by Alexandra Sellers

She came in search of adventure—and discovered passion in the arms
of tall, dark and handsome Hadi al Hajar. But once Kate Drummond
succumbed to Hadi's powerful touch, would she succeed in
taming his hard heart?

### "Kismet" by Fiona Brand

A star-crossed love affair and a stormy night combined to bring
Laine Abernathy into Sheik Xavier Kalil Al Jahir's world. Now, as she
took cover in her rugged rescuer's home, Lily wondered if it was her
destiny to fall in love with the mesmerizing sheik....

*Where love comes alive*™

Visit Silhouette at www.eHarlequin.com

PSSOS

community | membership

buy books | authors | online reads | magazine | learn to write

# magazine

### quizzes

Is he the one? What kind of lover are you? Visit the **Quizzes** area to find out!

### recipes for romance

Get scrumptious meal ideas with our **Recipes for Romance**.

### romantic movies

Peek at the **Romantic Movies** area to find Top 10 Flicks about First Love, ten Supersexy Movies, and more.

### royal romance

Get the latest scoop on your favorite royals in **Royal Romance**.

### games

Check out the **Games** pages to find a ton of interactive romantic fun!

### romantic travel

In need of a romantic rendezvous? Visit the **Romantic Travel** section for articles and guides.

### lovescopes

Are you two compatible? Click your way to the **Lovescopes** area to find out now!

*Silhouette®*

## where love comes alive—online...

Visit us online at
### www.eHarlequin.com

SINTMAG

Love and danger mingle in

### Silhouette

# DREAMSCAPES...

four dangerous and sensual romances that will
bewitch and enchant you!

**WHISPERS IN
THE WOODS**
by Helen R. Myers

**SILENT SCREAMS**
by Carla Cassidy

**SECRET OF
THE WOLF**
by Rebecca Flanders

**BENEATH
THE SURFACE**
by Evelyn Vaughn
*Book 2 of The Circle*

*Look for the dark side of love
at your favorite retal outlet
in August 2002.*

### Silhouette®

*Where love comes alive™*

Visit Silhouette at www.eHarlequin.com          RCDREAM8

Silhouette Books is proud to present:

# Going to the Chapel

**Three brand-new stories
about getting that special man to the altar!**

featuring

*USA Today* bestselling author

# SHARON SALA

*It Happened One Night*...that Georgia society belle
Harley June Beaumont went to Vegas—and woke up married!
How could she explain her hunk of a husband to
her family back home?

**Award-winning author**

# DIXIE BROWNING

*Marrying a Millionaire*...was exactly what Grace McCall was
trying to keep her baby sister from doing. Not that Grace had
anything against the groom—it was the groom's arrogant
millionaire uncle who got Grace all hot and bothered!

**National bestselling author**

# STELLA BAGWELL

*The Bride's Big Adventure*...was escaping her handpicked
fiancé in the arms of a hot-blooded cowboy! And from the
moment Gloria Rhodes said "I do" to her rugged groom, she
dreamed their wedded bliss would never end!

*Available in July at your favorite retail outlets!*

*Silhouette*®

*Where love comes alive*™

Visit Silhouette at www.eHarlequin.com

*A powerful earthquake
ravages Southern California...*

*Thousands are trapped
beneath the rubble...*

*The men and women of
Morgan Trayhern's team
face their most heroic
mission yet...*

A brand-new series from
*USA TODAY* bestselling author
# LINDSAY McKENNA

Don't miss these breathtaking
stories of the triumph of love!

Look for one title per month
from each Silhouette series:

**August: THE HEART BENEATH**
(Silhouette Special Edition #1486)

**September: RIDE THE THUNDER**
(Silhouette Desire #1459)

**October: THE WILL TO LOVE**
(Silhouette Romance #1618)

**November: PROTECTING
HIS OWN**
(Silhouette Intimate Moments #1185)

*Available at your favorite
retail outlet*

*Where love comes alive™*

Visit Silhouette at www.eHarlequin.com          SXSMMUR

**LONE STAR COUNTRY CLUB** EST. 1923

Where Texas society reigns supreme—and appearances are *everything!*

**Mayhem in Mission Creek!**
A mysterious woman shows up in town....
The Texas Mafia wants someone to pay an old debt....
Four eligible bachelors find a baby girl on the ninth tee....
And everyone is asking: Who's this baby's father?

**THE REBEL'S RETURN**
**by Beverly Barton**
**Available August 2002**

Millionaire and reformed bad boy Dylan Bridges had something to prove to his hometown. But all he wanted was Maddie Delarue. Would the richest woman in Texas give him the time of day?

*Available at your favorite retail outlet.*

*Silhouette*®
*Where love comes alive*™

Visit Silhouette at www.lonestarcountryclub.com     LSCCTRR

Coming in July 2002 from

#1 *New York Times* bestselling author

# NORA ROBERTS

Read the stories where it all began
in three mesmerizing tales of palace intrigue
and royal romance....

*Cordina's Royal Family*

a special 3-in-1
volume containing AFFAIRE ROYALE,
COMMAND PERFORMANCE
and THE PLAYBOY PRINCE

*Available at your
favorite retail outlet.*

Visit Silhouette at www.eHarlequin.com

PSCOR